ROTTEN
TO THE CORE 2

ROTTEN
TO THE CORE 2

**More Crime, Sex and Corruption
In Johnny Appleseed's Hometown**

•

MARTIN D. YANT

**Public Eye
Publications
Columbus, Ohio**

ISBN 0-9642780-2-2

Printed in the United States of America.

For the late Melodie Gross Wineland
and my mother, Margaret Yant,
whose supportive spirits
live on in these pages

&

The magical Diana Rankin, whose vitality
revived this writer and this long-dormant book.

Also by Martin D. Yant:

Presumed Guilty: When Innocent People Are Wrongly Convicted

Desert Mirage: The True Story of the Gulf War

Rotten to the Core: Crime, Sex and Corruption in Johnny Appleseed's Hometown

Tin-Star Tyrants: America's Crooked Sheriffs

Contents

Acknowledgments   9

Foreword   11

1. "Watch Yourself, Boy"   13

2. The Badge of Terror   29

3. Dr. Greed   97

4. The Tower of Babble   113

5. The Three-Ring Circus   135

6. The Power Brokers   147

7. Highway Robbery   165

8. Prison City   191

9. The End of a Beginning   201

10. A Personal Perspective   217

11. Is Mansfield Typical?   223

Acknowledgments

This book, like the original *Rotten to the Core,* would not be possible without all the good people of Mansfield who supported my attempt to shed light on the town's inner darkness. This was particularly true of the staff members of *The Ohio Observer,* who produced an innovative newspaper of quality and dignity under the most difficult of circumstances.

Of those, the late Melodie Gross Wineland remained a wonderful friend until her death in 1998. Jennifer Moore Hoffman and Brenda McGlone continue to be good and loyal friends. Brenda has actually been far more than that. She has been my biggest cheerleader and volunteer for whatever project I have been involved in.

I also am grateful to Barbara DeWolfe for her insights and help with *Rotten to the Core 2.* Although this book includes much of the information included in the original *Rotten to the Core,* I have rewritten, expanded and updated it so much that I decided it deserved a title of its own. This volume also includes a final chapter that documents how the corruption I stumbled upon in Mansfield is sadly typical of what one can find throughout the United States

❶

Foreword
By Steve Allen

Author's note: TV legend Steve Allen who died in October 2001, wrote this for the original edition of Rotten to the Core. *Allen, who was also an author, poet, playwright and one of the most prolific composers of modern times, remained an outspoken critic of corruption to the very end. It is an honor to include his words in this edition.*

A longtime staple of American fiction whether portrayed in novels, radio, television or film drama, is the story of the crusading young journalist who discovers corruption in his community, tries to expose it and pays a painful price for his heroism.

Martin Yant has written precisely such a story — a true thriller with the standard ingredients of action and suspense. But the most important thing about this shocking story is that every word of it is true.

Yant, formerly of *The Chicago Daily News,* moved to a small middle-America type of community that on the surface seemed to epitomize the advantages and virtues of small town life but which, in reality, was a cesspool of corruption.

Every student, every civic official — indeed every citizen — ought to read this book.

1

'Watch Yourself, Boy'

The snowflakes first hit the windshield of James Truly's steel-laden truck as he was nearing the end of his run from Cleveland to an auto factory in Mansfield, Ohio, 70 miles to the south.

"It was about 4:30 or 5 a.m. when I got off State Route 224 onto State Route 13," Truly said later. "It was raining all along, but then it turned to snow just like that and began blowing. I couldn't see, so I stopped the truck. Somehow I could see a pickup truck in front of me. It was stuck. I got out and helped the man push it out. Then I went back in my cab and waited."

As the snow continued to fall, the wind began blowing with unbelievable velocity and the roads quickly became impassable. Since it was still dark, bitterly cold and Truly didn't know the distance to the nearest building, he decided to stay where he was. That was a fateful decision. For as Truly dozed in his cab, the blizzard of January 26, 1978, became more and more ferocious as it pummeled the Midwest. Before it was over, it would be ranked as perhaps the worst blizzard in American history. The storm crippled the nation's midsection for days and set dozens of weather records in the process.

When Truly awoke several hours later, he didn't realize until he tried to open his door that the blizzard had buried both him and his 40-foot-long truck in a huge 20-foot-high snowdrift.

"I was hoping to get out and walk," Truly said later. "When I was ready to go, I couldn't get out and my engine had shut down. My first thought was, 'Would somebody come and start digging me out, please?'"

The 42-year-old father of two was getting desperate. He had no food, no watch, no blanket and no light. The native of Frostburg, Maryland, survived by eating snow, trying to contact help on his CB radio and praying. "I have a lot of religion in me," Truly said. He also gained solace, Truly added, by repeating a saying he had first heard at a brother-in-law's funeral: "Don't let the darkness of today cast a shadow on the sunlight of tomorrow."

So the three-packs-a-day smoker kept the faith in the darkness even when he got to his last cigarette. "I broke the last one in half and said, 'I'll smoke half now and the other half when I get out,' " Truly told reporters later.

Incredibly, it would be five maddening days, buried alive, before Truly had a chance to finish that cigarette off. And it was only because of his brother Donald's insistence on action that James Truly was rescued even then.

Donald Truly went to Mansfield after his family did not hear from James for some time after the blizzard had died down. Through a frantic process of elimination, Donald determined that his brother's truck was buried on Route 13, which he knew James usually traveled to the auto plant.

But Donald's requests to various authorities for help fell upon deaf ears. He finally persuaded some Ohio National Guardsmen clearing the road with a large snowplow they used to clear the nearby airport's runways to walk over the drifts with him to see if they could find some sign of a truck.

It was quitting time, and the Guardsmen were reluctant. But they finally decided Donald wasn't going to take no for an answer, so a few of them went with him. As Donald and the Guardsmen walked over James Truly's cab, he heard their boots crunching in the snow. It was the first sound he had heard since some snowmobiles had passed overhead earlier in his ordeal.

Realizing his sudden chance of rescue, Truly started pounding on the roof of his cab with a steel pipe. Those above couldn't believe their ears. They quickly cut a path along the side of the truck with their huge snowblower and dug open the cab's door.

"Nice to see you," James Truly said to his brother.

"Nice to see *you*," Donald Truly replied.

As James Truly stepped out of the darkness into sunlight, he also stepped from obscurity into fleeting fame. Photos and stories of his ordeal and rescue appeared on the front pages of newspapers all over the world. Radio and TV stations from as far away as Japan reported how he had survived temperatures as low as 55 degrees below zero while buried alive in his truck for 124 terrifying hours.

Truly's faith still came through, though, as he talked to reporters between gulps of water. "I never had given up hope," he said "I just had the feeling that I would be saved. I knew I had a brother who doesn't give up."

Truly never did have to light up the half-used cigarette he had saved for the occasion. One of his rescuers handed him one already lighted. He kept his half-used one, he said, "as a fond memory to a nightmare."

Fateful phone call

It was 11:30 p.m. when the phone rang in the newsroom at the Mansfield *News Journal.* It had been another long and hectic day, as they all had been since the blizzard first hit five days before. But this one had been even worse, as calls came in from news organizations across the country trying to get a fresh angle on James Truly's rescue.

Once the reporter working on the story finished, I could go home. Then the phone rang. Since everyone else had left and the reporter was on the other line, that left me to answer it.

I was 28 then, and had been editor of the *News Journal* for only a month. I had been slowly making my presence known, but had studiously avoided making overly rapid changes in the paper's content or editorial policy.

Lovell Stallard's call changed that — and my life — for good.

"I'm calling about that truck driver who was rescued today," Stallard said in an Appalachian drawl in his voice.

"How can I help you?" I asked, expecting another offer of aid like the dozens of others that had come in that evening.

"I don't know if I should get involved or not, but there's something you should know," Stallard continued.

"What's that?" I asked, my curiosity suddenly aroused.

"Well, you see, he could have been rescued four days ago."

"You're kidding."

"I wish I was. It makes my heart sick to think of all the suffering he went through and to know I could have done something about it if I had just made someone listen to me."

"What do you mean?" I replied with increased interest.

"Well, I live just down the road from where the guy was buried, and several people who stayed in our house during the blizzard told me they thought a trucker might be stranded up there."

"And no one would listen to you when you reported it?"

"That's right. All I got was the run-around," Stallard said. "The police said they would check it out, but they didn't. So then I called the street department, and they told me all the plows were already out. (I would learn later that one was being used to clear the parking lot of a powerful fraternal organization and another to clean city council members' driveways.)

"Then I called the sheriff's department," Stallard continued. "But the woman there told me she didn't know who to contact. I wish I could have done more. I tried to climb through the drift myself to see if I could find him, but that was impossible. I even tried to raise someone with a plow on the CB, but that didn't do any good either. So I finally decided that since no one would listen, all we could do was pray that no one was there."

I couldn't believe what I was hearing. If it was true, it certainly put a different spin on the Truly story. So I tracked down several witnesses whose names Stallard gave me that night and early the next morning. They all confirmed Stallard's story. Some also said they had made calls of their own and had gotten the same run-around.

When the story I wrote about the apparent negligence appeared in the paper the next day, it included strong denials from all the agencies involved. But that just caused a second wave of similar accusations from others who had been stranded in the area or who had heard Stallard's CB calls.

Soon Mansfield's officials were beginning to trip over their own lies. Even worse, those making the accusations were being intimidated. And harassed.

Stallard, for example, told me that he was warned by shotgun-toting Captain William Miser of the sheriff's department that he might end up going to jail if he didn't change his story — a threat, I later learned, that Miser and other deputies used all the time to get their way.

But the more Mansfield's officials tried to cover up the facts, the more foolish they looked. When I asked to hear the police department's recording of incoming calls during the blizzard, for example, it was discovered the system had malfunctioned at that time. As the backtracking and lying grew, I dubbed the affair "Snowgate."

Much to my amazement, though, Mansfield's politicians weren't about to change their tune.

They were too used to bullying their way out of controversies to do that. And they weren't about to change their style now, even if James Truly had almost lost his life because of their incompetence and callousness.

Richland County Sheriff Thomas E. Weikel's response was typical. Weikel told reporters that Truly deserved his fate because his truck was probably overweight and on the road illegally. Furthermore, Weikel said, Truly was a fool for staying in his truck, even though *The News Journal* had quoted survival experts as saying he had done the right thing and may have died if he had tried to escape.

Suddenly, James Truly, internationally famous victim, had become James Truly, dumb crook. Weikel even went so far as to try to have his deputies locate Truly's truck so it could be weighed and ticketed if it proved to be overweight. But his deputies didn't find the 18-wheeler until it had been unloaded. That's when I made the decision that would change my life. I did something that had previously been pretty much unheard of in Mansfield: I openly criticized the arrogant Weikel in an editorial. Weikel's response was fast and furious. Within minutes after the paper hit the streets, he was on the phone.

"This is Sheriff Weikel," he said angrily. "I just read what you said about me, and I don't like it."

"I'm sorry," I replied. "That's the way we feel."

But Weikel wasn't finished.

"Why don't you come over here and tell me what you wrote to my face?" he screamed.

"What difference would that make?" I asked.

"Why don't you come over and find out?" Weikel replied.

"I don t know why I have to tell you to your face," I said.

"Watch yourself, boy."

"What?" I asked in growing disbelief.

"I said you'd better watch yourself, boy. You might end up in court."

"For what?" I replied. "Telling the truth?"

"You don't know what the truth is, boy. You're just an immature young man, a baby, baby boy. What you need is four years in the Marine Corps."

I couldn't believe what I was hearing — especially from a man who had bragged to me at our first and only meeting that he was a retired Army officer, not a Marine officer.

But Weikel didn't care what I thought. He just kept shouting in an increasingly shaky voice, clearly not paying attention to my responses. I would later learn that this was standard Weikel fare when anyone crossed him, but it certainly was a shock the first time one heard it.

"I don't like you, boy," Weikel raged. "I've heard a lot of bad things about you. The trouble with this country is that too many people like you are in positions of power."

"People like *me*? I asked incredulously.

"I ought to write a letter and tell people what I think of you," Weikel continued.

"Be my guest," I replied. "I'll put it in the paper tomorrow."

"I ought to write a letter. . . . But you wouldn't print it," Weikel said, clearly not hearing my response.

Nor did the man behind the badge accept my invitation when I repeated it several more times before I hung up amid a torrent of profanities from the person I had been told was the most powerful politician in Mansfield, greatly because of just such intimidating tactics.

What made matters worse was that Weikel apparently always got away with it. But I was determined that he wouldn't this time. I waited a few days to see if Weikel would carry through his threat to write a letter to the editor. When none arrived, I decided to let the sheriff have his say by running the gist of our conversation as an editorial titled "The Sheriff Speaks," which I concluded with this postscript: "We never did receive a letter from Sheriff Weikel, so we thought the citizens of Richland County might be interested in the manner in which the county's chief law-enforcement official conducts his business." It was only later that I learned how people began calling others about the editorial shortly after *The News Journal* hit the street. The average Mansfielder had suspected Weikel of this kind of mentality, but this was the first full exposure of it.

Those who knew Weikel also couldn't believe he was actually being challenged this way. That led to a second reaction: a large number of calls with information about the antics of Weikel and his deputies. Before long, a mountain of allegations had poured in. They included everything from possible murder, drug dealing and brutality to theft in office, abuse of office and harassment.

Despite its external charm, Mansfield was quickly turning out to be quite unlike the ideal middle-American city I had expected to find when I left *The Chicago Daily News* to become editor of *The News Journal.* In fact, I had expected the complete opposite, based on the way Mansfield was portrayed in a series of articles in *The Daily News* I edited that had first piqued my interest in the town. Mansfield was used as a sounding board for political opinion in those stories, because, the paper said, it "represents a cross-section of American life."

Reporter Ray Coffey went on to portray Mansfield as "a town with 56,000 people, 200 churches and no massage parlors. It has a main street called Main Street [He apparently missed the Main Street lounge with a sign in its window saying, "Notice all Prostitutes and Pimps: Stay out of this bar!"] and a parking ticket here costs you 50 cents.

"Miss Ohio is crowned here every year, and this year she went on to become Miss America. Anyone old enough to be Miss America's father or mother might easily think of Mansfield as the place where Andy Hardy grew up."

Since my wife, Sigrid, and I had grown up only 70 miles south of Mansfield, and we had both become dissatisfied with life in Chicago, I decided to send *News Journal* publisher Harry Horvitz the series of articles the soon-to-die *Daily News* series on Mansfield and ask if he had any jobs available in his chain of several similar-sized newspapers.

When I was named editor of *The News Journal* six weeks later I thought it was a dream come true. But that dream turned out to be a nightmare instead. Before it was over I had lost my job, my house, my car, my savings, my health and, eventually, my marriage. I also had endured 18 months of threats on my life; rocks thrown through windows; continual surveillance by the sheriff's department; the intentional burning of a building used by the newspaper I started after Horvitz tried to muzzle me; break-ins of its newsroom; and, finally, smears on my personal and professional reputation.

In return, I gained some $150,000 in debts. Included in that amount was what seemed to be a relatively trifling $11,000 I owed the IRS that I paid several times over in the 20 years it took to get the issue resolved. But that was small potatoes compared with the $45 million in libel suits — all of which were eventually dismissed – that Mansfield's officious officials filed in an effort to shut me up.

Along the way, I also encountered a cast of characters more corrupt, brutal and venal than I could ever dream up. In addition to Sheriff Weikel and his Gestapo-like deputies, they included:

● A coroner who stole from the dead and jeopardized the lives of thousands around the world through lax testing procedures at his private medical lab.

● A national foundation that primarily promoted the interests, including prurient interests, of chairman Sammy Davis Jr. and Mansfield's elite before it collapsed with several million dollars missing — and barely a notice in *The News Journal.*

● City officials who openly dispensed favors to their friends and relatives and grabbed all the goodies for themselves that they could get their hands on.

● Judges who routinely faced allegations of drunken driving and domestic abuse only to have the charges dropped and who looked down upon those they judged through eyeglasses stolen from the U.S. government.

● A prosecutor who somehow remained oblivious to all of this, and who often sought to discredit those who tried to stop it.

● Finally, and most tragically, a newspaper that not only ignored this corruption, but also was actively involved in it.

The Daily News' Coffey – a masterful globe-trotting reporter of the first order — could hardly be faulted for overlooking this any more than I could for believing the Mansfield myth when I was wined and dined by Horvitz and general manger Robert Blake. Nor was the venerable Coffey the first to portray Mansfield as a typical American town or political microcosm.

In his 1947 best seller, *Inside USA,* John Gunther portrayed the city as a cultural as well as a transportation crossroads. Mansfield, Gunther wrote, "is on the main line of both the Pennsylvania and Erie railroads, with direct service to New York and Chicago both; it is on a branch line of the Baltimore & Ohio, and the New York Central is only 12 miles distant. A stone's throw away northward is Norwalk, a pure New England town; a stone's throw away southward is Mount Vernon, a pure southern town. Consider, too, crossroads in another dimension. Mansfield has 60 industrial plants, but it is the center of some of the richest agricultural areas on earth."

"That was followed in the 1950s by glowing portraits of Mansfield as the typical American town in *Life* and other magazines.

Syndicated columnist Neal Peirce was equally enamored of Mansfield's representative nature. Pointing out that it is such medium-sized cities that contribute so much to Ohio's typicality and conservatism, Peirce focused on Mansfield as their representative in his book *The Megastates of America* in 1972.

"A touch of glamour has long been applied to Mansfield," Peirce wrote, "perhaps separating it from many other smaller Ohio cities. More than a century ago, railroad financiers used to meet in Mansfield, and Abraham Lincoln's name was first mentioned in regard to the presidency at such a Mansfield gathering. Senator John Sherman of Antitrust Act fame was from Mansfield, and it was the birthplace of the late Pulitzer Prize-winning author, Louis Bromfield, who turned his famed Malabar Farm outside the city into a conservation showcase and gathering place for writers and entertainers. Kay Francis, movie star of the '30s, used to come and dance with her shoes off; another visitor was John Gunther while he was traveling the country to write *Inside USA*. But nothing more famous ever happened at Malabar than the 1945 marriage of Humphrey Bogart and Lauren Bacall; as if nothing were holy, their nuptial bed can still be viewed on daily tours of the home."

CBS-TV News continued the tradition of using Mansfield as a special sounding-board during the 1980 presidential campaign, as did *The New York Times Sunday Magazine* in a 1984 cover story by the late two-time Pulitzer Prize-winner J. Anthony Lukas.

'Touch of glamour' lost
Despite its typicality, Mansfield has had the "touch of glamour" Peirce wrote about since its beginnings in 1800, when one of its first settlers was John Chapman, better known as Johnny Appleseed, one of the best-known figures in American folklore.

Mansfield was soon designated the seat of Richland County, which derived its name from the richness of its soil. The city was named after the Surveyor General of the United States, Colonel Jared Mansfield. The surveyor general's namesake was originally platted as a square with Central Park at the center. Richland County's first courthouse was one of two blockhouses built in Central Park during the War of 1812.

Indian attacks were frequent during the war. In one instance, several settlers were killed in the Black Fork Valley east of Mansfield. When settlers who escaped the attack sought refuge in the Block House, they warned that Mansfield was the Indians' next target. That set the pioneers, few of whom owned weapons, into a panic. They decided to send a messenger to this Camp Douglas 30 miles away to ask for troops to protect them.

When a volunteer was sought for the risky journey, the barefooted Johnny Appleseed stepped forward. As Appleseed ran through the forest on his way to Camp Douglas, he warned those who lived along the way to flee to the Block House. The next day, Appleseed returned troops to guard the settlement, possibly saving young Mansfield in the process.

That was just a small part of the legendary Appleseed's legacy in Richland County, where he lived from 1810 to 1830 — often with his half-sister, Persis Chapman Broome. All the early orchards of Richland County originated in one or another of his nurseries.

Appleseed's reported eccentricities only added to his appeal. The Massachusetts native often wore a coffee sack with holes cut for his head and arms. He went barefoot most of the time, even in winter, and for a hat he wore a tin pan, which also served as a stew pan in which he cooked his food. Chapman chose to grow apples because they were particularly important to the early settlers. Apples were the easiest fruit to grow and to store for year-round use without adding expensive sugar.

Following the area's streams and their tributaries, Chapman planted apple seeds wherever he found suitable ground for a nursery. He enclosed these spots with fences made of brush.

Each year he returned to care for the growing trees and to plant new nurseries. When settlers came he urged them to plant trees and advised them as to what varieties to plant. He kept ahead of the settlements and each year planted apple seeds farther west. In this way he covered most of Ohio and came far into Indiana.

Chapman's visits to the settlements were looked forward to with delight and no cabin door was ever closed to him. To adults he was news carrier and oracle. He taught the boys how to make sleds and wagons, and brought bits of ribbon and calico for the girls. Appleseed reportedly was a strict vegetarian. He believed it was wrong to take life in order to procure food. This, no doubt, added to his zeal in urging people to plant and grow fruit. But Johnny Appleseed didn't just give away apple seedlings and seeds, as it is often suggested. He was a businessman, albeit a softhearted one. Appleseed charged the going rate of 6 or 7 cents for his trees. But if setters couldn't pay, he would accept cornmeal or old clothes or a promise to pay in the future. Appleseed used much of his profit for charity and to further his work rather than for his personal comfort.

The arrival of the railroad in 1846 – one year after Chapman's death – soon led Mansfield in a direction the nature-loving Chapman would not have appreciated. With the whole nation suddenly within their reach, the city's farm-equipment and stove manufacturing industries, led by the nationally known Tappan Company, were booming. These were followed in the late 1800s and early 1900s by a large steel mill, tire companies and a massive, multistoried Westinghouse plant that produced electric lights and home appliances. By the late 1920s Westinghouse was Mansfield's largest employer. The factory remained a local economic powerhouse until the 1980s, when it fell victim to its antiquated design and American heavy industry moved its production to cheaper overseas labor markets.

During the labor shortage caused by World War II, Mansfield's high-paying jobs at Westinghouse, Tappan and Mansfield Tire began to attract eager workers from impoverished Appalachia. I became interested in the roots of this migration shortly after I became editor of *The News Journal*. As I read the paper closely each day I couldn't help notice frequent references to Olive Hill, Kentucky, in many obituaries and other announcements.

When I asked about it, I learned that a large percentage of Mansfield's Appalachian community had its roots in tiny Olive Hill. I later sent a reporter and photographer to the tiny Eastern Kentucky town. They came back with an interview with the mayor, who had several brothers in Mansfield, and a photo of some kids playing in a park who turned out to be from Mansfield and were just visiting relatives there.

As the city grew and prospered, it developed into a fascinating amalgamation that, in addition to Appalachians, included WASPS, middle-class whites and a solid black community that dates back to the town's underground railroad days. When I arrived, the black community's councilman and spokesman was the Rev. Joel King, who unfortunately wasn't as courageous or effective as his famous nephew, Martin Luther King Jr. Between the famous names of Chapman and King were many others associated with Mansfield through the years. One of the area's early notables was Jedediah Smith, who lived just south of Mansfield in his formative years and went on to became the most famous of the legendary "Mountain Men" who explored the American West. Smith was among the first Americans to cross west over the Continental Divide, during which he rediscovered the forgotten South Pass, the key to the settlement of Oregon and California. Smith was also the first American to cross California's scraggy Sierra Nevada Mountains. He later became the first American to enter California by land from the east, by way of the Mojave Desert, and to cross the hot, expansive Great Basin Desert when he made his return trip. Smith was killed by Comanche warriors in 1831 while looking for water on the Santa Fe Trail.

Next to Johnny Appleseed, the most famous Mansfield of the 19th century was John Sherman, who came to Mansfield from Lancaster, Ohio, to study law. Sherman was first elected to represent the Mansfield area in Congress in 1854. During the next four decades, he served in both houses of Congress and as secretary of state and secretary of treasury. He is probably best known as the author of the Sherman Antitrust Act. John Sherman's brother was General William Tecumseh Sherman, who made history with his victory march through Georgia during the Civil War.

Richland County was later home for Charles Follis, who earned the distinction of being the first black professional football player when played halfback for the Shelby Blues from 1907 to 1910. Follis' feat later earned him a place in the NFL Hall of Fame in nearby Canton.

Richland County has also produced several notable writers, including Dawn Powell of Shelby, whom Gore Vidal has called "our best comic novelist." Powell was a vital part of Greenwich Village literary circles from the 1920s through the 1960s. Powell often wrote of small-town Ohio where she had a difficult childhood that she later fictionalized in her 1944 novel *My Home Is Far Away.*

Far more famous was Louis Bromfield, who won a Pulitzer Prize in 1926 for his novel *Early Autumn* and later returned to Richland County to develop his internationally known Malabar Farm, which is now a state park. It was Bromfield who first helped me realize that as Mansfield had gained so much during its boom years it had lost something in return. During my first visit to Bromfield's fascinating 200-year-old home at Malabar, I picked up a copy of one of his best-known books, *The Farm*, in the gift shop. The book is a history of Bromfield's family farm near Mansfield, which he referred to as "The Town," before "progress" almost destroyed both. In one passage, Bromfield wrote that his father could have had a successful political career in Mansfield except that "he had no gift for compromise, nor the chicanery which was necessary in a political life that was highly organized and all too frequently dominated by unscrupulous bosses or businessmen seeking privileges in return for money."

"The politicians had small use for him because he was too honest," Bromfield wrote. "Sometimes, they said, as if it were a reproach, that he did not know how to make money, and in the eyes of certain citizens that was the first fault of all."

But Bromfield saved some of his most bitter criticism for the average citizen who had let such a system thrive in the first place. Speaking of the death of his pioneer grandfather, he wrote: "For him, that was the bitterest evidence of defeat — the fact that the citizen, the man in the street, so long as he was prosperous, no longer cherished a sense of duty, of honor, of decency. . . . It was not as though they were hypocrites, but that, yielding, they came to believe that bargaining and compromise and bad faith were simply a part of the new political philosophy and must be accepted, for the general good but most of all for the good of business."

Bromfield wrote an equally disturbing portrayal of Mansfield in *The Green Bay Tree*, in which Julia Shane, daughter of The Town's founder, accurately predicts that her Cousin Charlie would never survive as county treasurer because of his honesty.

"You see," she continued, "in going over the books, Cousin Charlie discovered that the Cyclops Mills owe the county about five hundred thousand dollars in back taxes. He's sued to recover the money together with the fines, and he cannot lose. Judge Weissman and Mrs. Harrison have just discovered that, and they've come to me to call him off because he is set on recovering the money. He's refused to take orders. You see, it hits their pocket-books. The man who was treasurer before Charlie has disappeared neatly. There's a pretty scandal somewhere. Even if doesn't come out, the Harrisons and Judge Weissman will lose a few hundred thousand."

"And what did you tell them?" Julia's daughter Lily asked.

"Tell them! Tell them!" cried Julia Shane. "What could I tell them? Only that I could do nothing. I told them they were dealing with an honest man." . . . But I'm sorry for Charlie and Hattie, just the same. He'll suffer for it. He has killed himself politically."

"It can't be as bad as that!" Lily argued. "That can't happen to a man because he did his duty. The Town can't be as rotten as that!"

"It is, though," Shane replies matter-of-factly. "It is. You've no idea how rotten it is. Why, Cousin Charlie is a lamb among the wolves. Believe me, I know. It's worse than when your father was alive. The mills have made it worse."

I would later discover how right Julia Shane was. In fact, I found that Johnny Appleseed's hometown wasn't just rotten. It was rotten to the core.

A phone call my first day on the job gave me my first warning of that.

"Are you the new editor?" an older-sounding woman asked.

"Yes, I am," I said proudly.

"Well, I've got a question for you. Are you going to cover up everything that goes on in this town like the other editors did?"

"I'm not sure I understand," I replied, both confused and curious.

"You've got a lot to learn, son. Take a look at the lumps of dirt under your carpet. Then you'll begin to understand."

I got my first peek under the carpet a few days later during a get-acquainted meeting with reporters.

First sign of cover-ups

"Let's suppose I come up with information about a judge getting arrested for drunk driving and causing an accident," said a pipe-smoking George Constable, whom I would soon make a columnist. "Would you run a story on it?"

"Not only would I run a story, I'd run it on the front page," I replied.

"That's interesting," Constable mused. "I had a story like that killed by the higher-ups last year."

"Do you still have a file on the case?" I asked.

"You bet," Constable said with a smile.

"I'd like to see it when we're finished here."

When I did, I could see immediately why the story had been killed. The judge was Richard Christiansen — the paper's former lawyer and a close friend of general manager Robert Blake. Even worse, Christiansen was driving home from a Christmas party at the publisher's cable TV franchise.

When I asked Blake why the story on Christiansen was killed, he became visibly irritated. "First of all, it would have been embarrassing to us as well as to him," he snapped. "Furthermore, we don't run stories about an arrest unless someone is formally charged. Of course, it's pretty obvious why he wasn't charged, but we can't help that."

(I would later learn that this wasn't Christiansen's first brush with the law, and that the assistant city solicitor who pushed for the judge to be prosecuted in this case soon found himself out of a job.)

It was beginning to become pretty obvious that something was very wrong at *The News Journal* and that Blake had a lot to do with it. He proved that once and for all a few months later, when he told me he was to have lunch with Sheriff Weikel to see if he could get him to agree to straighten up his act before we ran the results of the highly- productive investigation of his department I had launched.

I was outraged that Blake would even consider proposing such a deal. But I would soon learn that such meddling in the news department was standard fare for the tall, imperious "Blowhard Blake," as some employees called him. To Blake, I learned the hard way, protecting Mansfield's business and political establishment came before almost all else. Blake proved that in a second incident during my first weeks at *The News Journal* when he called me into his large office, which was as bland as Sinclair Lewis' George Babbitt-incarnate was proving to be.

Blake proceeded to explain that he was a member of an ad-hoc committee to break local labor unions, which he likened to a cancer on the march of Mansfield's progress. As he sat behind his desk and placed his hands on the back of his head as he always did when he was feeling full of himself, the spectacled, silver-haired Blake informed me that Mansfield's huge Westinghouse plant was going to announce large layoffs that presaged its demise several years later.

"The head of the Westinghouse union is a radical who always twists what management says," Blake told me. "So when I give you the news release announcing the layoffs tomorrow, I don't want you to give it to the business reporter until it's too late for her to get the union's response before we go to press. She can do a follow-up on what the union says the following day. But I want the company to have its say first."

"That's not very fair," I told Blake. "You're putting us in a position of manipulating the news."

"That's one of the privileges of owning a newspaper," a red-faced Blake said. "So you'd better get used to it. It's part of your job."

That was news to me. Blake and publisher Harry Horvitz had apparently feigned the enthusiasm they showed when I told them in interviews before they hired me that I believed the modern newspaper had to be a fiercely independent, positive force in the community. A good newspaper, I told them, must make news as well as report news. One way to do that, I explained, was through aggressive reporting that left no stone unturned in its pursuit of the truth. Another was to get the newspaper's readers involved through an editorial advisory committee to make them feel that *The News Journal* was *their* newspaper. A third way was to set an agenda that the community could rally around, as I later did by launching a campaign to have Mansfield strive for the improvements needed for it to be named an All-American City.

I later realized I had spoken heresy to Horvitz and Blake, but it didn't seem to bother them at the time. They apparently felt that I could be controlled once they got me aboard, just as they had co-opted the long-time editor who preceded me. If they did, I thought as I left Blake's office that day, they were sorely mistaken.

But my immediate concern at that time was dealing with Sheriff Weikel. And that wouldn't be easy. I quickly learned that Weikel was a lot more than a bully with a badge. He was, as then-State Rep. and now-U.S. Rep. Sherrod Brown put it, "a wild man."

2

The Badge of Terror

By 1978, Sheriff Thomas E. Weikel had been in office for 14 years. And it looked like he would be there for many more, judging from his tremendous success at the polls, where he had run up huge victory margins every time he had run for re-election.

To some, Weikel seemed like the perfect lawman. He talked tough, looked tough and, most important, acted tough. No one pushed Tom Weikel around. That included anyone who so much as looked like a criminal — as well as attorneys who dared to defend those he particularly despised.

Weikel ran a tight ship. The average deputy had to toe the line and follow orders or else. Those who belonged to Weikel's inner circle, however, could get away with almost anything. That double standard eventually had much to do with Weikel's downfall.

Weikel's rise before that fall had been steady, if not spectacular. He was born on April 2, 1922, in a tough South Philadelphia neighborhood. After graduating from high school in 1939, Weikel joined the army, where he soldiered under General George S. Patton during World War II. Weikel later served as an infantry platoon sergeant in the Korean War, where he won a battlefield commission, a Silver Star and a Purple Heart.

It was Weikel's last assignment in the Army that brought him to Mansfield. He served as Army Reserve adviser there until February 1961, when he retired. By then, he had married the former Betty Dysart, whose father, Harold, was a Tappan Co. executive and a leading figure in the local Republican Party.

After working in the Ohio Bureau of Unemployment Services for a year, Weikel eagerly accepted an appointment as a deputy with Sheriff Richard E. Steele.

During the next 21 months, Weikel was moved in and out of several departments. According to several deputies who were there at the time, the reason for the shifts was that Weikel simply didn't seem to work out anywhere. In fact, Weikel's stubbornness reportedly caused more than one run-in with Sheriff Steele. After one of those arguments in January 1964, Steele told several high-ranking deputies that he was going to fire Weikel at the end of the month.

Four days earlier, however, fortune smiled on Weikel for the first of many times in Mansfield: Sheriff Steele dropped dead of a heart attack. Several days later, on February 4, 1964, the Republican Party Central Committee, at the urging of his powerful father-in-law, appointed Weikel sheriff.

Good sheriff at first

By most accounts, Weikel was a good sheriff during his first term in office. He appeared to be congenial and tried to get along with the deputies he had inherited from Steele.

"For the first four years he was in office, he did a great job," brother-in-law Robert Dysart, who served as Weikel's second-in-command for several years, told me. "He even drove his own car, not a county car. It seemed like after he was elected on his own in 1968, though, that there was a gradual change. The longer he was in office, the worse he got. I wasn't used to that. I could see things he was doing that just weren't right. I'll admit that some of his actions were also rubbing off on me. That's why I finally got out."

Dysart wasn't alone. The older, more experienced deputies began to leave in droves in the late 1960s. In their place, Weikel hired deputies whose loyalty to him came before all else.

One of the first of Weikel's new breed to join the force was Raymond Eugene Hart, who came aboard in 1967 at the age of 22. Another Weikel favorite was Shirley Whisler, who joined the force in 1968. It was those two young deputies, many sources said, who curried Weikel's favor more than anyone else in the coming years, and they eventually became his most trusted assistants.

Hart got off to a rocky start, however. Shortly after joining the department, according to news reports at the time, Hart wrecked the department's newest cruiser while allegedly pursuing a car that had no license plate. To make matters worse, Hart wrecked the car in the front yard of a county commissioner.

One month later, Hart was driving a cruiser at a high rate of speed while another deputy, Robert Pershing, was holding a gun on a person they had just apprehended. As Hart sped over a bump, the gun accidentally discharged, wounding Pershing in the foot, according to news reports. Weikel apparently was fed up. He reportedly gave Hart an angry dressing down, then fired him.

"If anyone had talked to me like that, I would never have gone back," a deputy who claimed to have overheard Weikel's tirade told *The News Journal* in 1978.

But Hart did go back. Several months later he turned up working as an undercover agent during a major drug raid in Columbus in which several Mansfielders were arrested. The next day, Weikel announced that Hart had never really been fired. He said Hart had been quietly transferred to the undercover job that had led to the arrests and would be rejoining the department.

Hart would later show that he would do almost anything to keep his job once he had gotten it back. He became a tough law-and-order man as he rose through the ranks.

After he was appointed second-in-command, sources said, Hart initiated a controversial car-stop program in which people were stopped without cause. They said Hart also established traffic-ticket quotas to increase the number of traffic citations issued by the department. At one time, several former deputies said, if a deputy hadn't written at least two tickets a night, he would have to go back out until he did.

But Hart was allegedly a law-and-disorder man, too. Ex-employees were quoted by *The News Journal* in 1978 as saying that he encouraged deputies to break the law if necessary to enforce it, that he sanctioned brutality, and that he became a participant in many of the department's myriad corruption schemes.

One alleged scheme was the publication of two "drug education" books financed by advertising from local businesses, which were eager to show their support.

The second book, for example, brought in $28,790. Although the books were collections of copyrighted articles, the book credited Hart for "preparations and comments," thus adding to his reputation as an expert on drugs. While the book was well-received in Mansfield, it wasn't by the state auditor, whose office had found that similar books printed for other sheriffs had resulted in substantial amounts of unaccounted revenue. The auditor apparently expected to find the same thing in Richland County.

But Weikel and Hart outfoxed him, former department members claimed. Several ex-deputies told *The News Journal* they were called into the department in the middle of the night before the auditor's office was supposed to make a surprise visit and asked to sign blank receipts to reconcile expenses with the books' proceeds. If true, the tactic worked. The auditor was unable to find any evidence of impropriety.

After the alleged cover-up was reported in the award-winning *News Journal* investigative series I launched in 1978, the auditor sought the records for a more detailed audit. But Weikel said the records had been destroyed by accident.

Controversial shooting

Hart became embroiled in another controversy at the same time the drug books were published, and the result was far more tragic. On March 15, 1970, Hart responded to a domestic-disturbance call. Moments later, 19-year-old Joseph Grove, estranged husband of the woman who had placed the call, was dead.

Hart had shot him, he later said, in self-defense after Grove had attempted to stab him, breaking his knife's blade in the process when it struck a pack of credit cards in Hart's shirt pocket. Five days later, Coroner Robert W. Wolford ruled that Grove's death was a justifiable homicide. But rumors that there was more to the killing than met Wolford's often-blurry eyes were still circulating in Mansfield when I arrived eight years later. It didn't take me long to find out why. In October of the same year of the shooting, I discovered, attorney Vincent Phelan — one of several attorneys reportedly harassed by Weikel's deputies — attempted to have Jerry Lee Clark, one of the four witnesses to the shooting, testify about what had occurred at the time of the incident during a court hearing on a different case involving Hart.

After Clark was sworn in, the judge ruled that his testimony would be irrelevant. But the judge did permit Phelan to enter into the record that, if Clark could testify, he would state that he and Grove's father-in-law were both restraining Grove when Hart "bent over so that he could place the revolver, which looked like a .38 snub-nosed revolver, against Joseph Grove's chest, . . . pulled the trigger and did then and there kill Joseph Grove." The statement added that "Hart was in such close proximity to the decedent that he could have struck the decedent upon the head with his revolver, and this was an excessive use of force under the circumstances."

Clark stuck to his story when he was interviewed in 1991. "Hart just walked inside the trailer without knocking and without anyone letting him in," Clark said. He immediately pulled his revolver when he entered the trailer. Hart immediately told Joe Grove, 'I'm going to shoot you.' . . . Hart was not in danger. . . . I was holding Joe from behind and he was bent over trying to shake me off when Gene Hart came over to within arm's length of Joe, held his gun with his arm fully extended, placed his gun to Joe's chest and shot Joe without warning. I was shocked. I didn't think anyone would be shot."

Earl Boggs, the former father-in-law of Grove, corroborated Clark's statement that the shooting was unjustified, even though he couldn't recall Clark restraining Grove.

"Joe had the knife in his hand and he always had the knife in a downward position near his side," Boggs stated in 1991. "Joe had no intention to use the knife. Joe was standing up and next to the couch when Gene Hart suddenly, and without warning, shot Joe. Joe never raised the knife, and I do not remember him ever threatening anyone while Gene Hart was there. . . . Immediately after Joe was shot I asked Gene Hart, 'What did you do that for?' I also told him, 'The boy needed help, not that.' " Margaret Boggs, Earl Boggs' wife, added that Hart was "gun-happy for sure."

As was typical at that time, Clark's proffered court statement never made the news. When I investigated the case nine years later, I called Hart for his side of the story, and got the same response I would in several other instances when I tried to obtain his side of the story.

"I'd like to ask you some questions about the Joseph Grove, case," I told him.

"The *what* case?" Hart asked, as if he had never heard Joseph Grove's name before.

"The Joseph Grove case — the guy you shot after responding to a domestic-disturbance call in 1970."

"That was a long time ago," Hart said. "I'll have to check my files and get back to you." Hart didn't, however, even after I left several messages for him. So I ran the story without his comments.

Accident or murder?

Three months after the Grove shooting incident, Hart allegedly was involved in yet another mysterious case, although possibly not as much as some claimed.

Just before 4 a.m. on June 11, 1970, a milk truck was driving along Route 97 one mile east of the small Richland County town of Butler. As the driver came over the crest of the hill, he saw a man lying face down in the middle of the road in a downhill position.

Unable to stop, the driver swerved so his wheels straddled the body. Unfortunately, the undercarriage hit the man's head, ripping the top completely off.

The victim was identified as Kelly Dean Gentry, a 20-year-old AWOL soldier whose family had moved to Richland County from the hills of Virginia a few years before. But several questions about Gentry's death didn't die with him. Among them were:

• How did Gentry come to be lying in the middle of a country road in the middle of the night in an uncomfortable downhill position?

• Why was he practically naked, save for a pair of coveralls that weren't his?

• Why did Hart try to get Gentry's best friend to plead guilty to murdering Gentry if someone didn't suspect foul play?

• How did Gentry come to have broken bones and blood and bruises all over his body that apparently predated the accident?

• Finally, what happened to the men several of Gentry's friends said were chasing him when they last saw him alive?

The beginning of Gentry's end came when he stole some gasoline from a school bus garage in nearby Lexington on June 7, and a motorcycle from an employee of the Hulcher railroad emergency service on June 8.

Gentry and several friends then went camping in a wooded area outside of Butler.

Captain Ray Herschler of the Lexington Police Department later said that officers from three police departments, the sheriff's department, members of the Naval Reserves and employees of the Hulcher company searched the area for three days before locating the Gentry gang on the afternoon of June 10.

No one could explain why so much attention was paid to the theft of one motorcycle and some gas, nor why the Hulcher employees and members of the Naval Reserves were brought into the search in apparent violation of the law.

All that was said was that the camp had been found, that three juvenile girls had been arrested, and that Gentry and the other boys had escaped.

But that was the official version. A more disturbing account was given to Lexington police by one of the girls, and it was later confirmed by several witnesses.

"Some boys were walking through the woods, ducking down like they were hiding," she stated. "Then, before any of us girls knew what happened, John Markley yelled, 'Run!' We started off; but the boys tackled us. Someone fired a gun and yelled halt. I thought he got Dean [Gentry] or one of the boys, so I turned around. The boys that got us were the Hulchers — the guys Dean stole the motorcycle from. I was cussing and everything at them. They took us up a hill and the fuzz was there. I was smarting off and calling them names because Dean's brother was there — he told where we were. But he had to – they put his family in jail."

I later confirmed that several members of the Gentry family were indeed taken to jail even though they apparently were never charged with a crime, never read their rights and never permitted to call a lawyer.

Members of the Gentry family later told me that the deputy who arrested the family and also transported Ronald Gentry, 16, to the area where he was forced to reveal his brother's hideout, was Gene Hart.

Kelly Dean Gentry, meanwhile, had fled with his friend, Michael Giffin. In a statement later given to the Lexington police, Giffin said that when he and Gentry heard gunshots, they ran through the woods to Route 97.

"We walked down 97 about a half a mile and stood there and hitch-hiked," Giffin said. "And then I saw a red pickup truck coming and I told Dean it was the Hulchers, so I hid down in the ditch and Dean stood there until [those in] the truck seen him. Then we both ran up over this little hill in the woods, and the Hulchers were right behind us, so I hid in this guy's garage and they went on past me still chasing Dean."

Giffin later managed to slip away. As he neared Lexington the next morning, however, he was arrested and taken to Richland County Jail. He had learned that Gentry had been killed just before his arrest, and at the jail he was told for the first time that Gentry's body had blood on it that was several hours old at the time of his death.

Giffin claimed he was then given a polygraph exam by Hart, who told him that the results showed he had killed Gentry and he should confess. Giffin said he refused, and that he was never bothered again.

But Giffin later stressed in several telephone interviews from his home in Florida that the Hulchers were carrying clubs when he saw them chasing Gentry only 500 yards from where he died. He speculated that the Hulchers caught Gentry, severely beat him and then dumped him in the road at a time when they wouldn't be seen. Almost every other friend or relative interviewed agreed.

Then-Coroner Robert W. Wolford must have had suspicions, too. Although Wolford never made his report public, he did record that Gentry had suffered multiple cuts, bruises and fractures on both legs that probably had been "previously produced" before the truck hit him.

Unfortunately, Wolford didn't seem any more interested in finding out how Gentry got all those injuries than anyone else. Nor was anyone interested in following up on a report by the first people to arrive at the accident scene that a car full of men they later identified as members of the Hulcher gang sped by jeering at Gentry's body almost within seconds of his death.

The witnesses, who asked to meet with me late at night so they would be less likely to be identified as my sources, told me they had seen the same car parked near where Gentry was hit a short time before the accident. They described the car as a black Pontiac. When I asked two of Gentry's friends to describe the car in which they saw some of the Hulchers as they fled the camp, both described it as being black and one said it was a Pontiac.

The two witnesses also told me that the first officers at the scene had remarked that Gentry appeared to have been beaten.

"I saw one of the cops bring a piece of wood down from the hill and put it in a plastic bag," one of the witnesses said. "It had blood and hair all over it."

When I tried to ask Hart why the case was closed with so much evidence of foul play, he once again said he would have to review his files before he could reply.

He failed to return several phone calls after that, and finally left a message referring all questions to his attorney, Robert Whitney, who, according to Mrs. Gentry, had told her at the time of her son's death that she had no legal recourse for all her family had endured.

Mrs. Gentry told me by telephone that the Hulcher gang used to ride their motorcycles around their house several times a week, and to tease her at her place of work about how they had killed her son. "We finally couldn't take it anymore and decided to return to Virginia," she told me between sobs.

After I revealed all this information in 1979, I pushed for an investigation of what very well could have been a murder in which law enforcement was peripherally involved and probably covered up. But no one seemed to care.

Ex-trooper comes forward

As it turned out, former Ohio State Highway Patrol Trooper Norman Helser *did* care. But because he was working undercover for the U.S. Customs Department in Florida when my stories appeared, he thought it was too risky to come forward at that time. When he finally left Customs in 1992 and returned to Ohio, Helser tracked me down to tell me my stories were accurate.

"There is no doubt in my mind that it was a homicide," said Helser, who originally investigated Gentry's death. "It *was just obvious* that this Gentry thing was a cover-up from the word go. Nothing that was happening made sense. I asked questions and didn't get any answers. I just got pushed aside, even though it was my case."

Helser said he had little doubt after looking at Gentry's body at Mansfield General Hospital that Gentry "was laid out in the road and the truck just finished him off."

"It was obvious that he [Gentry] had serious damage to his elbows and knees previous to the accident," Helser said. "It looked to me like someone had taken a 2-by-4, placed the end of it on his knees and elbows, then hit it with a sledge hammer."

Helser said the investigation was taken away from him by Sgt. Richard Petty, who was later elected sheriff after Weikel's conviction. Helser said he believed Petty originally took the case away from him "because he was going to crack it and it was going to be his claim to fame." But Petty's attitude changed, Helser said, after he talked to Herschler at the Lexington Police Department, who organized the search and was Petty's friend. "When Petty came back, I told him that I had some things I wanted to do on the case," Helser said. "But the next day was my day off; and Petty told me, 'Don't worry about it. I'll handle it." He just took the case away from me at that point. And that's not the way the Highway Patrol does things. The supervisor is not there to do the investigation. He's there to assist. But he absolutely took it away from me."

Petty strongly defended his investigation during a 1979 interview. "We covered every inch we could within our jurisdiction," Petty said. "As far as the circumstances leading up to the accident being strange, I reckon they are." But that part of the investigation, Petty said, was the responsibility of the sheriff's department. But Helser said he couldn't dismiss the case that easily. "This is something that has bugged me forever because I *know* that it was a vigilante deal and I *know* it was covered up," Helser said. "I even told Petty when this so-called investigation was going on to go down and grab some of those people at Hulcher's and put them on the hot seat. . . . And there again, he just shrugged me off."

When I reported Helser's comments about the Gentry case in 1994, Richland County Prosecutor James J. Mayer Jr. called to tell me he was going to talk to Sheriff James Stierhoff and the Highway Patrol about reopening the case. Stierhoff, who was a state trooper and was at the scene of Gentry's death, wholeheartedly supported a new investigation.

"There's no doubt in my mind that Gentry was murdered, Stierhoff said. "Since Gentry had two broken legs, the only way he could have got to the middle of the road was to pull himself there. So I walked up and down both sides of the road looking for signs of the gravel being disturbed and couldn't find any. As far as I'm concerned, Gentry had to have been dumped in the road. He didn't get there on his own."

Stierhoff, who also saw Gentry's body at the hospital, agreed with Helser's description of his wounds. "It looked like he had been beaten with 2-by-4s," Stierhoff said. Stierhoff said he also suspected that Herschler, the Lexington "super cop," who organized the search party and was known to have a vendetta against Gentry, may have been involved in his death or at least knew who was.

"When he walked into the hospital, Herschler took one quick look at the body and said it was definitely Dean Gentry," Stierhoff said. "I couldn't understand how he could be so sure, especially since the top of his head was gone and his face was badly disfigured. He acted like he knew [it was Gentry] before he even looked."

The investigative team assembled by Prosecutor Mayer eventually concluded that Gentry was indeed murdered, and that the two most likely suspects in the killing were Herschler and the Hulcher crew member who owned the motorcycle Gentry had stolen. Unfortunately, when investigators tried to locate the suspects, they determined that both were dead, so the case was closed.

In marked contrast to how the Gentry gang was treated for the relatively minor offense of one of its members is how deputies acted when they discovered a similar beer and pot party seven years later. This time there were no gunshots, no vigilante actions and no incarcerations of families. Instead, the youths involved were treated with kid gloves. Of course, the fact that one of them was Sheriff Weikel's kid may have had something to do with their much gentler treatment.

Weikel's law

Quite obviously, the Richland County Sheriff's Department was remarkably different from the norm. Its only standards were Sheriff Weikel's standards, and the only law was Sheriff Weikel's law.

By 1970, Weikel had begun to make that philosophy clear to all. He dressed down politicians, had those who opposed him harassed by deputies, allegedly subjected prisoners to physical and mental abuse, and, according to sources in a position to know, created a system of widespread corruption. But few seemed to notice. And those who did kept it to themselves. The reason, in a word, was fear: fear of what Weikel could do to them and their families or fear of what Weikel had on them — and that often was plenty.

Those who dared cross him often found themselves faced with what they claimed were trumped-up charges. Others said they had their livelihoods destroyed.

Then Weikel made the first of many missteps that would eventually terminate his reign of terror. In June 1977, 15 deputies dared to challenge Weikel's authority by forming an "association" to achieve better working conditions.

Weikel's reaction was predictable. He called a department meeting, during which he threatened to fire anyone who didn't quit the association immediately. When one of the group tried to explain why the deputies felt the need to organize, Weikel cut him off in mid-sentence.

"I ought to knock your goddamn teeth out," he shouted. Then Weikel went wild, obviously unaware that one of his "disloyal" deputies was tape-recording his performance.

"You're as bad as the people you're arresting each day," he screamed at one deputy.

"Without that badge, you've got a yellow stripe up your back a foot wide," he derided another.

Then he gave the deputies the same kind of advice he had given me: "What all of you need is four years in the service," he told the deputies, many of them military veterans.

And if they wanted a fight, he left little doubt that he expected to come out on top. "I'll be around here a lot longer than you," he predicted. "In fact, I'll probably eat the bird that shits on your grave."

But the deputies had taken all the intimidation, threats, corruption and brutality they were going to take. A few weeks later, they staged a sick-out and Weikel promptly fired them. Asked at a press conference how the deputies were being notified of their termination, Weikel replied: "They're being notified right now, through the media."

Yet Weikel later successfully argued in a court case that the deputies had resigned rather than been fired because they had turned in their badges and weapons the next day without being terminated in writing, which would have allowed them to appeal the action as civil-service employees. But Weikel was less lucky in defending himself before the Ohio Ethics Commission against charges by eight of the former deputies that he had illegally taken $500 from a $2,000 reward given the department's pistol team and had used it in his 1976 re-election campaign.

The commission determined that Weikel and Capt. Shirley Whisler had illegally entered the money into his campaign fund in the name of several deputies, and recommended the pair be prosecuted for their actions. They never were, but only because the offense would soon seem too trivial to bother. The fired deputies did not remain idle during the intervening months. With the help of fed-up citizens, they passed petitions demanding Weikel's removal from office. They also began to drop hints that there was much more wrong with the department than they had yet mentioned. But no one seemed to be listening. It wasn't until my publication of Weikel's threatening phone call to me and the subsequent outpouring of accusations that anyone would.

The truth seeps out
Some of the accusations were so serious that they had to be thoroughly investigated by the two young, aggressive reporters Bob Hiles and Ron Rutti — I had assigned to look into them. As the investigation progressed, I slowly realized that there was no reason that much of the material we were uncovering could not have been reported before. One of the first people I interviewed, in fact, complained that he had come to *The News Journal* before to reveal what was going on at the county jail, but no one would talk to him.

"Who did you ask for?" I asked.

"The managing editor. The guy right out there," he said as he pointed to managing editor Robert May out in the newsroom. "He told me there was nothing he could do about it."

(Sherrod Brown, at that point the youngest elected state representative in Ohio history, told me he had referred several people who had complained to him about corruption and brutality in the sheriff's department to May as well. But nothing ever came of their allegations, either.) This was a pattern I was to see time and again. Some of it seemed to be a deliberate cover-up, done perhaps out of fear more than friendship. Some was done out of a lack of vigilance, as in the case of Gary Lee Mossor, who died in a cloud of mystery four months before my arrival.

When I pulled the clipping on Mossor's death, I was surprised to see the story was a mere three inches long — not very much for a death in a jail in a county the size of Richland County, which then billed itself as "The Fun Center of Ohio."

So I asked the reporter who covered the sheriff's department at the time why nothing more was done with the story.

"Didn't you hear any of the rumors going around about Mossor's death?" I asked.

"Sure," he replied.

"Did you do anything about them?"

"Yeah. . . . I told the coroner about them," he replied sheepishly, apparently knowing full well that the coroner had since been dragging his feet on looking into the suspicious aspects of Mossor's death.

I was later told by a former assistant city solicitor that the same reporter had known that the assistant solicitor had been fired for trying to prosecute Richland County Judge Richard Christiansen on drunken-driving charges, but the reporter had apparently done nothing with that story either.

Neither did the previous editor, who admitted during a tape-recorded meeting with the fired deputies that, "we have Judge Christiansen's drunk-driving record, and we let them [the officials] know we have it." Unfortunately, *The News Journal* never let its *readers* know the newspaper had it. No wonder the tension grew as the investigation of Weikel's department proceeded. Things seemed to hit bottom when general manager Blake called me into his office one day and asked me to close the door.

"I have some bad news," he said nervously. "I've been told Sheriff Weikel is investigating *The News Journal* in an attempt to discredit us before we can discredit him."

"Is that a problem?" I asked suspiciously.

"Well, it could be," he replied to my disappointment rather than shock, based on what I had begun to learn about the paper's previously cozy relationship with Weikel and the rest of the powers-that-be. "There *is* one possible source of embarrassment," he continued.

"What's that?"

"It's nothing serious, but Weikel could make it look that way if he finds out. As you know, the city council regulates our cable-TV company, and somewhere along the line the company began giving the council members and other city officials free cable service."

"Isn't that illegal?" I asked.

"No, but I am taking some steps to make sure it looks as above board as possible. I'm going to formalize it as a 'monitoring program,' and have those who get the service file written comments on its program quality. I'll just back-date some of them to cover earlier periods."

I couldn't believe what I was hearing. Memories of Watergate came to mind, only this time it was a newspaper doing the covering up rather than exposing it. I took Blake's claim that the free-cable deal wasn't illegal at face value, however, and suggested that it might be best to just report the situation in some kind of routine story.

"I'd rather do it my way," Blake snapped.

"OK. . . . You're the boss. But if you change your mind, I'll be glad to cooperate," I said, as I headed for the door before I lost my cool. I went back to my office and closed the door. I scanned its plush decor, the matching chairs, the large conference table. Not many journalists had it this nice at 28, I thought. But I wasn't about to sell my soul to keep it. Somehow I had to get the TV deal publicized before Weikel used it to sabotage our increasingly frightening investigation.

I needed help. But from whom? Then it hit me. I picked up the phone and called the local FBI office and set up a meeting with Smokey Stover, the agent in charge. A short time later I was seated at a dark restaurant table across from Stover, who was far more congenial than most FBI agents, who usually acted like they would prefer death to talking to a journalist. The few conversations we had before had been cat-and-mouse games in which we both tried to get as much information as we could while giving out as little as we could.

This time Stover was a lot more open. I have since been told by one of the top law-enforcement sources in Richland County that the reason for his talkativeness was that he was wired at the request of the prosecutor's office and wanted to encourage me talk as much as possible about what exactly I knew. Regardless, I got out of Stover what I wanted.

"I hear the sheriff decided that since you were investigating him, he should investigate you," Stover said with a chuckle.

"Yeah, I got a call from a Mansfield native who works in the courthouse in my home town to warn me that some of Weikel's deputies were down there trying to come up with some dirt on me, but they didn't find any," I said.

"What about Chicago?" Stover asked.

"What about it?" I replied.

"Did you hear about [Captain] Bill Miser supposedly going up there and coming back with a story that you had been sent to Mansfield by the mob to get rid of Weikel so the Chicago family could move in?"

"That's news to me," I said.

"Besides," Stover said, "Mansfield is already spoken for by the Cleveland mob."

Indeed it was. I had already learned about how the bullet-riddled body of a Cleveland mobster had been found in the trunk of a car at a notorious Richland County truck stop on 1-71, and had assembled some interesting information on how the mobster may have met his end at the hands of Mansfield mob operatives. But the same Captain Miser who liked to tell about my imaginary mob links didn't want anything to do with the real thing.

A former deputy told me Miser made one trip to Cleveland concerning the death, and "when he came back, the case was closed. We were told it was being turned over to the police in the town where the victim lived, which was kind of strange." The murder was never solved.

But now I feared Weikel, Miser, and company might be pursuing a case they were a lot less likely to drop. So I told Stover that I had heard Weikel was apparently investigating *The News Journal,* since he couldn't come up with anything on me.

"Oh, you mean the free-TV deal," Stover said, to my surprise. "Weikel's already turned over the details to us, but I wouldn't worry about it going any further. So far, it doesn't look like it violates federal law. (He later determined it did, much to the publisher's chagrin, but a federal grand jury decided not to issue indictments when it considered the evidence.) Of course, I can't speak for state law, only federal."

That's all I needed to hear. I headed back to the office and informed both publisher Horvitz by phone in his Cleveland office and Blake that Weikel already had the goods on the free-TV deal, and the best thing to do was to report it before Weikel found someone who might try to embarrass the paper with an investigation.

After quite a bit of wrangling, I finally got them to agree to revealing the practice in a general story about cable TV. They only permitted the inclusion of two paragraphs, but at least I had gotten something into print. I later learned from law-enforcement sources that the cable giveaway was in violation of several state laws, including the one on bribery.

By then, I was publisher of my own paper, so I put the story where it belonged: on Page One. *The News Journal,* after first pointing out it had already run a "story" on the practice, eventually dropped the "monitoring program" when it thought I wasn't looking.

Unfortunately for *The News Journal,* I was. After my paper reported the cancellation, *The News Journal* announced the end of the practice as if the whole town didn't already know. But the free-TV deal wasn't the only problem I found myself facing at *The News Journal.* I began to learn why so many in Mansfield had looked the other way during Weikel's reign of terror when I received a late-night phone call at home a few days after I first attacked the sheriff in print.

"You're going to be dead if you don't stop minding other people's business," a gruff voice said.

"That *is* my business," I replied.

"Not in this town. Don't say you weren't warned," said the voice, followed by a loud click.

A few days later, I received an early-morning call from a syndication salesman who had taken me to dinner the night before, then driven me home.

"I just thought you should know that as I pulled away from your house, I looked in the rearview mirror and saw a car with its lights out pull up and park in front of the house next to yours," he said. "So I drove around the block to see what was going on. The car was a sheriff's cruiser. It looks like that investigation you mentioned must have someone really angry. Just be careful, pal."

"Thanks," I said before hanging up and heading for the front window. Sure enough, the cruiser was still there — as one seemed to be much of the time from then on, just as one seemed to be behind me wherever I drove.

I learned to live with it, but my wife never did after cruisers started following her, too.

"It sure is nice to have an escort," she said the first time she noticed. But she soon came to dislike the attention and to fear for our four children — Heidi, Freman, Kimberly and Martin Jefferson — as calls informing me I was going to end up dead if I didn't drop my criticisms of Mansfield's public officials and the investigation of the sheriff's department became a macabre nightly ritual.

Soon 9-year-old Heidi began paying a price for my actions. When we asked why her grades had taken a sudden nose-dive, she said that her teacher picked on her so much that she had started dreading going to school. As Heidi's fears and grades got even worse, I finally asked the superintendent to check into the problem. He called back a few days later with a touch of anger in his voice.

"It's not your daughter's imagination," he said. "I had the class monitored, and it soon became clear that the teacher was doing everything she could to make Heidi miserable. It turns out the sheriff's wife also teaches there, and Heidi's teacher is her best friend. I told her to keep politics out of the classroom from now on or else. I think she got the message."

She did. But not before her students had picked up her attitude toward Heidi and made life miserable enough for her that we finally transferred her to another school. Then I received yet another distressing call from my wife one day. "I think our phone's been tapped," she said.

"You're not getting paranoid, are you?"" I asked jokingly, as I worried that she actually was because her bitterness toward Mansfield — and me — seemed to grow worse by the day.

"Come home and see for yourself," she said, with a touch of sarcasm. I did, and decided she might be right.

"See all those footprints in the snow around the telephone pole?" she asked as she pointed out the kitchen window. "I know those weren't there when I washed some dishes just before dark last night. But when I looked out the window right after you left early this morning, there they were. And the phone's sounded kind of strange all morning."

"I'll go out and take a look," I said.

I followed our telephone link to the pole and looked up to see a small box attached to it. All the other lines were clear. walked back to the house and called the telephone company. The security director showed up a half hour later to check the device out.

"False alarm," he assured me. "It's just a line-testing monitor a repairman must have left there by mistake."

"How do you explain all the footprints that weren't here last night, though?" I asked.

"Probably just some teenagers horsing around," he shrugged. "Just don't worry. Your phone's fine. Take my word for it."

When I later told one of the fired deputies about the false alarm later, he laughed and said, "And you believed him?"

"Why shouldn't I?" I asked.

"Because the phone company's got lots of friends in the sheriff's department, that's why," he said.

Soon, the harassment was coming right into my office. On one occasion, Hart himself showed up to ask if we could have a private talk. I took him into my office and closed the door. "What's up?" I asked.

"I just wanted to see if we could call a truce," Hart said with the sincerity I had been told he could turn on and off at will. "I think I can smooth things out between the sheriff and the fired deputies if you'll just cool things on your end."

"My goal isn't to get the fired deputies their jobs back, even though they deserve that," I replied. "My goal is to get to the bottom of some serious allegations made against your department."

"You just don't get it, do you?" Hart said with a smirk. "The one who's going to end up getting hurt the most if this keeps going is you."

"We'll see," I said as he walked out.

I was suddenly a little bit scared. But I was a lot more angry. So, apparently, was Weikel. A few days after Hart's peace ploy, two deputies showed up in the newsroom with a terrified person I had interviewed a few days before about a beating he claimed to have suffered in the county jail.

"The sheriff found your name and phone number in his wallet and told us to bring him over to see you since you're such good friends," one of the deputies said sarcastically.

"Did you ask to see me?" I asked, as I led my shaking source to my office.

"Are you kidding?" he replied in a trembling voice. "When they found your name in my wallet and gave it to Weikel, he went crazy. He started slapping me around, then told them to bring me over here to tell you I was in jail again."

"What did they arrest you for this time?" I asked.

"Nothing! They just picked me up when I was walking out of a bar. Like I told you, you don't have to do anything at all in this town to get arrested."

"Well, there's not much I can do about it now," I said. "But let me know if they do anything else to you. I'm sure our readers would be interested," I said loud enough to be heard as I took the poor guy back to his escorts.

"Who'd believe *this* dumb hillbilly," one of the deputies laughed. "The sooner you learn how things work in this town, the better off you'll be."

"I'm learning, all right. But it's hardly a lesson in democracy," I said as I ushered them out of the newsroom.

If Weikel knew how much I had already learned, in fact, he'd probably have gone crazy. Every stone reporters Ron Rutti, Bob Hiles and I turned over seemed to produce not only what we were looking for but something else as well. Before long I had several other reporters working on the probe. My office began to look like command central. We had a map up on the wall to plot a mind-boggling number of trips deputies had made all over the country that we were able to trace through credit-card receipts in the county auditor's office.

I also had stacks of documents, affidavits and hundreds of invoices we had copied one day when we wheeled our own copy machine into the county building and began copying every sheriff's department document we could get our hands on before it disappeared. It took the threat of lawsuits, of course, before officials agreed that we had a right to the documents.

"I don't know what you're looking for, but you won't find it," one official told me. "Sheriff Weikel is an honest man."

"Then that's what the records will show, and no one has anything to worry about," I said.

"Yeah, sure," he replied with a sudden surge of doubt.

Death and corruption

As we had expected, and the official no doubt feared, the records showed that Weikel wasn't so honest after all. The documents smelled of corruption on a grand scale that matched the evidence we had accumulated of the callous and sometimes brutal treatment of inmates.

One example of the latter was the death of 18-year-old Lawrence Hawkins Jr., who succumbed to tuberculous meningitis in 1971. According to witnesses, Hawkins became seriously ill in late July, and could barely move from the bunk in his cell during his last six days in jail.

Rather than show concern when Hawkins couldn't move at all, deputies called him a "lazy nigger" and rolled him out of the bunk. When he was finally taken to the hospital, Hawkins was already in a coma. He died three days later, with no one expressing the slightest concern about why he was brought to the hospital at such a late point in what was obviously a serious illness.

A few months later, Weikel bragged in his newsletter that his department promptly provides medical attention to "anyone who needs it." For some reason, though, Hawkins didn't qualify. Perhaps it was because he was just a "lazy nigger."

On the other hand, the fact that Gary Lee Mossor was white didn't seem to be a particular advantage. In fact, his death probably said more about the callousness and arrogance of the sheriff's department than any other act. Mossor was a parolee and an alcoholic who was trying to straighten his life out with the help of a friend, Bob Whipple, who had given him a place to stay in his home.

The West Virginia native was arrested on parole violations at 9:50 a.m. on September 14, 1977. The Whipples said Mossor had only one beer before leaving their house at 4 a.m. that day. His whereabouts between then and his arrest could not be accounted for. But two hours after he was brought to the supposedly safe and comfortable confines of the new Richland County Jail, Mossor "just flipped out," one inmate said. "He started yelling about giant rabbits coming after him and a man's head sticking out the toilet," the inmate said. Added another: "I knew the man was sick. They wouldn't help him. He was begging for help."

Instead, deputies shouted at Mossor to shut up. When he got even worse, they threw him into an isolation cell known as "the hole," where his shouts wouldn't be as much a bother and the other inmates couldn't see him. But Mossor continued to get worse. He began pounding on the walls of the cell with his arms and then his head. The deputies just taunted him instead of providing aid.

The crying and pounding continued through the night, as did the shouting by increasingly irritated deputies telling Mossor to shut up.

Then, during one such episode just before dawn, the shouting, pounding and screaming got much louder. An eerie silence followed. When the jail "trusties" arrived with Mossor's breakfast, they found him lying dead on the floor, a final scream frozen on his bloodied face.

According to one of the first deputies on the scene, Mossor's stiff body had bruises all over it. His yellow-tinged tongue was sticking out the side of his mouth. He wasn't a pretty sight.

But shift commander Lt. Michael Spognardi wasn't all that shocked. After making a half-hearted attempt to revive Mossor, witnesses said, he began laughing and told the other deputies to shake hands with a dead man. Questions arose immediately in the jail about what had really happened to Mossor. Then came Coroner Raymond Thabet to save the day. Thabet would delay filing his autopsy report on Mossor for so long that Mossor was almost a forgotten man.

When Thabet and an assistant coroner performed the autopsy on Mossor, Thabet probably couldn't help but be concerned. It was bad enough that the body's condition indicated Mossor had suffered horribly before his death. But it was something else that presented the real problem. For as he and his assistant cut into Mossor's chest and examined the heart, he seemed shocked.

"Dr. Thabet, something is unusual here," a witness later quoted the assistant as saying. Indeed there was. Mossor's atrium, the muscular upper chamber of the heart, had been badly ruptured. And that, pathologists told *The News Journal,* was an injury that was virtually impossible to self-inflict.

Perhaps for that reason, Thabet seemed to delay filing Mossor's death certificate for months. Harold Jones, Thabet's investigator at the time, said he had to remind Thabet several times that he had promised the assistant coroner that he was going to submit Mossor's atrium tissue to outside experts for analysis. But Thabet waited for more than three months, until late December, when the county health department pressed him to complete unfinished business before the new year.

According to Jones, Thabet at first prepared a death certificate that didn't even mention the ruptured atrium. "When I reminded him of the problem, Dr. Thabet acted frustrated and said the matter had merely slipped his mind," Jones said. "Then he prepared a certificate listing the ruptured atrium as the immediate cause of death and acute and chronic alcoholism as the condition that gave rise to it."

When reporters Hiles and Rutti asked Thabet for a copy of the autopsy report on which he based those conclusions, he refused. "We don't show those to laymen," he snapped.

On March 22, 1978, *The News Journal* demanded a copy of the autopsy report in writing, pointing out that state law required him to honor such a request without delay.

A half-hour later, the report was in our hands.

Once we had gotten Thabet's report, we sent copies to noted cardiologists and pathologists across America. A few days later, I received a call from cardiologist Alexander Ormand of Akron.

"I've been going over the autopsy you sent me with several other specialists," Ormand said. "As best as we can determine, it's virtually impossible for a ruptured atrium to be self-inflicted. And the damage recorded to other organs suggests that Mr. Mossor was the victim of severe trauma."

"What does that mean?" I asked.

"What that means is that there is a strong likelihood that Mr. Mossor was beaten to death," Ormand replied.

Ormand expanded on his opinion in a letter on April 20, 1978. "The external examination significantly showed multiple bruises of both lower legs, both forearms and knuckles," Ormand wrote.

"The internal examination significantly showed multiple hemorrhagic areas in the intercostal spaces, which are the spaces between the ribs. This could not have occurred without some sort of trauma, presumably blows to the chest wall. Why the external examination did not show any, or record any bruises, I cannot say.

"The liver showed three areas of subcapsular hemorrhage. This would not occur unless some trauma had occurred. The heart showed this 'rent.' No one that I talked to believes that this could occur spontaneously. It could only occur as a result of trauma."

A day or two later, Hiles received a call from a prominent New York pathologist. "Could this man have been stomped on?" he asked.

When Hiles inquired why the pathologist was asking, he replied, "Because, while 10 percent of severe DT cases end in death, none that I have ever seen ended with an atrial rupture."

A heart specialist at the National Institutes of Health was equally surprised at the condition of Mossor's heart.

"I have never seen a case of a ruptured atrium," the doctor said. "It seems to make some sense there was foul play."

But such comments from renowned experts didn't seem to faze Dr.

Thabet. When one of the reporters asked Thabet if he was investigating Mossor's death, he replied: "I have more important things to do first" — perhaps stealing from the dead and fabricating lab-test results, of which he was later accused.

As soon as he had been forced to turn over the autopsy report to *The News Journal,* Thabet called Weikel. According to the dispatcher who took the call, the obviously worried coroner asked to talk to the sheriff on a line without a taping device.

A short time later, Thabet called his acquaintance, Cyril Wecht, the controversial coroner of Allegheny County, Pennsylvania, who had gained notoriety for his claim that President John F. Kennedy's assassination was the result of a conspiracy.

The reason we knew Thabet had called Wecht so quickly was that, almost immediately after obtaining the Mossor report, we contacted Wecht and asked if he would be willing to review it. Wecht replied that he had just been contacted by Thabet for consultations on the case and couldn't comment further. Thabet later told a special grand jury that Wecht had concluded that Mossor's atrium had been ruptured when the jailer first discovered his body and tried to revive him by pounding on his chest.

How this could happen when rigor mortis had apparently already set in wasn't explained, and pathologists I consulted said it would have been next to impossible. A few weeks later, though, Wecht proved he had more in common with Thabet than an unusual explanation of Mossor's ruptured atrium when it was disclosed that he had been using county money for some time to fund a generous "professional education fund" to be used at his discretion. Regardless, Wecht's analysis apparently kept the grand jury from issuing indictments in the case, despite the fact that Mossor had been mercilessly forced to die an agonizing death in a well-equipped and well-staffed jail.

Prosecutors reportedly considered seeking indictments for jailer negligence, but they couldn't decide who was responsible. That decision crushed the hopes of Mossor's family that his cruel death would be avenged. Pleas for action had already been made in Columbus and Washington, but responsibility was always shifted back to Mansfield. Mossor's brother Larry told me he was still plagued by nightmares about Gary's death. Noting that the funeral director in their native Tyler County,

Virginia, had shown him the bruises all over Gary's body, Larry said, "When I saw him lying there, I knew it wasn't right. His legs and arms were bruised and swollen."

Larry's wife, Sandy, added that "Gary was far from a hardened criminal. He was shocked at what he saw of prison life." It was that experience, she said, that caused Gary to experience a religious conversion while serving time for forging checks. "I have been going to church and I feel like a different person since I have been saved," Mossor wrote in a letter less than a year before his senseless death at age 32. "I don't feel alone now. Jesus said, " am the light of the world; he that followeth me shall not walk in darkness, but shall have the light of life.'

Mossor's family still believes that "light of life" was snuffed out needlessly at the hands of the callous Richland County Sheriff's Department.

Terror unleashed

The family of the late Timothy Thayer felt the same way, even though the details of his death are quite different and more confusing. The evidence seems to indicate that Thayer killed himself on January 31, 1977, with the same gun he had used to wound Deputy Jesse Owens. But the actions and comments of several individuals, plus a number of curious events in the aftermath of Owens' shooting, caused widespread rumors and suspicions.

One thing is certain: Thayer's shooting of Owens brought out the worst in Sheriff Weikel and his deputies. A chemist with an IQ 16 points above the genius level, Thayer supposedly was obsessed with Weikel's department. He told friends Weikel was a fascist, and that his deputies often used Gestapo tactics when they made arrests, many of which he said were unnecessary. Thayer was also obsessed with guns, and the combination of those two obsessions proved deadly when Owens pulled over the vehicle Thayer was riding in with two others for suspicion of smoking marijuana. The driver of the truck was Ted Troupe. He and his companion, Scott Huvler, had just finished moving a load of Troupe's belongings to a new apartment before picking up Thayer, who volunteered to help them move when he met them at a party the previous night.

They were headed for a second load when Owens pulled them over. Troupe admitted that the trio was smoking pot, so there was some reason for apprehension when Owens approached.

As Troupe reached into his glove box for his registration, Thayer had to move from his position on the console into the back. The next thing Troupe knew, Thayer had shot Owens in the arm.

Troupe and Huvler were stunned. They hadn't known Thayer had a gun, let alone an inclination to use one. Troupe made a desperate grab for the weapon, but couldn't get it. Instead, he pushed Huvler out of the truck on the passenger side and jumped out after him.

As Thayer fled from the truck, several squad cars arrived. Deputies and bystanders began kicking Huvler and Troupe as they lay on the ground. Thayer, meanwhile, was last seen alive as he ran across a snow-covered golf course. What happened after that is anybody's guess.

It doesn't take much guesswork, though, to figure what Weikel had in mind for him. According to several sources, Weikel came on the air just as deputies were arriving at the scene and issued this command to one of them: "When you find that guy, take care of him. You know what I mean."

Later that night, witnesses said, Weikel accosted the same deputy when he returned to headquarters several hours later and told Weikel he hadn't been able to find Thayer. "We're not going to use the taxpayers' money to clothe and feed this guy in jail," he said. "Now you get back out there and find him. And you know what to do when you do."

The deputy left in his cruiser immediately, witnesses said. A dispatcher said he radioed in a short time later to say he would be off the air for what turned out to be several hours.

Weikel, meanwhile, went to visit the slightly wounded Owens at the hospital. "You don't have anything to worry about," Owens later quoted Weikel as saying. "I told [the deputy] to take care of him."

Weikel's mood hadn't changed much the next day, either. "The only way I want to see him [Thayer] is face down on a slab in the morgue," Weikel told deputies during a department meeting. But most deputies didn't take Weikel seriously, because, some said later, he talked like that, mostly for effect, all the time. The sheriff got his wish 19 days later, however, when Thayer's body was found in a quarry not far from the shooting scene.

After much wrangling, the Mansfield Police Department detective squad, headed by the father of deputies Bill and Michael Spognardi, finally allowed me to review the photos of Thayer's body.

The corpse, which had been found by two boys, was, as the police report said, "in a reclining, seated position with the head thrown back and eyeglasses pushed back above the forehead." But the photos also revealed something that was odd, although not impossible.

After apparently blowing his brains out by shooting himself through the roof of his mouth, Thayer had managed to rest both arms on his chest, with his finger still on the trigger of his .22-caliber pistol.

Coroner Thabet commented at the scene that Thayer's death was an apparent suicide, but never ruled on the mode and manner of death. But several aspects of the case still bothered many in the department. For one thing, Thabet determined that Thayer had been dead since the day he shot Owens.

So how did several inner-circle deputies fail to find the body, which was discovered in an open area they had supposedly searched several times? Where was the deputy who was off the air for so long the night of the shooting? Why did he reportedly leave for an unscheduled Florida vacation at taxpayers' expense, our investigation discovered, the following day? Why was he promoted shortly after he returned? Why, according to the fired deputies, did he so frequently predict that Thayer would turn up dead on his birthday, which he did?

And why did several key deputies fail to respond to an auxiliary policeman's report of a man matching Thayer's description the day after he had shot Owens unless they thought he was already dead?

In an attempt to get to the bottom of the Thayer case and several others, I arranged for a secret meeting with current and former deputies who had raised such questions during earlier individual interviews. After we assembled as many pieces of the perplexing puzzle as we could, I finally put the question to them bluntly.

"OK, guys. Put aside your biases and try to look at this as professionals. How many of you think Timothy Thayer committed suicide?"

Only two or three of the 15 or so present raised their hands.

"OK, how many think he was killed?"

All but a few raised their hands.

"So who killed him, then?"

Silence, followed by nervous laughter.

"Come on, guys, you must have an idea. Most of you were on duty that night."

"Some things are better left unsaid," one of the group's leaders said. "We don't want to end up like Thayer ourselves."

Unfortunately, Coroner Thabet made it easier for the rumors and suspicions to spread because he neglected to record the size of the bullet wound in Thayer's skull or to note the size of the recovered bullet.

Shortly after the stories about Thayer's death appeared in *The News Journal,* for example, I was working late in my office when a man claiming to have worked for the coroner asked if he could talk to me about some important information he had. He seemed nervous as he was ushered into my office. When he gave his name, I recognized it as being that of someone who actually had once worked for the coroner. After a minute or so of small talk, I asked him what he wanted to tell me.

"It may not be much," he replied, "but did you happen to notice that Thabet didn't record the size of the bullet wound in Timothy Thayer's skull?"

"As a matter of fact, I have," I said.

"There could be a reason for that, you know," he said. "The only other person at the autopsy told me it was a .38-caliber wound, and Thayer was holding a .22-caliber gun. Now how do you figure that?"

I couldn't, of course. And attempts to find the witness to the autopsy who quit and left town soon after that proved futile. But in 1991, I discovered a Mansfield Police crime-lab report in the coroner's file that had not been there in 1978. The report indicated that the fatal bullet was, in fact, .22-caliber, as was Thayer's gun, causing me to conclude in the first edition of this book that Thayer probably had shot himself. Now I'm not so sure. What changed my mind was a telephone call from a man who claimed he was in the Richland County Jail at the time Thayer shot Owens. The man said he had gained the status of a "trustie" and was allowed to work on squad cars in the garage attached to the jail.

"I was out there one night, minding my own business when [the same deputy named by department sources] pulled in with Thayer and another deputy in the cruiser," the man said. "He went into the department, came out a few minutes later and drove off. When I learned the next day Weikel had told him to take a vacation to Florida, I figured that was his reward for killing Thayer. Later, a deputy whose name I'm not going to give you because there's no way he'd ever talk, told me that the [the deputy] came in to borrow some magnums [bullets] from him."

What impressed me about that was that the police-lab report said the shell of the bullet used to kill Thayer was a magnum. As best as I could determine, though, that fact had never been reported publicly. Regardless of how Thayer died, he probably experienced less pain that night than his two companions. It took me several weeks and countless phone calls to track down the still-traumatized Troupe and Huvler in faraway states, and several more to persuade them to talk about what had happened to them. The reason for their reluctance quickly became apparent. They were put through living hell.

After being assaulted at the scene of the shooting for several riotous moments by outraged deputies and members of a nearby VFW post, Troupe and Huvler were transported to the county jail in separate cars.

"When they put me in the squad car parked in the VFW lot, the deputy in the front seat said he felt like blasting my brains out," Huvler told me. Troupe described what awaited them at the jail as "a Nazi version of the Keystone Kops."

As Huvler was being escorted into the jail by two deputies, he said, an older deputy approached and asked if he was one of "those sons-of-bitches" involved in the Owens shooting. He then hit Huvler so hard with a leather blackjack that the weapon split open and the metal balls inside flew all over the hallway, causing incoming deputies to slip and slide the rest of the way into the building.

The stunned Huvler was then taken to the booking room, where he was told to lie down on the floor and keep his mouth shut. Troupe, meanwhile, was thrown against the wall as soon as he was inside the building. Someone then banged his head against the wall so hard several times that blood started coming out of his ears. Then he was taken to the booking room, too, and thrown onto the floor next to Huvler.

The next thing either remembered was being kicked repeatedly by Deputy William Spognardi. One of the first kicks to Huvler's head caused a snap so loud that a dispatcher across the hall in the radio room heard it through the window. As she looked up, blood splattered all over the glass. Huvler knew immediately that his jaw was broken.

Both of the helpless young men cried for mercy. But Spognardi kept up his attack for several more minutes. Then Troupe was taken into a conference room for interrogation. At one point, he told me, Spognardi slammed him against the wall and told him to "quit being so nice."

At another point, he said, Capt. William Miser told him he would be taken out "on a slab" if he didn't cooperate.

One of the fired deputies recalled that while Troupe was being terrorized inside the room, Weikel was outside urging the deputy to go in and "make him talk." He declined, and walked away. When Troupe was finally asked to sign a statement, he asked that he be allowed to see an attorney. But Troupe quickly learned what many who had made their way through Weikel's little shop of horrors already knew — that the U.S. Constitution and a suspect's Miranda rights didn't exist there. So Troupe's request for an attorney was denied.

"I signed it [the statement] because I feared what would have happened to me if I didn't." Troupe told me with a touch of terror still in his voice. Troupe added that Michael Spognardi made two comments about what was going to happen to Thayer: "If we find him, he'll be blown away," and, "If we find him, he'll be taken out feet first."

Huvler, meanwhile, was faring even worse than Troupe. He continued to be beaten despite his obviously broken jaw, until he was finally asked to sign a statement as well. Huvler also had the temerity to request an attorney and was granted another brutal kick instead. Huvler was then taken to a jail cell. On the way, Huvler and his escorts passed a crazed Weikel. "Is this one of those pricks?" Weikel asked. Told by one of the deputies that he was, Weikel stared at Huvler and shouted, "I'd like to bust your fucking head."

But Weikel didn't have to bother. Huvler's head was already pretty much broken. Despite his repeated requests for medical aid, however, Huvler wasn't taken to the hospital for another eight hours. When Captain Shirley Whisler found out that Spognardi had finally consented to the transfer, witnesses said, she tried to talk him out of it. They said she expressed concern that news of his injuries might leak out if they didn't have a good enough excuse, so a story was concocted that Huvler had slipped and fallen on some ice. It was quite a fall. He had a broken jaw, a broken nose, two black eyes, several bruised ribs and cuts and bruises all over his body. Several patches of his beard and hair had been ripped out as well. Huvler was in the hospital for 10 days. Not surprisingly, word of what happened to Huvler didn't leak out of Mansfield General Hospital any more than news of two deputies previously beating an inmate to a pulp in the emergency room did.

The only charge against the two men, who had no previous criminal records, was possession of marijuana. Each was ordered to pay an $18 fine and court costs. But they paid far more for the crime of being at the wrong place at the wrong time. It took months for either of them to talk about what happened to them that horrifying night. Friends said Troupe initially would break into uncontrollable crying spells when the subject came up. Huvler refused to say a word about it for three months. Both finally moved out of state to get away from nightmarish memories. "I had never been arrested before Tim shot the deputy," Huvler said. "It was a hell of a surprise that he did it. But so was what happened to me in jail."

Troupe and Huvler weren't the first, nor the last, to get such an unpleasant surprise when they went to the Richland County Jail. Dozens suffered similar or worse fates before *The News Journal* exposed the routine brutality of the sheriff's department in May 1978. As Weikel explained it in a speech to the Optimist Club a few days before the explosive series of articles started to appear: "One person you can tell to sit down and he will. Another you've got to teach the facts of life."

Weikel himself wasn't above teaching the facts of life to some residents of his "motel," as he referred to the jail, although former deputies said the coward usually preferred to get his licks in only when the prisoner had already been worked over by a deputy. One of the cases Weikel was allegedly involved in was the assault of Larry Gorman, who had turned himself in after an earlier escape. Several deputies who saw the incident claimed that after Hart whipped Gorman to the ground with nunchakus, a martial arts weapon consisting of two rods connected by a short chain, Weikel kicked him several times. Then he threw him in the drunk tank and ordered that he be fed only bread and water until his release. Gorman confirmed their accusations, with slight variations, in 1991.

"When I arrived at the Richland County Jail I was placed inside the drunk tank although I was not intoxicated," Gorman said. "Then Gene Hart and Sheriff Weikel entered the room. Just the three of us were in the drunk tank. I remember Hart had nunchakus in his hip pocket and then in his hand prior to coming inside the room. . . . Hart and Sheriff Weikel then began hitting me with their hands and feet. This beating lasted between 15 and 25 minutes. There was no way I could resist since I remained handcuffed with my hands behind my back. I laid on the floor and did my best to cover up.

"Hart hit me in the head with his fist numerous times and [Weikel] kicked me in the rib section and legs numerous times. I suffered a lot of pain and bruising due to this beating. I had no way to say anything to them and in no way did I provoke them. While Hart was beating me he said something like, 'You can't run from my jail.' I was left in the drunk tank for three or four days in the dark. . . . For the days I remained in the drunk tank I was given only bread and water to eat and drink. My family was not allowed to see me until I was removed from the drunk tank. Before and after my beating Gene Hart was heard by me and other inmates threatening to beat prisoners with his nunchakus."

Another alleged victim of Weikel's hospitality was Thomas Davis, who had a previous run-in with Weikel. In March 1976, Davis was escorted from his jail cell to Weikel's office by Deputy Joe Hetler.

"Weikel was waiting when the doors opened," Davis said later. "He grabbed me, threw me against the wall and punched me in the face with his fist. I believe he was trying to get me to hit back, but I didn't. He grabbed me again and pushed me against the wall and yelled to Hetler, 'Take this fucking punk back up to the D Cell.' I was in there for five minutes when Hart started yelling at me. He took the mattress out. Captain Bill Miser came in next and started screaming."

Davis said he had to sleep on the cement floor or bed springs for 19 days before his probation officer got him released. "When I got the release papers, I was sneaked out so Weikel wouldn't see me and get mad," Davis said.

But not all brutality took place in the safe confines of the county jail. Deputies didn't hesitate to take Weikel's brand of justice to the streets, either, as a federal lawsuit by 17-year-old Steven Burggraf documented. Burggraf's nightmare took place when he and his parents attended a graduation party at a community hall in June 1977. When neighbors complained about the party's noise, a deputy was dispatched to quiet it down. In the process, he "accidentally" hit a woman with his nightstick.

When an angry crowd formed around him, the deputy went to his cruiser and called for backup. Within minutes, more than two-dozen squad cars were on the scene. Burggraf went to see what was going on. He said he was shocked to see deputies kicking, beating and arresting everyone in sight. Another witness said that even two 8-year-old boys were handcuffed.

Then Burggraf saw one of his friends being manhandled and went to his aid. "They arrested me when I told a couple of deputies they didn't have to treat my friend so rough," he told *The News Journal*. "One of them twisted my arm behind my back, and the other started hitting me."

According to his lawsuit, Burggraf was thrown to the ground by Deputy Terry McMillen, who knelt on his head while handcuffing him. After McMillen had put Burggraf in the front seat of his cruiser, the teenager told him, "You're not much of a man to act like that." McMillen responded by bashing Burggraf in the mouth with a five-cell flashlight.

"There was blood all over the dashboard and teeth falling out of my head," Burggraf recalled. "McMillen said, 'Shut up or I'll tear your fucking head off.' I believed him. I thought he was going to kill me. His eyes just lit up." Burggraf later had to have his lip and the back of his head stitched. The intoxication charges filed against him were eventually dismissed in juvenile court.

McMillen later admitted in court to beating another 17-year-old, Charlie Bond, in November of the same year. Bond and Ralph Martin Meadows had been arrested for allegedly trying to cash a stolen check. In a vicious attempt to get the two to confess, Bond said McMillen "kneed me in the crotch. Then he just kept slapping me." Then he attacked Meadows by grabbing his hair, hitting him in the face and banging his head against the wall. McMillen was later suspended 12 days for the beatings.

But Burggraf and Bond got off relatively easily compared with Gobel Risner. Risner claimed that, after his arrest in February 1977 for allegedly shooting at a patrol car, a deputy stuck a pistol in his mouth and pulled the trigger. "Why it didn't go off, I don't know," he told *The News Journal* the following year.

Risner later claimed that he, his brother, and their wives, were forced to lie in the snow for 20 minutes without coats while deputies ransacked his house looking for the gun he allegedly had used to fire at the cruiser. When Risner's brother, Harold, was allowed back into the house, he said, he was forced to stand on a floor register. When his shoes started to smoke, he was told he would be killed if he moved.

Risner said he was then taken to the county jail where, he claimed, he was beaten by two deputies. A man who was in a nearby cell told us that he heard the deputies shouting questions at Risner.

When he didn't give them the answers they wanted, the witness said, "They beat the hell out of him. Later, I rubbed his back to try to ease the pain, and there must have been a bruise a foot wide."

Risner was arraigned three days later, but not for the alleged shooting. Instead, he was charged with the assault of a deputy in jail, for which he was fined $300. After his release, Risner was treated for a broken rib.

Bob Cushard was another man to be taught Weikel's "facts of life" after being arrested on charges that were later dropped. "They tied me to a chair and messed me up pretty good," Cushard claimed. "I had bald spots on my head from where they pulled out my hair."

Torture, Mansfield style

But the allegations of Risner and Cushard were mild compared with what Ricky Tucker claimed he went through in Weikel's wonderland. The origin of Tucker's problem was, believe it or not, two impacted wisdom teeth. Tucker was scheduled to go to the dentist to have the painful teeth removed on the same day he was arrested on a charge that, ironically, was later dropped. While awaiting trial in the jail, however, Tucker's teeth began causing unbearable pain. He said he repeatedly asked to see a dentist and was refused. When he reached the point of desperation, Tucker threatened to file a complaint against Weikel if he wasn't allowed to get treatment. He got the treatment, all right, but not the kind he had hoped for. Several deputies removed him from his cell and threw him into an unlighted, concrete drunk tank, where he remained for three days.

After Tucker was returned to his cell, he decided to take matters into his own hands. He and another inmate planned an escape. Their attempted jail break failed miserably, but not before Tucker and his accomplice, Marvin Frankfather, had gotten themselves into more trouble than they ever could have imagined. In their attempt to get on an elevator, Tucker and Frankfather had to use their only weapon, a jar stuck in a sock, on a deputy blocking their way. When Tucker struck Sgt. Stanley Popp on the head, Popp fell to the floor unconscious. Before the attack, however, Popp had jammed the elevator, blocking their escape.

That's when Tucker and Frankfather said they decided to give up. "We just went back into our own [cell] range and waited for the inevitable," Tucker wrote later in an affidavit.

"We didn't have long to wait, either. Within five minutes of our returning to our range, the jail floor hall was literally flooded with police from the Mansfield Police Department, the sheriff's department and the Highway Patrol." He continued:

"At the front of the range, every officer (15 to 20) had a shotgun, with one exception: Joe Taylor, from the MPD, who had a .357 Magnum pointing right at my head. We were made to crawl from the cell to the front of the range, and then they had us lie face down on the floor. . . . First, we were handcuffed behind our backs . . . so tight the cuffs cut into our skin and left welts for the following month. Joe Taylor kicked me a few times about the head and collarbones. Captain Miser was going back and forth hitting both Marvin and me with the butt of his shotgun, kicking us to the body and head, and yelling over and over that we were 'going to die.'

"Then we were dragged by our hair and the cuffs out of the range and up the hall. . . . Deputy Mike Spognardi had Marvin, primarily, swinging him back and forth by the handcuffs, and pausing only to hit him with his fist and shotgun. Captain Miser had me mostly, doing the same thing, and continuously telling us that we were going to die (and I was beginning to believe him by now). Then each of us was dragged through some blood from Sergeant Popp's wound, by the hair and cuffs. By this time, both of my eyes were bleeding; and I now have scars from those cuts, as well as one on my arm, my mouth, and a couple on my legs that I acquired along the path of that long, long day."

Tucker at that point had no idea just how long that day would really be. For, as incredible as it may seem, their torture had just begun. Nor, apparently, was Tucker's story exaggerated. It was corroborated by numerous witnesses, and the incident eventually led to several indictments. Tucker's story continues:

"When we finally got to the [drunk] tank, all of the aforementioned, and a few others, continued to kick us as we lay on the floor. Finally, they left. But later, Donnie Todd, Mike Spognardi, Dan Scheurer and a few others came in and asked us if we wanted a shower. . . .

"We didn't have to reply. They threw us under cold water, in our clothes, and threw us back in the tank. [This routine tactic was known as a "hillbilly shower" because most of those who received it came from an unincorporated   area   just outside Mansfield known as "Little Kentucky."]

"We could smell and see the puddle of Mace on the floor as we were heaved back in. I noticed the blood from Marvin's head and lip; and I was bleeding from my arm, eyes, leg and head.

"Later, Todd came in again with some others; I told him, 'At least you got *Popp* to a doctor.' He asked if I wanted to go to the hospital, and jumped on me again (we're still handcuffed behind our backs), this time slitting my upper lip completely down the middle. I have a scar from that one now, too. They left then; and, later, Miser came back to beat on us some more. He left, and later Sheriff Weikel came in and got his share, and then he left. Later Dan Scheurer, Bruce Armstrong, Jimmy Hoffer, and Bob Conley came in and dragged us out one at a time. I still haven't found out what exactly they did to Marvin, but here's my part: They dragged me into the 'shakedown' and shower room, threw me face down on the floor, ripped my personal clothing from me, and as Bruce Armstrong kept his knee in the small of my back, and Jimmy Hoffer had fun standing on my toes and feet, Bob Conley uncuffed me one hand at a time as he slipped some coveralls that were fresh with Mace over my shoulders. Every time I'd look back over my shoulder to see who did what, Conley would slap me. Scheurer had his Mace can out; so I can assume who sprayed the coveralls.

"Afterward, I was handcuffed again, and thrown back in the tank. In all, our persons were assaulted seven times the first day alone. (I counted; and in the days to follow, we were beaten a couple more times, though certainly not as bad as that first day.)"

For the next three days, Tucker claimed, he and Frankfather were kept handcuffed and were given neither food nor water. Use of a restroom was also denied them. They were kept in total darkness and forced to lie in a large puddle of Mace, which passing deputies added to by spraying under the door. Tucker and Frankfather were finally given their first meal at the end of their third day in special confinement. For two days, they would be given two slices of bread twice a day. Every third day, they were given one meal.

They did, however, continue to receive a steady diet of Mace. After two weeks, Tucker and Frankfather were finally taken to individual detention cells, where they were mostly left alone. Tucker was beaten one more time, however, when he balked at going to court without wearing his own clothes.

Tucker's attorney was Robert Whitney, who would later do a stellar job representing several of members of the sheriff's department against grand-jury indictments. But when Tucker asked Whitney to represent him in a suit against the sheriff's department for the abuse he had undergone, Tucker claims Whitney refused, implying, in Tucker's words, it would "reflect badly on his reputation with the court." Whitney did, however, manage to get the charges Tucker had originally been arrested for thrown out. But that hardly meant Tucker was free to go. He and Frankfather still faced assault charges for their escape attempt. Tucker claimed he was then treated even worse than before:

"After I left the courtroom that day of my theft arraignment, I was taken directly to the tank again. This time, with the material I was already donning, my feet were chained tightly together, I was handcuffed behind the back; and then I was bent over backward, and my hands and feet were chained together . . . 'hog-tied,' BACKWARD. The Mace returned (abundantly), and I was left just like that for the following five or six days. I wasn't given anything to eat, no water; and wasn't even permitted to use the john. Oh, again, I was also in darkness.

Altogether, Tucker claimed, he gained eight scars and lost 30 pounds through his long ordeal. He never knew why he was freed until much later, when it was reported that a dispatcher disturbed by Tucker's torture mentioned it to her husband, who was the police chief of a neighboring town. After seeing Tucker in the hog-tied position himself, the police chief called an attorney who had influence with Weikel and told him what was going on. When the attorney called Weikel, Tucker was freed. His tribulation was over.

While Tucker's experience was the extreme, the ordinary at Richland County Jail was bad enough. As with many jails, drugs and sex were commonplace. What set it somewhat apart from most was that deputies were heavily involved.

Former inmates claimed that a resident in favor with certain deputies could usually get drugs from them for a premium price. As late as only two months before Weikel's long-delayed ouster, when the department was being investigated by several agencies at once, a deputy was caught selling inmates drugs he had taken from the evidence room. He was promptly fired, probably not so much for what he was doing, but for doing it at such a delicate time.

A number of male deputies were also known to have sexual relations with female inmates, sometimes by force. One deputy became so infatuated with one female inmate that he left his family and moved in with her after her release. While male deputies apparently had no part of homosexual sex, they reportedly didn't interfere with its practice. They were even reported to play matchmaker by putting homosexuals together for a fee.

Some residents of Richland County outside the jail weren't treated much better than those inside. Almost anyone was susceptible to harassment or intimidation. The department's indiscriminate car-stop policy gave deputies ample opportunity to harass blacks, "hillbillies," longhairs, or anyone else whose looks they didn't like. Although the sheriff department's primary area of responsibility was supposed to be the county's unincorporated areas, many of the car stops were made in the city, where Weikel insisted he had equal jurisdiction with the Mansfield Police Department. Police officers constantly complained about the policy, but the mayor wouldn't tell Weikel to back off.

Many young people who were arrested often claimed that illegal searches were made of their cars and that small bags of marijuana were dropped, then "discovered" by deputies. They would then be taken in and booked for possession of drugs that they insisted weren't theirs. But the harassment went deeper than that. Political and personal enemies were all fair game. At the top of the list were lawyers who handled suits against the sheriff's department. Several former deputies told me they were often ordered to follow and arrest, if possible, any of several attorneys.

"Weikel told me to get [attorney] Vince Phelan on a traffic charge or anything else I could," he said. "I made myself as obvious as I could, however, so he'd be aware I was following him."

Another deputy finally did nail Phelan — for littering. But his real offense at the time was representing used-goods dealer Bill Knipp in a lawsuit against the department and Captain Bill Miser. Miser had gotten in a scuffle with Knipp during an auction at Knipp's house. When Knipp sued, the harassment began. Phelan, Knipp, and friend Denver Roof claimed they were all placed under 24-hour surveillance. Knipp's windows were broken. Pets and livestock were killed. Knipp even claimed that a helicopter Weikel had access to would frequently hover so closely over his house that it would knock pictures off the walls and blow burning ashes out of the fireplace.

Knipp claimed he finally left the state to escape Miser's revenge. But that just allowed deputies to turn their attention to Knipp's relatives, some of whom also were forced to move, he said.

Knipp returned for an interview in August 1978, during which he charged that Miser had offered to drop the charges against him in return for $2,000, and that Miser had shot at him several times during a car chase near his home.

He added that his problems stemmed not only from his altercation with Miser, but also from his refusal of a request by two deputies that he smuggle guns to Florida in his motor home and that he provide $6,000 worth of phony bills on parts to cover work allegedly done on sheriff's cruisers.

Knipp said it was his understanding that the deputies often transported guns to Florida in sheriff's cruisers and returned with large quantities of drugs. He said deputies also obtained drugs by stopping suspected smugglers on Interstate 71, confiscating their contraband and telling them to get lost if they didn't want to go to jail.

Knipp's allegations weren't as far-fetched as they seemed. In fact, Richard Petty, then an Ohio Highway Patrol post commander and later Weikel's successor, told me of a case in which smugglers who had been stopped by one of his troopers were turned over to the sheriff's department along with their trunk full of drugs, and that both seemed to disappear in quick order. "We kept waiting to be notified of a court hearing and never were," Petty said. "When we finally called, we were told that the charges had been dropped."

Hart's own favorite harassment target allegedly was a beautiful young woman named Allison Maher, who would become a successful international model after leaving Mansfield. On several occasions, Maher said, Hart took her in for questioning about her alleged involvement with drugs, then offered to drop the matter if she would go out with him.

"The closest thing I ever got to being involved with drugs was to write a letter to the editor disputing Sheriff Weikel's claim that marijuana was addictive," Maher told me. "But that was enough to start the harassment. Hart actually arrested me once for selling marijuana. Then he tried to get a confession out of me by threatening me with 30 years in prison if I didn't cooperate. I told him he was crazy, and he later dropped the charges."

Weikel rarely did his own dirty work in the field, but he didn't hesitate to go after someone on his own turf. Radio reporter Dean Lamneck's experience on August 18, 1977, was a good example. In a report filed with the Mansfield Police Department, Lamneck said he was showing his replacement how to go through arrest reports that day when Weikel came up to them and started accusing him of "bad-mouthing" him on the radio. Then Weikel threatened, not once but several times, to knock Lamneck's "fucking teeth out."

While Weikel often came off as a mental midget in uniform, sources said he was far from it. He was also a connoisseur of some of the finer things in life. And he allegedly used some of the county treasury to satisfy that desire. Corruption soon became wholesale, although it was anything but cheap. It started simply enough, with a free tank of gas here, a padded expense account there. But once Weikel and his closest associates discovered how easy it was, theft apparently became a major benefit of the job. By the early 1970s, Weikel had begun to think of himself as not just *a* sheriff but as *the* sheriff. So anything that belonged to the sheriff's department was also automatically Weikel's.

One manifestation of this belief was the assignment of on-duty deputies to work on his house. In fact, Miser spent so much time doing carpentry and remodeling work for "the big man" — almost every day for three straight months at one point, former deputies said — that he became known as "Captain Carpenter." On another occasion, the former deputies claimed, Weikel assigned an entire shift of on-duty deputies to lay cement in his driveway.

Weikel allegedly also used the county jail's kitchen as his private supermarket. According to several sources, the sheriff would come to the jail almost every Sunday after church, where he served as head deacon, and fill his car with whatever food he wished. Steaks were allegedly specially ordered for him. When he and his wife couldn't be bothered with food preparation themselves, the sources said, Weikel even had the jail cook prepare dinners for them.

Dining out was a real bargain for Weikel and his minions. They received discounts as large as 50 percent at several of their favorite restaurants. They also helped themselves to anything else they wanted. For example, the manager of one large restaurant said a deputy once asked him for a set of drinking glasses on display so he could give them to Weikel.

When the manager turned him down, he said the deputy replied: "How would you like for us to find some heroin in your car sometime?" The deputy got the glasses.

Weikel allegedly took advantage of a lot of other businesses in Richland County, but none was abused like a local electronics store. Unbeknownst to the absentee owner, Weikel had a willing accomplice in the store manager, who was also a special deputy. A former store employee and frequent customer both stated that when Weikel visited the store, he often left with a piece of merchandise for which he neither signed nor paid. The former employee also said he once was ordered to deliver a color television and other items to the homes of Weikel and Captain Shirley Whisler without the usual purchase slips.

The special deputy's ex-wife also said that when she and her husband visited Weikel's home, her husband usually brought a gift from the store with him. The deputy's generosity might explain Weikel's frequent practice of posting "For Sale" notices for things like televisions and stereos on the department bulletin board.

The special deputy's charity finally caught up with him, however, when the store's owner determined that several thousand dollars' worth of merchandise was unaccounted for and fired him. True to his tradition of helping special deputies who got into trouble, Weikel put his generous friend on his payroll until he found another job.

Another source of such items may have been Weikel's own evidence room. Both he and Hart were indicted for stealing a recovered stolen color television set and an expensive riding lawnmower.

How the latter indictment came about provided one of the few comical episodes in an otherwise tragic tale. It started with a phone call I received from a reliable source in the Mansfield Police Department.

"I've got a tip for you from one of the old-timers at the sheriff's department," he told me. "This guy wishes he could help more, but he says this is about the only thing he has personal knowledge of. Anyway, he says when they caught a local fence with three stolen riding lawnmowers in his truck, Weikel decided to keep one for himself after the department supposedly failed to locate its legitimate owner."

"I'll check it out," I said. Tell the old-timer I appreciate his help." I was soon able to corroborate the story and reported it in my investigative column "The Public Eye."

A week later, I reported that "one loyal reader of Public Eye appears to be Sheriff Thomas E. Weikel. Our sources tell us that when he read our report last week about his allegedly taking a recovered stolen lawnmower to his home after the owner could not be located, he quickly transferred it to the home of a loyal deputy until the heat is off."

By then, however, investigators were hot on the trail. That led to more Public Eye reports on the whereabouts of the mobile mower and two more moves by Weikel before Special Prosecutor Joseph Murray's sleuths caught up with it — and Weikel was awarded yet another indictment. But a lot more than expensive lawnmowers disappeared from the evidence room. Recovered guns were somehow lost almost as fast as they were brought in. So, too, were drugs, which solidified a theory many had that several deputies were recycling them for profit.

Opponent framed

While the idea of Sheriff Weikel being a fence for stolen property might seem humorous to some, wholesale-equipment dealer Anthony Sgambellone saw more irony in it than humor. Sgambellone and others claimed Weikel had him set up on just that charge when he found out that Sgambellone was planning to run against him in 1976.

When I checked the story out, the evidence indicated the framing of an innocent man was no figment of their imaginations. Several ex-deputies said Weikel complained during a meeting in 1975 that Sgambellone was thinking of running against him. "I'm going to have that SOB taken care of no matter what," Weikel was quoted as saying.

A short time later, Sgambellone was arrested and charged with felonious theft after buying a stolen stereo from Lewis Young, who had just been arrested for stealing the stereo from a Mansfield home. Young later admitted in court that he was told the burglary charges against him would be dropped if he agreed to set up Sgambellone.

Young said that, after coaching by an assistant prosecutor, he was taken to Sgambellone's wholesale store, and Sgambellone bought the stereo from him for $40. Young later told my sources that he believed Sgambellone had been set up to destroy his reputation. He also said the assistant prosecutor told him he would "never get out of jail" if he ever told what had happened.

THE BADGE OF TERROR 71

After Sgambellone's arrest, Deputy Michael Spognardi was overheard by several deputies as taking credit for the scheme. He added that Weikel had even awarded him with a Florida vacation for his efforts.

Although Sgambellone had no prior record, the presiding judge, who happened to be Weikel's friend, sentenced him to two to five years in prison, all but 30 days of which were suspended. He also was fined $1,000 and placed on three years' probation. One requirement of his probation was an 11 p.m. curfew. Another requirement prohibited him from being in a place that served alcoholic beverages. Combined, the two stipulations made it next to impossible for Sgambellone to run his popular family restaurant. The hard-nosed judge was later heard to remark to a deputy as he walked through the jail, "Well, we got Sgambellone, didn't we?"

Unfortunately, they lost a real criminal, Lewis Young, in the process. After the charges against him were dropped as promised, Young went on to commit two armed robberies, for which he was later arrested and convicted.

Because of the ease with which Sgambellone was framed for a crime he didn't commit, I later began to look for and write about similar cases in my column in *The Columbus Dispatch*. This eventually led to publication of my first book, *Presumed Guilty: When Innocent People Are Wrongly Convicted*. That, in turn, led to my career as a private investigator specializing in the cases of inmates with strong claims of innocence and the righting of wrongs in general.

Corruption expands

After Weikel went on to a smashing re-election victory in 1976, corruption began to spin completely out of control. Another special deputy, Kenneth Olson, became one of Weikel's favorite pocket-liners at this time until he was suspended in April 1978 from his medical-technician job at the National Guard post.

Investigators had found that Olson had been taking large amounts of supplies from the dispensary and giving them to Weikel and other deputies. Witnesses said Olson had taken whole cases of antacids and cold remedies to the jail, as well as prescription medicine and eyeglasses. The eyeglasses were apparently given to any sheriff's department employee who gave Olson a prescription. One claimed to have received four pairs.

Sources said Weikel, no doubt concerned that justice not be blind, also got some friendly judges free eyewear. The attitude of the commanding officer of the unit explained how this could go on for so long without being noticed. When asked to comment on Olson's generosity with the taxpayers' money, Col. Emerson Lewis refused to comment other than to say, "It's a little incident of no concern to the public."

Applicants and employees of the sheriff's department were also said to be given free medical examinations at the post, even though National Guard members had to pay for them and for most of the other things Olson gave deputies at no charge.

When Olson was finally suspended for 25 days for his pilfering, Weikel, once again helping a friend in trouble, put him on his payroll for the entire period.

Weikel also developed a multitude of ways to siphon off money from his employees, the public and his supporters, former deputies said. One of the easiest was a flower fund to which all employees were expected to give at least a dollar a month but which was rarely used to buy flowers. Another source allegedly was cash generated by a $2 fee charged for copies of accident and theft reports.

When one employee noted that a lot of the cash seemed to disappear, one of Weikel's top deputies told her: "Don't worry, little lady. It goes in the big man's pocket."

Many suspected that donations for the sheriff's annual ball went to the same place. Tickets were $10, yet the only real expense appeared to be the band. The food reportedly came from the jail's kitchen, and the dance was held at a rent-free building on the county fairgrounds. The 200 or so people who attended each year had to bring their own drinks, and ice and mixes were sold at a steep price. Yet records showed that the ball always broke even.

But if those kinds of schemes didn't produce enough additional income, there were others to fall back on. One was the regular use of phony receipts for reimbursement, sometimes from the Furtherance of Justice Fund, for business trips or attendance at training schools.

Many of those trips and schools, however, turned out to be as phony as the receipts. Most of the "training sessions" turned out to be trips to the home of one of Weikel's best friends, ex-Mansfield businessman Sheldon Shaffer.

After moving to Hollywood, Florida, Shaffer set up a drug-rehabilitation clinic called The Starting Place. It was there that favored deputies supposedly attended seminars.

The deputies would later fill out blank certificates of attendance that had been printed in Mansfield. The only problem was that The Starting Place wasn't certified to teach law-enforcement seminars, which were readily available in Ohio anyway. It turned out that the seminars never took place — unless boating, fishing, bar-hopping and woman-chasing could be considered seminars.

Ex-deputies suspected, but couldn't prove, that some of the deputies who made frequent trips to Florida took the department's confiscated weapons with them for sale on the black market in Florida and returned with a fresh supply of marijuana.

Street sources claimed that Colombian marijuana, for which Florida was then the main port of entry, suddenly became readily available at the same time deputies started to make their Florida trips. But there was a sudden halt in the supply in the summer of 1978, they said, when the trips were being investigated. Coincidentally, the sheriff's department made its first request for a court order to destroy confiscated drugs in several years at that time.

The most intricate scheme Weikel and his deputies purportedly devised was a kickback arrangement on the repair of cruisers. According to former and current employees of the sheriff's department and the town's Cadillac dealer, Cadillac driver Weikel benefited from the scheme through discounts on his personal vehicles and other forms of largess.

One former high-ranking deputy said in a signed statement saying that during the winter of 1975-'76 he was told by Weikel that he was going to have a hydraulic lift and new blade installed on his son's four-wheel-drive vehicle and that the work and parts would be billed to the county.

"Sheriff Weikel told me not to question the amount of money indicated on the bills and to OK all . . . that came to the Richland County Sheriff's Department so that the lift and blade would be paid for," the former top officer said.

"I did in fact OK a number of bills. . . that were received. To the best of my recollection. . . the amount of the lift and blade was in the neighborhood of $500."

Several employees of the dealership confirmed that the lift and plow were paid for by the sheriff's department. A number of other sources also claimed that a high-performance engine was later installed in the truck and apparently billed to the county. In yet another case, a second former high-ranking deputy told of how a car bearing the same squad-car number received two complete tune-ups in one week, a claim verified by invoices. According to the ex-deputy, the first car was actually Weikel's. He said the sheriff's car was randomly assigned a squad-car number without anticipating that the one bearing the number would receive the same service a few days later.

But such favors were possibly only small potatoes compared with the overall double-billing scheme, from which the proceeds were allegedly split between Weikel and the dealer. To camouflage the plot, the department reportedly sent a car in for each time a bill was produced, but no work was actually done the first time. When deputies complained that the car still wasn't running right, it would be returned and repaired for a second full charge. A former service manager we tracked down in Texas also explained how phantom parts and repairs were routinely added to invoices, and how a special code hid the practice from auditors.

Since Weikel spent $10,000 a month on cruiser repairs — almost twice the amount spent by similar-sized departments — the profit potential of such a scheme was significant. But documenting it proved difficult because of the intricacy of the scheme, a key source said.

During our investigation, we eventually crossed paths with the Ohio Bureau of Criminal Identification and Investigation and its dedicated director, Jack McCormick, which was compiling evidence against Weikel as well, and we began exchanging information.

Two days before our investigative reports were scheduled to start running, two BCI agents took a summary of their own findings, which greatly duplicated ours, to Prosecutor William F. McKee and offered to aid any probe he might initiate. McKee's response left them dumbfounded. He laughed out loud, both agents said later in affidavits, and lectured them on the poor credibility of the "hillbillies and niggers" who were among the sheriff's department's most numerous accusers. At the same time, the sheriff was defending himself in Columbus before the state's ethics commission, which was considering charges by the fired deputies that he had forced them to make an illegal contribution to his campaign fund.

When Weikel returned to Mansfield from Columbus that night, he attended a Masons meeting. Afterward, the sheriff bragged to a number of members at the meeting that *The News Journal* had started backing off its criticism of him after he had intimidated the paper's "punk editor."

But Weikel's attitude had changed dramatically by the next morning. Within hours of the prosecutor becoming aware of the kind of information we probably had on Weikel, the sheriff had launched a counteroffensive.

First he canceled his subscription to *The News Journal.* Then he called some of those he apparently suspected of spilling the beans and threatened to destroy them. Weikel spent the rest of the day in a meeting with his most trusted aides and advisers. He also refused once again to talk to Rutti and Hiles, who had been trying to reach him for several days.

The stage was set. The first stories were finalized that afternoon. Accompanied by a reproduction of Weikel's badge and the series title, "Badge of Terror," the investigative series began appearing in the May 7, 1978, edition. The public's response was amazingly positive. The phones rang off the hooks with congratulations and more information. Criticisms were sparse.

Almost everyone in Richland County seemed to be glad that the truth about Weikel was finally coming out. Almost everyone, that is, except those in the county building — and at *The News Journal.* Instead of being enthused, a surprising number in the newsroom and other departments seemed sullen. They acted as if this just wasn't their way of doing things. It was almost as if they would have preferred doing nothing at all.

Two events pounded that home. One was a call I received from the aunt of the badly brutalized Scott Huvler.

"I'd like to thank you for finally running the story on Scott," she said.

"What do you mean, *finally?*" I asked.

"Because I gave all the medical records and the photo you printed of Scott lying in the hospital bed to one of your reporters several months ago," she replied. That was news to me. Bad news.

"When was this?" I asked incredulously.

"Right after it happened," she replied. "I called him several times after that and he finally told me he couldn't. I had given up hope."

I later discovered that *The News Journal* had also ignored information on the horrifying abuse of Ricky Tucker, which would eventually lead to several indictments. In his previously quoted affidavit of July 29, 1977, Tucker said:

"Earlier this year, my father sent me a clipping from the Mansfield *News Journal* from the Public Letters section, entitled 'Needless Cruelty.' I wrote a response to Sheriff Weikel's response, entitled 'Nothing to Hide,' and I gave a brief description of the same things I have mentioned in this statement. But, thanks to some undercover member of the 'Weikel Image Committee' at *The News Journal*, my letter wasn't ever printed for the public to see. Maybe because I *signed* my letter, and challenged the sheriff to call *me* a liar."

It is no wonder, then, that when Weikel was packed off to jail more than a year after the first stories appeared, a Mansfield man would charge in a letter to the editor that:

"It must be recognized that *The News Journal* was partially responsible for the situation which developed with the Sheriff's Department in the years since Weikel took over. Prior to Marty Yant becoming editor, Weikel was portrayed in this paper as the savior of Richland County who could do no wrong. This characterization persisted even though some knowledgeable persons believe that the newspaper had received tips and accounts of brutality and corruption in the sheriff's department dating back a considerable period of time. These accounts and tips were ignored."

The truth hurts

After what happened to me when I started publishing those accounts, I began to understand why Weikel's corruption was ignored. Investigative reporting in a small city like Mansfield almost invariably leads to problems. In my case, it led to big problems. Those problems came to a head over Weikel's suspect arrangements with the Cadillac dealer. Several days before the story detailing the scheme was scheduled to run, general manager Blake called me into his office.

"I've just found out that the dealer has threatened to organize an advertising boycott if we run the story about him," he said. "He's also threatening to file a libel suit. Under the circumstances, I'm not sure the story's worth it."

"Tens of thousands of dollars being stolen from the county treasury, and the story's not worth it?" I asked, dumbfounded.

"Look, I think the town and the staff have had about all they can bear. Let's cut it off while we're still ahead," Blake said sternly.

"OK, OK. Just give us through Monday."

"Monday and no later. Then you can move on to other things."

I'd like to think Blake hadn't realized how prophetic that last comment was. Then again, he very well could have. As the final deadline neared, the story on the cruiser-repair scam suddenly hit a brick wall in the person of the paper's libel attorney, whom the general manager had insisted would have to approve it before it could run.

When I read the final version to him over the telephone, he suddenly raised a flurry of what seemed to be superfluous questions. He asked that I have the story rewritten, and then drive to his office in Lorain, some 50 miles to the north, so we could go over it in person in the morning. I agreed, but only reluctantly. Before leaving that morning, I left the general manager a memo explaining that the story had been held at the attorney's request, but that it should be ready after we met.

A few minutes after I arrived at the lawyer's office, Blake called to ask him if I was there. I naively thought he was concerned about my safety. As it turned out, he just wanted to know if I was conveniently out of the way, which probably was the way he had it planned all along.

After getting the attorney's approval to run the story, I headed for a scheduled meeting with the publisher in Cleveland. When I arrived there, I called editorial page editor Terry Mapes to make sure there were no problems with an editorial on the sheriff's department that I had left for that day's edition.

"I don't know," Mapes said hesitantly. "I was told it was going to be changed — something about the conclusion of the series."

"There's been a change of plans, though," I told him. "I just got the OK for the final story to run tomorrow."

"Good. I'll try to get things straightened out," Mapes said with a touch of uncertainty still in his voice.

I would later find out that the conscientious Mapes did indeed try to get things straightened out. But Blake had engineered a coup and had taken control of the newsroom with the eager assistance of managing editor May, who had once told me that he never trusted the general manager and resented his interference in the newsroom. It's amazing how a chance for a promotion can change one's perspective.

To Mapes' consternation, May rammed through an editorial announcing the end of the investigative series and *The News Journal's* intent to turn over the rest of the evidence reporters had unearthed to the prosecutor, which was like turning over the keys of the chicken coop to a chicken.

While all this was happening, ironically, I was listening to the publisher tell me what a great job I had been doing.

When I arrived back in the newsroom, it felt like I had just entered a morgue. After I saw how I had been undercut, I headed for Blake's office, only to find he was gone for the day. When I got to him first thing the next morning, I expressed my shock at what he had done.

"Tough," he said. "I call the shots here. If you don't like it, there's the door."

"I don't believe this," I replied. "You never had any intention of letting that story run, did you?"

"I told you it wasn't worth the risk, and I meant it," he said, as he waved me away. I went back to my office and called editor friends in Chicago and elsewhere asking for advice. None of them could believe what had happened. One suggested I call the editor of *The Akron Beacon Journal,* which I did. He was sympathetic, and offered to discuss job possibilities with me. But, he said, he also would like to have a story written about the investigation and its aftermath.

"It may do more harm than good to me, but I can hardly try to censor a story about censorship," I said.

As soon as the publisher found out the next day that *The Beacon Journal* was working on a story about the premature ending of the series, he called Mapes and dictated a contradictory editorial saying the series that the paper had pronounced dead a few days before was being revived. "It's not over yet," the headline trumpeted to the paper's undoubtedly confused readers.

I foolishly took heart and started work on the auto-repair story. But both the readers and I had been duped again. The day after *The Beacon Journal* story about the controversy ran, Horvitz called me into Blake's office and ranted that I had "lost perspective" on the kind of newspapers he published.

What he really meant, I suddenly realized, was that I had *gained perspective.* My discovery of their cable company's sweetheart deal with city council and the cover-up of Judge Christiansen's drunken-driving arrest had caused me to realize that Horvitz and Blake were no Woodward and Bernstein. I also realized that my discussion of investigating other politicians and the suspicious financial collapse of a Mansfield-based national foundation that garnered only a brief story in *The News Journal* also frightened Blake and Horvitz. They acted as if I was getting too close for comfort.

"If that's the way you see it, then I have no choice but to resign," I said as I walked out the door. My resignation because of "philosophical differences" was announced on the front page the next day. As I tried to make sense of what had happened, a call I had received from a woman a few days before suddenly came back to me.

"By Mansfield standards, you're a lot like Christ," the caller told me. "And you know what happened to him." The first part of her analogy definitely didn't fit. But the second part was now painfully apparent.

I realized then that I should have taken Neil Peirce's word for it in *The Megastates of America* when he wrote: "Radical change in Mansfield hardly seems in store, even as it heads into the late 20th century. A generally conservative and Republican tone is set by the Mansfield *News Journal* part of a chain owned by Harry Horvitz, a man whose home is in Shaker Heights near Cleveland. It is this same alliance of business-industrial interests with the organs of public opinion that seems to keep so much of Ohio on a steady, conservative course — avoiding, at all costs, open social conflict."

Honest journalism causes open social conflict at times, and Harry Horvitz hadn't changed since Peirce wrote his book: He still wanted nothing to do with it — especially at the time he was in the process of suing his two brothers over control of their $700 million empire, which *Cleveland Magazine* said was "truly among the great American fortunes."

When Harry, Leonard and William Horvitz's father Sam began building the empire, the magazine said, "the money never came without a fight," which he almost always won by "crushing the opposition."

The way Sam Horvitz came to own *The News Journal*, I would discover later, fit that pattern. Horvitz first got into the newspaper business with *The Lorain Journal* to get back at Raymond Hoiles, publisher of *The*

Lorain Times-Herald, which had questioned how Horvitz's paving company had won a lucrative city contract.

A few years later, Horvitz extended his vengeful battle to Mansfield, where he started the Mansfield *Journal* to compete with Hoiles' *Mansfield News*.

In 1928, a bomb destroyed the front porch of Hoiles' new Mansfield home. When dynamite was found rigged to Hoiles' car a year later, he threw in the towel. Hoiles sold his Lorain and Mansfield papers to another publishing company, which in turn sold them to Horvitz, who merged them with his own newspapers. The result of the merger in Mansfield was the profitable *News Journal*, which at first was called *The Journal-News*.

When Sam's three sons divided up responsibilities for their father's empire when he died in 1956, Harry took over the newspaper division, which he quickly expanded by buying several other moneymaking newspapers. Leonard concentrated on the construction company and William moved to Florida to run the family company that was developing Hollywood, Florida, into a large, affluent city.

The brothers behaved themselves until their mother, Hattie, died in 1977. Then the gloves came off, just as I was about to become editor of *The News Journal*. When Leonard, who was not a trustee of the estate; and trustees William Horvitz and Frank Kane, Sam's longtime accountant, started meddling in trustee Harry's newspaper kingdom, Harry sued to stop them.

By the time the suit was over in 1987, Harry had lost badly, and got beaten up in the process.

In a deposition, Harry's brother Leonard described a man I had seen glimpses of during my six months of working for him.

"He is sick," Leonard said of his publisher-brother in a deposition. "The man goes into uncontrolled fits of temper. He absolutely can't control himself. He attacked me physically since this litigation began. He tried to kick me in the balls in the office. He scratched me and pulled my hair. And he swore at me."

Fortunately, Harry never kicked me in the balls. But he did knife me in the back and would later keep me from getting a top editing position with a major metropolitan newspaper. So I didn't particularly feel sorry for Horvitz when the litigation he started ended with his being forced to sell his precious newspapers in 1987.

Weikel's deputy dogs were ecstatic when they heard I had resigned. Their celebration at a local bar got so far out of hand that it ended in a brawl that got those who started it suspended by a suddenly less-permissive sheriff. Weikel also filed a written reprimand against Hart, who, *The News Journal* quoted witnesses as saying, was "tending bar" at the time. Weikel knew he couldn't tolerate such nonsense anymore. Although he had said, after the investigative series started to appear, that he was "sure that after an appropriate investigation, this department will be cleared of any wrongdoing," Weikel knew *The News Journal* had opened a can of worms that would be hard to close, even if I was gone.

Most Mansfielders had a quite different reaction to my resignation than the deputies. Many were outraged, and expressed their anger on the local talk-radio station. Dozens wrote or called to express their support. *The News Journal* received so many letters protesting my departure that Blake decided it had to publish some to regain a semblance of credibility.

"A breath of fresh air had been brought into our town when Martin Yant came to *The News Journal*," one letter said. "Mr. Yant had the courage to bring out into the open what had been rumored for a long time. His departure makes it very obvious that pressure is being brought on people. . . . Where is freedom of the press in Mansfield, Ohio?"

A letter signed by three readers said my "refreshing approach — commonly known as truth — to the stagnation and corruption in the Fun Center of Ohio was a welcome relief after years of Pollyanna journalism. . . . If the 'philosophical differences' leading to the resignation center on Yant's muckraking journalism, such objections are invalid. Apparently there is plenty of muck to rake. Mansfield has been known as a center of criminal activities and political corruption for years, but the gutless wonder of the fourth estate rarely mentioned anything more embarrassing than traffic accidents or sewer rates. "Although the excellent series on corruption on Sheriff Weikel's private army is, we suspect, the crux of the 'philosophical differences,' " the letter added, "*The News Journal* has also challenged Mansfield to live up to its potential. Editorials urged the adoption of a coordinated plan for the restoration of Mansfield's dismal downtown and encouraged businessmen and private citizens to partici-pate in a cleanup/fix-up campaign. Under Yant's leadership, several new columns focused reader attention on the interests and accomplishments of their fellow citizens.

"The citizens' review committee Yant organized would have provided readers a voice in the organization and function of Richland County's only major daily. The entire newspaper had a newer, bolder, fresher appearance."

As nice as all the letters and phone calls were, my first reaction to being forced to resign had been to get as far away from "The Fun Center of Ohio" as I could. Within a few days, I was in California for a job interview. Then I got a phone call from Sandy Schmidt, a Mansfield real-estate agent. "A lot of people are really upset about what happened to you," she said. "And some of them have the power to do something about it."

"That may be," I said. "But the only newspaper in town isn't for sale."

"But there doesn't *have* to be just one paper. That's why I'm calling. Some people with money to invest want to talk to you about starting a *new* newspaper. I realize that sounds far-fetched, but all I ask is that you come back and hear them out." I was on the plane for Ohio the next morning. As the letters and phone calls of support kept coming in, I decided that the idea of starting a new newspaper wasn't as ridiculous as it had first seemed. Unfortunately, my enthusiasm and ego got the better of me, and I decided the paper should be a six-days-a-week daily with a Sunday-like Saturday edition rather than a weekly. I saw the opportunity to carry out the much-needed journalistic revolution of providing not just Mansfield, but eventually many other one-newspaper cities in Ohio with an innovative, statewide second daily newspaper. Hence the name *The Ohio Observer* — and hence, with the help of circulation sabotage, arson, intimidation of advertisers, threats on financial supporters and libel suits, the paper's ultimate failure. But much good happened before then, thanks to the extraordinary efforts of staff members, community volunteers and more than 100 investors — including a high-school student, a woman in her 80s who sold subscriptions door-to-door and a couple who said they and their friend Louis Bromfield considered starting a second Mansfield paper after he returned to Richland County and saw how bad *The News Journal* was.

Noticeably absent were several of the wealthy people who had originally talked me into starting *The Observer*. Some admitted they had been pressured to withdraw their support, leaving me holding the bag with a mere $64,000 in it to start a daily newspaper.

But it was too late to turn back then, so I went the only direction I could — straight ahead. The day *The Ohio Observer* first hit the streets on September 11, 1978, excitement filled the air. People waiting in cars to get a first edition caused a traffic jam, and when the papers arrived some paid $20 to get one of the first ones off the truck. Getting the tabloid with a contemporary design to that point hadn't been easy, but we had done it.

"What kind of newspaper will *The Observer* be?" I asked rhetorically in a front-page editorial. "Quite, simply, it will be a newspaper that will never compromise the truth."

I then told how self-censorship had forced me to leave *The News Journal* and it was exactly that kind of thinking we intended to avoid by fulfilling the newspaper's vital role as a watchdog against public and private corruption.

"As a people's paper," I concluded, "we will praise those who deserve to be praised and damn those who deserve to be damned rather than the other way around."

Unfortunately, that policy ended up damning me as well. The next several months were pure hell for me, my family and my staff as *The Observer* — despite its editorial excellence and growing circulation — was brought down, just as I had been warned it would be.

One of the first warnings came from a woman whose boss was a good friend of Prosecutor McKee. She told me her boss had told her that McKee had said he was going to get me before I got him. George Constable, then a *News Journal* columnist, passed on a similar warning. No matter where I ended up, he quoted McKee as saying, they would find me "when the lawsuits hit." As will be detailed in the next chapter, McKee apparently also tried unsuccessfully that summer to have ludicrous charges filed against me for failure to report a crime to law enforcement that I wrote about in *The Akron Beacon Journal.*

The threats on my life became more and more numerous as the first publication date neared. But I still didn't take them seriously until I was walking out of the office late one day with State Representative Sherrod Brown. As I looked across the street, I saw a man sitting in a car with a telephoto lens pointing at us. He snapped a couple of quick shots and sped away, but not before I got his license plate number.

When I got home, I had a source get me the name of the person the car was registered to. I checked the owner out the next day and learned he was a local steelworker. A few days later a Mansfield businessman stopped by to see me. "When I stopped to get some gas at the truck stop out on 1-71 yesterday, I decided to go to the men's room," he said. "As I walked in, I saw two guys looking at a picture of you walking out of your building, and one of them was saying something like, 'This is him.' It may just have been my imagination at work, but these guys didn't look like the friendliest people in the world, so I thought you should know."

"Thanks," I said. "I'll check it out."

After the businessman left, I called my best police source and told him the details of what had happened. The next day, the officer showed up at my office with a bulletproof vest.

"We checked out your photo bug, and he's a small-time gambler who owes some big-time people in Cleveland a lot of money," the officer said. "I want you to wear this and let me and my buddies give you a ride to and from work for a while."

"Thanks, but you don't really think anyone would be that stupid, do you?" I said.

"If the rumors are true that you're investigating the Highway Safety Foundation, anything is a possibility," he smiled.

"Well, there were some definite mob links there," I replied.

I only wore the vest once or twice and I am still alive. But the rides to and from work those days sure were appreciated.

The message from all of this was clear: Investigative reporting was not appreciated in Mansfield, and the one who might suffer the most from revealing corruption would be the messenger. If President Nixon had included McKee and Weikel on his team, Woodward and Bernstein could have gone to prison rather than Haldelman and Erlichman.

Among the more humorous things that happened as *The Observer* was being developed was a sudden interest in our building. The small downtown structure had been on the market for $50,000 without a nibble from a potential buyer for several months when the owner agreed to rent it to me.

Shortly after we moved in, though, I saw Horvitz and Blake standing across the street pointing at the building during an involved discussion. Within a day or so, the owner got a call from an unidentified "out of town buyer" who offered him $70,000 for the building, supposedly sight unseen. Fortunately, he turned the offer down.

A similar offer would be made three months later with the same result. But after *The Observer* folded and therefore couldn't be evicted by a new owner, the building sat vacant for almost a full year and then was knocked down. As the first day of publication neared, things got increasingly hectic. In order to get our computer system, we had to fly to New Jersey, rent a truck and deliver it ourselves. The politically connected telephone company, meanwhile, managed to get our news-wire machines functioning at only the last moment even though the order had been placed six weeks earlier.

Because of a tight budget, most employees couldn't start work until a day or two before the first edition was produced. That created chaos, which turned into havoc when the computers malfunctioned. Many of us worked more than 24 straight hours to get that first issue out, which we finally did several hours late. Many kept up that pace for several days before we finally got all the bugs worked out.

The reaction of the readers is what kept us going. They liked what they saw, and subscriptions came pouring in. Within a few weeks, *The Ohio Observer* had a circulation of 17,000 — almost half that of the long-established *News Journal.* Before *The Observer* was brought down eight months later, it had managed to keep the heat on local officials — and *The News Journal* — to push for a thorough investigation of Weikel's department.

36 indictments

After the appointment of Special Prosecutor Joseph Murray and an intensive four-month-long investigation by BCI agents, a special grand jury issued 36 indictments on 68 counts of assault, violations of civil rights and theft in office against Weikel, Hart, Whisler and Miser; deputies Dan Miller, Bill Spognardi and Gary Bush; and former deputies Michael Spognardi, Terry McMillen, Earl Korn, Donald Todd and Timothy McClaren.

Weikel was indicted on two counts each for assaulting inmates Larry Gorman, Thomas Davis, Ricky Tucker and Marvin Frankfather. He was also indicted for five private trips to Florida paid for by taxpayers. Hart was named in five counts for theft in office and two counts of aggravated assault and interfering with the civil rights of Gorman. The indictment accused him of using a deadly weapon, nunchakus, to beat Gorman.

The theft-in-office charges against Hart included trips to Florida and Washington, D.C., and selling handcuff cases to deputies without turning the money into the county's general fund. Miser was named in the alleged assaults of Tucker and Frankfather, and Whisler for taking an unjustified trip at public expense to Florida in 1976. Many of the indictments against the deputies and former deputies contained multiple counts. Most dealt with alleged assaults or Florida trips.

With the apparent legal advice of the Richland County prosecutor's office, however, Weikel's lawyers got Common Pleas Court Judge Max Chilcote, Weikel's longtime friend, to throw out the indictments on a technicality.

Chilcote bent over backward to allow the department's attorneys to prove that the grand jury had been illegally impaneled and that the jury's secrecy had been violated by the press. He held reporters Rutti and Hiles in contempt for refusing to turn over their notes and name their sources, a decision later overruled by an appeals court.

Then Weikel went too far, even for Chilcote. Just after I invoked the same state shield law that had failed to protect Rutti and Hiles while being asked to name my sources on the grand jury proceedings, Chilcote stunned those present by announcing he had just been informed that the courtroom had been bugged. He ordered Deputy Michael Sheline to approach the bench, then asked him if he was wearing a body microphone. Sheline admitted he was. Chilcote then ordered two officers to remove the device, which Sheline said he had been ordered to wear by Hart that morning so the proceedings could be transmitted to Weikel's office. At a hearing later that day, Hart and Weikel admitted they had ordered Sheline, and Miser on two previous occasions, to bug the courtroom with a device that, ironically, Weikel had purchased during a taxpayer-paid vacation to Florida for which he had already been indicted.

Calling Weikel and his deputies his "friends," Chilcote said he had no choice but to hold them in contempt. He then ordered Weikel to serve 10 days in jail and pay a $500 fine. Hart got a four-day sentence and Sheline a one-day suspended sentence. The vacationing Miser was later sentenced to three days in jail.

Weikel, Hart, and Miser hardly suffered during their stays in Mansfield City Jail. They were placed in separate unlocked cells and could order any meal they wished. Weikel even sent a jailer out for a second milkshake when the first one didn't meet his standards. All three "crime fighters" were paid during their incarceration. When Chilcote threw the indictments out and ordered a new grand jury impaneled, Murray quickly obtained 27 felony and 11 misdemeanor indictments. Chilcote threw out indictments dealing with the theft of up to $27,000, however, because the 12 counts didn't specify exact amounts.

Having done about all he could do for his "friends," Chilcote ordered the trial to be heard by Vincent Barbuto, a notorious wheeler-dealer judge in Akron. A short time later, Weikel and his deputies entered Barbuto-brokered no-contest pleas on no more than two misdemeanor charges each and were sentenced to six months in prison. Barbuto also stipulated that they could never hold a position in law enforcement again, but that didn't keep either Weikel or Hart from later running — very unsuccessfully — for sheriff in Richland County.

It would become clear a year later just why Barbuto could let such brutal criminals off so easily when Geraldo Rivera, then a serious investigative reporter, revealed on the ABC-TV show *20/20* that Barbuto was a criminal himself. Rivera's dramatic investigative report revealed that Judge Barbuto a former prosecutor, had given reduced sentences to prostitutes in return for sexual favors, had run a house of prostitution from his judicial chambers and regularly sold confiscated weapons left in the custody of his court.

Barbuto was eventually convicted on charges similar to Rivera's revelations and sentenced to prison. Rather fittingly, Barbuto took another sheriff down with him. On June 6, 1980, Summit County Sheriff Anthony J. Cadarelli pleaded guilty to three misdemeanor charges of dereliction of duty and one misdemeanor charge of obstruction of justice. He was given a suspended 360-day sentence and placed on probation with the condition that he never seek or hold office again. In return, four felony counts against the sheriff were dismissed. The charges were related to the mishandling of guns seized as evidence and the termination of an investigation by two of his deputies of reports of Barbuto's sexual misconduct.

In a second, related proceeding, William G. Brooks pleaded guilty to one count of obstructing justice after being charged with intimidating five female witnesses in Barbuto's trial. Brooks received a suspended 30-day sentence on the condition that he "remove himself from Summit County and not return for at least 10 years."

Chilcote sure knew how to pass the buck to a judge who appreciated one — and how to corrupt others as well.

Nonetheless, Weikel's reign of terror was over, although Weikel tried to revive it when he ran as "the best sheriff Richland County ever had." shortly after his release from jail. But the voters weren't about to fall for Weikel's bluster again.

He got less than 10 percent of the vote in the 1980 Republican primary and headed for Florida and well-deserved obscurity at the age of 58. Weikel died in Deland, Florida, in 1998. According to his former daughter-in-law, who lived with Weikel's son near the former sheriff, Weikel didn't exactly turn over a new leaf. "He had a terrifying temper, and he was perpetually angry," she told me.

Hart also ignored Judge Barbuto's stipulation that he never return to law enforcement. After spending five months in the Franklin County Jail before he was released, Hart got a Richland County judge to expunge his record and order all investigative records on his case sealed. With a clean slate, Hart started searching for a new job in law enforcement, as if all was forgiven and forgotten.

Hart learned that wouldn't always be the case in May 1980, when the Columbus suburb of Minerva Park announced it was hiring him as its police chief. While all might have been forgiven, it had not been forgotten when news broke about Hart's controversial past.

In one story, Jack E. McCormick, superintendent of the Ohio Bureau of Criminal Identification and Investigation, whose agency aided the grand-jury investigation of the sheriff's department, told the *Columbus Dispatch* that Weikel and Hart should never be able to serve in law enforcement again. McCormick, a former FBI agent, added that Weikel and Hart had presided over the worst corruption and abuse of power in law enforcement he had ever seen. Two days later, Minerva Park officials said Hart was not going to be hired after all.

Petty corruption

Unfortunately, the "reform" candidate elected to replace Weikel's interim successor eventually fell into the same corruption trap. Richard Petty, a former Ohio Highway Patrol post commander in nearby Ashland, was convicted in 1987 on two counts each of tampering with evidence and obstructing justice.

The Richland County jury that heard the case before a visiting judge convicted Petty after hearing evidence concerning Petty's failure to act on a 1984 arson confession from Debra Bush, the daughter of Petty's former campaign manager. Bush, who had since pleaded guilty to arson, admitted to Petty several months after the fire that she had hired a Mansfield man to burn her house in order to fraudulently collect $11,900 from an insurance policy.

When Mansfield police found the confession in Petty's desk after obtaining a search warrant based on a tip on Petty's cover-up, the sheriff claimed he had held onto the confession as part of an investigation into a second 1984 fire that killed a 4-year-old boy.

Petty resigned a few days after receiving a concurrent two-year prison sentence for obstruction and one year for tampering, which the judge said he would reduce to two years' probation if Petty gave up his office. Petty was also fined $2,000 and required to pay the costs of prosecution.

Petty was replaced by fellow Democrat Dale Shetler, who ran into trouble himself in 1991 when a special prosecutor was appointed to investigate his handling of a theft case. Shetler's troubles began when a deputy was caught pocketing $285 in bond money. After an administrative hearing, Shetler decided to drop the matter if the deputy paid the money back and resigned, which he did. The special prosecutor was asked to investigate whether Shetler was negligent in the performance of his duties by not charging the deputy with theft.

That wasn't the end of Shetler's problems, however A few days before the 1992 primary election, Prosecutor James J. Mayer Jr. asked the Mansfield Police Department to investigate reports in *The News Journal* — by then under different ownership — that Shetler had made 150 personal calls at county expense, billed the county for other personal expenses, used deputies to run personal errands and dispatched cruisers to pick up his wife at their home some 20 miles away and bring her to work at the courthouse.

Some of the non-reimbursed phone calls, *The News Journal* reported, were made to Shetler's barber and his mother. But most were made to a woman who said she had a personal relationship with the sheriff. Shetler insisted that the calls, as well as numerous trips in a county car to the woman's home in another county, involved official business.

(According to one rumor, part of Shetler's "official business" was strolling through the streets of the town where the woman lived holding her hand. According to another rumor, which I confirmed, a car wreck by Shetler near his home in Shelby occurred while he was drag racing one stepson in a new convertible owned by his other stepson. Shetler claimed he was forced off the road when an oncoming car swerved left of center.)

The News Journal also reported that, between 1989 and 1991, Shetler had spent more than $11,000 on promotional items such as balloons, star-shaped key fobs, and business cards featuring his color portrait. In this case, the people didn't wait for the courts to pass judgment on their sheriff's alleged transgressions. They did so themselves in the Democratic primary in June, which Shetler lost to a retired Mansfield police officer. Three months later Shetler resigned to avoid prosecution. "It's the easiest, smartest and most economical solution for everyone, Shetler said. "Why should I have to put my family through a trial?"

His agreement with the special prosecutor also stipulated that Shetler pay the county about $400 for an FBI ring, plaque and coffee cup he allegedly bought with money from the always-troublesome Furtherance of Justice Fund. Shetler added that he would not have made the deal if he had won the primary and that he should not be compared with Petty and Weikel. "I walk out of here with my head held high," he said. "If I had more time left in office, I'd say, 'I'll see you in court.' "

Given the records of his predecessors, Shetler's alleged transgressions did seem minor. But one of those eager to take advantage of ouster was the newly reconstituted R. Gene Hart, who had announced his candidacy for sheriff in the 1992 Republican primary in February 1991.

"I'm announcing early because of the perceived reputation I have to live down among people who don't know me personally but who just know my name," Hart said when he declared his candidacy. He added that he would work hard to dispel his inaccurate tough-guy image, which he said started when he had to break up bar fights as a young deputy. I'm going to say within probably a two-year period, I must have hit a dozen to two dozen people over the head with my flashlight and grabbed them by the collar and dragged them out to the cruiser," Hart explained. "When you do that enough and people see these six-cell flashlights come down on somebody's head and batteries fly all over the place, you get a reputation from that."

Hart admitted to hitting inmate Larry Gorman, a charge to which he had pleaded no contest as part of a deal to avoid prosecution on the more serious charges against him, all of which he said were unfounded.

"These indictments were based on rumors and accusations, and if there was any validity to them, believe me, the capable prosecutor, Joe Murray, would have gone after them," Hart said. "If Joe Murray could have gone forth on any charge that would have been a felony, he absolutely would have gone forth."

Hart's statement came as quite a surprise to Murray. "The plea bargains came because the case was getting very expensive and the sheriff was still in office," Murray told *The News Journal*. ""We had to get him out of there. That doesn't mean there was no validity to the other pending charges." Murray added that, "If I lived in Richland County, I wouldn't vote for him. The fact remains, he did six months in jail for simple assault on an inmate. If that's the kind of person Richland County wants as sheriff, so be it."

When I recounted the long-ago-published allegations against Hart in a column in *The Columbus Dispatch* after he had announced his candidacy, Hart demanded a retraction. He claimed he had been cleared of wrongdoing or wasn't involved in the incidents I had mentioned other than the one with Gorman. After reviewing my files, attorneys for *The Dispatch* refused his request. Hart then filed a libel suit.

"I've never met or talked with Martin Yant, but over the years he has accused me of wrongdoing apparently on the basis of untrue and unsubstantiated rumors and through guilt by association," Hart said. He said the filing of the lawsuit two days after the 1991 election, when attention would focus on the 1992 primary in which he was a candidate, was coincidental. He said his attorney had been too busy to file his five-page complaint, two pages of which were a recapitulation of my article, any sooner.

As it turned out, Hart fared even worse in the Republican primary than Shetler did in the Democratic primary: He finished a distant third among four candidates. Two days later, Hart dropped his libel suit, as he had offered to do after an April pretrial conference at which *Dispatch* attorneys gave an idea of the substantial evidence they had to back up my allegations — plus much more. The suit was dismissed with prejudice, which means Hart had agreed to take no additional action against me and/or *The Dispatch*.

Hart tried, but failed, to get *The Dispatch* and me to agree not to make any public comment on the suit after its dismissal. I could certainly say plenty more than I have, but won't. The fact that Hart dropped the suit speaks volumes for me. So did his rejection by the voters, who apparently saw Hart's campaign slogan, "Proven Tough on Crime," as an ominous reminder of his past.

True to form, *The News Journal,* which had given prominent play to Hart's filing of his suit, did not report its dismissal. *The Dispatch* was almost as petty, as newspapers usually are when it comes to reporting about themselves. When Hart filed the suit several months after I had left the newspaper, it ran a story in which my name was prominently mentioned to make clear that I was responsible for the supposedly libelous column. When *The Dispatch* reported that the suit had been dismissed, and the substance of the column therefore vindicated, my name was nowhere to be seen.

But that wasn't the end of Gene Hart. Hart worked as an auxiliary policeman wherever he could until he got a chance to move up. That happened in Clinton Township, a small chopped up entity surrounded by the city of Columbus. Hart started working there in 1994, where he reportedly impressed the powers-that-be. When the chief's job became open, Hart applied. As he filled out the job-application form, Hart stated that he had never been convicted of a crime. Although Hart was less than forthright, his answer was technically true because his record had been expunged. Hart may have stretched the truth, however, when he explained why he left the Richland County Sheriff's Department.

"Sheriff left office [Hart didn't say he left to go to jail] and I went back to school full-time to get my degree," Hart wrote on the application. While Hart eventually did get a degree, he certainly didn't go "back to school" as soon as his answer implied — unless the Franklin County Jail offered college courses. When I revealed in *Columbus Alive* that Hart had a criminal record, Trustee Larry Wilkes jumped to the new chief's defense. "Everyone deserves a second chance," said Wilkes, who himself was convicted of a public-indecency charge in 1999. "Hart has done more for this township in a few months than anyone else has done in years."

Wilkes added that Hart had been professional almost to a fault and that he turned down his first raise because he said he would rather see the money go toward improving the department.

A marked increase in traffic citations once Hart took over quickly created a stir, however. Wilkes said that, while ticket revenue has increased from approximately $3,500 to $10,000 a month, the police department's goal was enforcing the law, not making more money. But a memo from Wilkes to Hart I obtained suggested that increased revenue was also a motive.

"As you are aware traffic citations are an important part of our operating revenue," Wilkes wrote. "Monies received from those citations could mean the difference between maintaining the recent changes in the department or going back to business as usual."

According to a township police officer and other sources, all of whom agreed to interviews on the condition that they not be identified, Hart backed Wilkes' emphasis on traffic citations by setting ticket quotas that each officer was expected to meet. If an officer didn't meet the quota, the sources said, Hart made them ineligible for special duty, which many officers used to supplement their income. Ironically, deputies and former deputies who provided much of the information that led to Hart's downfall in Richland County said one of the first things Hart did when he was promoted to chief deputy there was to institute stringent ticket quotas.

The Clinton Township sources said Hart also ingratiated himself with the trustees by issuing them badges. Wilkes confirmed that Hart gave the trustees badges so they had official-looking identification. He said other township trustees had similar badges.

Hart reportedly told his officers that they had jurisdiction throughout Franklin County, and if they saw someone break the law outside their jurisdiction they could still pull them over. In April 2002, Hart practiced what he preached when he pulled over a motorist in downtown Columbus. When a Franklin County Sheriff's Lieutenant Mark Gilbert saw an unfamiliar unmarked car pulling over another car, he decided to see what was going on.

"I had no idea if this might be a drug deal going bad or what, so I pulled in behind the unmarked car and turned out my headlights with my parking lights on," Gilbert wrote in a report. "As (Hart) approached the vehicle it became apparent that he had simply made a traffic stop and was lecturing the driver of the suspect vehicle. . . . I believed at this point I either had a private security officer playing policeman or that this individual was a 'wanna-be' impersonating a police officer."

Gilbert, who was also in an unmarked car but in uniform, said he blew his horn and motioned for Hart not to leave as Hart got back into his car. Gilbert said Hart ignored him and turned across several lanes of traffic at least twice in an effort to avoid pursuit before he finally stopped and identified himself.

"I asked why he would be making a traffic stop in Downtown Columbus and so far out of his jurisdiction," Gilbert reported. "He quickly became defensive stating that the [Ohio Revised Code] said he could do so anywhere in the county." Gilbert said he told Hart that he could only make stops for serious offenses.

Hart later denied trying to evade Gilbert and stood by his interpretation of the law. "We're constables, and under Ohio law, a constable has jurisdiction in the county where the township is located."

Franklin County Prosecutor Ron O'Brien disagreed. In a letter to Hart, O'Brien said that state law made "it perfectly clear that neither the chief nor the constables of Clinton Township have any warrentless arrest or detention authority in any other jurisdiction" except in cases of hot pursuit or on highways adjacent to the township.

Noting that the prosecutor's office represented Clinton Township, O'Brien wrote that he "wanted to make sure they were aware of what the law says." Trustee Wilkes said that the township and the police department accepted O'Brien's opinion. "As of this afternoon, when I talked to the chief, what's in that letter is now our policy," Wilkes said. "We want to do what's right and what's legal."

Not according to the Ohio Civil Rights Commission, however. In August 2002, the commission agreed that evidence existed that the township discriminated against a part-time police officer of Middle Eastern heritage. Officer Abdeljalil "Abdul" Aburmaieleh, of Jordanian descent, had argued that Hart, Wilkes and Lieutenant Anthony Pfeifer discriminated against him because of his national origin.

"There is some form of evidence to substantiate that discrimination has occurred in violation of the law," on both complaints, spokeswoman Connie Higgins said. Aburmaieleh said he would use the decision to bolster a lawsuit he had filed against the department in Franklin County Common Pleas Court. In his suit, Aburmaieleh accused officers of calling him a terrorist after the September 11, 2001, terrorist attacks and said that an internal memo referred to him as "Abdul Bin Laden."

The suit also claimed Aburmaieleh was subjected to unwarranted investigations and unjustified discipline. "They've been retaliating against him mercilessly," said Aburmaieleh's attorney, Frederick M. Gittes. "We now have an independent agency that has confirmed what he has been going through for quite some time."

Aburmaieleh also complained that Wilkes made unwanted sexual advances against him. Witnesses confirmed that Wilkes frequently discussed his sex life in his work place, the commission report said.

Hart's problems mounted in other ways that same month, when the township's trustees announced that his department would overspend its $850,000 budget by $200,000 to $300,000 that year. The trustees said the extra money would come from the township's general fund. Noting that the department had expanded from 17 officers to 66, including 18 volunteer reserves, since Hart became chief in April 2001, the trustees said they probably would have to put a 3-mill levy on the November ballot to prevent a similar deficit the next year if Hart didn't stanch the spending increases. They said that would be in addition to the seven existing police levies, which total 9.7 mills and would raise $675,000 that year.

Hart's biggest booster, fellow former lawbreaker Trustee Wilkes, claimed the township of 4,500 was in the midst of a crime spree and needed a larger police force. But Karon Wing, a resident since 1954, said the crime spree was a figment of Hart's and Wilkes' imaginations. In all that time she had lived there, the outspoken Wing said, "I've never had nothing but a plastic Uncle Sam stolen out of my yard."

Township statistics did show a marked increase in police activity after Hart became chief. Traffic citations rose from 2,989 traffic citations in 2000 to 10,406 in 2001, and crime reports rose from 1,210 reports to 5,386. But some officers said the reason for the increase was more a matter of Hart's penchant for paperwork than crime-fighting.

In October, Township Clerk Rebecca Christian announced that, despite orders to the contrary, Hart was still overspending his budget, mostly on salaries for 45 part-time officers. "The police department is basically out of money," Christian said. "The whole point is the police chief was hired to manage the department. He's overspent for four more payrolls now. At what point does this stop? I'm not against the police department. I just think it's a chief's responsibility to manage and to meet a budget. When he does blow the budget, there should be consequences."

There finally were on April 17, 2003, when Hart resigned after losing the support of trustees for still breaking his budget and the support of full-time officers, who stopped talking to him. Hart blamed the trustees for the morale problems, which he said started when they shut down the detective bureau he established in May 2001.

The problems came to a head when the trustees left Hart out of a private session at which they met with representatives of the police union and the Franklin County Sheriff's Office. Among the topics discussed was an investigation of the possible misuse of the state's confidential law-enforcement database.

Bill Capretta, president of the Fraternal Order of Police Capital City Lodge No. 9, said the eight full-time officers represented by the union had complained that Hart "mistreated and intimidated them." In a subsequent column in the FOP local's newsletter, Capretta said a review of the department's personnel records indicated that "little background work was done prior to hiring part-time and reserve officers." Indeed, my own review determined that at least two of the officers Hart hired did not have the certification required to be a police officer. Another officer Hart hired was John Clark, a former Fairfield County sheriff's lieutenant who had recently admitted in court testimony against former Sheriff Gary K. DeMastry that he had signed false affidavits. Clark also admitted that a state audit that prompted public-corruption charges that eventually led to DeMastry's conviction originally found that Clark owed the county $33,000 for dubious expenditures.

After Hart resigned, longtime resident Wing, who had tried to get Hart ousted once his criminal record became known, blamed the trustees. "They let him do anything and everything he wanted," Wing said. Given Hart's history, that was a prescription for disaster, as the people of Richland County knew all too well.

3

Dr. Greed

When it came to damaging people's lives, Richland County Coroner Raymond Thabet hardly took a back seat to Sheriff Weikel.

The only difference was that the harm Thabet allegedly caused stretched around the world and was much harder to calculate. The consequences of fabricated results on Pap smear, blood and urine tests are hard to calculate, but the potential of harm was certainly great.

But Raymond Thabet apparently was at the point in his life that he didn't care. After a long struggle, he was finally a financial and social success. That was something that had eluded him before. A native of Charleston, W.V., Thabet graduated from the Medical College of Virginia before becoming associate pathologist and director of laboratories at Grant Hospital in Columbus. But Thabet didn't seem to fit in well in the state capital. There was no doubt that he was a brilliant pathologist, but he was suspected of cutting too many corners and for being too greedy.

But Thabet considered that kind of attitude his detractors' problem, not his. He wanted to be both rich and powerful. And since money buys power, he concentrated on getting rich first. Thabet's road to riches led him to Mansfield in 1963, where he became chief pathologist of Mansfield General Hospital.

Unlike in Columbus, Thabet quickly fell in with the powers-that-be. One of these friends was Richard Wayman, whose Highway Safety Foundation was the town's most respected organization before it collapsed in 1974 with several million dollars missing — as well as Way-

After learning how his newfound friends had gained their wealth, Thabet set about gaining his. The chosen vehicle was Automated Medical Services of Ohio. Automated, or AMSO, was an instant success. Just as he established it in 1967, doctors, hospitals and Planned Parenthood units across the country began using private medical laboratories like AMSO to conduct tests for them.

Outfitted with sophisticated equipment and allegedly high standards, such medical labs were supposed to do a far better job than overburdened hospital labs.

Fired by hospital

So Thabet had no problem attracting business for his lab once he had set it up in an old house near downtown Mansfield. He did have trouble keeping his job at Mansfield General, however. After five years, in 1968, his temper tantrums and bizarre behavior caught up with him. Although the dispute that caused his termination ostensibly concerned hospital policy, the fact was that many of Thabet's former friends had become fed up with him.

So the hospital board voted to let him go. Guards reportedly were posted at the lab entrance to keep Thabet out. Undaunted, Thabet became chief pathologist at the city's much smaller People's Hospital, where he remained until 1974. It was then that Thabet's lab moved into a $325,000 two-level building he had built on land purchased from the Sterkel estate, which had been left primarily as a site for a Catholic hospital and ended up with everything on the land but that.

When Thabet had announced the planned construction the year before, he called it "an attempt to make practical the concept of rapid, high-speed laboratory services and make it available in this area of Ohio." Thabet stressed that a new computer would greatly enhance the accuracy of Automated's work, and that error would not exceed "one standard deviation from the federal government's requirement for accuracy in laboratory data." Later events would make that boast seem terribly empty.

But four years of good times preceded the bad ones. Automated continued to grow and prosper. It received a number of federal contracts, and by 1978 had attracted 345 customers in Ohio and 113 customers in 14 other states. Thabet had made it. He began telling friends and relatives that he was a millionaire many times over.

Once he had money, Thabet went after power. In 1976, he ran as the Republican Party's candidate for coroner. With the support of almost the entire medical community, Thabet was elected over Dr. Gordon Morkel, who had been openly critical of the Mansfield medical establishment, its doctors, hospitals and their greed for many years.

Thabet could have been satisfied, but he wasn't. His journey to success had been costly. His marriage had begun to fall apart as the beatings of his wife and children took their toll. (One daughter had to wear a brace in her mouth for several months after Thabet broke her jaw.)

Thabet's first case as Richland County coroner typified the callousness with which he approached the job. In January 1977, one of the coldest months in history, Eugene Kuhn of Mansfield froze to death after the local electric company discontinued his service because of unpaid bills. (The business of Mansfield, after all, was business — not social service.)

As news of the Kuhn tragedy spread across the country, and protests to the electric company's actions began pouring in, Thabet arrived at Kuhn's home to pronounce him dead.

After doing so, Thabet helped himself to Kuhn's pornographic-magazine collection, stamp collection, coin collection and several bottles of wine. He also filled some boxes with a variety of items, including a winter coat and a toilet-bowl repair kit, and took them to his then-$150,000 home in the best section of Mansfield.

Why would such a wealthy man steal such junk from a dead man? Because it was there, most who knew him agreed. Thabet, they said, was a near-kleptomaniac. "If he came to your house and you had a few coins on the table next to where he sat, the coins would most likely be gone when he was," one former aide said.

Others gave an additional reason: greed. Thabet, after all, had both a stamp and coin collection. And the only way he could find out whether Kuhn had some kind of hidden treasure in the collections was to take them. He probably decided to take the rest of the items as an afterthought.

Shortly after I reported Thabet's theft of Kuhn's possessions in *The Akron Beacon Journal*, the Mansfield Police Department began an investigation and developed what detectives told me was an "airtight" case against Thabet. Among the evidence were statements by Thabet's estranged wife and two daughters stating that Thabet had brought the stolen items home and refused Mrs. Thabet's requests to return them.

But a funny thing happened to the case on the way to trial. It got into the hands of Prosecutor William F. McKee. The once-airtight case no longer was.

After holding off presenting the case to a grand jury for several weeks, McKee acted, according to one source, more like a defense attorney than a prosecutor when he finally did.

Those called to testify said his questions were superficial and often irrelevant, and McKee seemed to be questioning their motives more than Thabet's.

The result was no indictment, despite the preponderance of evidence. That included most of the stolen items, which had been located in Thabet's home or office. Mansfield-style justice had struck again.

But that was just a minor aspect of the problems Thabet would face over his private laboratory, which began coming undone in July 1978. Before the dust had settled, the FBI, U.S. Air Force, state attorney general's office and even syndicated columnist Jack Anderson would be on the case, all of them confirming what I had reported in *The Beacon Journal.*

The FBI was the first aboard. In 1977, the agency had received a letter from a former lab employee charging that a number of testing irregularities had occurred there on the processing of Pap smear tests for the Air Force. In July, U.S. Attorney James Williams announced in Cleveland that Pap smear tests conducted at Automated had a high incidence of error. In Washington, meanwhile, the Air Force issued a worldwide alert that all women in the service during the years Automated conducted the tests, 1973 through 1977, should have a new test done as soon as possible if they hadn't had one since then.

But that was just the tip of the iceberg. Former executives, technicians and employees, some of whom admitted they had not been qualified to perform the tasks they did, told me that inaccuracies and irregularities went far beyond the Pap smear tests. Among their allegations:

• Results for many Pap smear, urine and blood tests were falsified or altered, and too little time was spent on many of the tests.

• Unqualified personnel — including a chemist, a veterinarian and maintenance supervisor — performed procedures at the lab that should have been done by a doctor, including autopsies, cutting and diagnosing human tissue and reading Pap smears.

• Sanitary conditions were poor. For example, fetuses obtained from abortion clinics under a federal contract and fetuses from other medical customers accumulated in boxes in the basement of the lab, despite the foul odor they gave off. Just before a federal licensing inspection in 1976, Thabet had about 500 of the fetuses buried behind the laboratory building.

"People are paying for tests that aren't done properly, or, in some cases, aren't done at all," one former supervisor at the lab said.

Corner-cutting had been a trademark of Automated since its beginning, employees said. But it was when the lab began receiving lucrative and poorly policed federal contracts that standards really began degenerating.

Automated's first federal contract was awarded by the Federal Aviation Administration in 1972 for the study of air-traffic controllers' stress levels through blood tests. When Thabet bid on the contract, he indicated Automated had the needed equipment, when it actually did not, a former aide said. It was not until Automated had actually won the contract that the required equipment was purchased, he added. And then it was operated by unqualified personnel.

When Thabet finally did hire someone with the proper credentials, it turned out that the employee had fabricated them to get the job. When I tracked the former employee down in Rhode Island, he admitted that he had been unqualified to conduct the tests required by the contract, but that he would have been able to do them properly if he had been permitted the proper amount of time.

Jack Anderson takes note

But time was of the essence. Syndicated columnist Jack Anderson, intrigued by Thabet's ability to continue getting federal contracts despite his poor performance, reported in September 1978 that the FAA had become impatient with the progress of the test after 10 months and attempted to withdraw it from Automated.

Anderson quoted an FAA attorney as saying that Thabet argued that the work was impossible to perform, even though the Navy had been doing it for years. The case was eventually settled out of court. But when the FAA retrieved the frozen blood samples, the attorney told Anderson, it turned out that they had been refrozen and were useless. "We just had to drop the whole project," the attorney said.

But that didn't prevent Thabet from getting an even better federal contract for Automated. In 1973, he was awarded a $570,000 Air Force contract to analyze Pap smears from Air Force personnel throughout the world. One year later, the lab also obtained part of a $320,000 contract from the U.S. Environmental Protection Agency to determine whether aborted fetuses contained traces of cancer-causing pesticides.

In 1977, Thabet also obtained a $300,000 state contract to analyze through urinalyses the progress of patients at methadone clinics throughout Ohio. All three projects were fiascoes. But the Air Force Pap smear project was more than that. It was a biological time bomb bound to explode when it became known that hundreds of human lives may have been endangered in the name of profit.

That time bomb first hit when the Air Force finished a preliminary study of the tests conducted at Automated. It showed that as many as 23 percent of the tests were done improperly and that 3 percent of those showed major abnormalities needing immediate medical attention, even though Automated had originally reported them as being normal.

Former employees were not surprised at what the Air Force found. They said Pap smear tests were routinely processed more rapidly than stipulated by contract or medical standards, and in some cases weren't conducted at all. The results, they said, were merely fabricated.

Several employees told of one incident, for example, when a number of slides were lost in the mail although the paperwork arrived. They said Thabet became irate when the Air Force was going to be informed that no tests could be conducted until new Pap smears were obtained. He reportedly said he couldn't afford to wait for the new slides and filled out the forms showing that all the Pap smears were normal.

In a second case, about 100 Pap smear slides were accidentally damaged in two washing accidents. Since the Air Force had already been informed of the first accident, Thabet refused to allow employees to inform the service of the second one. He ordered the paperwork processed, and negative results given.

"He said he couldn't afford to have the Air Force think he ran a sloppy laboratory," one ex-employee said of the incident.

But testing irregularities by then had spread to virtually all procedures, including urine and blood tests and the examination of aborted fetuses and tissues.

The experience of two of the lab's many conscientious employees explains how this could happen. When they noticed an unqualified employee pouring blood and urine samples down the drain rather than doing the required tests, they said they took their case to Thabet. He ignored them at first. When they kept complaining, Thabet fired *them* instead of the employee with lax standards.

As far as the state contract for urine tests was concerned, one employee termed it "a joke." Unqualified people right out of high school were hired for the job.

The EPA contract for the analysis of fetuses for traces of pesticides also became engulfed in controversy. Questions were raised about whether the fetuses came from the required geographically diverse areas, whether the women who underwent the abortions had signed the required consent forms for testing and whether the tests were properly conducted.

It appears that the test failed on all three counts. Rather than coming from all over the country, the fetuses apparently came primarily from two locations — abortion clinics in Cincinnati and San Francisco. Thabet was so concerned about keeping this information from becoming known that he forced his wife, who was strongly against abortion, to pick up the shipments in each city.

It was apparently some time later that Thabet realized the fetuses did not have the required consent forms. He was heard by several employees to ask the person in charge of the tests one day where the forms were and he was told there were none. As for the test itself, one former high-ranking employee referred to the doctor in charge as "a jelly," and added: "I would not be able to account for the results' authenticity. My opinion is that the results were pretty screwed up. It was very easy money."

Thabet, of course, was not directly responsible for everything that went on in his lab. But he did ensure poor quality by hiring unqualified personnel, establishing dangerous cost-cutting procedures on chemicals and by permitting unsanitary conditions to exist for long periods of time.

Take the Pap smear tests as an example. Cytologists who read the smears were to classify them between one and five. Anything classified from three to five was considered serious and was to be read by a pathologist, namely Thabet. But Thabet assigned others to look at the smears for diagnosis of a possible malignancy instead of doing the job himself.

One person who handled the job was a veterinarian who would turn the paperwork back into Thabet for his signature. "Half the time, he wasn't checking anything at all, if you want to know the truth," said a former top aide. The veterinarian was only one of several employees over the years who performed delicate tasks in violation of professional standards and sometimes the law. Another analyst was a Ph.D. in chemistry who worked for the lab for two years in the early '70s. According to the man's ex-wife, Thabet forced him to do so many functions of a doctor that he began using the title to avoid suspicion. In fact, many in Mansfield's medical community expressed surprise when I revealed that he wasn't a medical doctor at all.

When Thabet was resident pathologist at People's Hospital, the chemist's ex-wife said, her husband was required to analyze frozen tissue samples and prepare reports under Thabet's signature. She said he was also ordered to perform autopsies at a hospital in nearby Millersburg with which People's had contracted to perform the procedures, which the chemist did in violation of state law. Only an elected coroner or a certified pathologist can perform that task, and the chemist was neither.

But other employees were equally overworked and forced to do things they didn't like. One who quit several months before the dam broke at Automated said she left because she "couldn't take it anymore the tension and knowing what I knew." Asked what that meant, she said she was referring to the improper reading of Pap smears and the suspicion that the clinic was receiving fetuses that seemed to have been illegally aborted. She said the fetuses that came in from one clinic in particular often seemed to be six or seven months old.

"We couldn't believe it," she said. "On top of that, we were running behind in our tests both downstairs and upstairs, so the fetuses were lying all over the place."

She and most others agreed that the cytotechs were pushed behind beyond the point of medical quality when it came to reading Pap smear slides. Another former AMSO employee agreed. "They're supposed to spend two minutes per slide, but I doubt if they're spending 15 to 20 percent of that time on them," she said.

Other employees complained of a host of other poor conditions at the lab, including bad ventilation in the basement, where employees worked with noxious and flammable chemicals.

One ex-employee said that when she complained to her supervisor about a malfunctioning hood used in tuberculosis tests, she was told: "Don't worry about it. The hood's exhaust fan is working fine. You can feel the air as it goes into the men's room."

Lab officials tried to cut down on supplies as well as cleanliness to save money. Technicians, for example, were ordered to dilute various chemicals and reagents, which also tends to cut down on the accuracy of the tests they are used in.

One former employee related how she and some others were dubious about the accuracy of an inexpensive rubella test kit the lab was using, so they conducted a test on the same sample on two different days to see what happened. As they feared, the results were diametrically opposed. They presented their evidence to Thabet, to no avail.

It was then that the technicians began to suspect that the tests were being used as a medical justification for abortions for welfare clients, since abortion on demand had been eliminated for welfare recipients. They also noted that all the tests seemed to come from one doctor, and that Thabet often encouraged them to give a reading that indicated the possibility of rubella. That, after all, was all the doctor needed to charge the abortion to the government.

With standards like those, it is no wonder Automated had a high turnover of employees — as high as 72 percent a year. Both the lab's working conditions and standards were hard to stomach.

"It wouldn't surprise me if the wrong diagnosis went out to the wrong person quite often," said one ex-employee. "Hardly a day went by that something didn't go wrong."

The crowning blow for many was Thabet's mass burial of about 500 fetuses that took place just before an inspection by the national Centers for Disease Control.

While the disease centers appear to do well with its highly publicized monitoring program on flu epidemics, it was not known then for being a particularly tough on-site inspector. Visits like the one in 1976 are generally known about in advance. That gave Automated plenty of time each year to be cleaned up for about the only time until the next inspection.

Before the clean-up got very far in 1976, however, something had to he done with the 500 fetuses stored in the basement. This was a new problem.

Previously, fetuses and human tissue had been disposed of in an incinerator at a local hospital. But Thabet quit that practice to save money. Instead, the material began being burned in the open on Thabet's farm outside Mansfield. Old tires and other junk were sometimes thrown in for good measure. For some reason, however, the disposal job had been neglected through most of the summer, and the fetuses were piled up in the basement. That led to their mass burial. Gruesome, yes. Illegal, no, I discovered.

But Thabet's degenerate disposal practices went far beyond fetuses. Several employees claimed that urine from the tests his lab did or did not do on drug addicts was routinely dumped in a ravine behind the building. Some of it, they add, contained hepatitis, a highly infectious disease that could have been spread through the water.

It didn't stop there, either. Cultures containing organisms such as salmonella and shigella were also buried behind the lab. Former employees fear that an epidemic could break out if any of those organisms ever reach water level.

Although no one could pinpoint a law Thabet had broken by his disposal policies, he was clearly embarrassed by it. The week before my newspaper stories first brought the practice to light, a bulldozer was seen behind the building covering the land with more dirt.

It is somewhat ironic that Thabet would become concerned about something that was apparently not illegal when he had so consistently flouted the law. For example, the coroner had not bothered to obtain an Ohio driver's license in the 27 years he had lived there. He told his wife that, first as a doctor and then as coroner, he didn't need one. Nor did the lack of a license prevent Thabet from submitting mileage expenses to the county auditor for reimbursement.

But other vouchers in the auditor's office proved more controversial. They showed that his lab had submitted thousands of dollars worth of bills to the county for services rendered to Thabet as county coroner.

Thabet began sending the coroner's work, such as tissue analyses, to his own lab shortly after taking office. In the first six months, the lab billed the coroner's office for $2,551 in tests.

The amount rose to $4,245 during the next six months. The purchase orders, in at least one case signed by Thabet, were for toxicology analyses, tissue slides and blood-type tests.

Former employees said many of the tests were unnecessary, but they knew better than to say so to Thabet. The tests may have been more than unnecessary. They may have been illegal. The Ohio criminal code at the time said no public official shall "authorize or employ the authority or influence of his office to secure authorization of any public contract . . . in which he has an interest." Violation of the statute was a felony and carried a fine of up to $2,500 and a jail term of between six months and five years.

Thabet's practice of assigning business to his own lab may also have violated Ohio's ethics law, a first-degree misdemeanor that carries a maximum penalty of six months in jail and a $1,000 fine.

When I first brought this practice to light, County Auditor Freeman Swank immediately froze all payments to Automated and asked for a legal opinion from County Prosecutor McKee. McKee said Thabet might be in violation of the law if he could not show that the services were not available elsewhere or at a lower price.

Thabet was asked to submit evidence of this or to discontinue his practice of giving Automated the coroner's business. But the issue was never resolved. Thabet resigned before it could be.

Timely resignation

The reason Thabet gave for his resignation in November 1978 was poor health after undergoing triple-bypass surgery. But Thabet's mounting personal, financial and professional problems probably had a lot more to do with his departure.

By the end of the year, Thabet would be facing four lawsuits filed by women claiming that Pap smear tests conducted at his lab had failed to detect their cervical cancer at a time it would have been more easily treated. Total damages sought were $2.5 million. Revelations of Automated's mishandling of Pap smear tests caused Planned parenthood centers in Cleveland, Columbus, Mansfield and Akron to send letters to almost 50,000 women whose tests had been sent to the lab that they should be re-tested.

The centers also used radio and television announcements and posters to spread the word. "It's possible the laboratory reports on some Pap tests didn't give sufficient information and we want to take precautions," the head of Cleveland's Family Planning Program said.

Meanwhile, the joint Air Force-FBI investigation was moving along, although not as rapidly as many would have liked. In fact, it seemed headed for a quiet death after the initial onslaught of publicity. The reason, according to a source close to the investigation, was that the only way Thabet's complicity could be proved would be to also prove the negligence of the Air Force.

"There's no doubt that Thabet was bending and breaking every rule in the book, but the Air Force wasn't much better," the source said. "That's why they made such a big deal of it in the beginning: to make it look like all the blame rested with Thabet."

For a while, Automated was also investigated by the state because of abrupt increases in its Medicaid fees. But that also was bust. Other investigations proved more worrisome, though. One, of course, was the Mansfield Police Department's inquiry into Thabet's alleged theft from Eugene Kuhn. During one interrogation by detectives, Thabet reportedly began to shake uncontrollably as the questions became more pointed.

Even more serious, from a financial point of view, was an investigation of Automated by the Centers for Disease Control. The probe was ostensibly launched to determine whether the lab's license to conduct Pap smear tests should be renewed. But it may also have been an attempt by the Atlanta-based agency to obfuscate its own poor performance.

Pressed for details of the findings of past inspections of Automated, CDC finally released records that revealed a long list of problems discovered there. One 1972 report, for example, showed there was concern even before Automated got the lucrative Air Force contract about whether Pap smear tests were conducted and screened properly.

Another report revealed that CDC refused to renew the lab's license to "receive and process" out-of-state blood samples for the purpose of testing for triglyceride [fat] levels. A routine CDC review of the lab's proficiency for doing such tests revealed that the results at the lab "were not within a range considered acceptable," the CDC said.

The CDC ban against the company remained in effect until April 2, 1974, one year after the company first applied to regain its license. Automated passed three successive proficiency tests at that time, and the license was renewed. Then, on July 27, 1976, the CDC pulled the lab's license to test specimens for the presence of bacteria. The license wasn't renewed until almost a year later.

The last action the CDC took against Automated was its belated attempt to pull the lab's Pap smear test license some seven years after the lab's proficiency had been questioned. One reason for the action was the alleged "discrepancies" found in the Air Force tests. Another was Automated's refusal to turn over slides to the CDC for re-evaluation. But the question was soon to become moot.

Thabet quietly leased his lab's facility in late 1978 to Med-Serv Inc., a Cleveland-based testing firm. Automated seemed to have disappeared, until I looked closer. Then it appeared that the only thing that had changed was the lab's name. The facility, personnel and procedures were pretty much intact.

Then I discovered that Med-Serv had quietly been taken over by two of Thabet's relatives and perhaps by Thabet himself. Thabet would later deny that, of course. But he would also admit in the same breath that it was his idea for his relatives to invest in Med-Serv, and, in fact, that he had made the first contacts to bring the buyers and sellers together.

Mrs. Thabet's divorce attorneys elicited all of this from her husband during a deposition. They were attempting to show that Thabet had neatly camouflaged his substantial assets in another company, thus removing them from their grasp and those suing Automated. But the judge wouldn't buy that argument. Justice, after all, is often overly blind in Mansfield.

The judge went on to demonstrate that in his final decision. Despite the fact that Thabet had ignored his order to pay temporary child support, and paid $5,000 to his mother, $3,000 in one day to a clothing store and $3,000 on a Caribbean cruise, the judge assessed no penalty against him. And despite the fact that Thabet had earned $127,000 the previous year and often bragged that he was a millionaire but no one would ever prove it, the judge determined that Thabet's heart surgery had hurt his earning potential and that his other problems had cost him his fortune. As a result, his wife of 25 years was awarded no alimony at all and child support of $50 a week for each of the couple's three children still at home. Years later, his former wife said Thabet never paid a penny. One of his daughters was so embittered that she changed her last name.

So the good doctor had proven once again he was still a slick operator. His predecessor as coroner wasn't much better. And in some ways he may have been worse. Thabet's sticky fingers may have led to a few problems, but never to the extent of those faced by Dr. Robert W. Wolford.

Mansfield police officers told me of several instances where Wolford was caught shoplifting. No charges, of course, were ever brought against him.

The police also looked the other way several times when Wolford was picked up for drunken driving. Worse yet, the higher command never looked into allegations made by two officers that a suitcase full of money found in the home of a dead man appeared to be missing a large amount of money when the coroner, to whom they entrusted it, brought it into the station later that day.

Asked why an investigation wasn't conducted to determine how some of the money apparently had disappeared while in Wolford's possession, my police source shrugged his shoulders and said: "I guess because he was the coroner." No wonder Thabet thought the position gave those who held it a license to steal.

Wolford reportedly received another favor from the police when he was picked up on a prowling complaint. The officers who caught him in the act took Wolford home instead of to jail.

But Wolford's problems finally caught up with him, as they did with Thabet. Rumors about his kleptomania, as well as his alleged drug addiction, had made Wolford a political liability. To make room for Thabet, Wolford was appointed county health commissioner. It wasn't too long before his sticky fingers got him in trouble there, too. When it was determined that he had used some health-department funds for his own benefit, Wolford was forced to resign.

Shortly thereafter, Wolford married one of his health-department employees who had also been caught in some financial improprieties. Little did he realize, however, that his new wife had provided investigators with some of the information that caused his downfall, apparently when their on-again-off-again relationship was in the off cycle.

When Coroner Thabet resigned, Richland Countians hoped for the best and feared for the worst about whom the Republican Party's Central Committee would appoint to fill out the term. They got neither the best nor the worst: Instead, they got Dr. Milton Oakes, a 73-year-old eye, ear, nose and throat specialist, a field about as far removed from pathology as you could get.

Given pathologists Thabet's and Wolford's performances, perhaps that was not as bad an idea as it seemed. But the GOP passed over a better candidate to pick Oakes.

The favorite candidate among many Republicans was Deputy Coroner Charles Butner, who had performed capably during Thabet's long absences. Several sources said Butner's appointment was blocked by a few party stalwarts because of his support of then-State Rep. Sherrod Brown, a Democrat, over the his inept Republican opponent in the recent election.

Controversy causes reform

As bad as Thabet's private lab was, the controversy it generated ultimately helped lead to something good. One of those who watched the story closely was Walt Bogdanich, then a reporter with *The Plain Dealer* in Cleveland.

After having an accurate story saying Teamsters president and Cleveland heavyweight Jackie Presser took kickbacks and was an FBI informant retracted by *The Plain Deal*er when its gutless Horvitz-like owner buckled under to mob pressure, Bogdanich moved to *The Wall Street Journal.*

Bogdanich later told me that my revelations about the lax standards at Thabet's private lab helped inspire him to start looking into the then-$20 billion national clinical laboratory industry in the mid-1980s.

Bogdanich soon learned that the Thabet's lab wasn't any worse than many others. The resulting series of articles eventually won Bogdanich a well-deserved Pulitzer Prize in 1988 and led to his important 1991 book *The Great White Lie: Dishonesty: Waste and Incompetence in the Medical Community.* More important, Bogdanich's articles spurred hearings by three congressional committees on the clinical-laboratory industry.

"Millions of Americans routinely undergo laboratory tests to determine the source of their medical symptoms or to provide early detection of cancer," said Sen. William S. Cohen of the Government Oversight subcommittee. The Maine Republican said Bogdanich's articles "demonstrate that faulty laboratory tests are truly a life-or-death issue that deserve much closer scrutiny by the Congress."

Congressional sources said they were particularly concerned about Bogdanich's report that 20 percent to 40 percent of Pap tests fail to detect cervical cancer or precursor cell aberrations. The article reported that Pap smears often were processed at home by unsupervised technicians or at "Pap mills," where technicians were forced to process an excessive number of tests.

The story also noted that Pap tests were the only common lab procedure for which technicians were not required to pass a proficiency test.

The hearings that Bogdanich's reports spurred eventually led to enactment in 1988 of important amendments to the Clinical Laboratory Improvement Act to "ensure the accuracy, reliability, and timeliness of patient test results regardless of where the test was performed."

The amendments established quality standards and a regulatory structure for all clinical laboratory testing. They also required laboratories to conduct proficiency tests designed to identify those with systematic problems.

Clinical laboratories also were mandated to report errors that harmed, or had the potential to harm, a patient.

Patients whose tests were processed by Automated Medical Services of Ohio should have been so lucky.

4

The Tower of Babble

Across the street from the Richland County Courthouse, from which Sheriff Weikel ran his reign of terror, is a building of remarkable contrast known as the Mansfield Municipal Center.

While the courthouse at least gives the impression of being open and inviting, Mansfield's city hall does not. It is much taller, darker and forbidding. Except for the ninth floor, where the mayor and his top aides have their offices, the building is virtually windowless. So while the city's political powers-that-be are able to look over the city they pretend to control, its citizens are symbolically prohibited from looking in.

In the late 1970s, it was perhaps just as well they couldn't. Corruption and favoritism were of such frightening proportions in city hall that it is surprising the building didn't collapse under its weight. In fact, those familiar with the back-scratching and corner-cutting that went on when the building was constructed say that is an eventual possibility anyway.

The building's problems stem from the selection of an architect. Former Mayor Richard A. Porter, who had the appearance and demeanor of a flat-topped Marine drill sergeant, insisted that the job go to his good friend Martin Bricker. Although Bricker's architectural talents were heavily debated, his political abilities were not. The fact that his interior-decorating specialist was Porter's wife didn't hurt either. So Bricker got the job, and Mansfield got its monstrosity.

But not before some significant cost overruns and construction delays put the building's debut way behind schedule. Rumors about the cost overruns were rampant.

The FBI apparently thought they might be more than rumors when it began looking into possible irregularities in late 1978, but nothing came of the probe, as usually seemed to be the case when the placid Mansfield office of the FBI looked into anything.

Mayor Porter's association with Jess Byrd the owner of the city's only ambulance service also began undergoing FBI scrutiny at that time. The FBI was curious about how Porter's relationship with the company's owner seemed to bloom at the same time Porter became steadfastly opposed to the development of a public paramedic program in the city.

In fact, the Porter administration issued a directive prohibiting the fire department's rescue squad from transporting accident or fire victims except in extreme emergencies at the same time most fire departments across the nation were expanding their emergency services. The order was issued by Public Safety Director Clayton Long, a former Byrd Ambulance employee.

Porter and Byrd, meanwhile, had become so cozy that they took several trips together, including one to Russia.

It should surprise no one, though, that the Byrd family was the regular recipient of favors from the Porter administration. The most important favor of all may have been helping the company drive its only competitor out of business.

Ex-employees of that company contended that Byrd Ambulance received preferential treatment in being notified of the need for emergency service.

Long had also been known to come to bat for one of Jess Byrd's brothers who regularly ended up in jail for public intoxication and related offenses. The police department did likewise. When the wayward brother allegedly broke into a neighbor's home and stole a bicycle, for example, the neighbor got nothing but the run-around when he tried to press charges.

The city law director's office also played the game. City Law Director Robert K. Rath forced one of his most respected assistants into resigning because the assistant was unwilling to let Byrd's brother off on charges involving firearms violations.

After all, Rath reportedly told the assistant, 1979 was a municipal election year. And you don't take people like the Byrds on in an election year.

So the FBI shouldn't have had trouble finding evidence in its investigation of the Byrd-Porter alliance. In fact, it already had in its possession a recording of a conversation in which Byrd's brother threatened to blow the whistle on the allegedly cozy relationship. Unfortunately, as is so often the case in Mansfield, nothing ever came of the probe.

Porter's favoritism to an architect who had the good sense to hire Mrs. Porter wasn't all that unusual. Almost everyone in city hall was related to someone else then. One study, as a matter of fact, showed that at least 100 of the city's 600 employees were related to at least one other city worker.

Even worse, the higher you went up the ladder, the more prevalent was the nepotism. Law Director Rath's secretary, for example, was his wife, who used his city-owned car for him because he couldn't drive. To keep it all in the family, Rath's intern one summer was his daughter.

There were other examples. One was Safety Director Clayton Long's fiancee, who was chosen over three other candidates who had scored higher on the civil service test to become secretary to Long's subordinate, Police Chief Matthew Benick. Then there was the case of Service Director Peter Zimmerman hiring his mother-in-law.

Mansfield's City Council wasn't much better. Its open meetings were full of such high comedy that members tried to discuss their more serious business behind closed doors.

That is exactly what Mayor Porter and a number of council members were doing one night before a scheduled meeting in the spring of 1978. As they merrily cut a deal on a major piece of legislation, however, two reporters caught them in the act.

When the participants were informed that such meetings were in violation of the state's open-meetings or "sunshine" law, they ignored the warning. They simply finished their dress rehearsal and entered council chambers, where no citizens were waiting because the meeting had been canceled and then quietly rescheduled.

The once-divisive bill they had discussed was passed this time around without a hitch. Or so the conspirators thought.

Let the sunshine in

But, as editor of *The News Journal* at that time, I instituted a lawsuit against the council for violation of the sunshine law.

A short time later, Judge James J. Mayer Sr. ordered the council to revote the legislation after open public debate, which it did reluctantly. The legislation passed once again, but an important point was made that lawmakers shouldn't be lawbreakers at the same time.

But not all council members limited their antics to legislation. They often mixed their council duties and private interests into a very fine mixture of muck. Take their relationship with *The News Journal's* cable TV company. Five of the council's 11 members were reported to be receiving free cable service from the company even though it was the council's duty to regulate the service and vote on proposed rate increases.

The arrangement, which began just before council voted in 1975 to raise cable rates by 20 percent, was in apparent violation of state ethics laws. The company, Multi-Channel Cable TV, claimed that the free service wasn't provided as a gift but as part of a "monitoring program" on the quality of service. But, as already detailed, that excuse was a mere ruse devised by *News Journal* general manager Bob Blake when Sheriff Weikel reported it to the FBI.

Another recipient of the free service was Service Director Zimmerman, who was responsible for making sure workers compensation and liability insurance coverage for the company was at statutory levels. Zimmerman also had general authority to supervise the cable company's operations. Zimmerman at first tried to deny he received the free service, but the cable company and several council members all confirmed that he did. Then Zimmerman said he couldn't remember if he did or didn't.

While all of the councilmen involved in the arrangement said they saw nothing wrong with it, Council President William McCarrick admitted that they had private concerns. He said three of the recipients asked him if the program shouldn't be dropped before it became public.

While both the cable company and the council members publicly pooh-poohed speculation that there was anything wrong with receiving the free service, they privately decided to deep-six the payoff plan.

Shortly after the program was revealed by *The Observer,* it was canceled because of "adverse media criticism." But there may have been more behind the move than that. The FBI had begun looking into the giveaway shortly after it had been made public, and it determined the practice may have violated federal law. The case was eventually taken before a federal grand jury, but no indictments were issued.

One of the unrepentant recipients of the free service was Councilman Dan Stevens. While some of the members who received the service said they would abstain from any votes concerning an increase in the cable service charge, Stevens' response was quite different. "Hell, no, I wouldn't abstain," he said. A look at some of Stevens' other council votes shows why he would have no such misgivings. Several votes he cast in 1978 to benefit the developer of a shopping center, for example, also paid off for Stevens when he sold a piece of property he had bought only a year before to the same developer for a profit of 250 percent.

Stevens and his son bought the parcel of property for $28,200. They later optioned it to the developer for $75,000. Before that option was signed, however, Stevens participated in several votes to make the development possible. Two months after Stevens bought the land, city council, with Stevens present, unanimously voted to extend water service to make the development possible.

Three months later, Stevens seconded and voted for a motion approved by the quasi-governmental Greater Mansfield Area Growth Corporation for industrial revenue bonds not to exceed $3.9 million for the same development. Six weeks after that — and nine days after the option on the property was signed — Stevens seconded and voted for a GMAG motion authorizing industrial-revenue-bond financing for a shopping plaza by the same developer on the same side of the road as his property.

Stevens saw no conflict of interest in his votes to ensure construction of a development that would make him a handsome profit. "It's a private matter," he said.

Ohio law seemed to clearly indicate that it was a *public* matter, but no official pursued the case after it was revealed by *The Observer.*

Mansfield has a long history of land deals that seemed to benefit everyone but the people at large. Sometimes even legitimate land purchases smacked of politics.

One such deal concerned land bought to build the city's main fire station. City Council was in such a hurry to buy the land from the Republican Party chairman that it neglected to get the required property assessments.

When the federal government, which footed the bill for the building, ordered the belated assessments, the two real-estate agents asked to conduct them by the Republican Porter administration were both active Republicans.

Needless to say, they arrived at the same fair-market price as the one already paid by the city. To do otherwise would have meant that the whole project was jeopardized or that the city would have had to make up the difference between the market price and the purchase price.

The real-estate deals that didn't come off are sometimes as interesting as those that did in those days. One concerned Mansfield's ill-fated attempt to persuade Miller Brewing Co. officials to locate a new brewery they were contemplating building in the city.

Real-estate agent Sandy Schmidt made an aggressive attempt to interest Miller on a well-situated piece of land near Mansfield's main crossroads, Rt. 30 and I-71. Repeated calls and letters to Porter for his assistance, however, went unanswered. And without some interest expressed by the city administration, the project had little hope.

Later, Service Director Peter Zimmerman arrived at my office to unveil a top-secret proposal the city had made to Miller. The biggest difference in the city's proposal and that of Schmidt, who was a Democrat, seemed to be that the agent representing the city's proposed location was one of the same Republican real-estate agents who had retroactively assessed the land purchased for the fire station.

Long's short arm of the law

Mayor Porter's politics didn't stop at the police department door, either. Porter and Safety Director Clayton Long, for example, both received copies of all confidential reports filed by police officers, no matter how sensitive or politically damaging the information contained therein.

Long's appointment as safety director in 1976 probably did more than any other move to inject politics into the department, which had slowly recovered from a scandal in the mid-1960s to the point of respectability. After going through the farce of interviewing over 20 candidates, most of whom had far better credentials than Long, Porter selected Long, whose major accomplishment up to that point had been to work longer than almost anyone else for the scandal-ridden National Highway Safety Foundation of Mansfield.

Since Long had used politics to get the safety director's job, it should not be surprising that he used politics to keep it. That became apparent in the fall of 1978, when *The Observer* revealed the contents of a tape of an April 1977 conversation between Long and several officers.

The tape was later introduced as evidence in a suit brought by officers that succeeded in having regulations barring officers from public comments declared illegal.

The officers revealed what was on the tape to show the kinds of things they could bring to the public's attention without a gag order. The tape transcript revealed Long ordering the police to stop making arrests for underage drinking at certain politically connected nightclubs. Long was quoted as saying: "We're going to hit trouble spots, not the best places in town."

To which one officer replied: "Director, we're hitting every place in town."

"Yeah," Long replied, "but we're not now."

Long went on to lecture the cops on the art of politics, Mansfield style. He told them that one of the bars they had raided was owned by a city councilman who could be instrumental in getting them a new raise. Take your pick, Long seemed to be saying: money or conscience.

"I'm not telling you who to arrest and who not to arrest, but we've got to use a little discretion," Long lectured the officers. If they knew of any gambling or prostitution going on at some of the protected places, Long said, they should notify him and he would tell them to "knock it off." After all, many of the patrons at these places were members of the city's elite inner circle of businessmen, lawyers, judges and politicians — including, Long might have added, himself.

If Long hadn't made himself clear that "you don't go over there and bite the hand that feeds us," Mayor Porter certainly did to two officers later that night. The two former officers claimed Porter came up to them on the street after they had just checked out the councilman's bar.

"He acted like he could do everything but walk on water," said one of the former officers. Both agreed that Porter told them "to learn to follow orders on who you arrest." Asked what he meant by that, Porter allegedly answered, "You know what I mean."

One of the two former officers said that when he told Porter, "What you are telling us is not to arrest certain people," Porter replied: "That's right." It wasn't right, of course, only politically correct. But Porter had learned in his previous career as a powerless, undistinguished educator that you had to play politics to get power. And since might made right, politics superseded justice.

While Porter and Long were ordering the police not to arrest the powerful on one hand, they were ordering them to show no mercy to the powerless on the other. Porter and Long spent many an evening playing cop. They proved to be real crime fighters, too. Long, for example, once ordered a police officer to ticket a teenager for gunning his engine.

While the Starsky and Hutch of Mansfield were quick to spot alleged violations of the law, however, they always called in officers who had never seen the crime committed to make the arrest because they didn't want their names on the arrest reports.

Porter, for example, once reported an illegally parked car by city hall and ordered it "taken care of." After a patrolman wrote out a ticket, an angry Porter called police headquarters again and said he wanted the car towed. The officer refused, however, unless Porter was willing to have his name recorded on the complaint. But a sergeant informed him that the mayor's name could never be used that way. After all, it might cost him a vote.

Porter's tough approach to illegally parked cars at city hall, however, didn't apply to everyone. When the Rev. Joel King, the fifth ward councilman, had his car towed because it was in a spot reserved for the handicapped, Porter came to his rescue. As he entered the office of the night-watch commander, Porter demanded to know who had ordered King's car towed. He also wanted to know why King had not been notified in advance.

That was a mistake on Porter's part. The commander presented him with a copy of written order from Service Director Peter Zimmerman commanding police to tow all illegally parked cars immediately, without any attempt to warn the owner.

"OK, you were ready for me this time," Porter conceded.

In the style of a Chicago alderman, Porter flicked the ashes from one of his always-present cigars onto the officer's desk and stormed away to give King a ride to the wrecker service lot to which the car had been towed. The furious King, Porter realized, had to be placated at all costs. King was too crucial a vote for Porter's pet projects to have him become alienated by a towing fee, so Porter paid it for him.

The politicization of the police department disturbed the rank-and-file officers to no end. Given time, they feared it could become like the sheriff's department across the street.

Fear and confusion seemed to rule the department already. Officer distrusted officer. No one seemed to know for sure who supported Porter's way of doing things and who didn't. Many of the best officers left as a result. Police Chief Matthew Benick gave those contemplating blowing the whistle a lesson that two could play the game. As pressure mounted for an investigation that would focus on allegations made against the department's upper echelon, Benick issued an order prohibiting the street cop's own form of petty corruption, the acceptance of free services or discounts.

The investigation that wasn't

But pressure continued to mount for a full-scale investigation, so Benick issued a directive one week after the banning of gratuities announcing that the Ohio Bureau of Criminal Identification and Investigation would assist the department in an "impartial investigation" of a variety of allegations.

The average officer at first seemed encouraged by the announcement. But suspicion and mistrust soon replaced their optimism when they learned that Long and Porter would have access to the investigators' files. The ones who might end up suffering, the officers feared, would be those who talked. Not too many talked as a result, even though they had plenty to say.

Among the accusations they would have liked to make but did not were:

● Several cases of covering up the arrests of prominent citizens or politicians.

● Instances of direct intervention by the Porter administration in the cover-up of illegal activities of politicians and city officials.

● Involvement of members of the Porter administration and city council in gambling, theft in office, bid-rigging and the receipt of illegal compensation in the form of discounts, gratuities, free cable service and a multitude of other favors.

● Several cases of payroll fraud by both high-ranking officers and patrol officers.

● Widespread cheating on promotional exams, as evidenced by the fact that a Byrd Ambulance Co. executive who served on the Civil Service Board had been caught trying to sell answers to police department exams.

• Suspected payoffs to high-ranking officers that had resulted in tip-offs to a number of establishments about to be raided.

Any hope the police still had in the investigation, however, seemed to fade when the state BCI decided to pull out when it failed to get a letter from Prosecutor William F. (See No Evil) McKee confirming that he would prosecute anyone found to have committed a crime. The BCI wanted McKee's commitment because of his general reluctance to prosecute politically powerful individuals.

The BCI was also miffed at a report that McKee had tried to persuade at least one Mansfield patrolman that the state's top law-enforcement agency was connected with organized crime (an allegation he would later make against me, as well) and couldn't be trusted.

McKee seemed delighted with BCI's withdrawal, and suggested the local office of the FBI as an alternative. The suggestion no doubt made sense to both. The local office was already overwhelmed with investigations. It was also greatly dependent on both the police and the prosecutor for assistance. So it no doubt could be more easily controlled.

But that was a faulty assumption. Local FBI agents would never be confused with "The Untouchables," but they had managed to become a little more aggressive after assisting in the investigation of the sheriff's department and leading the charge against Coroner Thabet.

So when Benick started pushing for the FBI seal of approval for his department only three weeks after the investigation started, he got the brush-off. As a matter of fact, the FBI had been quietly waiting for its chance to inspect the workings of city hall, and now that it had been invited in, it didn't plan on leaving too quickly.

Soon though, Benick announced that the investigation had been concluded without the finding of any wrongdoing. Benick hadn't told the FBI of his decision. In fact, he timed his announcement for when the agent in charge was in Washington.

Benick's whitewash came as no surprise to me any more than it did to the BCI or his officers. I had begun to have my doubts about the chief after meeting with him to discuss off the record the possibly illegal activities of his boss, Clayton Long, when he worked for the Highway Safety Foundation.

Rather than taking the accusations seriously, Benick, who also worked for the foundation, took them straight back to Long.

After all, Benick told me when he called to tell me of Long's denials, Long was his friend as well as his boss, so he felt obligated to tell him. No wonder so few police officers were willing to talk.

A lot of people who did offer to talk, however, reported what they had to say often fell on deaf ears, if any ears at all. And the few investigations that did appear to be making progress seemed to slowly get lost in the shuffle, which is probably just what had been planned all along.

This wasn't the first whitewash of corruption in the Mansfield Police Department. In 1965, a grand jury investigated charges by an officially appointed citizens' committee that corruption was rampant in the department and that Mansfield had become an "open city" for gambling, prostitution and related crimes.

No one was surprised, however, when the grand jury returned no indictments. The jury was leaking information as fast as it was compiling it. "Everyone in the department knew what had gone on there every day," one former policeman said. "It was a controlled deal from the beginning. There was plenty of ammunition there, but no one expected the grand jury to use it." It didn't, either. No indictments were returned, but there might have been if the grand jury's investigation hadn't been sabotaged by the prosecutor, who told one of his assistants that it took everything in his power to keep the jury from doing so.

By this point, Porter was clearly getting fed up with *The Observer's* own investigations of his administration and those it inspired. In an article about *The Observer* in *The Akron Beacon Journal,* Porter was quoted as saying those who worked for or supported *The Observer* were "sickies and dissidents, a vocal minority who like to bask in the glory of someone else's chastisement."

How much corruption existed in city hall during the Porter era probably will never be known. But some of it may have been of considerable proportions.

One thing I was looking into just before leaving the city was its expensive police-communications system. Although a supplier with better equipment also had a lower bid, the contract went to another company. Money and gifts, I was told by several sources, went to a few of the company's friends in city hall as a result.

But just as interesting was the cleverness of the schemes devised by lower-ranking employees, who were apparently inspired by their bosses.

One of the cleverest was developed by the man in charge of the city's garbage disposal system. He simply created a bogus company and underbid the city and other private scavenger firms for several contracts, and then put his customers on city garbage-truck routes.

It was easy money while it lasted. When he finally got caught, the only price he had to pay was with a slap on the wrist and his job. The penalty no doubt wasn't so much for what he had done, but for getting caught at it. Or, perhaps, that he didn't share the wealth of his idea with others. At any rate, the garbage grab went unnoticed by most Mansfielders, since no announcement was apparently made of what an investigation had dug up. Too many people thought of city hall as a garbage dump, anyway. There was no reason to confirm their suspicions.

Faced with that kind of attitude, Porter made the only intelligent decision of his political career: He decided not to run for re-election and pretty much faded from the scene.

Not so Clayton Long. In 1997, Long became the source of more controversy when he resigned his position of director of transportation for Lexington Local Schools after being accused of sexually harassing several of the district's female bus drivers. Long had held the position for 18 years.

Although the harassment allegedly had gone on for years, officials in the district just south of Mansfield said they first heard about it when driver Phyllis Schumacher told an assistant superintendent about it. Long was immediately placed on administrative leave. His resignation was unanimously accepted by the board of education five weeks later. Long reportedly received $20,000 in severance pay. The bus drivers who claimed to have been harassed by Long were upset that Long was paid anything and that no investigation was conducted of their accusations.

One of those irate drivers was June Eckard. "[The administration] had five weeks to investigate this and they didn't do one thing," Eckard said. "During that time [Long} was collecting money and they let him retire." With twisted logic, Superintendent William Swartzmiller said that the accusations against Long couldn't be investigated because Long's decision to resign five weeks after he was suspended "took it out of [the district's] arena." Swartzmiller didn't say why the investigation wasn't done during the five weeks before Long quit, but Long's accusers had a good idea.

They said Swartzmiller had known about the problem for several years and did nothing about it because he and Long were friends. They added that the school board's president, attorney Robert Whitney, was also a friend of Long's and helped him get the job 18 years before.

Eckard said Long started harassing her in 1985. "He put his arms around me and pressed his chest against my back, and I told him not to touch me," Eckard said. "That started a war between him and me that lasted 12 years."

Phyllis Schumacher, who first blew the whistle on Long's alleged misconduct, said she was constantly harassed for years by Long. Among the things she was subjected to, Schumacher said, was having Long scream at her on the job and calling her late at night asking her for sex. "He even threatened me, saying he knew people who could make me disappear," she said. "I was scared to death. I didn't stay at home for four weeks."

Schumacher claimed that when she once went with the school band on an out-of-state trip, Long showed up at her hotel door and told her he'd heard she didn't like sex but that he could change her opinion.

Kathy Carns, another bus driver, said she witnessed Long's mistreatment of several women who worked at the district's bus garage. "I know what he's done to the girls," Carns said. "He's made their jobs hard."

Mansfield's police officers and firefighters who worked under Long could appreciate that statement.

New mayor brings change

Fortunately, things began to change for the better when city planner Edward Meehan was elected to replace Porter as mayor and people like Clayton Long were out of a job. Professional attitudes suddenly replaced political bickering in much of city hall, and Mansfield's image began to improve. The Meehan years were hardly scandal-free, however. The long-troubled police department continued to be a source of embarrassment.

In 1981, three officers were tried but acquitted on charges of beating an inmate. And in 1987, City Finance Director L. Norman Walker resigned after pleading guilty to two counts of theft in office and resigned. Walker admitted that he had improperly billed the city for a private trip to Toronto and sought reimbursement for gasoline used on a trip to Indiana even though the fee had already been paid for with a city credit card.

Then, in 1988, Police Lieutenant Charles Oswalt was convicted in the strangulation death of Margie Coffey, who had filed a paternity against him, a fellow officer was charged with helping Oswalt dispose of the body, and three others were disciplined for mishandling the investigation.

That prompted Meehan to appoint a task force to seriously study the department's problems and he rode in cruisers to learn from officers why the department had been troubled for so long. Meehan said their answers were blunt and instructive: fear; too much finger-pointing; a lack of training direction and teamwork; and little respect for authority.

Later, Meehan hired former FBI agent Robert Greenhalgh to investigate possible police involvement in up to 21 unsolved homicides in the area. In his 1989 report, the Columbus private investigator revealed that several Mansfield officers were sexually involved with Debra Lee Miller, an 18-year-old whose 1981 murder was one of those never solved. But Greenhalgh said he could find no police involvement in the slayings. He did, however, raise serious questions about the department's standards, particularly in homicide investigations.

That seemed to finally seal Chief Matthew Benick's fate. After Benick was nudged into retirement, Lawrence Harper, who became Mansfield's first black police officer when he joined the force in 1948, was named chief in December 1989.

Harper, who held the department's longevity record of 41 years at that time, had seen it all in his career. It now was his job to change much of it, which proved to be quite a challenge.

The continued mishandling of the Debra Miller homicide case was a good example why. When I asked to review the Miller case file in late 1995, it was discovered that most of its contents had somehow disappeared. The case summaries that remained, however, indicated that a former Ohio State Highway Patrol trooper who resigned the year before after only a month on the job told investigators that he had visited Miller at 11:30 p.m. on the night of her murder. The former trooper said he had sex with Miller and left for work at 3:20 a.m.

Richland County Coroner Milton Oakes said the temperature of Miller's body at the time it was found indicated that she was killed at approximately 2:30 a.m. Paul Jolly, chief deputy coroner of Hamilton County, placed the time of death at approximately 1 a.m., two hours after Miller ate some mushrooms at a nearby restaurant at 11 p.m.

Both estimated times of death were within the period the ex-trooper said he was with Miller that night. But with many crucial documents missing, it seemed unlikely that Miller's family would ever see anyone brought to justice for her murder.

Betty Dyer's family was a little more fortunate. When Detective John Wendling was asked to review the file on Dyer's disappearance from a laundromat on December 31, 1972, he was surprised at what he saw. As in the Miller case, the name of one possible suspect stood out. Yet there was nothing in the file to indicate that the suspect, Lawrence Davis, was ever questioned, even though he had been the prime suspect in several other rapes in which the victim was abducted from a laundromat.

"There were several people . . . who positively identified Lawrence Davis as being their assailant," Wendling wrote in a report. "It is unknown to this officer, and I can't find anything in the case anywhere, where he was prosecuted for those rapes. . . . In 1973, he was prosecuted for an 'aggravated assault' where he allegedly tried to take [a] female out of the laundromat in the early morning hours, which would coincide with the MO of the other rapes."

Although it would take several years, the Dyer case revealed that a detective finally did decide he should travel to Louisiana to interview Davis, who was serving a 60-year sentence there for the murder of a woman in 1978. But his travel requests were turned down because of a lack of funds. Money *was* made available in 1979, however, when a detective requested permission to travel from his vacation in Arizona to California to consult a psychic who purportedly had helped police locate bodies in the past.

The psychic, Katherine Rhea, charged nothing for her consultation, which was what it proved to be worth. Rhea told the detective that Dyer was buried north of Mansfield in a shallow grave "with one hand sticking out of the grave," the detective's report said. Rhea sent detectives on a wild goose chase that focused on an area north of the city's airport, where they could find no grave with a hand sticking out of it.

When Wendling and Prosecutor James J. Mayer — who had made solving Richland County's numerous unsolved homicides a priority — later became the first officials to question Davis about Dyer's disappearance, he greeted them by saying: "I've been waiting for you to come for 20 years. What took so long?"

Davis quickly admitted to abducting Dyer from the laundromat, killing her and burying her in an area far from where the psychic had pinpointed in 1979. When Davis was brought to Mansfield in March 1995 to plead guilty to Dyer's murder, however, he changed his mind and would only plead no contest. Davis then tried to show officials where Dyer was buried, but he had trouble being precise enough for the body to be found.

In 1999, Prosecutor Mayer's Richland County Unsolved Homicide Unit began to look into another case that cried out for justice — the November 1978 murder of Judy Bruce. Led by investigator/lawyer Scott Reinbolt, the task force eliminated two suspects and began to focus on Judy Bruce's husband, Larry. Reinbolt and detectives James Gadd, Mike Viars and Jeff McBride carefully went through the original investigative file and interviewed all of the 87 people mentioned who were still alive. The investigators slowly developed evidence that Larry Bruce was involved with another woman at the time of his wife's murder and that he had admitted to a relative he had once tried to kill "the little bitch" by throwing her down the stairs. In May 2002, the damning testimony of the state's 30-plus witnesses led to Larry Bruce's conviction for the murder of Judy Bruce. He was sentenced to a prison term of 15 years to life.

In the Dyer and Bruce cases, justice was definitely delayed but not denied. Ironically, there is some question whether justice *was* denied in the conviction of Police Lieutenant Charles Oswalt in the Margie Coffey murder case that brought the unsolved-homicide issue to a head. The case against Oswalt seemed convincing when he was tried in 1988. But the credibility of the two most important prosecution witnesses against him — FBI fiber expert Michael P. Malone and Charlynn Sawyer — later became somewhat dubious.

Malone testified that two foreign fibers found on one of Coffey's leg warmers and her jacket matched the carpet fiber in the police cruiser Oswalt drove the night he allegedly killed her. Malone lived up to his reputation as a convincing witness, which was why prosecutors often were eager to have him testify. In the 20 years he worked in the FBI crime lab until 1994, Malone testified as an expert witness in about 500 cases. He made headlines for his work in the *Fatal Vision* appeals of Jeffrey MacDonald, the Green Beret Army surgeon convicted of murdering his family, and the case against John Hinckley, who shot President Reagan. He also helped put defendants on death rows across the country.

But Malone's persuasive testimony on hairs and fibers was already starting to unravel by the time he testified against Oswalt. In 1987 and 1988, the Florida Supreme Court threw out murder convictions that hinged on his hair testimony. Then, in 1989, William Tobin, the FBI's chief metals expert, detailed 27 instances in which Malone made "false," "completely fabricated," or "inaccurate and deceptive" testimony. Malone survived Tobin's attack on his credibility, but it set the stage for a much more serious one. In 1997, Malone's work — and that of 12 other FBI lab examiners — came under fire in a report by the inspector general of the Justice Department. The report found that Malone sometimes testified beyond his area of expertise, misled juries about the scientific basis for his conclusions, misstated FBI policy and kept notes that were inadequate to support his conclusions. No wonder prosecutors asked Malone to testify so many times. As Senator Charles Grassley said after hearings on the FBI crime lab's problems, Malone was willing to "provide testimony on hair and fiber that no one else would." Professor Peter DeForest said Malone "tended to overstate the evidence."

That apparently was the case in the 1992 trial of Anthony Bragdon of Washington, D.C. In May 2003, the conviction of Bragdon, who spent 10 years in prison for intent to rape and use of a firearm in a violent crime, was overturned because Malone gave inaccurate testimony and withheld important evidence. "If the jurors had known that Mr. Malone testified falsely . . . the outcome of the trial reasonably could have been different," the judge who reversed the conviction wrote. Malone testified that carpet fibers he found on the clothing of a woman who was raped linked her to Bragdon's apartment.

As in Oswalt's case, the fibers were the only physical evidence presented against him. Then, in 2001, prosecutors informed Bragdon's lawyers that Malone testified falsely as to the absence of other possible sources of the fibers found on the victim's clothing; that he failed to disclose the existence of non-matching fibers found on the victim's clothing; and that he didn't perform tests to support his conclusions.

The Associated Press reported in March 2003 that a Justice Department review had identified about 3,000 cases that could have been affected by the questionable work of Malone and other FBI lab employees but that only 150 defendants, including Bragdon, had been notified of problems.

It now appears that Oswalt's is one of those 3,000 questionable cases. Documents obtained by a Freedom of Information Act request show that an independent scientist who reviewed Malone's work on Oswalt's case determined that:

• Malone did not conduct tests that he "could and should have utilized." As a result, the scientist said, "It is difficult to agree that [the fibers] are 'absolutely the same,' as the examiner testifies."

• "Testimony that the fibers have the 'same dye' and 'were made by the same manufacturer' is much stronger than the conclusion of 'consistent with' stated in [his] report."

• "Testimony that the microspectrophotometer absorption curves for [the fibers] are 'absolutely the same' is not correct."

• "Testimony that 'if you can match an unknown fiber and known [fiber] to the same dye, then you have cut it down from one of 7,000 different dyes' is misleading if not incorrect."

• "It is impossible to answer the hypothetical question posed on Page 795 [of the transcript], but this witness did. No one can determine or estimate with any accuracy the number of fibers that may have been on the victim's clothing 10 days before she was found. There is no scientific basis for doing so and published articles point out that it is an impossible task."

Even if Malone had given accurate testimony in Oswalt's case, there is growing skepticism about the value of hair and fiber evidence. DNA tests have often proved identification of hair to be wrong. If hair identification is inaccurate, it is safe to assume that fiber identification is as well.

The other key witness against Oswalt was Charlynn Drye Sawyer of Columbus, daughter of the late Bun Drye, Mansfield's former king of vice. On June 14, 1988, when Oswalt's trial was well underway, Prosecutor John Allen disclosed that Sawyer had provided important new information about Coffey's murder. Allen said Sawyer did not come forward with the information — that Oswalt had told her he had murdered Coffey — until she called Assistant Prosecutor Catherine Goldman at 10:30 p.m. on June 8. Actually, in a 1996 deposition taken by investigators conducting a mayoral investigation of Columbus Police Chief James G. Jackson, Sawyer, whose last name was then English, said the first official she told was Mansfield Police Lieutenant John Wendling, another crucial witness against Oswalt.

Columbus investigators questioned Sawyer-English and Wendling after I quoted Wendling as saying that when she approached him to tell him about Oswalt's alleged confession she identified the man driving the car she exited as Jackson, then a deputy chief. This interested the investigators because Sawyer-English was believed to have been an employee of a Columbus escort service at the time — a fact she confirmed in her deposition. Sawyer-English also admitted that Jackson would regularly visit her at her Columbus townhouse while he was on duty. Given the importance of Sawyer's testimony about Oswalt's alleged confession to her, it is interesting to note that the Columbus investigators quoted Wendling as saying she was a "habitual liar, very convincing, a manipulator."

After Allen's disclosure about his surprise witness, Judge Max Chilcote canceled proceedings to consider whether to allow Sawyer to testify. He ruled she could the following afternoon. The next morning, Sawyer testified that Oswalt told her he killed Coffey and that another officer dumped her body where it was found 10 days later. Although Sawyer told the detectives who interviewed her and the grand jury that she initiated contact with Oswalt shortly after he was released on bond on March 11, she testified at the trial that Oswalt contacted her first. Sawyer said they met at a north Columbus hotel, had a few drinks at a bar and then went to her nearby home. There, Sawyer said, Oswalt told her that Coffey flagged him down on January 21, got into his cruiser and started talking about the paternity suit she had filed against him. Coffey then threatened to tell Oswalt's wife about the suit. Sawyer said Oswalt told her that this led to a heated argument, during which he ended up strangling Coffey.

During cross-examination, defense attorney Robert Whitney played a recording of a phone call Sawyer made to a Mansfield detective on March 23 in which she said Oswalt was with her the night of the murder. Sawyer said she had since changed her story "because I have a conscience." Perhaps that is why Sawyer called Oswalt's appeals attorney, R. William Meeks of Columbus, in 1989 and told him her testimony was untrue. According to Meeks, the most important part of his recorded conversation with Sawyer went like this:

Sawyer: The truth is . . . he did meet with me here in Columbus and he denied everything. . . .

Meeks: He denied having anything to do with this woman?

Sawyer: No, he has never denied ever having anything to do with her. He denied the fact that he *killed* her.

Sawyer also told Meeks that she was pressured into giving false testimony, adding: "My conscience has caught up with me and it caught up with me after I did it. That is why they sent me out of state, they sent me away."

Sawyer claimed that "John Allen wanted to make a case because of all the people in Mansfield who had been murdered and unsolved. . . . The prosecutor and them took me to General Hospital because my nerves were so bad I started throwing up, OK? And they kept feeding me valiums the whole time I was on the stand. If you look, I had a cup of water in front of me. My conscience is bothering me because I lied about a good friend, you know? He's in jail now maybe because of what I said."

If Sawyer's conscience got the better of her that day, it soon lost its influence. Sawyer later denied any such conversation with Meeks ever took place, even though he had it on tape. She refused to discuss the case when I contacted her in 2003.

A comparison of the investigative files I obtained from the Mansfield Police Department, the Richland County Sheriff's Department and the prosecutor's office with what Prosecutor Allen turned over to defense attorney Whitney revealed that Allen — a disciple of former Prosecutor William F. McKee — withheld what Oswalt referred to as "extremely exculpatory evidence." One potentially important document Allen apparently didn't turn over was a report by Margie Coffey's neighbor that he saw a truck with three white males in it leaving Coffey's property on the night she disappeared.

'Scannergate,' lost accreditation

Corruption continued into the new millennium. Three officers pleaded guilty in 2000 to charges of altering hand-held scanners to eavesdrop on private telephone conversations and, in one case, that they recorded a phone-sex encounter. It was also speculated that three or more arrests might have occurred based on information illegally obtained with the scanners. Each of the three officers convicted in the scandal was sentenced to suspended six-month jail sentences, $1,000 fines, a year of probation and 160 hours of community services with Habitat for Humanity.

A fourth officer, who went to trial, was found guilty on two counts of falsification and one count of obstructing official business. Several other officers were disciplined for their role in the scandal.

The turmoil caused by Scannergate, pressure on Chief Harper to retire and the department's failure to integrate certain procedures into its operations cost the department its accreditation with the Commission on Accreditation for Law Enforcement Agencies in March 2002. Under Harper's determined leadership, the department had earned the distinction, which was held by only 5,000 of the nation's 100,000 police agencies, in 1996. Then, as Harper's age caught up with him, things began unraveling.

"More than one member of the department, including members of the command staff, described the department as 'dysfunctional,' " a report by the organization said.

"Clearly, the turmoil is a major distraction to members of the department, which is making it difficult to focus on the prevention of crime, the delivery of police service, and to meeting the requirements of accreditation."

Harper, who had already agreed to retire at age 76 in July 2002 when the report was released, noted that the department had met compliance in all but six of the 74 areas considered.

"We got an education out of it," Harper said of the accreditation review.

"We're trying to make progress and move forward with it. Overall we're in pretty good shape, but there is always room for improvement."

A few weeks later, Mayor Lydia Reid announced that Captain Phil Messer had been selected to become the police department's 18th chief. Messer took command on July 19, 2002.

Harper, the department's first black officer and chief, left after a remarkable 54 years of service, during which he overcame blatant and subtle discrimination of all kinds.

Messer brought some baggage with him to the chief's office. As project director for the 10-county METRICH Drug Task Force in north central Ohio, Messer had been the target of a substantial number of accusations in recent years. Among them were:

• Evidence developed by METRICH that a Mansfield city councilman's bar was involved in a gambling operation disappeared.

- A Mansfield police lieutenant assigned to METRICH threw a party involving illegal gambling and liquor-law violations at the Fraternal Order of Police Lodge, but no charges were filed against him.
- Messer took his family for out-of-state trips in METRICH vehicles.
- Messer's son drove his METRICH vehicle and once used it to chase down a Police Athletic League (PAL) employee with whom he had an argument.
- METRICH received gratuities from companies that do business with the drug-fighting task force. On one occasion METRICH received Cleveland Indians tickets and used a PAL van to take favored city officials to the game.
- METRICH contracted for the use of vehicles that were overly luxurious for police work.
- METRICH employees attended high-cost schools and seminars in Florida, Las Vegas and Arizona while average officers' requests to attend less-expensive training opportunities were routinely turned down.
- Messer wrote a letter to the Ohio attorney general's office stating that a man had been an auxiliary officer for the Mansfield Police Department, meaning he was qualified to run for sheriff in Morrow County. Subsequent reviews found the man had never served as an auxiliary officer.
- Playground equipment obtained through grants for a city school went, instead, to a school attended by Messer's son.
- Allegations of the theft and use of confiscated illegal narcotics by METRICH detectives were covered up.
- Allegations that METRICH officers also used modified hand-held police scanners to intercept cell phone and cordless phone calls were covered up.
- Grants that were supposed to be distributed to law-enforcement agencies that were part of METRICH were never received.

Messer found out almost immediately that I had received the allegations and called me to deny them. He attributed the accusations to a few disgruntled officers. The proof of Messer's true character will be in the pudding as he puts his imprint on a police department that has had more ups and downs than a roller-coaster.

5

The Three-Ring Circus

If Mansfield's political tragedy stopped with Sheriff Weikel, Coroner Thabet, Mayor Porter and assorted hangers-on, it would be bad enough. Unfortunately, it didn't. Where it ended, if it ended, is anybody's guess. But it certainly was pervasive enough then to qualify Richland County as a legitimate (perhaps illegitimate might be a better word) three-ring political circus.

And while Weikel, Thabet, Porter and Clayton Long were the stars of sordid show, the ringleader was Prosecutor William F. McKee. It was not so much what McKee had done to deserve this role as what he had not done.

Although he held a position that many have used to do good or further their careers, McKee had been content to use it as a vehicle for protecting the powerful, prosecuting the powerless and investigating anyone who would have it any other way.

That, no doubt, was why he laughed at the charges about to be made against Sheriff Weikel when they were presented to him in advance by two BCI agents. And when those charges resulted in indictments, he tried to argue that they weren't the same charges at all, even though the package he was presented revealed that the allegations were very much the same. McKee had been presented evidence of possible election-law violations by Weikel even before that. The ex-deputies who tried to present the information found McKee greatly uninterested. They said he gave them a considerable run-around before he finally referred them to someone else for more of the same.

When they got no satisfaction there, the ex-deputies sought out their own attorney and filed a complaint with the state ethics commission, which agreed that a probable violation of the law had occurred.

McKee's investigation of theft-in-office charges against Coroner Thabet was equally undistinguished. As the police investigated the incident, they were ordered by Captain William Spognardi Sr. — whose deputy sons were soon to plead no-contest to charges brought against them — to investigate me and a reporter for *The Akron Beacon Journal* who had first made public the allegations against Thabet. The charge: failure to report a crime to a law-enforcement officer.

At the urging of McKee, the officers told me, Spognardi had even sent out letters to several law-enforcement agencies to determine if we had reported the crime to them.

If McKee knew the law as well as he knew dog racing, he would have known that the state reporter's shield law specifically exempted journalists from the requirement to report a crime if they would have to reveal a confidential source or only had second-hand knowledge that the crime had been committed.

McKee always on attack

McKee apparently was still obsessed on his incorrect interpretation of the law when a reporter asked him if he was going to investigate the practice of city councilmen receiving free cable TV service. Probably not, McKee replied, since any violation of the law that might have occurred would be a misdemeanor and his office only handled felonies.

What, the reporter asked, if the acceptance of the service was a felony?

If it was, and the reporter had knowledge of it, he would have violated the law himself by not reporting the crime to a law enforcement officer, McKee snapped. The reporter, somewhat new to Mansfield, was stunned. It seemed that he was being told that if he pushed the issue he might be the one to suffer. Unbelievable — except for McKee.

If McKee was the great protector to some, he was just the opposite to many others. He and his bloated staff of assistants pursued many petty criminals with a vengeance. Mercy was not one of their trademarks. "Law and order" was. As for McKee himself, he was quite often "out of town."

That often meant he was attending another convention, which he often paid for out of his Furtherance of Justice Fund, a special account each elected law-enforcement official gets to combat crime. McKee was quick to point out that this practice was not illegal, although legislation was later passed to ensure that the money went to direct crime-fighting practices. McKee's FOJ funds had been the source of considerable controversy. He and the Ohio Prosecuting Attorney's Association finally reached an out-of-court settlement with the state auditor's office, which subpoenaed some of McKee's records because of the strikingly similar amounts checks were made out for.

The defendants claimed the records must be kept secret to protect the names of informants. Yet all the amounts in question were made out either to McKee or his assistants.

Despite all the controversy surrounding McKee's FOJ fund, his request for an additional $2,000 was approved in November 1978 by three of the county's four common-pleas judges.

The fourth judge, the late Judge James J. Mayer Sr., wasn't even consulted because his vote wasn't needed and he might start asking questions about what McKee had done with the other $13,000 he was given for the year. When the news broke about the additional grant, McKee was conveniently out of town — at a convention.

Drunken judge gets break

It is no wonder McKee felt safe asking the county's three common pleas judges for more money.

They were all bona fide members of the Richland County buddy system. In fact, Probate Court Judge Richard M. Christensen was — and remained until his death in November 2001 — one of its main men. Many considered the former minority whip in the state House of Representatives, in which he served from 1960 to 1972, the county's most powerful Democrat. Christensen, who became probate judge in 1973, took a back seat to no one, even when he should have.

Christiansen certainly should have taken a back seat on January 24, 1977, when he was arrested for driving under the influence of alcohol returning home from a party at Multi-Channel Cable TV. (Christiansen once was a lawyer for the cable company's parent organization, *The News Journal.*)

The judge was found by officers sitting in his car after a minor accident. He reportedly refused to take a Breathalyzer test as well as a straight-line test, saying he was too shaken by the accident. But one arresting officers later said Christiansen appeared to be intoxicated. According to the accident report, Christiansen had "a strong odor of alcoholic beverage, eyes very bloodshot, speech slurred . . . Often not understandable."

Despite the fact that he was arrested for DUI after an accident and refused to take a Breathalyzer test, Christiansen was only charged with speeding and with failure to stop within an assured clear distance. He paid an $18 waiver fee and the matter was quietly forgotten. So was the assistant city solicitor who had approved the case for prosecution with the more serious DUI and accident charges. His decision was overruled by City Law Director Robert Rath, Christiansen's fellow Democrat, and the assistant city solicitor was fired when he protested the cover-up.

That wasn't Christiansen's first scrape with the law. On February 7, 1971, the then-state legislator was arrested after police were called to his home by his wife, who told the officers that he assaulted her. The two police officers dispatched to the scene reported that Christensen appeared to be drunk and had slurred speech.

When one of the officers asked Christiansen if he had another place to stay for the evening, Christensen assumed a favorite role for many local powers-that-be.

"Young man, do you know who you are talking to?" he asked arrogantly.

As if to pound his point home, Christiansen repeatedly tapped the officers' badges, saying they "could kiss them goodbye." At the police station, Christiansen refused to enter a jail cell, allegedly stating that he was a state representative and could not be incarcerated. Christensen wasn't too far off the mark about his influence The next day, the two arresting officers were called in the office of Police Chief John Butler and told to drop the charges against the powerful legislator.

"You're going to do more harm than good," Butler allegedly told the officers as he ripped their report up.

Sheriff Weikel had his chance to help out Christiansen in May 1977 when his office covered up a violent domestic quarrel, during which gunshots were reportedly fired, between Christiansen and his wife.

Deputies dispatched to the scene were ordered to file a confidential report on the case rather than an offense report, and no charges were filed. The confidential report showed that deputies found bullet holes on the exterior of the house. The inside was allegedly "torn apart."

But all deputies except one were taken off the case. The deputy left to handle the situation was the Christiansens' son Jody.

Christiansen did not, needless to say, suddenly transform into a sober model of probity when he donned his judicial robe. Probate court was Christiansen's personal fiefdom for almost 30 years, and he used it to dispense justice as he saw it, which was often through distorted lenses. A case brought to my attention in the mid-'90s was a good example. Before it was over, a woman who was left her aunt's house had lost it to a distant relative who hadn't seen the woman in years. But the distant relative had something going for him that the Mansfield woman did not: He was represented by one of Christiansen's legal cronies. In Christiansen's court, that was more than enough to tip the balance, and it did.

Christiansen was hardly the only Richland county judge with a drinking problem, and it perhaps was a sign of progress that one caught driving in that condition in 1985 was actually convicted of drunken driving. Municipal Judge George Murray spent 10 days in Ashland County Jail as his sentence, then was suspended 30 days without pay in January 1986 by a state disciplinary board.

The five-member Board of Commissioners on Grievances and Discipline of the Judiciary said Murray had exhibited "conduct which brought his judicial office into disrepute."

Judge Angelo Gagliardo, the Ohio Supreme Court's disciplinary counsel, said Murray was the first judge to be disciplined by the commission since July 1983, when the high court adopted new rules governing the state's judges. Under the old rules, Murray would have been disciplined as an attorney, not a judge.

Unfortunately, the discipline didn't work. Murray was charged with drunken driving again in October 1987. This, it turned out, was the sixth time since 1970 that the judge had been charged with drunken driving. Three of those charges ended in conviction, including the 1987 one. Murray was sentenced to 30 days in jail, fined $200 and had his license suspended for a year. Even Murray's Republican Party had become fed up with him before his latest arrest.

He was defeated in the party primary the previous May and had 66 days left in his term at the time of his arrest.

Murray was first elected to the bench in 1981, and had publicly acknowledged his alcoholism. But he refused to remove himself from hearing drunken-driving cases, just as he refused to believe that Sheriff Weikel was a mere mortal the first time I met him.

That was at one of a series of meet-the-editor meetings I hosted for members of the community after becoming editor of *The News Journal*. As I was discussing my editorial philosophy, an apparently inebriated Murray suddenly interrupted me and said, "You'll never get anywhere investigating Tom Weikel."

"I wasn't talking about Tom Weikel," I replied nicely and tried to return to my subject.

"I'm just telling you you're wasting your time going after him," Murray persisted. "I'd be willing to put money on it."

"We'll see," I said, and returned to my subject once again.

The county's other judges weren't the political heavyweights Judge Christiansen was then, nor were they the embarrassment Judge Murray was. But that didn't keep them from having fun. Nor did it keep them from compromising their integrity, as they did when they accepted free prescription eyeglasses from the Ohio National Guard medical technician who was giving them to everyone in the sheriff's department where he was a special deputy as well.

The fact that they were receiving stolen goods in the process didn't seem to bother the judges' consciences, but having a conscience wasn't a prerequisite for success in Mansfield, either. In fact, it could sometimes be a hindrance.

Judge James J. Mayer Sr. could testify to that if he were still alive. Mayer died in 1979, several months after he lost a close election contest to retain his seat on the bench after becoming the first judge in state history to be removed by the Ohio Supreme Court for health reasons.

Mayer's problems began in the early 1970s, when he was diagnosed with cancer.

As he underwent chemotherapy, Mayer was forced to temporarily discontinue the use of lithium to control his manic depression. Without it, the popular judge's moods began to swing up and down the emotional scale.

Before long, Mayer was lashing out at the corruption and favoritism rampant in Richland County, much of which he accurately blamed on Christiansen and McKee. Mayer sometimes chose the wrong forum for his outbursts and his attacks may have been exaggerated at times. But they also were laced with truth, the kind of truth Mansfield's powers-that-be didn't particularly want exposed.

So McKee and Christiansen, two knights in grimy armor if there ever were any, got the Ohio Bar Association to file a complaint against Mayer with the Supreme Court.

As the controversy dragged on, Mayer was able to resume taking lithium and his manic depression stabilized. Mayer once again became a productive and efficient judge and apologized for much of what he said. But it was too late. Mayer had crossed the power brokers' path and had to go. The Ohio Supreme Court agreed when it decided Mayer was unfit to hold office.

After an appeal to the U.S. Supreme Court was denied, Mayer took his case to the people. Neither party would touch him, of course, so he was forced to run as an independent.

His two opponents had a lot more money and support from those who counted. Nonetheless. Mayer managed to finish a strong second to Max Chilcote, McKee's former assistant, who had thrown his hat into the ring after taking out petitions to run for judge in another county. McKee and Christiansen had succeeded in getting rid of their outspoken nemesis Judge Mayer.

But there is more than a little irony — to say nothing of poetic justice — in the fact that 25 years later the man holding McKee's office was James J. Mayer Jr. and the man holding Christiansen's was the late Judge Mayer's other lawyer-son, Philip.

As for Chilcote, the man who had seemed like everybody's nice guy proved to be anything but that after he had won. As soon as he took the bench, Chilcote began adopting an arrogant approach to the media, lawyers and his own supporters.

Chilcote got miffed at me after I published a statement from him admitting that McKee had taken him on a two-week junket to Hawaii in 1975 to attend a prosecutors conference paid for with FOJ funds. Chilcote noted that the trip came near the end of his career in the prosecutor's office and wasn't all that beneficial to him or taxpayers.

"I'll admit it — it was nothing but a vacation," Chilcote said. But I had been handling over 200 criminal cases a year and only making $16,000-$17,000 a year, so I thought I deserved it."

Two Richland County judges generated controversy over religion in the courtroom during the 1990s and into the 21st century. In July 2000, Common Pleas Judge James DeWeese put up a "Rule of Law" display in his courtroom that included the Bill of Rights and quotes from Abraham Lincoln, Thomas Jefferson and James Madison, and the Ten Commandments. DeWeese reportedly included the Decalogue as a lesson in the supremacy of divine law over human affairs.

The judge ended up getting a lesson of his own in the supremacy of the U.S. Constitution and the federal courts. On June 11, 2002, U.S. District Judge Kathleen O'Malley declared DeWeese's display unconstitutional, and ordered it removed. The ruling came in response to a lawsuit filed by the American Civil Liberties Union of Ohio against DeWeese and the county commissioners after Bernard Davis, a longtime Mansfield attorney risked raising the ire of a judge he often appeared before by complaining that the display made him feel that DeWeese was forcing religion on him. O'Malley agreed. She said that DeWeese's intentions were "generally laudable," but that his display was nonetheless unconstitutional "because the debate he seeks to foster is inherently religious in character."

DeWeese responded that he was "confident of the legality and correctness of the challenged conduct and welcomed the opportunity to take the case before a higher tribunal." The federal appeals court in Cincinnati declined to interfere with O'Malley's order that DeWeese remove the poster until it ruled on DeWeese's appeal, which he filed with the help of a group founded by Pat Robertson. Robertson is a strange ally for a supposedly impartial judge. The former presidential candidate and creator of the Christian Coalition once said the court system of which DeWeese is part was "merely a ruse, if you will, for humanist, atheistic educators to beat up on Christians." Robertson also came under attack in 2001 for agreeing with Jerry Falwell's view that the 9/11 terrorist attacks occurred because Americans allowed abortion, feminism and pornography. He created another furor in 2002 when he said Islam was a violent religion that wanted to "dominate and then, if need be, destroy."

But while DeWeese injected religion into his courtroom, he didn't seem to let it seep into his rulings.

Many Mansfielders felt the same could not be said about Juvenile and Domestic Court Judge Ron Spon. Attorneys and average citizens complained that Spon's fundamentalist Christian beliefs often affected his rulings in divorce cases, where women often seemed to come up on the short end of the stick. "Spon doesn't believe in divorce, and he often does everything he can to delay them," one attorney said. "His religion also believes that women should be subservient to men, so his rulings often unfairly favor the husband."

Spon has also been accused of arbitrary and discriminatory practices in the management of the Richland County Juvenile Justice Center. In one example, a discrimination complaint filed with the Ohio Civil Rights Commission in 2003 claimed that two black employees were terminated after being charged with misdemeanors. Yet a white man, who reportedly was a friend of Spon's son, was employed for two years after serving 1½ years in prison for drug trafficking.

When one of the blacks reapplied for a job several years after the charge against him was dismissed, he was told the position he applied for had been filled. When the applicant learned he was turned down because of the same dismissed charge that cost him his job at the juvenile center years earlier, he filed a racial-discrimination complaint. In response, Spon's minions claimed that there was no racial discrimination because the job went to a black applicant with a college degree. But the only black or white person with a college degree working at the facility signed an affidavit stating that he was hired several months *before* the applicant was was denied employment.

Municipal Court Judge Jerry Ault added another chapter to Mansfield's history of troubled judges in December 2003, when he pleaded guilty to two first-degree misdemeanor counts of deceiving physicians in attempts to get double doses of painkillers. The judge's plea agreement said he "sought treatment for pain and was taking properly prescribed pain medications but became dependent on controlled substances . . . and he again resorted to the use and likely abuse of alcohol." Ault said he took "full responsibility for what happened." Delaware County Municipal Court Judge David P. Sunderman, who was appointed by the Ohio Supreme Court to hear the case, gave Ault a suspended sentence of 120 days and placed him on probation for two years. Ault was also fined $1,000.

The period covered by the charges gave the impression that Ault's history of painkillers was relatively recent, beginning in 2001. Yet I had been told in 1998 about Ault's possible misuse of painkillers for several years prior to that and was provided a copy of a prescription for Ault to obtain Tylenol with Codeine (No. 4) signed by a psychiatrist in December 1993. Codeine is a narcotic and, "even if taken in prescribed amounts, can cause physical and psychological addiction if taken for a long enough time," one medical reference source says. "Addiction may be more of a risk for a person who has been addicted to alcohol or drugs." Why would a psychiatrist subscribe such a potent painkiller to a man long suspected of having a drinking problem? Because powerful people like Ault, then a first assistant county prosecutor who helped form the local drug task force, often received such favors, my source replied.

Taxpayers revolt

When Max Chilcote, then judicial candidate and later a judge, told me in the fall of 1978 that he felt he deserved a "vacation" to Hawaii at taxpayer expense, a lot of hard-working people in Mansfield probably would disagree. They certainly disagreed with the Richland County Commissioners' decision in 1979 to enact a half-percent piggyback sales tax. The required number of signatures was quickly gathered to force the issue onto the ballot that fall, and the tax hike was soundly rejected by voters. It seemed as if the average citizens of Richland County had come to the realization that corruption costs money and the current fiscal crisis was only a symptom of a bigger problem.

The commissioners, for example, ignored the fact that cost overruns in Sheriff Weikel's and Prosecutor McKee's offices in recent years would have accounted for the $574,000 deficit of the preceding year that caused the commissioners to approve the tax hike, just as they or their successors ignored the overspending and its causes when it was accrued.

At the very time the debate about the tax was going on, for example, Weikel bought five new cruisers for a department in which a captain was provided a cruiser to drive to and from home. Instead of complaining about things like that, the commissioners usually chose to complain about the cost of Special Prosecutor Joseph Murray's investigation of corruption in Weikel's department.

Murray said he went for such a soft deal with those indicted in the scandal because he was under so much pressure to bring the investigation to an end. Actually, the commissioners could have exposed Weikel themselves if they wanted to. They certainly had some knowledge of what was going on in the sheriff's department. But to bring it out in the open would have taken courage, and courage was a rare commodity in the commissioners' office. Commissioner Art Touby definitely seemed to know that something was amiss in the sheriff's department. "I could tell you things about sheriff's department that would make your head spin," Touby told me. But he never did. Another commissioner with some insight was Dale Cook, who defeated Touby in 1978. Cook's own son reportedly had some problems with the sheriff's department, but when reporters tried to get him to talk, he said his father had told him not to because it might hurt his election chances.

But Touby's and Cook's lack of courage paled in comparison with the misconduct of one of their successors. In February 2004, recently re-signed County Commissioner David Swartz pleaded guilty to felony sex charges involving a teenage girl. Swartz reportedly admitted to authorities that he had sexually abused the girl since she was 6 years old or earlier.

Ironically, Richland County seems to end up with many such people in power because their lack of character proves to be an asset. When someone *with* character manages to get into a position of power, attempts often are made to control him. The police chief of the village of Lexington, for example, was cooperative in helping me unravel the mystery surrounding the death of Kelly Dean Gentry, which an official investigation years later determined was indeed a murder and not an accident. But because the stories reflected poorly on at least one former Lexington policeman, as well as a local company, Lexington's city council tried to muzzle the chief for his candid comments. The fact that someone may have been murdered wasn't important. What was important was Lexington's image.

If it seems there is no end to Richland County's three-ring circus, that is because there is none. The powers that be liked it that way in 1978, and, judging from the people they helped put in power 25 years later, they liked it that way in 2004. While all eyes are on the county's clownish political puppets, of course, no one is watching who is pulling the strings.

6

The Power Brokers

Located in an alley behind the beautifully renovated Mansfield-Richland County Library in downtown Mansfield is a tidy, gray, nondescript building.

The building's address is supposed to be 51 Library Court. But neither the address nor the name of the organization inside are affixed anywhere on the building. Those who need to know its location, do; those who don't, don't. It is in this building that Mansfield's inner circle of power brokers break bread daily and discuss political and economic issues and the general state of the world.

My interest in the Fifty-One Club was sparked during my research on Mansfield before I moved there when I came across a portrayal of its members in author Neil Peirce's *The Megastates of America*.

"They are a conservative and cautious lot who meet to make (or fail to make) the essential decisions for Mansfield at places like their exclusive Fifty-One Club in an old downtown building," Peirce wrote in his popular book.

When I asked reporters and editors about the club after becoming editor of *The News Journal*, I was surprised to learn that no one even knew the club existed even though it was located only about two blocks away. And if reporters don't know about something, you can bet few in the general population do. The members of the Fifty-One Club liked it that way, though. Most felt that the less the public knew about them and their private retreat, the better.

Members denied that, of course. When *The Ohio Observer* did a story about the club. They claimed it was just a quiet place for men with similar interests to get together for lunch. The fact that the club membership list read like Who's Who in Mansfield was a mere coincidence Anyone could apply for membership, although that didn't mean he would be accepted.

The names of politicians were noticeably absent from the membership list, because, one member said, they are reactors more than they are actors. Besides they usually come from the lower end of the social-economic scale.

"I don't think politics is where the power is in Mansfield," the member said. It lies more with the lawyers and businessmen. They are the ones who really get the ball rolling. The politicians just carry out what they started."

The Fifty-One Club opened in a converted barn in January 1951. It had 51 charter members who paid $51 for an annual membership to be able to get away from the rigors of daily work.

In the late 1970s, the exclusively male club still had 51 members. The number of charter members was down to 13 and annual dues were up to $400. Members included almost every important banker, lawyer or businessman in town.

Despite this, members played down the club's influence "No decisions are made there, believe me," said the club's treasurer. He insisted that discussions involved general topics and that any matters concerning groups like the Greater Mansfield Area Growth Corporation or the Chamber of Commerce were a matter of hindsight rather than foresight

At least one member disagreed. "Any time you put such a group of powerful men together in a private setting, opinions are undoubtedly going to be influenced and decisions definitely made," he said. "There's nothing sinister about it, it just happens."

Chamber does it to Mansfield

If the Fifty-One Club's power was informal, the Chamber of Commerce and Greater Mansfield Area Growth Corporation (GMAG) were anything but. They were all business.

In the late 1970s, at least, the chamber was anything but a force for progress.

One of its major roles before then, old-timers charged, was to keep out industries that would drive up the local wage rate or compete with established industries. In the late '70s, however, the chamber became more active and more the spokesman for small business. Discussions at some board meetings even concerned how the chamber could control the more conservative GMAG and make it more responsive to the community.

One of the chamber's more visible efforts for change when I became editor of *The News Journal* was its "Do It In Mansfield" campaign designed to get people to shop in the city's struggling downtown area. While the chamber's hierarchy didn't see how "Do It In Mansfield" could be open to misinterpretation, even though "do it" had been used as a euphemism for having sex for decades.

Young people, with the words of the Beatles song *Let's Do It In the Road* relatively fresh in their minds, jokingly interpreted the chamber's slogan as an invitation for people to come to Mansfield to have sex. The town is lucky it didn't end up hosting a huge love-in in Public Square. Then there were the cynical letters-to-the-editor writers who interpreted the slogan to mean that business wanted to "Do It *To* Mansfield" rather than *In* Mansfield.

Quite a bit of money was spent on the project. Bumper stickers, posters and billboards covered the city and the campaign even won some awards for its originality. But its effect on downtown was negligible at best. Part of the reason for campaign's failure was the mentality and defensiveness of the project's supervisor, a high-ranking executive at one of the local banks. The woman had become so involved in the campaign that any criticism of Mansfield was taken as criticism of her slogan and herself. This paranoia, not untypical of Mansfield's power brokers, was once exhibited to me when Miss Do It In Mansfield asked me to lunch at the time *The News Journal* was running a series of articles on Mansfield's problems and opportunities. With few social pleasantries beforehand, Miss Do It In Mansfield got down to business.

"We'd like to know when you'll be through destroying Mansfield with your articles so we can begin to build it up again," she said through a fixed smile. Such insecurity was typical of Mansfield's self-appointed leaders. Criticism was never constructive, only destructive. Mansfield would build from its current shaky foundation rather than one strengthened by new ideas.

Shortly after our friendly luncheon, the chamber began a new campaign to drive the point home: "Be A Doer, Not A Critic. Do It In Mansfield," the posters proclaimed.

The chamber might have used an ostrich with its head stuck in the sand as the campaign's symbol. It was not until several of Mansfield's major industries and retailers closed their doors over the next few years that the chamber started taking a more positive approach, and it began to have some success.

The chamber of the late '70s was not above politics, either. Several of its top members and officers took an active role in fostering the campaign of Republican John Buker for state representative.

The incumbent was State Rep. Sherrod Brown, who had been first elected in 1974 when he was 21 and straight out of Yale University. Two terms later, Brown was still the youngest legislator in the state, a liberal who could attract conservative votes with his earnestness and honesty, which often took the form of criticizing big business for taking advantage of consumers. Big business, in return, made Brown a prime target in the 1978 election. Since Mansfield's Republicans had already tried to beat Brown with an older, more experienced candidate and failed, the GOP and some of the town's biggest business interests decided to go with young Buker.

Buker was portrayed as an old high-school rival of Brown and a more responsible voice of youth. He was good looking and his family was well-known. The only problem was that Buker didn't have the slightest idea what most of the political issues of the day were, and he couldn't articulate them if he did. Buker's backers tried desperately to improve his speaking ability. They videotaped him as he practiced speeches at the chamber's downtown office, showing him where his presentation went wrong. They also poured a large sum of money into his campaign treasury, all to no avail. Brown drubbed Buker, and the chamber along with it.

The Greater Mansfield Area Growth Corporation was a different story than the chamber. GMAG was a quasi-official organization with real authority: It could recommend industrial revenue bonds for new development. Much of the future of the area therefore lay in its hands. I have already noted how one Mansfield city council member used the power of GMAG for his own benefit, and it is likely he was not the only GMAG member to do so.

One reason a seat on the board was so coveted was the opportunity it provided members to feather their own nests under the guise of a "community improvement corporation" established to aid the expansion and location of industry.

The whole world in his Hand

No one better epitomized the character and make-up of Mansfield power brokers than GMAG president Avery Hand Jr., who at one time or another held a similar position at the Fifty-One Club, Mansfield General Hospital, the Ohio State University-Mansfield advisory board and just about every other important organization in town. That included the Highway Safety Foundation, which collapsed in 1974 with several million dollars and Hand's friend Richard Wayman missing. Hand was a member of the foundation's initial board of trustees. He also introduced Wayman to a woman whose high salary at the foundation after Wayman hired her was strongly criticized in a state attorney general's report as payment for her talents in the bedroom.

On top of all these positions of influence, Hand was president and chairman of the board of the largest and the last independent bank in Richland County, First National Bank of Mansfield, which is now part of KeyBank of Cleveland. Hand didn't earn his powerful position the hard way. Instead, he inherited it from his grandfather in 1962. But therein lay the root of his influence. "By the fact that he is the chief executive officer of the largest bank in town, Avery Hand has everybody hanging from his financial string and he's not afraid to pull it when he has to," said one local businessman.

Or, as Mansfield Safety Director Clayton Long once put it, "Avery Hand runs this town." A *News Journal* survey of Mansfield power brokers that put Hand at the top of the list confirmed Hand's reputation as the go-to man when you wanted to "Do It In Mansfield."

When Hand died in 1997, Rex Collins, retired president of First Buckeye Bank, observed that, "Locally, what he said was almost gospel." But Hand's gospel was based on power more than the New Testament.

While few could point to any one act by Hand where he used or abused his influence with their organization, the cumulative effect of Hand's influence and interests were so broad that it would he difficult to know for sure. That, no doubt, is the way Hand preferred it.

When all his influence failed him, Hand had been known to take his ball and go home. That is exactly what he threatened to do in 1979, when Mansfield's downtown redevelopment plan did not turn out to his satisfaction.

To show his contempt, Hand announced plans for his bank to move its headquarters to a suburban location despite his previous commitment to redeveloping downtown and the substantial amount of property owned there by both himself and his bank.

Hand's threat infuriated city leaders. "There are just too many people who are so-called leaders who just won't come forward to do what needs to be done for this community," said City Council President E. William McCarrick. "The bank owes something to the community, to the customers who have banked with them,"

Councilman-at-Large Robert Boling said the city had worked with Hand "every step of the way, including tax abatement and getting the gas company to lift their freeze for certain downtown properties."

"We were led to believe that work was going to start a year ago, Boling added. "Just when we thought things were going along nicely with downtown, this came along."

Hand's involvement with Mansfield General Hospital put him in touch with one of the last vestiges of old power in Mansfield, the sophisticated and generally well-meaning Black family, which made a fortune through the city's longest-operating company, Ohio Brass, The Blacks' generosity has had much to do with the growth of Mansfield General. They controlled hospital policy through a relative by marriage, Philip Wisdom, and the medical community by their control over physician's privileges. But the Blacks pretty much let the doctors run things themselves, and that was a mistake.

It didn't pay for physicians to get out of line with the clique of doctors who controlled things, lest they wished to be faced with working at the city's only other medical facility, People's Hospital, which most people discounted because of its impoverished conditions. MGH somehow managed to get everything and People's nothing.

But People's was at least allowed to exist, — at least until 1998, when it was finally forced to close. St. Elizabeth's Hospital, which was to be built on land left by a wealthy woman by the name of Justine Sterkel never got off the ground.

Despite intense interest in the idea and a choice piece of property on which to build it, St. Elizabeth's never had a chance. Mansfield's powers-that-be did not want a hospital to compete with the one they controlled, so everything possible was done to prevent it. The local community appeal charity organization, for example, decided not to give it financial support even when several unions threatened to withdraw from their participation in the appeal's fund-raising activities.

So St. Elizabeth's died aborning, and Mansfield General prospered. Conditions there were considered by many employees to be less than ideal for the patient. Nurses in particular had a long list of complaints about some of the things they had seen. But they were told to mind their own business, which is what they thought they were doing.

As a result, Mansfield General suffered with a bad reputation right up to the present. In 1991, for example, the hospital was one of 161 in the nation to show up on a list of hospitals that federal officials said had death rates substantially higher than they should have been. According to the study, Mansfield General should have had a death rate of 7.8 percent for its 2,284 Medicare patients in 1989, but the actual rate was 10.7 percent.

Hospital officials blamed the fact that Mansfield General admits more seriously ill patients than the government model would project for the 10.7 percent rate. One example of the problems at MGH was the rape of a patient in the spring of 1978. When a reporter picked up on the incident from someone who had heard about it in a barbershop, MGH administrator Wisdom tried to have the story scuttled.

While admitting that the rape appeared to have been committed by someone who entered during visiting hours and remained, indicating a weakness in the hospital's security system, Wisdom nonetheless tried to persuade us not to run the story because there was still a possibility that the victim had "imagined" the rape. (When this was mentioned in the article, Wisdom called back furious. He hadn't really *meant* that, he said.)

After failing to get the story killed himself, Wisdom had Police Chief Matthew (Whitewash) Benick call to persuade us that printing it could jeopardize the police department's investigation. Knowing the incident already was being discussed on the street, we decided the best thing to do was to publish the facts rather than having the incident be blown out of proportion by rumors.

Ironically, we later learned that the hospital had already had a chance to correct the problem quietly when another patient was raped under similar circumstances only a few weeks before. With no adverse publicity, however, there was no action. Publicity about the second incident brought action. Three years after I left Mansfield, I met a nurse who had attended Mansfield General's nursing school. "Are you the Marty Yant who was the editor in Mansfield?" she asked.

When I told her I was, she continued: "I'm sure glad you exposed those rapes in the hospital. We had one in our dorm just before that, and they told us that if anyone talked about it to anyone on the outside we would be expelled because it would hurt the hospital's image.

Medical maverick

One of the few doctors to buck the Mansfield medical establishment was a man who brought hatred (or was it envy?) to the eyes of most of Mansfield's most taciturn physicians.

They called him a "quack," a "charlatan" and much worse, and it was his candidacy for coroner that ensured someone like Robert Wolford or Raymond Thabet their undying support.

The good doctor's name was Gordon Morkel. The late Morkel's original sin was writing a thinly veiled novel in 1958 called *Harvest of the Bitter Seed,* which exposed the incompetence and lack of principle of his colleagues and the administration of Mansfield General Hospital. Morkel not only raised some serious questions about the quality of health care in Mansfield, he did it in a way that made his attacks all the more difficult to swallow. Statements like, "There will be more whores in heaven than doctors from this town" helped seal Morkel's fate.

Already denied privileges at MGH for several years by the time his book was published, Morkel would continue to be denied them for decades to come.

But the medical establishment went further than that. It attempted to have Morkel's medical license withdrawn for his use of paramedics in his office and field. In 1973, the state medical board ordered the suspension of Morkel's license for 60 days. The board found him guilty of "gross immorality and grossly unprofessional conduct" for charging a fee for services he didn't perform and lending his name to an "illegal practitioner of medicine," namely, a paramedic.

The Fifth District Court of Appeals, however, later ruled that the charges against Morkel were too vague, that he was never told what he had done that was "grossly immoral" and that there didn't seem to be a law against "gross immorality," whatever *that* was.

Before Morkel was vindicated, he spent some $70,000 in legal fees to defend his plan of staffing well-equipped ambulances with highly trained paramedics who would make house calls and emergency runs while in contact with a doctor. If Morkel's projections were correct, his service would have been able to eventually better serve the entire Mansfield area with far fewer doctors.

Like many visionaries, Morkel's problem with this idea and many others was that he was way ahead of time. Thirty years after the medical establishment tried to punish Morkel for the use of paramedics in electronic communication with doctors to make house calls, "telemedicine" became one of the hottest topics in medicine. On May 7, 2003, for example, several reports on the progress being made in telemedicine were presented as part of the "Telehealth on the Hill" series in Washington. The conference was kicked off by Senator Kent Conrad, who cited the tragic events of 9/11 as a telling example of the need for the merger of medicine and telecommunications.

But Morkel was only courting disaster with ideas like that in the early 1970s. Not only was he developing an ambulance service to compete with all-powerful Byrd Ambulance, but he was developing a system to deliver medical services to the home for a fraction of the cost of the more traditional system. That meant less demand for doctors and less income for them as well.

It was one thing for Morkel to ridicule the medical establishment and still manage to have the largest private practice in Mansfield. But it was quite another to threaten doctors' whole way of life.

If it hadn't been for Morkel's equally threatening promises in his campaigns for coroner, a lot of doctors would have been happy to let him have the job to get him out of their hair.

But when he started talking about performing autopsies on anyone who died less than 24 hours after entering the hospital or having surgery, supporting him for coroner became an impossibility. He might discover the kinds of needless deaths he had written about in his book and that nurses still talked about in hushed tones at Mansfield General.

Morkel argued that his autopsy policy would assure a more accurate assessment on the patient's cause of death and, if errors proved to be a contributing factor, steps could be taken to avoid them in the future.

Three decades later, Morkel's vision proved to be accurate once again. A 1998 article in *The Journal of American Medical Association (JAMA)* estimated a 40 percent error rate in the cause of death listed by doctors on death certificates. Two years after that, *JAMA* published a study that said medical treatment was the third-leading cause of death in the United States. Among the causes of death Dr. Barbara Starfield included in reaching that estimate were unnecessary surgery; medication errors in hospitals; other errors in hospitals; infections contracted in hospitals; and adverse reactions to prescribed drugs.

For more than 30 years, the outspoken Morkel lived as an outcast from the medical establishment because he stood his ground against everything the powers-that-be could throw at him. Morkel also gave the good doctors a little of their own medicine, such as the time he arrived at a medical association meeting with a machine gun. When he rose to speak, the famed gun collector placed the weapon on the table before him and joked: "The greatest thing I could do to improve the quality of medical care in Richland County would be to pick up that gun and start firing."

Many also liked to attribute a comment to Morkel that he allegedly made when he learned of the death of a local brain surgeon who had shot himself in the head. "That's the best brain surgery he ever performed," Morkel supposedly said. Morkel disavowed the comment, however. "I wish I had been clever enough to think of something like that, but I didn't," he said. No one was sacred to Morkel. His one-liners were delivered to all by the big-hearted man with an even bigger laugh. When Mayor Porter once incredulously asked the doctor if it was true that he had supported his re-election campaign, Morkel said it was. When Porter asked why such an outspoken Democrat would support a rock-ribbed Republican like himself, Morkel replied: "Because I figured you'll do less damage to Mansfield in the long run as mayor than you would as an educator."

Unfortunately, Morkel's legacy has been overshadowed by that of Coroner Thabet. In fact, one doctor took Thabet's willingness to endanger lives for money a step further and apparently *ended* a life for money.

On December 31, 1989, Dr. John F. Boyle Jr. allegedly killed his wife, Noreen, wrapped her body in a tarp and drove to a house he had just bought in Erie, Pennsylvania. There, Boyle put the body in a hole he dug in the basement after breaking through the concrete with a jackhammer he rented in Mansfield. Boyle then filled in the hole with fresh cement and covered it with cheap indoor-outdoor carpet. He told his two children that their mother had run off with another man.

But if Boyle thought he had committed the perfect crime, he soon found out otherwise. Once Noreen Boyle's disappearance became known, two important tips came in. One concerned the jackhammer he paid to rent with a check. The other came from the real estate agent who sold Boyle the house in Erie, who reported that Boyle had asked her if he would be able to raise the basement ceiling.

The concrete wasn't even completely dry when Noreen Boyle's body was located. Boyle's fate at his 1990 trial was greatly sealed by the testimony of his 12-year-old son Collier, who said he heard what sounded like a body being thrown against a wall and a scream coming from his parent's bedroom at 3:30 a.m. on the day Noreen Boyle disappeared. Prosecutor James Mayer contended that Boyle killed his wife because she planned to divorce him and he did not want her to get half his assets.

Boyle didn't go to prison to serve his 21½-years-to-life sentence quietly. He quickly launched a newsletter to advocate his innocence and asked me to look into his case. I saw too many holes in his claim and declined. Boyle was persuasive and persistent, however. He finally persuaded *The Akron Beacon Journal* to bolster his claim that the body found in the basement of his new home in Erie was not Noreen Boyle's. *The Beacon Journal* helped create enough doubt that the body was exhumed.

Tests confirmed that the body was, indeed, Noreen Boyle's. But Boyle wasn't about to give up. He had some of his supporters in Mansfield contact me, then wrote to me himself. Boyle complained that the Akron attorney who successfully represented him in his effort to get the body exhumed would no longer take his calls or respond to his letters.

As clever as he was, Boyle did not get away with murder. But another Mansfield doctor may have — at least as of this writing. A pulmonary physician was a prime suspect in the murder of Gatha Bowman since shortly after her disappearance on February 15, 1993.

Bowman's murder has been one of Mansfield's most perplexing mysteries, since the attractive 38-year-old owner of a medical-equipment supply company's body was found by a Delaware County engineer at the edge of a gravel pit near Alum Creek State Park north of Columbus a month after her disappearance.

On the day she disappeared, Gatha called best friend Mary Frazier and asked if Frazier would watch her two children until about 10 p.m. According to investigative records, Gatha told Frazier that she didn't want to take the children home to husband Gary, as she would have to if she used her regular baby sitter. Gatha told Frazier that she and Gary had been fighting a lot and she didn't want to be late for a 7 p.m. meeting with the doctor. In fact, employees later said Gatha and her husband had an argument that afternoon after Gary learned that their company, Primedica Health Care owed between $8,000 and $10,000 in withholding tax.

Gatha told Frazier she hoped to get enough business patients from the doctor, who ran a sleep lab, to put Primedica solidly in the black. Gatha said the doctor might take her to Columbus because he didn't want his employees to know about the meeting. Frazier told investigators that Gatha seemed nervous about the meeting and allegedly made the comment, "I hope I come back." A Primedica employee told investigators that Gatha also told him that she had an important meeting with the doctor that night.

Gary Bowman looked over the books until 6:40 p.m. He later told investigators that he then went to a shopping mall to have his eyeglasses fixed, which a receipt verified. Gary said he then ate at a Wendy's and called his parents from a pay phone. While on the phone, Gary said, he saw a co-worker and they waved to each other. The co-worker later verified this.

According to those present, Gatha left Primedica's office about five minutes after her husband that day. She told the employees she was going to a meeting — she did not say with whom — that she hoped would breathe new life into Primedica's business. One way or the other, the meeting may have cost Gatha her life instead. Gatha's minivan was found parked on the far south end of the parking lot of a motel she frequented two days after she disappeared. The Mansfield area had eight inches of snow starting at about midnight the night Gatha went to her ill-fated meeting.

The van was covered with snow, but there was none underneath it. That indicated the van was parked there before midnight. Inside, investigators found the clothing Gatha had worn to work, indicating that she had changed in the van.

When Gatha Bowman's body was discovered, its condition added to the mystery. Apparently to blend in with the snow, the body was painted white. It was also covered with trash that contained a receipt dated two days after Gatha's disappearance that was traced to an apartment complex not far from the doctor's residence.

When Gatha's body was found, it was lying face-down. She was wearing a skirt One of Gatha's friends told investigators that Gatha once told her that the doctor, with whom several of her friends said Gatha had an affair before she married Gary five years earlier, had previously asked her to wear a skirt to a meeting in a motel room. When her body was found, Gatha's purse, shoes and coat were missing. One front tooth was chipped half off. The cause of death was listed as strangulation.

While Gary Bowman's explanation for his whereabouts checked out, the doctor's were more suspect. Despite Gatha Bowman's claims to the contrary, the pulmonary physician insisted he was not scheduled to meet Gatha the night she apparently was killed. The physician said he and his wife spent the evening visiting friends, which they confirmed.

The doctor's message-service records indicated he had another doctor take his calls — supposedly because he wasn't feeling well — from 6:10 p.m. until 9:30 p.m., when he called to report in. But when a call came in at 9:48 p.m., the doctor did not answer. The operator then called his pager, which could pick up messages in a 25-mile radius. The doctor didn't respond to the page until 10:08 p.m. Several People's Hospital employees said that, on or about the day after Gatha Bowman disappeared, the doctor came to work unshaven and that he had what appeared to be a scratch on his face.

The legal eagles

Mansfield's legal community was and is pretty much cut of the same cloth as its medical community. It is very traditional, very money-oriented and generally apolitical. A relatively small percentage of the town's lawyers tend to get involved in politics beyond the positions where a law degree is required.

They would apparently prefer to leave local government in the hands of legal illiterates who have to turn to the lawyers to get them out of a bind — for a fee, of course. Fees, after all, are a big part of the reason many of Mansfield's lawyers are lawyers to begin with.

Many courts are run in assembly-line fashion for the benefit of the attorneys. Drunken-driving charges are often very expensive for the client, who paid several hundred dollars for a few minutes' work. For a little higher fee in the 1970s, some attorneys could promise to beat the rap for their clients whether they were guilty or not. Of course, part of the fee went to the judge. And if money didn't entice the judge, photos of his sexual encounter with a young woman at election victory party apparently worked for the select few lawyers who supposedly had them. The line between justice and injustice might he thinly drawn in almost all communities, but in Mansfield it was often nonexistent. Power, after all, knows no bounds.

Nor does it know any morals. Mansfield is a town with a definite double standard that goes far beyond the excesses of a few politicians. Ironically, most of the community's immoral leaders hide behind the guise of born-again Christianity because of the instant acceptance that can bring in a city that has more churches per capita than any other in Ohio. But while Mansfield's average citizens practice their faiths, their leaders do anything but.

Drinking, gambling and woman-chasing are all stock of their social trade. A visit to one of the elite's watering holes would leave little doubt about that, even if it is less blatant now than in the 1970s.

One of the city's richest individuals, president of a company with offices around the world, for example, could be seen at one popular restaurant at least once a week for several months with the city's highest-paid prostitute.

Gambling at these establishments or nearby was also commonplace. During the infamous recorded discussion with Safety Director Clayton Long, for example, it was mentioned that one of the town's top lawyers had won $1,000 at one establishment, which the police told Long was frequented by a judge as well.

When the situation became more heated, the power brokers moved their poker games to a vacant house near one of their favorite restaurants where they could play in peace.

In *The Best Suit in Town,* his generally saccharine memoir of his days on the Mansfield Police Department, former chief John P. Butler nonetheless says that in the 1950s and '60s, the late vice king Bun Drye was "the most influential man in the city and county." Butler wrote that Drye "owned a house of prostitution and gambling on East Sixth Street, which was exclusively for white folks, and the Vets Club on North Main Street for gambling and drinking for the colored. . . . Bun also had connections in the county. He ran a place call 'The Farm' outside of the city. It offered prostitution, gambling and liquor for white people."

Another common man who apparently wielded uncommon power in Mansfield was Tony (The Godfather) Mollica. Mollica's base of operations was a rundown Main Street bar and restaurant that was one of the establishments Safety Director Clayton Long was referring to in his tape-recorded orders for police officers to leave alone. When *News Journal* columnist George Constable told me that Mayor Porter frequently had lunch with Mollica in his restaurant, which did little daytime business, I had to see it to believe it.

Sure enough, Porter and Mollica were breaking bread together the day Constable and I went to lunch at the almost-empty joint. Equally interesting, Mollica was doing most of the talking and the normally motor-mouthed Porter was doing the listening.

Prostitution and gambling and other vices were just as prevalent among Mansfield's elite in the late 1970s as they were in the days when Bun Drye was king. The president of one of Mansfield's largest industries typified the hypocritical activities of many of his wealthy colleagues. A good, born-again Christian who has made a number of major contributions to churches in the area, the executive was also known to keep several mistresses handy for when his faith failed him, which was quite often.

One of those women was generally selected from those who worked at his factory. She was usually in her early 20s and ambitious. But other women were usually maintained for his evening excesses. They, too, were often quite young. The story of one such woman tells a lot about what can happen in these relationships. According to a statement the woman gave to the Mansfield Police in the fall of 1970, she met the executive when she was 20. She was introduced to his best friend, another prominent businessman, about one month later.

A few weeks after that, the woman said, she was invited to accompany them to Florida "for business and for pleasure." The relationship with both businessmen continued for about six months. Although she admitted to having sex with both men, she said only her involvement with the older of the two ever came close to being "of a romantic nature."

In June of that year, however, the one-time hairdresser fell in love with a much younger man and attempted to break off her relationship with her sugar daddy. Another reason for breaking off the affair, she said, was that, "I can't take the strains and hassles anymore. No matter what I did or whatever I said, I had to answer to him like he was my keeper."

But breaking off a relationship with someone used to getting his own way didn't prove easy. Several attempts were made to get her back.

The last attempt occurred when the businessman's friend called her to ask if she could come to a local restaurant to help get his friend, who was heavily intoxicated, home.

Although she didn't know it, the woman's new boyfriend followed them to the man's mansion, which was one of Mansfield's most distinctive. When the friend heard the boyfriend's car approaching, he took a .25-caliber derringer he had just loaded, went outside and apparently fired two warning shots at the boyfriend. That prompted the woman to call the police, which is how she ended up giving her revealing confidential statement.

When the responding officers arrived, the woman said, the friend told them that her boyfriend had shot at him even though he had earlier admitted to her that the only shots fired were his. Both of the older men, she noted, seemed to be "high" and one of them showed her some pills he had taken. She added that the one who fired the two shots seemed to have enjoyed it and that he had a love affair with guns in general. Included in his collections, she said, was a sawed-off shotgun. "I mean, it was really sawed off," she said. "Like 16 inches."

Pornography enters the picture

But that apparently wasn't the only thing that her former sugar daddy loved. Asked if he had an interest in pornographic materials, the young woman replied: "I have never seen any, I only know that they have . . . I've been offered, you know, if I ever want to see them, we'll have a party."

"What about any film that was made by the Mansfield Police Department?" the interrogating officer inquired.

"He has made reference to that, that he does have it and I told him that I was upset with the incidents, the way it was handled at the time. So he gave me his opinion and asked if I would like to see them"

"And by that, you mean the one that was taken at Central Park several years ago in regards to homosexual activity?" the investigator asked.

"Yes," that's correct" she replied

"Did be ever state to you directly that he has this film?"

"Yes, he made it clear that he can get a hold of it or that he has it."

The woman's lover wasn't alone in that, however. The film, which was used to break up a homosexual ring in Mansfield and was then marketed by the Mansfield-based Highway Safety Foundation as a training film for police vice-squad officers, reportedly has been known to be shown in some Mansfield's best mansions, where part of the entertainment reportedly was guessing who some of the poorly disguised participants were.

That may have been the first Highway Safety Foundation film to be used more for prurient rather than safety interests, but a number of sources claimed it wouldn't be the last.

And it wasn't a coincidence, as it turned out, that the young woman's sugar daddy apparently had access to the film on the restroom activities of homosexuals in Mansfield's Central Park, as well as other pornographic films. He was, after all, the brother of one of the Highway Safety Foundation's founders and part owner, along with him, of the company that processed the foundation's films.

7

Highway Robbery

A few days after I left *The News Journal,* I received a phone call from a well-connected news source. "A very important person would like to meet with you as soon as possible," the source said. "He says he's got some information you might be interested in."

That very important person turned out to be a politically powerful judge who somehow managed to inhabit the inner circle of Mansfield's power structure without losing his integrity.

"I've heard all kinds of reasons why you were forced out," the judge told me when we met at a restaurant that night. "The way I see it, only one of them makes sense: The sheriff's car-repair deal put you on thin ice, all right, but I suspect that they were more afraid that you might start digging into the Highway Safety Foundation."

"That's an interesting theory I hadn't really thought of," I said. "But you may be right. I started talking about investigating the Highway Safety Foundation after someone who called with information on the sheriff's department ended up telling me a lot more about the foundation. But why would they want to force me out over that?"

"Because of what went on there and how many big toes you would end up stepping on," the judge said. "The sheriff's department is small potatoes compared with the foundation."

"So how do you know so much?" I asked.

"Simple. I presided over the divorce of a woman I think you will find was in the thick of the whole mess. And enough came out in the divorce hearings to convince me this thing is big — and ugly."

That almost proved to be an understatement once I started pursuing some of the leads the judge gave me.

The origins of the Highway Safety Foundation are a little confusing. In his 1999 book *Mental Hygiene: Classroom Films, 1945-1970,* Ken Smith quotes business partner Earle Deems as saying that the foundation's founder, Richard Wayman, became interested in highway safety after a friend was killed in a car crash. In his memoir *The Best Suit in Town,* former Police Chief Butler says Wayman's interest started when the partner in the prestigious international Cleveland-based accounting firm Ernst & Ernst (later Ernst & Young), accompanied Mansfield Police Officer William Spognardi Sr. to the scene of an accident in 1954. As Spognardi photographed the accident scene with a "city furnished, Mickey Mouse camera," Wayman asked if he could do the same with his state-of-the-art color camera.

When the department expressed gratitude for his superior results, Wayman started snapping photos of accidents he encountered during his travels all around Ohio. According to *Hell's Highway,* Bret Wood's 2003 feature-length documentary on the foundation and its gory films, Wayman recruited Phyllis Vaughn to also take photos of crash sites. *The* (Cleveland) *Plain Dealer*'s Sunday magazine ran a cover story on Vaughn's newly found passion on May 27, 1956.

In 1958, photos taken by Vaughn and Wayman were assembled into a slide presentation that was shown at the Richland County Fair, to school groups and elsewhere. The reaction was so good that Wayman, who earned an estimated $300,000 to $400,000 a year, sent a free copy of the presentation to every state patrol post in Ohio.

"The police were impressed," Smith wrote in *Mental Hygiene.* "One of the patrol superintendents learned that Wayman also owned a 16 mm motion picture camera and reportedly asked, 'Did you ever think about making a movie?' Apparently Wayman hadn't, but the idea appealed to him."

Wayman recruited Vaughn's sister, Dottie Deems, and John Domer, a reporter for *The News Journal* whom Wayman had met at accident scenes, and bought a second movie camera for Domer to use. The film footage they took at accident scenes, along with some contributed by state troopers, resulted in a 1959 movie titled *Signal 30,* the Ohio State Highway Patrol's code for a death on a highway.

"You are there when stark tragedy strikes," Smith quoted from a brochure about the film. "It is an ugly film. It is meant to be. It is designed to drive home to those who see it that an accident is not pretty." Smith says the brochure also "playfully noted that the film was shot 'in living (and dying) color.' "

Charity for profit

Smith says that accounts vary on whether *Signal 30* was an instant hit. But what his book calls "the first highway safety gore film" did win a National Safety Council Award and the endorsement of the Ohio State Highway Patrol. *Signal 30's* success prompted Wayman and friends to start a for-profit production company called Safety Enterprises Inc. In 1960, Wayman launched the nonprofit Highway Safety Foundation. Among the trustees listed were Police Chief Frank Story of Cleveland, Scott B. Radcliff, superintendent of the Ohio Highway Patrol, and Wayman. Statutory agent was Bernard H. Little, an executive with the Ohio Brass Co. in Mansfield, where the foundation was located because Wayman had several major clients there and that is where Vaughn lived.

The foundation then sold the films throughout the country, which required additional prints. Part of that job was assigned to Allprints Photo, a company taken over with Wayman's financial coaching by one-time foundation president John D. Bolesky. Several individuals had thus built a structure that permitted them to control both the profit and non-profit aspects of producing films on highway safety. This apparent charity-for-profit scheme, known as self-dealing, was possibly illegal based on several civil-court precedents, a spokesman for the state attorney general's office told me. Nonetheless, the foundation's trustees and officers got away with it. It wouldn't be the only questionable activity some of them got away with, either. One of those activities allegedly was the making of pornographic films. The other, some suspected, was murder.

The Highway Safety Foundation, meanwhile, was becoming increasingly well-known. Its bloody films designed to shock the viewers into better driving habits that followed *Signal 30* included *Mechanized Death* and *Wheels of Tragedy,* in which actors from a Mansfield dinner theater reenacted the fatal mistakes of accident victims before the film switched to the gory aftermath, were shown in driver's education courses and at civic functions all over the country.

All told, the foundation said, some 40 million people had seen one of its films by the mid-1970s.

The films have had such a lasting impact that, 40 years after they were made, the satirical online newspaper *The Onion* ran a supposed news story on March 27, 2002 that began:

Driver's Ed Class Finally Gets To See Legendary Safety Film

NEW BEDFORD, MA — After months of eager anticipation, the second-period driver's-education class at Lincoln Memorial High School finally got to see the legendary highway safety film *Wheels Of Tragedy* Monday. . . .

Purchased by the school in 1973, *Wheels* combines grisly footage of actual car wrecks with dramatic reenactments of safety missteps committed by the victims in their final minutes. Driver's-Ed teacher Vernon Fait has shown the 22-minute, 16-mm film to every class since he began teaching the course in 1982.

Student reaction was positive.

"It was awesome," said Craig Martsch, 16. "There was one part where this woman turned around to yell at her kids in the back seat and—*wham*—she slammed right into an oncoming truck. It's not on the level of *Texas Chainsaw Massacre* or anything, but for something you see in school, it was pretty damn gory." . . .

Wheels Of Tragedy is just one of many short films produced in the '60s and '70s by the Highway Safety Foundation. Others include *Signal 30, Drive And Survive, Highways Of Agony, Mechanized Death* and *The Last Prom*. . . .

To discourage hysteria in the days leading up to the film's showing, Fait has had a longstanding policy of not revealing the exact date it will be shown.

Six months after *The Onion's* farcical article appeared, the Ohio Department of Public Safety released a tamer new version of the foundation's first film, *Signal 30*. A spokesman said *Signal 30: Part II* was needed because demand for the original version was outstripping the supply. "The combination of graphic content and shock approach to safety made *Signal 30* a mainstay for driver-education schools, safety groups, high schools and others, not only in Ohio, but nationwide, upon its release," said Lieutenant Governor Maureen O'Connor.

"To continue to reach young drivers aged 15 to 20, it was important to update the film to teach a new generation of drivers that bad choices can and do end with fatal results."

Unlike the shock-effect technique of the original, however, the new version of *Signal 30* blurred images that might disturb viewers and surrounded the footage with disclaimers. Ironically, the lack of graphic gore that made the original *Signal 30* and the Highway Safety Foundation famous apparently didn't seem to matter. Colonel Kenneth Morckel, superintendent of the Ohio State Highway Patrol, said focus-group research indicated that the tamer new film still got the safe-driving message across to teenagers, who are more likely to be in fatal crashes than others.

With cult-like success for Safety Enterprises' films like that in the offing, Wayman incorporated the Highway Safety Foundation Inc. in 1968. Like the older foundation, this was also listed as a charitable, non-profit corporation.

But while the Highway Safety Foundation was primarily engaged in film distribution, the Highway Safety Foundation Inc. employed research teams to develop data on the causes of highway accidents, conducted classes on driver's training and raised funds for the operation of both organizations.

Big names sign on

In his memoir, former Mansfield police chief Butler says Wayman "could sell iceboxes to Eskimos," which Butler probably could, too, judging from how he glosses over Mansfield's many scandals in his book and snows director Bret Wood in the documentary *Hell's Highway*. So Wayman didn't have trouble selling the Highway Safety Foundation Inc. The initial board of trustees reads like a Who's Who in Mansfield and Ohio. Among it members were Governor James A. Rhodes, John D. Bolesky, principal owner of Allprints and president of Therm-O-Disc Inc.; Colonel R.M. Charimonte, head of the Ohio State Highway Patrol; James C. Gorman, president of the Gorman-Rupp Co.; Avery C. Hand, president of First National Bank; his brother, Charles Hand; Charles Nail Sr., president of Lumbermens Insurance; and W.R. Tappan, chairman of Tappan Stove.

Many of these individuals reportedly were only peripherally involved in the foundation and may not even have known of its more unseemly activities.

The same certainly was the case when the foundation began to include people like Mario Andretti, Roy Campenella and R. Burt Gookin, president of H.J. Heinz. When Sammy Davis Jr. became national chairman in the early '70s, a big-name entertainment committee, including the likes of Lucille Ball, Joey Bishop, Carol Burnett, Jimmy Durante, Debbie Reynolds and others was also formed. (Davis' interest in the foundation originally came from the fact that he had lost an eye in an auto accident early in his career. But he, Wayman and some others involved in the foundation also apparently had one other thing in common — an appreciation of pornography. Davis even devoted a chapter to his favorite pornographic films in his 1980 book *Hollywood in a Suitcase.)*

The prestige of the foundation peaked on Memorial Day 1973, when Sammy Davis Jr. hosted a national telethon with Monte Hall featuring appearances by the likes of Muhammad Ali, Paul Anka, Joyce Brothers, Ray Charles, Dick Clark, Howard Cosell, Richie Havens, Danny Kaye, Jerry Lewis, Hal Linden, Rich Little, Minnie Pearl, Boots Randolph, Tex Ritter, Nipsy Russell, Sally Struthers, Ben Vereen and Lawrence Welk to raise $5 million for the organization. But the telethon lost a small fortune instead. That was the beginning of the foundation's end.

The roof caved in the following year. In July 1974, *The Cleveland Press* revealed in several front-page stories that:

• The foundation had somehow become $5 million in debt and had no funds with which to meet its liabilities.

• Wayman's firm, Ernst & Ernst, on the advice of counsel, had agreed to pay two outstanding loans of over $5 million to Cleveland Trust and First National City Bank of New York.

• Many of the pledges Wayman had submitted as collateral to obtain those loans had been forged.

• Wayman and his associates had been profiting through their involvement in the foundation by self-dealing with companies they owned.

• Wayman could not be located at his home in Cleveland. He was later reported to have surfaced in California as Sammy Davis Jr.'s business manager.

Despite the front-page exposure of the stories in Cleveland and the heavy involvement of many of Mansfield's most prominent citizens in the foundation, as wells as the Mansfield Police Department and several local politicians, *The News Journal* limited its coverage to one small story.

The article stressed that Ernst & Ernst was paying back the missing money and that the foundation's operation would continue under the leadership of Wayman's biggest apologist, former Mansfield Police Chief John Butler.

Had *The News Journal* dug a little deeper — and since John Domer had returned to the newspaper as an editor, it certainly had a resident expert — it could have unearthed a story with all the elements of a good murder mystery made even better because it was true. Here's how the story unfolded:

One week after *The Cleveland Press* revealed the questionable financial dealings of the foundation and its sudden $5 million debt, one assistant attorney general and two accountants were dispatched from the Ohio attorney general's charitable division to the HSF offices in Mansfield.

Irregularities uncovered

They soon learned that in late February 1974, the HSF's board was notified of a meeting to authorize and increase the foundation's indebtedness. One trustee, Richard Baker of Ernst & Ernst, reportedly took time to study the question. He didn't like what he saw. Baker then ordered an independent audit of the foundation's books by a rival accounting firm, Price Waterhouse, which uncovered a number of financial irregularities.

Accountants for Price Waterhouse and the attorney general's office were hampered, however, by a lack of vendor's invoices, documentation supporting a substantial number of disbursements, a lack of bank statements, inadequate personnel files supporting payrolls and a lack of inventory records.

This led them to the doorstep of Mansfield certified public accountant Benjamin Czajka, who supposedly audited the foundation's 1972 financial statement. Czajka admitted to the Accountancy Board of the Ohio that HSF financial statements attributed to him had been prepared by Wayman. Czajka collected $1,800 for putting his signature on Wayman's work. For doing so, Czajka was later expelled from the national and state CPA associations and had his license suspended for one year. The magnitude of the misrepresentation of the 1972 financial report was tremendous, as indicated by a 1974 Price Waterhouse statement. In that year, auditors were forced to write off or write down assets totaling $3.15 million.

The net worth of the foundation declined from a plus $750,000 to a minus $4.6 million. Assets declined $3.4 million to $195,000 and liabilities rose from $2.7 million to $4.9 million. From what little information could be obtained from the foundation's records, it was decided the attorney general's office would investigate the organization's telethon, golf tournaments, bank loans, payments to "consultants" and the foundation's forged pledges.

It was the HSF telethon broadcast from New York City on Memorial Day 1973 that brought the foundation its national fame as well as its eventual downfall. The telethon was a big event in Mansfield. Several local HSF employees, including Clayton Long, who was later to become the city's public safety director, appeared in films shown during the program. Several parties were held around town to celebrate Mansfield's brief moment in the sun. Out of civic pride, many Mansfielders pledged substantial sums of money to help make the telethon a success.

Their generosity, however, wasn't enough. Investigators determined that the cost of the telethon had been $1.2 million and the actual pledges received amounted to only $525,000, for a net loss of $675,000. When the trustees learned this, they quickly canceled a telethon planned for the following year. Former Mansfield Police Chief Butler, who had been recently appointed executive vice president of the organization, said it was decided the telethon was not "financially feasible" at that time.

Davis' ego leads to disaster

What was never revealed was that the 1973 telethon need not have been a failure if it had been properly managed. The investigators later pointed out in a confidential document I obtained from a news source that the major error made by the organizers was their failure to limit the telethon to television stations in the nation's major markets, which would have substantially reduced the $400,000 spent to rent TV stations.

"Those responsible for producing the telethon for the foundation were aware of such a problem but apparently that was of no concern to Sammy Davis Jr.," the investigators wrote. "As the entertainment chairman and master of ceremonies, he would not participate unless a sufficient number of stations were lined up. Therefore, although 20 stations made good economic sense, it was not satisfactory as far as Davis' exposure was concerned."

On Davis' insistence, the report added, the telethon was eventually scheduled for 52 stations.

Another major error was in not raising enough money before the telethon to ensure its success. It is a common practice to pre-raise pledges that are announced during the telethon. So when the host makes his "prediction" at the beginning of the show, it is a well-calculated estimate.

The third and most questionable area of mistakes made was in the expenditures permitted to the participants and staff in New York. While the major stars were not paid, all of their costs, which were sometimes substantial, were reimbursed. "No expense was spared, nor did anyone volunteer to refuse to accept reimbursement," the investigators commented in their report.

Sammy Davis Jr., for example, occupied a $350-a-day (in 1973 dollars) suite for four days. His manager stayed in a $130-a-day suite. All costs, including personal costs not related to the telethon, were charged to the foundation. A purchase made at the exclusive Cartier Jewelers, for example, was charged to the room of one of the performers.

Sammy Davis Jr.'s entourage, meanwhile, was well-paid, even if he supposedly was not. Among those rewarded were his manager, PR people, band leader, the band leader's wife and, in the words of the investigators, "an assorted number of hangers-on."

In his book's chapter on Wayman titled "The Most Unusual Man," Butler's only hint of the foundation scandal came when he said a problem arose because of the cost of the telethon. "Ritchie had made a mistake, and his company, Ernst and Ernst, would be required to pick up the slack as many pledges were not fulfilled," Butler wrote.

After the story about my Mansfield experience appeared in *Time* magazine, I was surprised to receive a complimentary letter from Steve Allen along with a copy of the latest of a long line of books from the prolific author, songwriter, *Tonight* show creator and unparalleled comedian. The book was called *Ripoff: The Corruption that Plagues America.*

I wrote back to Allen to thank him for his compliments and the book. Because of his interest in corruption, I enclosed my original articles on the Highway Safety Foundation. A short time later, I was surprised to receive a thick envelope from Allen. The cover letter said it was about time someone exposed the foundation. He went on to relate that he went along with his wife, Jayne Meadows, who appeared on the telethon.

As he stood backstage, Allen said, he began to dictate his observations into a tape recorder, which he was famous for carrying to try to preserve the thoughts of his incredibly active mind. The enclosed document was a summary of Allen's observations that day, and they weren't very flattering to the Mansfield-based foundation. Allen noted the presence of a number of apparent organized-crime figures and thuggish-looking hangers-on backstage. And although it was not shown on TV, Allen noted that Joe Colombo Jr., son of the recently assassinated mob leader, presented Davis a check for $10,000 before the theater audience. (Davis was one of the first people to arrive at the hospital after Joe Colombo Sr. was shot during a Columbus Day 1971 rally. "He's in our prayers," the shaken Davis said of his good friend the Godfather.) Allen said in his letter that when he returned to Hollywood, he told his friends that this is one charitable organization it would be wise not to attach their names to.

Golf tournaments fail, too

The state investigation found that the foundation's golf tournaments, unfortunately, weren't any better managed than the telethon. One tournament was a one-day celebrity fund-raising affair in 1972. Participants in the Candyman Golf Tournament were supposed to pay $1,000 to play, but many never did. The foundation also got stuck paying for the participants' travel, lodging and meals, as well as new golf shoes and accessories. The state audit found that the tournament lost $18,000. Butler nonetheless claims in his book that the tournament named after Davis' sugary hit song "was a very successful money-raising venture."

Wayman was apparently undaunted by the Candyman Tournament's loss. Shortly afterward, he signed up the foundation as co-sponsor of the Greater Hartford Open in 1973. Despite a great amount of work on the part of several foundation personnel, state investigators determined that the tournament netted only $2,000. A film made about the tournament cost the foundation another $100,000, an expense it apparently never recouped. But the disingenuous Butler claims in his book that, "Money would be made by all including the Highway Safety Foundation."

But the bad experience didn't dissuade Wayman. One of his first tasks when he left the foundation and joined Davis in California was to set up the Hartford tournament as one bearing the entertainer's name, which it did for several years.

Although the foundation was generous to a fault with participants at its benefits, it was even worse when it came to its consultants and employees. Take the case of Stanley Fields, who was in charge of the foundation's New York City office. Although Fields was supposed to be a full-time employee, he concurrently ran another business from the same office. Fields also charged his second business' long-distance calls to the foundation and had his own stationery printed with the HSF office address. For his dedication to the foundation, Fields was paid $50,000 a year for two years.

Stranger yet was the case of Arthur Konvitz, who was listed on the foundation's letterhead as national director. Wayman later admitted to state investigators that the "public relations consultant" was connected with the underworld, but he said he was too frightened to fire him. Konvitz, in the words of the investigators, was "an ardent advocate of nepotism." His secretary, whom he paid $800 a month to type on a typewriter purchased from his wife for $300, was none other than his daughter. But Konvitz sank to a new low when the foundation began falling apart and he attempted to spirit away $8,000 worth of the foundation's furniture.

Fortunately, the locks had been changed before he could pull off his caper. You would have thought $50,000 a year to do nothing would have been enough, but apparently not.

At least Konvitz didn't go as far as a consultant who was found to be on welfare at the same time. The consultant was Mary Stephens, a 24-year-old Cleveland woman hired to promote the foundation's goals among blacks. Although investigators were later to determine that Stephens "made no tangible or intangible contribution to the foundation," she was paid $20,000 a year for her efforts at the same time she was on welfare. She even had the audacity to use her welfare identification card to cash her hefty HSF paychecks. When Stephens' fraud was uncovered, she was indicted and convicted on charges of welfare fraud. She avoided going to jail, however, when her attorney produced a $4,000 check from Richard Wayman to pay her fine.

The mysterious Miss X

Of all Wayman's "consultants," a woman I agreed to identify only as "Miss X" in order to get details on her activities from family members was the most intriguing.

As the confidential attorney general's report on the foundation's activities put it: "Her rise through the foundation ranks could only be described as meteoric. According to Wayman, her talents were many. She at various times was reported to be a fund-raiser, secretary, taping specialist, bookkeeper, accountant, would-be grant writer and general Girl Friday. The attorney general's investigation revealed that she was worth no more than a minimum-wage secretary whose talents were confined more to the bedroom than anywhere else.

"Over a period of three years, the foundation paid her $182,000. It is interesting to note that the Internal Revenue Service found those payments to her were not made for the benefit of the foundation but for the personal advantage of Richard Wayman."

Wayman apparently first met Miss X in 1968, when she was working as a secretary for First National Bank president Avery Hand Jr. According to relatives and friends, when Miss X became pregnant despite the fact that her husband was sterile, Wayman arranged for her to have an abortion in New York, the only state to have legalized the procedure at that time. Shortly afterward, Wayman helped Miss X set up a secretarial service by arranging loans from Hand's First National Bank.

Wayman also got Miss X most of her first clients. The largest was the Highway Safety Foundation, which she billed $10 an hour. Another client was Safety Enterprises Inc., the profit-making firm owned by Wayman and several other Mansfield businessmen and foundation trustees that produced most of the films the foundation marketed.

Other clients for the Mansfield secretarial service included the Cleveland Growth Association, in which Wayman was active, and Automated Medical Services, which was owned by Wayman's friend Dr. Raymond Thabet.

In addition to starting the secretarial service, Miss X also began working as a fund-raiser for the foundation. This involved trips to places like Chicago, Las Vegas, Phoenix and California, where she would often rendezvous with Wayman on his plush Highway Safety Foundation bus, which was driven by Clayton Long and Jim Turner, later public safety director and police dispatcher in Mansfield, respectively.

Wayman reportedly used the bus to tour the country because of the discomfort his inner-ear caused him when he flew, although one former employee said the problem seemed to be more one of fear than the ear.

A major part of the attractive Miss X's job, and later that of the secretarial service employees, reportedly was to entertain potential contributors to the foundation. This service was at first highly informal, but it was later to become a regular part of the HSF fund-raising efforts, according to former employees and relatives of the participants. Miss X's "girls," sometimes recruited through a local personnel firm, were regularly bused or flown to fund-raising events all over the country. In addition to serving as the scene of such fund-raising parties, the HSF bus was also used, according to several sources, as a studio for filming pornographic films.

Until I fully disclosed the foundation's activities in 1978, two years after its final collapse, the HSF bus would still make regular visits to Mansfield. The Ohio license plate it bore was registered to Wayman at the address of Miss X's beautiful secluded home in Bellville south of Mansfield.

One of Miss X's girls apparently was a woman then known as Estelle Cunningham. I first learned about Cunningham from George C. Gilfillen, chairman of the E.F. MacDonald Co. in Dayton. In August 1979, Gilfillen contacted me after he heard about the series of articles I had written in *The Ohio Observer*.

Gilfillen said he had met the relatively young Cunningham while she was working for a small Atlanta-based aviation company he used to travel. During the few dates he had with her, Gilfillen said, Cunningham regaled him with stories about Wayman, who, she claimed, was almost like an uncle to her when she grew up in Mansfield. Gilfillen said Cunningham bragged about Wayman's connections with Sammy Davis Jr. and the Teamsters union, which Davis was hired by in the 1970s in an effort to improve its image.

Gilfillen said Cunningham bragged about delivering suitcases of cash to Teamsters President Frank Fitzsimmons in Detroit, how Wayman helped cover up the huge Central State Pensions fund scandal and, most important, how Wayman and Davis were involved in film pirating.

Miss X, meanwhile, became increasingly adept at raising funds, or at least pledges of funds, for the foundation. Her biggest accomplishment, she said in testimony during court hearings on her first husband's petition for divorce, was helping the foundation acquire a $300,000 grant from the U.S. Department of Transportation, for which Wayman paid her a commission of $15,000, a payment of dubious legality.

Former foundation employees told me the $300,000 was squandered rather than being used for its stated purpose.

Despite the receipt of a few generous grants and donations, the foundation's wild spending habits made it increasingly hard for the HSF to pay its bills. Wayman solved this problem, he hoped, by negotiating credit agreements with the Cleveland Trust Co. and the First National City Bank of New York. The total borrowed over a six-year period was $4.8 million. During the same period, on the other hand, only $800,000 came in from public contributions and $190,000 from film sales.

Investigators were intrigued by how Wayman managed to obtain these loans. According to Wayman, the loan from Cleveland Trust was not secured, but "collateralized" with corporate pledges to the foundation. The First National City Bank loan, on the other hand, was neither secured nor collateralized. It consisted of a series of demand notes guaranteed by the wealthy Wayman. Investigators later discovered that the foundation's $6 million in pledges used to collateralize the Cleveland Trust loan — with the exception of four amounting to $185,000 — were either false or uncollectible. Just who was responsible for this proved to be a mystery. Contained in the bank file were letters from a fund-raiser named John Haskell. But when the companies and a foundation whose pledges were listed were contacted, all said the same thing: They had never heard of John Haskell, nor had they made the pledges he attributed to them.

Investigators then attempted to find Haskell at the address on his letterhead, but it turned out to be a vacant lot in Chicago This led them back to Wayman, who told them Haskell was really a man named Jack Silverman, who, he said, may have been hired by Wayman's enemies to destroy his credibility.

Asked where Silverman was, Wayman said he had, ironically, been killed in an auto accident. The attorney general's office later spent a great deal of time, its final report said, trying to determine if the true author of the forged pledges was Wayman. But analysis by handwriting experts proved inconclusive because no original documents could be found.

Despite all the evidence of apparent fraud and reckless spending, including $800,000 in government grants and public contributions, little legal action was taken against the foundation's ringleaders. Wayman, Miss X, Long and Turner were all ordered to pay some back taxes, but that was the extent of any penalties.

Wayman and the others escaped responsibility for paying back the fraudulently borrowed money because Ernst & Ernst paid the two outstanding loans of almost $5 million in order to avoid embarrassment to the firm.

As for the attorney general's investigation, it concluded that Wayman's conduct and spending habits "certainly bordered on negligent." But no legal action was recommended because an amount at least equal to the $800,000 received from the public and government, over which the attorney general had jurisdiction, had been spent on highway safety endeavors. "As far as actions by other parties are concerned, it would be a private matter for which the attorney general has no concern," the report concluded as it washed its hands of the whole mess.

That attitude reportedly was not shared by many in the attorney general's office, however. The investigation of the Highway Safety Foundation was not something at least some people there were particularly proud of. They believed stronger action could and should have been taken and more loose ends should have been tied together.

But those involved in the foundation were not without power and influence. So Wayman became the scapegoat for the laxity and complicity of the foundation's board of trustees and employees, some of whom probably benefited from the chicanery as much as, if not more, than Wayman. "Although it can be said that the trustees of the foundation may have been lax in their duties by not paying closer attention to the activities of Richard Wayman, they neither participated in or were knowingly a party to any negligent conduct," the report concluded. "There is no doubt that there was only one person responsible for the rise and fall of the Highway Safety Foundation: that person is Richard D. Wayman. He misled and deceived those who came in contact was no indication that he benefited monetarily from funds the public contributed."

Wayman, of course, was long gone by the time the investigators leveled their criticism at him. Shortly after Price Waterhouse was asked to conduct its independent audit of the foundation, Wayman took $65,000 from the treasury he said was the repayment of a loan and headed to California to become Davis' business manager. Butler's book seems to portray Wayman as Davis' financial savior. "Sammy had no tax shelters and, if general, was making a lot of money but giving most of it to the government," Butler writes.

Actually, Davis, who had a history of spending money as fast as he made it, had a long history of *not* giving the government a lot of money. That apparently didn't change under Wayman's guidance. According to news reports and comments made to me by a movie producer who became friends with Davis' wife Altovise after his death, Davis died virtually penniless and owed millions of dollars in taxes.

Shortly after his burial, the Davis family was so desperate for money that Altovise reportedly had to have caretakers at Forest Lawn Cemetery dig Davis up so she could remove the estimated $70,000 in jewelry Davis had on when he was originally buried.

When Davis was nonetheless lionized in death as being someone quite different from the irresponsible self-destructive man he was in life, I decided to set the record straight in a column I wrote for the May 20, 1990, *Columbus Dispatch*.

"Poor Mark Anthony," I wrote. "His statement that "the evil that men do lives after them; the good is oft interred with their bones" has been turned on its head in celebrity-obsessed America.

"Consider the case of Sammy Davis Jr.

"When the superstar died last week, his obituaries were justifiably full of praise of his remarkable skills as an entertainer. But they were fairly skimpy in details on the self-destructive lifestyle that undoubtedly contributed to his death at age 64.

"And they were virtually free of facts on his fawning friendship with murderous mobsters, his unabashed love affair with pornography and those who make it, and his involvement in financial fiascoes."

Davis' association with organized-crime leaders, I wrote, was generally ignored by the news media. I noted how Davis along with mentor Frank Sinatra, performed free at Chicago gangster Sam Giancana's restaurant and raised money for mobster Joseph Colombo Sr.'s Italian-American Civil Rights League, which successfully pressured the FBI to stop using "anti-Italian" terms like Mafia.

I also noted how Davis' blindness to crime and corruption also showed in his involvement with the Highway Safety Foundation and his relationship with *Deep Throat* star Linda Lovelace, to whom he was introduced by the breakthrough porn film's mobster-connected producer and his claim that he "gave the premiere of *Deep Throat* in several countries."

That attitude was indicative of the decadent life of drugs, booze, sexual excesses, flirtations with Satanism and financial irresponsibility that Davis confessed to his 1990 best seller, *Why Me?* Davis also proclaimed his rehabilitation in the book, I wrote, but his two-fifths-a-day battle with the bottle and three-packs-a-day cigarette habit had taken their toll.

"Davis died a tragic figure greatly of his own making," I concluded. "But he was also the making of a star-struck society that not only permits but seemingly encourages such excesses among its celebrities.

Several days after the column appeared, I received a call at home from actor-dancer Gregory Hines, one of Davis' closest friends in his later years. "I just wanted you to know that the Sammy Davis I knew was a warm, wonderful human being and a tremendous talent," Hines said. "I don't deny that he made a lot of mistakes. But you have to keep in mind how tough it was for him, as a black, to rise to the top when he did."

I agreed — to a point. But it's also true that Hines' contention that past injustices excuse a person's later indiscretions is one we hear far too often these days. You name the offense and someone has an excuse for it. If society wasn't at fault, then something or someone else was.

Even federal drug czar William Bennett fell into the alibi trap a few days after Davis' death when he blamed Satan, whom he called "the Great Deceiver," for the national epidemic of drug abuse.

I'm sure there is evil in the drug world. But to blame the whole problem on Satan invites pleas of "The devil made me do it" from a people always quick to blame their problems and choices on everyone or everything but themselves.

Under this approach, no one is responsible for anything. And that is pretty much what happened with the Highway Safety Foundation. Even the scapegoat, Wayman, walked away unscathed.

Rumors persist

When the state attorney general's office issued its whitewash, the Highway Safety Foundation case was officially closed and, those involved hoped, forgotten. But it didn't work out that way. Too many had seen too much, particularly in Mansfield. Rumors continued to circulate about the foundation long after it was gone. Many of those rumors concerned the alleged interest some of those involved in the foundation seemed to have in pornography.

According to a former Mansfield post commander of the Ohio Highway Patrol and several employees of the foundation, the headquarters of both the foundation and Safety Enterprises in the lower level of the home of Phyllis Vaughn became a regular hangout for state troopers and Mansfield policemen. The apparent reason for the headquarters' popularity, the former post commander said, was the availability of pornographic films rather than highway safety films.

When the former commander learned that some of his men were also borrowing the films and showing them elsewhere, he said he ordered the HSF headquarters off-limits. According to several sources who attended parties at Vaughn's home, pornographic movies were viewed there by some of Mansfield's elite, a fact confirmed by the foundation's former statutory agent during a deposition in August 1979.

A Mansfield businessman was one of several sources to claim that some of these pornographic films were made at the headquarters as well as watched there. "One night back in about 1961, when I was still in high school, we were raising hate and discontent," he said. "There was a party at Phyllis' so we parked nearby at my friend's house and walked up to the windows and found that there was a pornographic film being made there. . . . The short time we were there, we saw two different couples engaged in sexual intercourse. . . . We couldn't see who was filming it with the way they had the lights positioned."

Pornographic films apparently continued to be made throughout the history of the foundation, judging from the comments of one woman, whose ex-husband, a respected Mansfield businessman, became involved in the foundation in 1970.

"First my husband started bringing the films home to show me, then he admitted he had filmed many of them himself," she said. "When he began encouraging me to participate in one of the films myself, I decided it was time for a divorce."

While most of these films were apparently made for local consumption, some might have been marketed in Cleveland or Detroit, sources said. How the making of pornographic films developed is unclear. Most of the dozens of sources interviewed on this aspect of the foundation's activities seemed to believe it started when Safety Enterprises made a film for the Mansfield Police Department on homosexual activity in the restrooms under Mansfield's Central Park in 1962.

The blunt Butler displays more than a little of his antiquated view of life in his book (he generally refers to African-Americans as "colored") when he expresses disdain for those caught in the act during the investigation. "If some of these people had as many pricks sticking out of them as they had stuck in them, they would be a porcupine," he wrote. "And we wonder how AIDS gets spread."

(The star-struck Butler apparently isn't aware that the man he almost deifies in his book, the "colored" Sammy Davis Jr., admitted to homosexual activity in his first autobiography, *Yes I Can*! He apparently also missed the scene in Linda Lovelace's *Ordeal* in which she relates how Davis had her teach him the "deep throat" technique she performed in her movie, after which Davis practiced it on her manager-husband.)

The film helped convict dozens of men on charges involving illicit sex. The foundation also released an edited version of the film called *Camera Surveillance* in 1964. Although the film was supposed to be used to train detectives on how to conduct such investigations and was to be released only to law-enforcement agencies, copies reportedly ended up in civilian hands and the film became an underground hit.

The surprising success of the public-restroom film inspired Safety Enterprises to produce a series of police-training and crime-prevention films in the mid-'60s. *The Shoplifter* (which could have starred former Coroner Wolford or the wife of a *News Journal* editor but didn't) was the first. It was followed, in quick succession by the graphic *Child Molester; A Great and Honorable Duty,* a tribute to police work; *Plant Pilferage* about inventory control; and *The Paperhangers* about check fraud.

According to several sources, the underground demand for the restroom film also inspired the production, by some foundation employees, of a series of pornographic films, in which they had a prior interest. The films were allegedly made at several locations, including the foundation's Leland Hotel headquarters in downtown Mansfield, the Highway Safety Foundation bus and Phyllis Vaughn's home, which also served as the headquarters of Safety Enterprises. Given the foundation's role in filmmaking, it was rather appropriate that Vaughn's attractive white house was located on fashionable Hollywood Lane. Most of the pornographic films apparently had limited circulation, but the market reportedly expanded later. In the early stages, at least, sources said the films were processed at Allprints.

If they were, the processing was in violation of the company's stated policy but apparently not of the practice of some of its employees, particularly on the night shift. Meanwhile, the more visible safety and police-training films continued to be made around the Mansfield area. Cameramen, including Clayton Long, often rode ambulances to the scene of accidents, where they filmed the aftermath in frequently gory detail.

The release in 1965 of *Carrier or Killer,* a film that featured graphic footage of fatal truck accidents, proved to be a real boon to the foundation when John Butler, a year before he became police chief, got an order for 50 prints from Teamsters union president Jimmy Hoffa. A year later, a *Time* magazine photo showed Hoffa testifying about road safety to a congressional committee while holding a print of *Carrier or Killer* in his hands. In 1967, the foundation got a large number of Mansfielders in the act by lying along State Route 13 as a camera mounted on a platform passed over them. The documentary *Hell's Highway* reports that the footage was initially taken for the film *Research for Safety* to dramatize the number of people killed in auto accidents, but that it ended up being used in the 1969 classic, *Highways of Agony.*

Byrd Ambulance benefits

Byrd Ambulance Service was, not surprisingly, a major beneficiary of the foundation's largess. Founded at approximately the same time as the foundation, several people involved with the Highway Safety Foundation were among Byrd's original backers.

It is no wonder, then, that the foundation reportedly paid handsomely for the privilege of riding to accident scenes in Byrd ambulances, just as it should be no surprise that Byrd always seemed to receive favorable treatment over its competitor, B&B Ambulance, which was started in 1964.

Shortly after Wayman joined Davis in California, they established a new version of the foundation. Called the Sammy Davis Jr. Foundation for Highway Safety Inc., records in the California secretary of state's office showed that it was suspended in 1977 for failure to comply with the franchise tax. Yet Miss X still claimed to be an employee of the foundation during a deposition in 1979.

The purpose and function of the new foundation were unclear. One Mansfield resident said he was brought out to California by Wayman to write a screenplay for a safety-related film, but nothing ever came of it.

Mysterious Miss X, meanwhile, was spending a lot of her time in 1979 making copies of just-released films, which she reportedly quickly sent back to California. The work could have been for a company Wayman started that was, Butler says in his book, among the first to put movies on videotape. But they also could have been used in the lucrative field of film-pirating, which George C. Gilfillen, chairman of the E.F. MacDonald Co., was told by a woman who apparently worked for Miss X that Wayman and Davis were involved in.

As for the foundation's continuing influence on Mansfield, a pornographic movie filmed by a man later named the town's "businessman of the year" demonstrated the permissive atmosphere it helped create. The film reportedly was quite popular at Mansfield stag parties because its "star" was a well-known mentally retarded man, which supposedly generated a lot of laughs. As if that wasn't bad enough, the man wasn't paid the $100 he had been promised for his performance, because, he was told, the film didn't come out. Shortly after I printed clips from the film to prove its existence, the expensive home of the man who made it was destroyed by fire later ruled to be caused by arson. Although the case was never solved, several knowledgeable sources reported it was possibly set after the businessman refused to turn over his extensive library of Mansfield-made pornographic films to certain individuals who feared I might obtain them. The fire, the sources said, was probably set to destroy the films and to teach their owner a lesson in Mansfield-style cooperation.

Enter Linda Lovelace

The foundation's apparently long-standing interrelationship with pornography, meanwhile, was confirmed by Linda Lovelace, star of the most popular pornographic film of all time, *Deep Throat*. In addition to relating how she was coerced into becoming a porn star through hypnotism, beatings and threats on her life, Lovelace also related in her highly praised book, *Ordeal,* how she was befriended by Sammy Davis Jr. at the time he was chairman of HSF. Lovelace was introduced to Davis by *Deep Throat* producer Lou Peraino, who later was sentenced to six years in prison on obscenity charges. Since I was in Miami at the time *Ordeal* was published, I wrote a story that verified many of Lovelace's accusations about the making of *Deep Throat*. Lovelace later referred to my findings in her second best seller, *Out of Bondage.*

In Ordeal, Lovelace recounts how she first met Davis on the eve of the Highway Safety Foundation's ill-fated national telethon in 1973, which she says Davis even asked her to appear on at the last minute. The fact that Lovelace would have, had it not been for the objections of the owners of the theater where the telethon was being held, is certainly a fitting commentary on the foundation's sordid history.

Equally disturbing, though, was the mysterious death of Phyllis Vaughn, whose Hollywood Lane home served as the organization's headquarters.

I was first made aware of the questions some had about her death when a reader called me in the midst of the sheriff's department *expose.* He told me he had some information about the sheriff and asked me to come to his home that night.

It turned out that the information on Weikel wasn't all that significant, but I listened attentively and took notes.

"Is that it?" I asked as I stood up to leave.

"Not really," the man said nervously. "I guess what I really wanted to talk about was the Highway Safety Foundation."

"I'm all ears," I said as I sat back down in my chair.

"Do you know about Phyllis Vaughn?" he asked.

"I know she played a key role in the foundation until she died in 1971, but that's all," I replied.

"That's what I want to talk to you about I think she may have been murdered."

"Murdered?" I asked incredulously.

"Murdered."

"Tell me why you think that."

"You see, Phyllis was like a second mother to me. We were really close, and I used to stop by her house just to visit. In the weeks before her death, she started acting kind of scared, you know? She also told me the foundation was doing a lot illegal things and stuff. Then, just before her death, she asked me to put a taping device on her phone because she was getting threatening phone calls. So I did. The next day, I was called in to Police Chief Butler's office. The next thing I know, Butler had me pinned to the wall and was asking me why I had put the tape on Phyllis' phone. When I told him it was because of threats she was receiving, he told me to take it off anyway.

"A few weeks later, I stopped by Phyllis' house to see if the calls had stopped. She came to the door crying and told me she feared for her life because she knew too much about what was really going on and had threatened to go public with it. She said the others would be at her house that night to discuss the problem, and she feared she may not be alive when it was over. The next day she was found dead. I just couldn't believe it."

One source I talked to, however, told me he had stopped by Vaughn's house after the meeting and that Vaughn was alive, but "stone drunk" when he was among the last to leave.

But my original source wondered, then, how Vaughn was supposed to have been found tucked neatly into her bed — a fact I confirmed with a witness — where Vaughn's housekeeper found her the next morning.

"When Phyllis was drunk, she usually didn't even make it to the bed," the source said. "And when she did, she would barely make it at all, let alone tuck herself neatly inside."

Several Mansfield police officers on duty that night told me they were also suspicious about Vaughn's death because of the steps higher-ups took to limit access to her home.

Medical murder?

As I pursued my investigation, I eventually received a call from a woman I had been trying to locate because she was supposed to have inside information on the foundation's activities.

"You know you're playing with fire, don't you?" she replied when I asked if we could meet.

"I know, but the truth has to come out for everybody's sake, I replied.

"OK, we can talk. But not in an office. I'll meet you near the pond at Kingwood tomorrow at noon."

Kingwood Center is one of Mansfield's proudest possessions, a nationally known horticulture exhibit on the grounds of one of the city's most beautiful mansions. It was a sunny, warm October day when I met my long-pursued source. I sat down on the bench and took in the beauty.

How could a city with so many beautiful places and wonderful people have such an ugly interior? I wondered. Then a woman approached and sat down beside me.

"Beautiful day," she said. "Are you sure you want to spoil it by talking about the Highway Safety Foundation?"

"I really hope we can," I replied.

"All right, you ask the questions and I'll try to answer them."

I started with some obvious ones, then moved to increasingly sensitive subjects. She confirmed much, but offered little.

Finally, I asked, "Was Phyllis Vaughn murdered?"

Silence. She took in the scenery for almost a minute before answering.

"I don't know," she finally replied. "All I can tell you is that I was told by someone in a position to know that Phyllis died after a doctor who's now dead injected her with something that wouldn't turn up in an autopsy. Apparently Phyllis was insanely jealous of Wayman's new mistress and was talking too much and threatening too much for her own good."

So how *did* Phyllis Vaughn die?

The cause of her death was reported to be a heart attack, and her best friend insisted the report probably was right, because Vaughn had a history of heart problems. Vaughn's death certificate, though, listed the cause of death as uremia caused by kidney failure. On the other hand, an attempt to kill a troublesome woman by injection was a story I had heard before. Dr. Raymond Thabet's former wife, Catherine, once told me that, at a time she was being equally vocal about certain things going on in Mansfield she didn't like, she had been injected by surprise at a party of Mansfield's elite at her home and that she didn't awaken until late the next day Mrs. Thabet said her husband insisted she had passed out after having too much to drink, but she said she had almost nothing to drink.

Later, she said, she found a needle in a wastebasket and had it tested by a doctor she trusted. She said the residue proved to be an untraceable substance that can be fatal in the right dose. Hers, fortunately, was not. Phyllis Vaughn may not have been so lucky.

When the first edition of this book was released in 1994, I hand-delivered a copy to Pete O'Grady, a well-connected lobbyist who headed the Ohio Department of Public Safety during the foundation's early years.

"I see you have a chapter on the Highway Safety Foundation," the affable O'Grady said as he leafed through the book.

"Does it mention anything about its executive director supposedly being killed by an injection?"

"If you mean Phyllis Vaughn, yes," I replied.

"No, I'm talking about a man named Sachs who had the job before she did," O'Grady said, to my surprise. "There were a lot of rumors in Columbus at the time that Sachs was killed. He was only in his 40s, but supposedly died in his sleep."

Wayman lived a lot longer than that. He was almost 74 when he died of a heart attack in California in 1983.

8

Prison City

The Richland Shield called it "Mansfield's Greatest Day" when the cornerstone for the Ohio State Reformatory was laid November 4, 1886. Some would dispute that, given the prison's checkered history. But it certainly has brought the city its share of fame. The prison's six-tier-high East Cell Block was listed in the *Guinness Book of World Records* as the world's largest free-standing steel cell block. Parts of four major movies — *Harry and Walter Go to New York, Tango and Cash, The Shawshank Redemption* and *Air Force One* were filmed there and brought in stars like James Caan, Elliot Gould, Diane Keaton, Michael Caine (*Harry and Walter*), Sylvester Stallone, Kurt Russell, (*Tango and Cash*) Tim Robbins and Morgan Freeman (*Shawshank*).

Before its early and recent glory days, though, the Ohio State Reformatory had its share of inglorious ones as the prison gained a reputation as a violent, dehumanizing place to be incarcerated or to work. In 1978, the Counsel for Human Dignity decided to do something about it. The coalition of civic and church groups filed a federal lawsuit that claimed that OSR's 2,200 inmates' constitutional rights were being violated by being forced to live in "brutalizing and inhumane conditions."

In February 1979, I reported that OSR's abysmal living and working conditions was causing rising violence. Past and present employees and independent observers revealed that overcrowding and poor-quality food and medical care for OSR's 2,500 inmates, combined with high employee turnover, corruption and favoritism in the administration of Warden Frank Gray had turned the state's largest prison into a potential powder keg.

Critics said Gray's attitude toward his employees was exemplified in a letter to an OSR teacher in which he said he was suspending him because it was "the ultimate penalty at my command, since drawing and quartering is no longer in vogue."

Gray wasn't nearly as tough on himself or his cronies. One example was Gray's ordering that a masonry class was shut down and the students were taken to Gray's state-owned house to build a fireplace. Gray reportedly had a mechanics' class canceled so employees could fix his personal truck. Employees said Gray also regularly had his personal autos fixed by state employees while on state time and at no charge.

Employees also contended that the warden, an alleged devotee of antique furniture, had taken an antique clock and carved hall furniture from OSR to his home, a charge Gray emphatically denied.

Employees claimed that Gray had an equally cavalier attitude toward anything involving his circle of friends inside the prison walls and beyond. One example of favoritism inside the prison was an employee who reportedly got caught stealing food from the prison kitchen. The employees said Gray had the accused person's uncle investigate the allegation, and he was cleared. An example of favoritism to those outside the prison walls employees occurred when a confidante of Gray's ordered the prison recreation department lend state equipment to the corrupt Richland County Sheriff's Department. Former recreation director Larry S. Pauley claimed that, when he tried to get the equipment back, Gray's confidante told him to forget it because the sheriff's department did them "a lot of favors."

But if you were not on Gray's limited list of friends, watch out. A minister who also worked at the prison, for example, was suspended for 30 days essentially for failing to be two places at once. A judge apparently thought that such a miracle would be hard to perform, even for a minister, and reversed the suspension with back pay.

The tension that Gray fostered among employees and inmates alike seemed to come to a head with the beating of inmate Samuel Moore Jr. on March 30, 1979, by several guards and an assistant superintendent. After spending 10 days in OSR's hospital, Moore was transported to a prison hospital more than 100 miles away in Lima. Officials there said Moore was dead when he arrived. Two autopsies determined that Moore died when blood clots possibly caused by some of the numerous injuries on his body traveled to his lungs.

Seven guards and the assistant superintendent later pleaded no contest to misdemeanor assault and violation-of-civil-rights charges. Each was sentenced to five days in jail and ordered to pay a $500 fine.

Moore's death gave renewed impetus to the lawsuit filed over conditions at OSR. It finally was settled in 1983, when state officials agreed to improve conditions while preparing to close the cell blocks by December 31, 1986. The closing date was extended by the court because of delays in the construction of the Mansfield Correctional Institution. The prison was officially closed in December of 1990 because of a court ruling OSR no longer met current federal prison codes.

New prison quite a contrast

When the Mansfield Correctional Institution opened, it created almost as much enthusiasm as the groundbreaking for OSR more than a century before. State officials estimated that 20,000 people took a self-guided tour on September 21, 1990, through what was then Ohio's newest, most secure and technically advanced prison. The $70 million prison had "the thickest walls, the heaviest doors, the most sophisticated electronic system available," its first warden bragged. The prison was designed with eight units that each contained a pair of two-story "pods," each containing 60 cells. Corrections officials said that violence would be reduced by keeping prisoners in smaller groups rather than in the world's largest free-standing steel cellblock at OSR. Its single-cell capacity was 1,200, about half the number incarcerated at OSR during its peak.

But ManCI soon proved to be plagued with the same kinds of problems as its predecessor. The prison's design to reduce violence proved to be only moderately successful. That became painfully obvious in June 1992, when inmate Roy Slider attacked correctional officer Thomas Davis Jr. with a padlock and stabbed him with a piece of sharpened steel.

The 47-year-old Vietnam veteran later died of misadministered megadoses of steroids at Mansfield General Hospital. The first rationale for the attack to surface for the unprovoked attack on the popular Davis was that Slider was a member of the Aryan Nation, a white supremacist gang. Davis was black.

But Slider gave a different explanation during his trial on attempted murder charges in August 1993. Slider blamed Davis for plans to move him out of the honor cellblock, where inmates have more privileges.

"I felt Davis singled me out," Slider testified. "I decided if I was leaving the pod, so was Davis." Slider also testified that he didn't want to kill Davis, just permanently put him in a wheelchair "so he could think about me the rest of his life."

Several of Slider's fellow White Aryans backed Slider's claim that Davis picked on him. But their testimony was suspect. One of those who testified for Slider told me earlier that he might be asked to do something to help Slider that he didn't want to do, but he would have no choice. "If you're told to do something and you don't, you're fair game and you never know what will happen to you," the inmate said.

Slider's strategy worked. The Richland County jury that heard the case found Slider guilty of felonious assault rather than attempted murder, which is what he was charged with. Judge James Henson gave him a maximum sentence of 12 to 15 years on top of the 18 to 65 years he was already serving for the stabbing death of a Columbus car salesman.

But a credible ManCI source gave me a different explanation for why Slider attacked Davis in 1995. "Tommy suspected that another White Aryan was having an affair with the unit manager and reported his suspicions just before he was killed," the source said. "He told me and several others about it and said something had to be done. He said the inmate was in the unit manager's office all the time when he shouldn't be and was even answering the phone for her. When the inmate found out Davis had turned him in, he put out a hit on him out of revenge. Slider was the man who got the job. After the attack, they found all kinds of love letters and cards in the unit manager's desk. They also found [disciplinary] write-ups on Slider that she had intercepted and several shanks hidden under her copy machine. But the whole thing was swept under the rug because it would have implicated management in Tommy's death for not taking action when he reported the problem. I had pretty much the same thing happen to me when I reported that an employee might be involved with an inmate. Instead of launching an investigation, management simply told the employee of my report and warned her to stop whatever was going on. A few days later, the inmate came at me shouting about turning them in. Fortunately, that's all he did."

One of Davis' closest friends confirmed Davis' concerns about the unit manager's alleged relationship with the inmate. "I went with him when he reported it," the correction officer said.

"We were told something would be done about it, but nothing was. The whole damn thing was covered up after Tommy was killed. I don't know if that caused a hit to be put out on Tommy, but it certainly wouldn't have improved the White Aryans' attitude toward him if they found out he had turned one of them in. And it doesn't take much of an excuse for those people to strike back. That's what makes them so dangerous."

Ironically, the inmate suspected of ordering the hit testified at Slider's trial about Slider's alleged beef with Davis. He was later released. When an article I wrote appeared in *The Ohio Observer*, which I revived as a statewide magazine in 1994, it created a stir. Warden Carl Anderson said he ordered Correction Officer Luther Spencer to remove a copy of the article from a display in the prison's lobby in Davis' honor because it was considered inappropriate. Anderson said a female employee took offense to the article being included in the memorial. Spencer was prevented from holding a news conference at the prison at which he planned to criticize Anderson's decision. The U.S. Constitution's guarantee of freedom of the press and free speech apparently didn't apply to ManCI.

The controversy occurred amid an investigation of corruption at the prison that resulted in the conviction of eight people, including William Mack, the prison's former deputy warden for security. Mack was found guilty in U.S. District Court on two counts of mail fraud and one count of wire fraud for accepting an airline ticket and signing business agreements with inmate and con-artist *extraordinaire* James D. Crow III, the key figure in the case. Crow and six others pleaded guilty to charges involving fraud, bribery and the smuggling of drugs into the prison by placing them inside soup cans. The investigation also led to the demotion of ManCI warden Dennis Baker. Reginald A. Wilkinson, director of the Department of Rehabilitation and Correction said Baker "mismanaged the affairs" of the prison and "failed to supervise senior staff."

One of the six to plead guilty in the scandal was William N. Spognardi Jr., who previously had pleaded guilty and was sentenced to six months in prison in 1979 for his involvement in the scandal in the Richland County Sheriff's Department. Spognardi, whose private investigation business was once glowingly featured on the front page of *The News Journal* in a story that failed to mention his conviction and prison sentence, was indicted by a federal grand jury on charges of bank fraud and making false statements on a mortgage application.

The grand jury said Spognardi provided Richland Trust Co. with fraudulent documents in order to obtain a $101,200 loan for Crow's trucking company that was used instead to buy four Mansfield houses from Spognardi. Spognardi's plea bargain saved him from serving up to 60 years in prison and a $2 million fine if he had been convicted after a trial.

During Mack's trial, officials revealed that then-state Rep. Frank Sawyer, a Richland County Democrat, was at one time a target of the investigation but he was not indicted. Sawyer was on the board of Second Chances, an organization formed by Crow to provide low-cost housing for the families of Mansfield inmates. Sawyer, who had historically been more sensitive to inmates' sometimes sincere claims of being the victims of injustice or mistreatment than most other state legislators, was an easy mark for a master swindler like Crow, who used an aptly named cell phone to run his businesses from the prison.

Sawyer became implicated when Crow had a package that contained drugs and a gun hand delivered to Sawyer's residence to prove his boast that he could get anything, including guns and drugs, out of the prison. At the time, Crow, who was serving an eight-year sentence for passing bad checks and insurance fraud, gained the support of Sawyer and many others in his bid for clemency, which was denied. "I should have listened to my wife. She told me, 'He's bad news, stay away from him,'" Sawyer told *The Columbus Dispatch*.

Crow was called "a dangerous man" by federal prosecutors, was sentenced by U.S. District Judge Kathleen O'Malley in January 1997 to 87 months for the fraudulent schemes he started while he was a ManCI. Crow pleaded guilty the previous July to racketeering and firearms charges by using his company, J.D. Crow Inc., as a front.

Raymond Hulser of the U.S. Justice Department's Public Integrity Section told Judge O'Malley how Crow used his charm and the phone to purchase houses and run a trucking company. Hulser said the U.S. Justice Department has taped phone conversations that show that Crow is a "very good con man. I shudder to think of this man's ability to manipulate others," Hulser said.

On the same day that she sentenced Crow, Judge O'Malley also sentenced Valerie Hamilton, Crow's former girlfriend, to 10 months of electronic home arrest and two years of supervised probation.

Hamilton had previously pleaded guilty to charges of possessing drugs, wire fraud and possession of a firearm with the serial number obliterated. Hamilton told how, at Crow's direction, she obtained the gun and delivered it in a package to Sawyer's home. Hamilton's attorney, Edward Marek, told O'Malley that Hamilton had never been in trouble before she met Crow. "Her life was intact until she read an ad in the personal columns of the Mansfield *News Journal*," Marek said. Tragically, Hamilton's life ended in suicide a short time later. She was only 29.

Death row riot

The year 1997 was eventful for ManCI inside its walls as well as in court. On September 5, a riot occurred in a section of death row, which was moved to ManCI from the Southern Ohio Correctional Facility in Lucasville in 1995. The incident began when inmates overpowered three correctional officers, seized their keys and freed other condemned inmates. Five hours later, a tactical squad fired tear gas into the unit and regained control. Three guards and four inmates were reported to have been injured.

Officials later said that inmates convicted for involvement in the deadly 1993 Lucasville prison riot were among those involved. The day after the riot, officials indicated that the target of the inmate's wrath was Wilford Berry, who had volunteered to become the first inmate executed in the state since 1963. They said that Berry suffered severe injuries at the hands of his fellow inmates during the riot. But Sonny Williams of the Ohio Prisoners Rights Union told the *Youngstown Vindicator* that administrators had ignored warnings for months that there could be problems on death row. He said inmates were not provided proper medical care and that some had been arbitrarily denied privileges, such as access to televisions and radios, that were granted to others.

It later was reported that all injuries to guards had been minor, but that several inmates were seriously hurt. George Skatzes, an alleged ringleader of the Lucasville riot whose death-penalty case I was appointed to investigate for the defense at Skatzes' request, said that he saw no inmate-on-inmate violence and nothing that could be used as a weapon other than one unlocked body chain. "All they [corrections officers] had to do was come in," Skatzes said. What Skatzes claimed happened next sounds like a scene out of Sheriff Weikel's Richland County Jail.

At about 10 p.m., Skatzes said, he looked through the window of his cell into the corridor and saw men in gas masks. Then a canister came through the cell window and hit Skatzes, causing minor cuts on his arms. Skatzes said that at least five canisters were shot into his cell. As his cell filled with tear gas, he said, he hit the floor and thought he was going to die. When the tear gas dissipated about 15 minutes later, Skatzes said he stood up and tried to get some air through the hole in his cell window and got a dose of Mace instead. An hour later, Skatzes said, two masked guards told him to stand and put his face to the wall. He said a guard went into Jason Robb's cell next to his and told Robb to strip to his underwear. Skatzes said Robb was then beaten without provocation.

The Marion native said at least three officers stormed in and began beating him. He said he rolled into a ball to protect himself, but the officers forced him to straighten out, face down. He said they then bent back his wrist and fingers trying to break the bones and one hit him in the head several times, causing cuts on his jaw and above his eye. Skatzes said that after the officers handcuffed him behind his back, one of them jumped on his groin. He said the officers then picked him up by the handcuffs and half walked, half dragged him out of the cell. He said an officer then grabbed him by the hair and banged his head against the wall. He said he was hit in the head several more times before they put him into a cell with three other inmates. As two officers walked Skatzes to a nearby warehouse, he said one complained that, "This man is saturated with that shit." He said the other officer then told him that he was "a good man." When the officers cut the plastic handcuffs off to put an orange jump suit on him and then re-cuffed him, Skatzes said, one noted how swollen his hands were.

The inmates from the DR-4 section in which the riot occurred were forced to lie on the warehouse floor for about three hours. A nurse treated the most seriously injured inmates, but no one was permitted to wash off the tear gas and Mace on them, nor would they be able to shower for five days. Skatzes and 10 other death row denizens were later transferred to the super-maximum Ohio State Penitentiary at Youngstown for disciplinary reasons.

Mansfield became an even bigger part of the "prison-industrial complex" in 1998, when the medium-security Richland Correctional Institution opened on 78 acres not far from ManCI.

In 2003, RCI had more than 2,000 inmates, 431 employees and a $34 million budget. ManCI also had more than 2,000 inmates, almost 700 employees and a $55 million annual budget. Prisons were big business to Mansfield, proving that crime sometimes *does* pay.

Despite the 1997 disturbance, Ohio's death row continued to be a growth industry. In 2001, the state announced it was expanding to make room for increasing numbers of condemned inmates. ManCI Warden Margaret Bagley said the institution was gaining three to five new death row inmates a year, even after Wilford Berry's execution in February 1999 ushered in a new era of executions. Bagley said 39 new death row beds would be available by midsummer and that cells for another 39 inmates would be made available in the near future.

Death row seems to bring the worst out in people, and Warden Bagley was no exception. The events of February 17, 2002, are a good example. Early that evening, Columbus attorney Cliff Arnebeck, the Rev. Gary Witte and Bob Fitrakis arrived at ManCI's entrance. Arnebeck, who was making a novel attempt to stop the scheduled execution of John W. Byrd on February 19, asked to see Bagley so he could serve her with a subpoena and to request permission to take a dying declaration from Byrd. Arnebeck sought the statement from Byrd for a wrongful-death lawsuit he planned to file after Byrd's execution that would be based greatly on evidence of Byrd's possible innocence that Fitrakis and I developed for an award-winning series of articles in *Columbus Alive*.

Captain Elmer Hale informed Arnebeck that Bagley's whereabouts were unknown and that Arnebeck could not see Byrd. According to affidavits signed by several corrections officers who saw Hale turn Arnebeck, Witte and Fitrakis away, Bagley came out of a closet-sized office in the entrance building after the trio left and thanked Hale for following her orders so well. Dishonestly ducking a subpoena and denying access to an attorney representing a soon-to-be executed inmate fit with the overall arrogance Bagley displayed in my dealings with her as well as the way she was alleged to treat ManCI's employees and prisoners.

OSR's new lease on life

With two nondescript, teeming modern prisons on either side of it, the deserted, century-old Ohio State Reformatory looks positively quaint, which explains why it has become a significant Ohio tourist attraction.

The Mansfield Reformatory Preservation Society, which owns the 175,000-square-foot prison, says it is the largest castle-like structure in Ohio and one of the five largest in the United States.

In 2001, the society kicked off a $1.5 million fund-raising drive to finance the restoration of the former prison, which was placed on the National Register of Historic Places in 1987. Board president Dan Seckel, an architect whose firm provides in-kind support, said the first restoration phase would include the guard room, where *The Shawshank Redemption* dining-hall scenes were shot, and the warden's quarters. He said additional restoration would be done later with a $2 million national fund-raising effort.

Shawshank, in particular, spurred new interest in the reformatory as a visual setting for entertainers. The rap group M.A.D. filmed a video there that urged young people to stay out of prison. The prison even made Broadway in a video featuring an *avant-garde* Dayton dance troupe. And *Details* magazine featured a Mansfield Reformatory fashion layout of grotesque shock rocker Marilyn Manson. The Canton native's bizarre appearance probably would have fit right in with the reformatory's popular ghost and haunted-prison tours — if he didn't scare the ghosts away.

9

The End of a Beginning

When people kept warning me that I was playing with fire by writing about the Highway Safety Foundation, they probably had no idea how accurate they would prove to be.

On December 1, 1979, *The Ohio Observer's* circulation building was burned down, and with it went most of our back issues, several new desks and chairs and all of our circulation route mailboxes. Two trucks parked nearby were also damaged.

The fire didn't come as a complete surprise, however. I had been tipped off a few days before that our building was under surveillance by an individual who worked for a former trustee of the Highway Safety Foundation. We had instituted several precautions because of that, but they proved for naught.

Needless to say, Clayton Long's fire department proved less than enthusiastic about solving the crime. Even though I gave the department's arson investigator the name of the individual who had reportedly been watching our building and later told him that the man's mother had called to tell me that her son was responsible for the fire, the investigator never got around to interrogating him before he skipped town several weeks later. But the investigator *did* manage to have the time to question several *Observer* employees about my personal life, including whether I had affairs with any women, under the pretense of the investigation. Just routine questions, he told me. I later learned the investigator had also been caught investigating the personal lives of firefighters active in their local union. So perhaps those questions were routine by his standards.

The night of the arson had been bleak even before I got the call informing me the building was on fire. I had been forced the week before to announce that *The Observer* was switching from a daily to a weekly so it could survive. The difficult decision only quickened rumors of the paper's imminent demise. It *did* seem hopeless, I thought, as I fell asleep.

Scare backfires

The next thing I knew, the phone was ringing. It was Eileen Switzer, a longtime supporter and strong foe of Sheriff Weikel. She had been up late listening to the police scanner when she heard the call from a police officer asking that the fire department dispatch a truck to *The Observer* building because it had just burst into flames.

My heart sank. That's it, I thought. At least it's going out in style. I was so numb from lack of sleep that, for a moment, I even thought it was perhaps better that way. I changed my mind, though, when I arrived at the scene. It was not the main building after all, just the circulation building. And that made me and the rest of the staff more determined than ever to continue the fight.

No one really said it, but almost everyone who remained seemed to have suddenly realized that something bigger than Mansfield was at stake. Freedom of the press was, too. If *The Observer* was going to die, it would be from exhaustion and not fear.

"Our job of bringing the truth to this community has not been easy," I wrote in the next issue's editorial. "The long hours, the payless paydays, the physical threats have definitely taken their toll.

"Nonetheless, those who remain are now more determined than ever to stick this out and overcome our difficulties. We believe that our own personal problems are not the issue here. Of far greater importance are the principles of freedom of speech. . . . That is why we go on. And our opponents should understand once and for all that we do not intend to be defeated. So if our opponents want to continue their senseless tactics, they should realize that they will only strengthen our resolve to continue to tell the truth at all costs."

Those costs had already been very high, and they would get higher. *The Observer* was the target of dirty tricks from the first day it hit the streets. The first problems were with circulation. No distribution system is perfect, and ours was far from it.

But it wasn't nearly as bad as the number of circulation complaints would indicate.

Many papers, we quickly discovered, were disappearing as rapidly as they were being distributed. Others were being ripped into shreds and stuffed back in their roadside tubes by sheriff's deputies in their cruisers. Bundles left in front of unopened stores each morning were being stolen, as were copies left in our vending boxes.

In another case, the bundles delivered to a large apartment building kept ending up in the dumpster. Each day it was something different — and usually worse.

Just as we seemed to be getting circulation under control, our opponents turned their attention to advertising. *The News Journal,* to be sure, applied pressure wherever it could.

Some advertisers said its salesmen were even telling them that if they advertised with *The Observer* they would never advertise with *The News Journal* again. It was over just that kind of tactic that WMAN, the first local radio station, sued *The News Journal* many years before and finally prevailed in an important ruling by the U.S. Supreme Court that such threats were illegal.

But our worst problems came from elsewhere, including Donovan Pore, whose wife worked for Judge Richard Christiansen, against whom we filed suit for threatening advertisers with a boycott and other actions if they didn't stop supporting "that scandal sheet."

As if that wasn't bad enough, some advertisers were threatened with physical violence and even death by anonymous callers if they didn't pull their ads from *The Observer.* Finally, one of our best advertisers had a fire set outside his business a few days after our building was burned down.

Slowly but surely, the tactics worked. Since most of our advertisers were small to begin with, they were susceptible to scare tactics. They simply couldn't risk their business just to support *The Observer.* Some who stopped advertising bought stock instead.

Then came the social and political pressure on supporters and potential supporters. Many were warned not to throw their money away on *The Observer.*

So investments that we had been pledged never materialized or became a smaller amount. That created problems meeting payroll, causing the first signs of inner turmoil.

The long-threatened libel actions soon followed suit. Coroner Thabet had already demonstrated the ludicrous litigation response of Mansfield's powers-that-be against anyone who revealed their corrupt habits a few months before. He sued *The Akron Beacon Journal,* which had published my story on his illegal and life-threatening activities, and *The News Journal,* which "revealed" the same accusations the following day, for a total of $27 million. The only difference between that suit and the ones against *The Observer* was the size of the defendant. Thabet soon realized the foolishness of his taking on two powerful newspapers and dropped his suit as soon as his original anger had diminished. *The Observer,* on the other hand, was an easy target. Since it was barely surviving as it was, the lawsuits were hoped to be the final blow, which in the long run they were, at least in part.

The first to file suit was Prosecutor McKee, who had been talking about doing so since the week I left *The News Journal.* Since McKee's suit was so weak, he tried to cover that up with sharp language about my "well known" reputation for "malice and inaccurate journalism," as well as the shocking amount he sought in damages: $25 million. My alleged offenses against McKee included a charge that his office — McKee was not even mentioned in the story — had helped frame a potential election opponent of Sheriff Weikel. Despite McKee's claim to the contrary, this accusation was far from fiction. It was based on several interviews and a proffered statement in court by the person who entrapped Weikel's opponent that McKee's office coached him exactly on how to do it.

The other statements that McKee claimed were libelous were all backed by affidavits of witnesses, court and other official records that demonstrated my reasonable belief in their accuracy. And court decisions have held that such articles about public officials that can be backed with even the flimsiest evidence, and mine was far more than that, cannot be deemed libelous. The court's decision in this case, however, would be months, possibly years, down the road. The damage the suit caused was immediate. People now realized that the powers-that-be were playing for keeps, and some began running for cover.

Libel suits filed by John D. Bolesky and his photo processing company, Allprints, didn't help. Bolesky sought $10 million in damages for falsely accusing him of being involved in the sordid activities of the Highway Safety Foundation.

In doing so, Bolesky ignored that I had accused him of no such thing. The only time his name was mentioned was in regard to the legally documented positions he held with the foundation and related enterprises. His suit also ignored that I had stated at the beginning of the articles that many of the foundation's officers were unaware of its more questionable practices.

As for Allprints, it also sought $10 million in damages for one indirect reference about pornography being processed there. I could have said much more. I had in my possession, for example, a pornographic film in two Allprints cans and with Allprints' name on the leader that I had indirectly obtained from an Allprints night-shift foreman. But I had chosen not to make an issue of the evidence because I believed such processing was a thing of the past.

In 1995, I learned during a review of a confidential, unsanitized version of retired FBI agent Robert Greenhalgh's report on his investigation of possible police involvement in several unsolved homicides in Mansfield that I may have been wrong about Allprints' processing of pornography having ended.

According to Greenhalgh's unedited report, one person he interviewed during his investigation told him she had quit working at Allprints in 1985 because she was forced by the night-shift foreman to process pornographic films. The Allprints-processed pornographic film starring a well-known retarded Mansfield man that I obtained in 1978 came to me by way of a relative of the same night-shift foreman.

'Observer' fights on

Despite the libel suits, *The Observer's* talented staff kept its promise of prevailing against all odds for several more months. By switching from a weekly to daily, *The Observer* showed new sparks of life and purpose.

I'll never be able to forget the dedication and purpose of managing editor Melodie Gross Wineland, who left *The News Journal* after my resignation; the impeccable typesetting and whatever else it took to be done by Brenda McGlone and Jennifer Moore Hoffman; the sterling photography of Steve Stokes; the creative art work of Chris Contra Berger, Brad Cook and Tim Gabor; the stellar sports reporting of young Mike Hostetler, now a sportscaster; the refreshing style of writers Larry Sawchak and Jane Wirick Drake; and the technical mastery of Dan Moore.

Our incredibly loyal readers responded to our plight with the beauty I had come to expect from them. Some bought more shares of stock. Others redoubled efforts to get subscribers. One doctor came into the office on a bleak Sunday and handed me $2,000 "so you can keep saying what should have been said years ago." Several of our most active volunteers even organized a well-attended benefit dance that raised a few thousand dollars.

But as public support grew, advertising support diminished. Several who stopped advertising were at least honest about it. They said they had received too many threats to make it worth the risk.

My final hope for survival was a new stock offering of $25 a share, of which several supporters said they felt they could sell a large number of the paper's supporters. Our application for approval from the state securities department dragged on so long, though, that I finally went to Columbus to find out why.

I was shocked to learn there that our application apparently had been conveniently "misplaced" and we would have to start the application process all over again. The file disappeared at the same time that Prosecutor McKee, always on the lookout for crime, told the Columbus Police Department that he suspected *The Observer* was "under the influence of organized crime" and asked that its stock records be checked at the securities department.

Records showed the file was checked by Columbus Police on October 19 and that it had not been seen since. Captain David Dailey of the Columbus Division of Police said McKee picked up the records a few days later, just before he filed his libel suit against *The Observer* on November 3. The records, obtained under the color of his public position, were later used to ask me questions during a deposition for McKee's personal libel suit. The deliberate delay in getting the new stock offering approved proved deadly for *The Observer.* Although the paper was actually moving toward making a profit, it now faced a major money crunch without the influx of stock revenue. The staff, exhausted and depleted as it was, kept working week after week and often had to forgo a paycheck for the privilege of doing it all again the following week.

Creditors close in

The inevitable finally came the first week of March 1979. The final blows came in quick succession.

First, upon arriving home one evening, I learned from my now totally bitter and withdrawn wife that we were going to lose our home if we didn't sell it by the end of the month. Then, when I went to get into my car the next morning, it wasn't there. It had been repossessed on the very day I had made arrangements to trade down to a cheaper car to pay ours off.

I obviously wasn't happy when I got to work that day, and a disgruntled ex-employee brought my feelings to a head. As with a number of former employees, I had been slowly paying what I owed him in back wages. But that was no longer acceptable, he told me.

"You're getting rich off this while everybody else is going payless," he smirked.

"Oh, I am?" I asked angrily. "Is that why I'm losing my house and just had my car repossessed?"

"Oh sure, but I've been told how you're stashing money away at the same time you're pleading poverty." he said.

Before I realized what I was doing, I was throwing my can of pop at the wall across the room and stood up in a fury.

"Get out," I screamed, as months of pain and frustration poured out of me as if I were a living volcano.

"Not until I get my money," he said with another smirk.

I asked him to leave several more times, but he wouldn't budge.

Finally, I said, "If you don't get out, I'll throw you out."

"Try it," he said as he stood up.

To my amazement, I did. I shoved him through my office door with such force that he crashed into the wall across the hall.

"Now get out." I shouted.

"Not until I get my money," he shouted as he picked himself off the floor. I then picked him up with a strength that amazed me and threw him toward the steps. Then I shoved him down the steps several times as he kept trying to come toward me until we were on the first floor. Finally, I opened the door and threw him out onto a pile of snow.

"You're in real trouble now," he said. "I'm going to the police."

But first he headed for *The News Journal* where, I learned later, he had been before coming to *The Observer*. It smelled like a set-up to me, conveniently planned to coincide with when a *Time* magazine reporter was in town to do what turned out to be a positive story save mention of the ex-employee's filing of an assault complaint against me.

But police determined the complaint was without merit after members of my staff confirmed that I had asked the troublemaker to leave several times before throwing him out.

After slamming the door after ejecting the malcontent, I headed for my office. As I sat at my desk, my suddenly tapped emotions continued to pour out of me, and I started to cry so hard I was shaking. I walked into a storage area off my office, sat on the floor with my back against the wall and continued to cry for several minutes. Then my wife walked in to console me.

"It's over," she said. "Let's get out of this town before it kills you. I decided I'm leaving with or without you."

"All right," I said as I regained my composure. "I'll tell the staff it's over."

Staff rises to the occasion

The Observer's finest hours were its last. The staff, upon hearing my decision, resolved to put out one final edition whether they were to be paid or not. On the final pages of the March 7, 1979, edition, the members of the staff bid *The Observer's* readers farewell.

"We were giving Mansfield a new newspaper which the people could believe in," wrote managing editor Melodie Gross. We made mistakes, but we learned from them. We tried so very hard. For most of us who made it from the beginning or near the beginning to the bittersweet end, The Observer has so totally consumed our lives that we feel the loss much the same as one feels the loss of a loved one at death. . . .

Melodie added that the staff kept hoping for a miracle so this would not be *The Observer's* last edition.

"But this is the last one," she reluctantly conceded. "And we're all very sorry. We feel sorry for each other. We feel sorry for the community. We feel sorry that ideal like "doing the right thing" and "printing the truth" are not strong enough to overcome the hard realities of not enough financial support to meet printing costs or to get supplies or to meet the payroll. Yet those who remain today have worked on despite the payrolls that have been missed even when some staffers had dependents at home to feed, clothe and shelter. And in the midst of it all, there is Martin D. Yant, a man we believed in on Day One and a man we will all continue to love, admire and believe in for the rest of our lives. . . .

"This is goodbye. This is the end. But if *The Observer* has given Mansfield even 'just one brief shining moment' we will be satisfied and proud, knowing our work was not in vain."

L. Allen Sawchak, who went on to a career as a respected radio newscaster in the area, admitted in his column that he originally came to *The Observer* because it offered him chance to earn more money and get in on the ground floor of a new newspaper. But he soon learned, Sawchak said, that "there was much more to the paper than just the weekly paychecks and the cold, hard facts spit out by the wire service printers and set into print by the typesetters. I learned of the people who sacrificed their hard-earned money to keep the paper in printer's ink and those who gave freely of their time to see that the money was there to meet expenses. There were also many who placed their lives in jeopardy so the truth could be known."

Always-outspoken and articulate typesetter Jennifer Moore Hoffman wrote that she could at least understand those who fought *The Observer* because its revelations might put them behind bars.

"There is/was something that scares me more," Jennifer wrote, "than those who were obviously against us — apathy, and the people purported to be friends and supporters, those who worked here and knew the situation and who subsequently turned on Martin Yant and "The People's Paper" and those of you in Mansfield who listened to the quitters and got a rather warped point of view. . . .

"I could never say that Martin Yant was an easy man to work for. He demanded perfection. Just when we thought we had done our best he was asking more of us, even when the company owed us a few paychecks. . . .

"Martin Yant is a very moral person with the strongest sense of obligation I've ever seen. For better or worse he feels obligated to this city and the people who literally cried out to him for help. In his heart he will never leave this city and its people behind, but there is only so much one person (and family) can bear. . . .

"Between our expected enemies, those who turned on the paper viciously and general apathy, *The Observer* now dies. Maybe this obit edition will wake some people up."

Once I had made the decision to close *The Observer* I couldn't bear to stay to watch the newspaper into which I had poured so much money and energy die.

I also thought that its staff members, who, unlike myself, were Mansfield-area natives, had a right to give the last edition their own imprint. So I called an editor friend on the West Coast who had offered me a job when I was starting *The Observer* and flew out immediately for a job interview.

As it turned out, my wife and I liked the city and the paper but wanted to return to Mansfield to decide whether to accept my friend's generous offer. We had many kind messages of support and thanks waiting for us when we returned, but no miraculous offers of financial support. Mansfield was a thing of the past.

Or so we thought. The day after I had accepted the job out West, I found that the Mansfield jinx was still with me. After I had already sold our house at a huge loss (although we had to sell anyway to avoid foreclosure), my editor friend called and told me as nicely as he could that he would have to retract the offer because *News Journal* publisher Harry Horvitz had learned of the offer and called his newspaper's publisher, who decided he didn't like my image as "a troublemaker."

I realized then that Mansfield would haunt me for a long time. So I decided to haunt it a little longer too.

The question was how. The answer was a newsletter called *The Public Eye* after an investigative column I had written for *The Observer* by the same name.

On April 16, 1979, I published a sample edition of *The Public Eye* in which I reported that, "Contrary to all the rumors you may well have heard about my whereabouts, I am alive and well and still living in Mansfield, much to the chagrin of Sheriff Weikel, Prosecutor McKee, *The News Journal* and others." The response to the first issue of *The Public Eye* was overwhelming. Almost a thousand subscriptions came in during the first two weeks, many with letters of praise and gratitude.

As the number of subscriptions grew, however, so did the threats and harassment as well as the financial problems.

Closing out *The Observer's* books was a full-time job in itself, one that my wife quietly and efficiently handled. But it was a mistake to let her carry so much of that burden alone.

Dealing with frequently hostile creditors and the mounting debts — topped off with the harassment — caused more anguish than she could bear.

The last straw was a threat from Captain William Miser over the telephone one morning ("I'm going to come and get you if you keep publishing that stuff about me.") followed by almost constant obscene phone calls over the next few days. The pressures, as well as my preoccupation with them, had become too much for Sigrid. She left to go grocery shopping with our four children one day and didn't return. It wasn't until late that night that I was able to find out that she had gone to our hometown of New Philadelphia and had no intention of returning.

I followed her there and agreed to her request that I enter the hospital, because she correctly surmised that you don't work 100-hour weeks for 10 straight months without some ill effects. After a brief scare, everything checked out in time to return to Mansfield to give a high-school commencement address. As I returned to our townhouse before heading for the school, debating whether to return to Mansfield or not, the answer was lying on the floor. A large boulder that had been thrown through the living-room window had landed halfway across the house in the family room. Shattered glass was everywhere. What Mansfield's rotten core had done to that window, I realized, it had also done to my family and my life. But unlike glass, a life can be put back together again.

So I headed for the school and announced my decision to turn the fight against corruption and injustice over to the graduates' generation. I quoted the warning by Thomas Jefferson, my favorite historical figure, that "the time to guard against corruption and tyranny is before they shall have gotten hold of us," then read this brilliant statement by Charles Morgan Jr. sent to me by a Mansfield reader: "It is not by great acts but by small failures that freedom dies. The sense of justice dies slowly in a people. They grow used to the unthinkable, and sometimes they may look back and even wonder when 'things' changed. They will not find a day or a time or a place. Justice and liberty die quietly, because men first learn to ignore injustice and then no longer recognize it."

"Please don't let that happen to you," I urged Mansfield's next generation of leaders. A short time later I was on my way out of Mansfield. It was my 30th birthday — a good time, I thought, to start putting my life back together again. In a letter I wrote to subscribers announcing the premature end of the rapidly growing *Public Eye*, I wrote that my search for the truth had to be suspended because keeping my family intact was more important.

"That doesn't mean I am not disappointed that I could not carry through with *The Public Eye,* I wrote. "I am. It certainly would have been satisfying to bask in the glory it might someday have brought me. But as Will Rogers put it a long time ago, 'It great to be great, but it's greater to be human.' I hope that explains why my family must come first after being last for the past year."

I eventually took a job with *The Miami Herald* and tried to put Mansfield behind me. But it would still take countless hours in court and out and thousands of dollars of my libel insurance company's money before attorney Martin Sandel and I managed to get the libel suits filed against me dismissed by the spring of 1980.

Prosecutor McKee's was the first to go. At a hearing in January of that year, the visiting judge informed McKee that his suit was becoming a waste of the court's time and McKee wasn't going to win much, if anything, in the end. The judge then asked Sandel if he thought I would be agreeable to a statement that the disputed allegations against McKee had only been meant to question his professional judgment and not his personal integrity. Although we had accumulated ample evidence to prove the accuracy of my accusations, I agreed it would be best to go along with the judge's proposal to avoid continued court battles at which I was at a distinct disadvantage since I was then living in Miami.

Several weeks later, a similar agreement was reached with Bolesky and Allprints. In return for dismissal of the suits, I issued a statement that said I had neither stated nor meant to imply that Bolesky had been involved in any of the Highway Safety Foundation's improper activities, which I hadn't. Concerning Allprints, I stated that company executives insisted that the processing of pornographic material was against Allprints' policy so that "any unauthorized processing which may have occurred would have been without the authority of Allprints." Far from denying such activity went on, the statement actually reiterated my belief that it did, even with the company's disavowed approval of it.

'News Journal' slants news again

Although this paragraph was the entire crux of the case and many hours were spent negotiating its wording, *The News Journal* conveniently ignored it in reporting the case's dismissal. Even worse, it ignored the statement's all-important final paragraph, which said:

"In all other respects, we have no reason to doubt the accuracy of the stories or reasonable implications to be drawn therefrom."

The News Journal's standards obviously hadn't gotten better since I left town. In fact, it did a pretty good job of covering up the sweetheart disposition of a vehicular-homicide case against Thomas Brennan, who later would become editor, within months of my departure.

The News Journal reported in only the briefest detail the fatal accident itself, which occurred at 12:05 p.m. on July 28, 1979, when Brennan's car struck and killed 14-year-old bicyclist Timothy R. Eyerly of Shiloh on Ganges-Five Point Rd. Eyerly died the following Monday.

The Ohio Highway Patrol report shows that Brennan was less than forthright when questioned about physical impairments that may have led to the accident. Asked if he had "any physical impairments other than the ear infection" he had mentioned earlier, Brennan replied, "No."

According to a transcript of the interview, the observant trooper then noted that, "You read very close. Do you have any visual problems?"

A. I do when I read. I wear bifocals to read with. I have macular degeneration.

Q. Does it affect vision other than close up?

A. It affects my ability to pick up detail, either close or far.

Brennan's case languished in Mansfield Municipal Court until December 21, 1979, when the charge was plea-bargained down to reckless operation and improper passing.

Brennan pleaded no contest to the charges and was found guilty by Judge Ralph Johns. He was fined $100 plus court costs on both counts and his license was suspended pending retesting.

News of this rather minor penalty for killing a 14-year-old boy on a bicycle was later reported in small type in the reckless operation section of *The News Journal's* municipal court report. A $14,000 settlement in a wrongful-death action filed by the victim's parents was apparently not reported. The parents of Eyerly later told me that they saw Brennan at school events on numerous occasions after the accident and he never offered his condolences for their loss, let alone an apology for his role in it.

As Jennifer Moore Hoffman predicted in the final edition of *The Observer*, I could "never leave this city and its people behind." And I am happy to report that, viewed from a distance, Mansfield is generally a better town as I write this than it was in 1979.

I'd like to think my work and those who supported me had something to do with that, and perhaps that is partly the case. Mansfield's old-guard politicians started disappearing in quick order as their corrupt network was exposed. They were replaced, with some exceptions, by generally more intelligent, dedicated public servants — several of them former supporters of The *Ohio Observer.*

As the crooked politicians migrated southward, usually to the west coast of Florida, they were followed by the last vestiges of home-grown power brokers who sold their generations-old companies to conglomerates such as Fuji, which acquired Allprints and changed its name.

Unfortunately, *The News Journal* became worse after Harry Horvitz was forced to sell it. While the paper sometimes seems more aggressive than in the past, it is selective in choosing its targets and still gives many the impression that it covers up almost as much as it covers. Pay reportedly is relatively low and turnover of reporters high.

Other companies once closely associated with Mansfield, such as Tappan, have disappeared altogether.

So did White Westinghouse when it shut down its huge washing-machine production plant in 1991. That cost Mansfield 300 jobs at the facility, which employed almost 8,000 people in the early 1950s.

When the Frigidaire plant closed a year later at the cost of 196 jobs, it clearly symbolized the end of an era. The plant was the last in Mansfield to make ranges, which began being produced in the city in 1883.

But revival-minded investors were already in the process of planning to generate new jobs at the old laundry appliance complex, which they bought for $1 million almost as soon as it was closed. Called the Mansfield Commerce Center, the 40-acre complex's investors said they would concentrate on two areas of development — the office and warehouse areas and the manufacturing plants.

At the same time that the White Westinghouse plant was taking its last breaths, the newly created Carrousel District was taking its first when it welcomed the first new, hand-carved indoor wooden carrousel built in the United States in 60 years. This merry-go-round has 52 wooden animals and two chariots. The district spurred the careful restoration of several Victorian-era buildings, which house restaurants and gift shops. It also became home of the Arts and Science Discovery Center at the Richland Academy.

Promoters said the center's blend of science, art, and technology is the nation's very first center to showcase techno-art.

The Carrousel District followed in the footsteps of another major downtown draw, the venerable Renaissance Theatre, which turned 75 in 2003. Restoration of the former Ohio Theatre began in 1980. A $2.25 million capital improvements campaign launched in 1984 financed to the complete refurbishing of the theater and construction of a glass-enclosed skywalk connecting the theater to the then-new Holiday Inn. In 1991, the theater's board received the deed to the property from the Fran and Warren Rupp Foundation. Six years later, it merged with the Mansfield Symphony, forming the Richland Performing Arts Association, which changed its name to Renaissance Performing Arts in 2003 to signify its service to several surrounding counties. By then, the Renaissance was home to the Miss Ohio Scholarship Program, the Mansfield Symphony Orchestra, the Renaissance Broadway Series, the Summer at the Renaissance Series and a variety of special programs.

In an exciting similar vein, ground was broken in 2000 for Johnny Appleseed Heritage Center & Outdoor Historical Drama on a 45-acre site in Mifflin, just outside Mansfield. After its scheduled completion in 2002, the center was to become home to a musical dramatization of Appleseed's life by playwright/composer, Billy Edd Wheeler and arranger Dennis Burnside. Wheeler previously wrote *The Hatfields & McCoys*, one of the nation's longest-running outdoor dramas.

On the employment front, Mansfield got a major break in 1993 when Armco announced plans to build a $100 million thin-slab steel casting facility at its Mansfield plant, a move expected to maintain about 1,400 jobs.

Unfortunately, Armco's decision to merge with AK Steel, a company with a history of unfriendliness toward labor unions, led to a sometimes violent three-year lockout of 600 workers in July 1999 that was reminiscent of a fictional violent strike by workers that Louis Bromfield wrote about in *The Green Bay Tree,* a novel set in Mansfield. AK Steel ended the lockout in November 2002 as the company neared completion of a new contract with United Steelworkers of America Local 169. Mayor Lydia Reid said the lockout was devastating to Mansfield in many ways and caused an increase in domestic violence and alcoholism in addition to leaving families without paychecks.

Reid added that police overtime and other costs related to keeping peace at the plant's gates and the reluctance of new businesses to locate in an area with labor unrest cost Mansfield dearly. Richland County Commissioner Daniel Hardwick called the three-year lockout "a sad chapter" in the area's once-grand history.

So Mansfield still needs a break to become the ideal town many from the outside have viewed it as being, and no town that suffered through the kind of leadership it had in the past deserves a break more.

Johnny Appleseed symbolically planted the seeds for a flourishing Mansfield area long ago, and Louis Bromfield gave them the proper cultivation. Mansfield's citizens must now nurture them back to life after a bitter winter highlighted by a brutal blizzard of official deceit and economic degeneration.

10

A Personal Perspective

Mansfield is definitely a different place than it was when I arrived there 25 years ago. But when corruption and brutality run rampant, as it did in Mansfield for many years, it can cost lot more than money. It can also cost lives.

While many victims of the Richland County Sheriff's Department's corruption-inspired brutality lived on life's margins, not all of them did. Some of the victims of Richland County's corruption were so unlikely that what happened to them didn't even become generally known. In 1997, I received a letter from Jane Cocanour Miller that put the hidden costs of Richland County's corruption in tragic perspective. Miller is a talented and successful free-lance writer in Pittsburgh, so it's best to let her tell her own sad story.

Dear Mr. Yant:

I just read your book *Rotten to the Core,* and I knew I had to write to you. My parents got me a copy for Christmas.

I have lived in Pittsburgh for 15 years, but I remember well your *News Journal,* the original *Ohio Observer,* and the horrible, awful events you unearthed.

There are so many ways that I feel connected to your book. Although I am a journalist myself, I don't know if I can write about all of these concisely and coherently. It was such a personal catharsis to read this book that I wanted you to know how much it meant to me.

My own family had experiences with the Richland County Sheriff's Department, the county coroner and Byrd Ambulance that, had you known about them, may have ended up in your book. These people were responsible for the death of my grandfather when I was about 13 years old. After that, I lost faith in our country's justice system.

A transforming experience

It happened in 1969 — a good year to become a radical at a tender age. I grew up on a farm in Richland County, several miles from State Route 13 (the road that entrapped truck driver James Truly, whose ordeal you tell at the beginning of your book.)

On July 4, 1969, there was a flash flood. The Blackfork Creek tributary, which you could normally walk across without getting your feet wet, flooded its bank. It swept a nearby house totally off its foundation.

The next day, my parents and I, along with many other neighbors, helped the family that lived there salvage what could be saved of the home's contents. As a 4-H club, some of us met at the house of a neighbor who had an old-fashioned wringer washing machine to wash clothing items far too muddy to wash in an automatic washing machine.

My grandfather, a robust farmer in his early 70s, also came to help. He was under treatment for a heart condition, but mostly he was quite healthy. While talking with my dad, my grandfather had a heart attack. Immediately, my father began resuscitation and another neighbor ran across the road to her home to call an ambulance and my mother, a registered nurse who had just gone back to our home, the next farm down the road.

Within a minute, my mother returned. At that time my grandfather was very much alive. A nearby state highway worker supposedly had placed a call to Gilberts Ambulance in Ashland. Although we lived in Richland County, we were 35 minutes from downtown Mansfield. Ashland, on the other hand, was only six miles, or less than five minutes, away in an emergency.

Five minutes passed. The ambulance did not arrive. My mother ran to the nearby highway worker's car to find out what happened and to have another call placed. That's when she found out that, when the worker placed the original call, it was intercepted by Byrd Ambulance and he was told that an ambulance from Mansfield would be dispatched.

My mother asked the highway worker to call the ambulance from Ashland. Even with the day, it would still get to my grandfather much faster. When another five minutes passed and no ambulance sirens could be heard, my mother once again ran over to the state highway vehicle and heard, over the two-way radio, the ambulance driver reporting that three Richland County sheriff's deputies had met his ambulance at the county line, about a half mile away, and barred it from reaching us.

Sheriff Thomas E. Weikel came on the radio and informed the ambulance service that the "body" belonged to a Richland County ambulance. The outraged ambulance driver shouted at Weikel that there was no "body" — this was a call for a man who was alive. But the gun-toting deputies threatened the men in the ambulance with their lives if they crossed the county line. Weikel confirmed their threat over the radio.

My mother then got on the radio with Weikel. He insisted, although the Ashland ambulance was there and the Byrd ambulance wasn't, that the "body" be brought to Mansfield. My mother, a former head nurse at Mansfield General Hospital, informed Weikel that this was not a coroner's case, that an emergency call had been placed for a man who was having a heart attack. She added that, if Coroner Robert Wolford thought this was a coroner's case, he was required by law to come to the scene.

"I don't give a goddamn what she says," Wolford shouted back over the radio. "I have duty at the emergency room and I can't come."

Although the deputies finally permitted the Ashland ambulance to drive to where my by-now-unconscious grandfather lay, they blocked access to the house. Finally, the Byrd ambulance medics arrived, entered the house and put my grandfather on a stretcher. As they were coming out of the house, though, they dropped him onto the ground. Weikel then relented and told his deputies to allow the Ashland ambulance to transport my grandfather. But he still insisted that he be brought to Mansfield, where he was pronounced dead on arrival. Later, the still-shocked driver of the Ashland ambulance told my mother that he had never, in 40 years of emergency work, had an experience like this one. It became my mother's mission that nobody else ever go through an experience like the one we had. As the 1969-'70 school year began, I remember my mom writing, writing and rewriting about this experience as she prepared a letter to the editor of *The News Journal*. Before her revisions neared final form, she bought our family's first typewriter.

I do want to note that one good thing did happen quickly. The hospital had the evidence to remove Wolford from his emergency room job for conflict of duties and double-dipping. My mother had told a doctor friend about her intentions to write about Wolford's actions that day of my grandfather's death, and he had said, "Let me take care of this one. We've been trying to get rid of him for years." (My mother said that, while she was head nurse at the hospital, it was well known Wolford had his own room where he "dried out" from drinking binges, and other nurses reported he often walked through the hospital corridors in his pajamas.)

Story covered up

Early in September, my mom delivered her letter to *The News Journal* office. Several days later, I came home from school just as a *News Journal* reporter was leaving. He had assured my mother that, although the editor couldn't print her letter, they would conduct a thorough investigation of her charges.

Months passed. She contacted the editor, and learned there had been no investigation. Yet everyone she talked to acted as if they knew about her letter. My mother became convinced that *The News Journal* was involved in a plot to cover up the wrongdoing of all involved!

Martin, I must say, you cannot imagine her delight nine years later when your investigative series confirmed that she was right! She called your office to share our own experience, but her call was transferred to general manager Robert Blake. Blake told her that if you were interested, you would call her. (After reading your book, my mother said, "Now I know why he never called! He never got my message!")

Months later, the editor of the school newspaper I supervised as a teacher, Scott Davis, insisted that we call you at *The Observer*. Scott said you would be interested in telling out tragic story. But, by that time, my mother was worn out, and you had shone a light and told stories of people who were far more brutalized than our family.

Going back to 1969, my mother was not about to give up because of media corruption. It was then that she decided to file a lawsuit. Although my family's faith did not believe in settling disputes in court, my parents selected an attorney known for his prosecution of wrongful-death suits. Since this was a violation of a civil right (the right to life, obviously) the suit was filed in U.S. District Court in Cleveland.

It took two years before the case was heard. My parents pulled me out of school on the day of the hearing. They thought it would be a great educational experience. It really was.

Years later, as I contemplate my unusual delight in lawyer jokes and derision of the profession, I know it began there. The shenanigans could have been part of "The Three-Ring Circus" chapter in your book. At the end of the day, the judge determined that there was insufficient evidence for a trial.

The state highway worker who testified, my parents were convinced, was not the same one who dispatched the calls: This man couldn't even remember his name or where he lived. The death certificate had the time of my grandfather's death as an hour before any ambulance had been called. The owner of Byrd Ambulance accepted the witness fee that came with his subpoena but sent his lawyer to say he couldn't be in court that day.

The whole experience is a black hole. There was ever so much that I had blocked from my mind, and it was just too painful for my mother to talk about again as I gently prodded her memory so I could share this experience.

My only memory of that day is sitting on a bench, surrounded by the darkened oak-paneled wall, watching our once-powerful attorney act like a babbling, incoherent, crooked-tie slob. In the two years since he had taken on my parents' case, our attorney had become an obvious alcoholic. Years later we found out that he had received death threats because of our case.

Faith in system destroyed

At a young, impressionable age, I lost faith in our system of justice, although I know that this experience — and your example — later gave me courage to do what I needed to do as a reporter. We all moved on with our lives and never talked about that time between 1969 and 1972 ever again — until your book came out. Since it was Christmas time, a number of people received your book as a gift from my mother!

When I opened the gift-wrapped copy of the book, my mother remarked to me, "You know, we were quite lucky. After reading this book, I'm surprised they didn't set fire to our fields, kill our livestock or bomb the house."

The second time I read your book I enjoyed your wonderful storytelling abilities and didn't shake or feel traumatized, although there was still a certain sadness that these things happened.

Thank you always for being the person to bring it all to light. Although I felt myself so immobilized by recalling this painful experience that it took two years to finish this letter, I can finally say that there has been a great deal of healing in my own life — thanks to you and *Rotten to the Core*.

Sincerely,
Jane Cocanour Miller

11

Is Mansfield Typical?

After Sheriff Weikel's resignation, *Time* magazine ran an article in its August 6, 1979, issue about my ordeal under the headline, "Just a Typical American Town — A Persistent Editor Wins a Painful Victory." The article noted that I had arrived in Mansfield full of hope 19 months earlier.

"Since then," the article said, "[Yant] has been the target of telephone threats ("You're going to be dead") a mysterious fire, a five-pound rock thrown through his living room window, and $45 million in libel suits. He has lost his job and his life savings, and his wife and four children have left him."

But, the story continued, "This month Yant's lonely crusade began to bring results. A second grand jury returned a new round of indictments against Weikel.

"A petition was filed, signed by 6,580 citizens, calling for Weikel's removal. Last week the sheriff pleaded no contest to various misdemeanor charges and resigned from office. . . . Says he:

"You can be crucified for only so long by the news media. How the hell can I fight them?"

In the last paragraph, I was quoted as saying: "I came here thinking this would be the typical mid-American city. The sad thing is, it just may be."

The Mansfield of today certainly doesn't seem as bad as the one I encountered in 1978, when corruption had been allowed to fester on the city's body politic for years.

Then again, as noted, two of Weikel's elected successors in a row were forced out of office amid scandals, albeit none as serious as his.

In addition, a Mansfield police-brutality scandal came to light in 1981. A Mansfield Municipal Court judge was suspended from the bench in 1986 after a drunken driving conviction and was arrested on the same charge a year later. The city finance director resigned in 1987 after pleading guilty to two counts of theft in office.

A Mansfield police lieutenant was convicted of voluntary manslaughter in 1988, and three officers were disciplined for mishandling his case. A retired FBI agent's conclusion in 1989, after a lengthy probe, that there was no evidence of police involvement in a series of unsolved homicides left many doubters, and I reported in 1995 that the file on one of the most suspicious of those cases had disappeared. The state prisons in Mansfield remained a continual source of brutality, murder and corruption that often spilled over into the community. Corruption and strife continued into the 21st century with the previously mentioned police "Scannergate" eavesdropping scandal.

But that, sadly, is somewhat typical of the kind of official misconduct and corruption that goes on across America. Thomas Jefferson warned that, "The time to guard against corruption and tyranny is before they shall have gotten hold of us."

But Americans didn't heed his warning, and corruption and tyranny now have more than gotten hold of us. They have gotten a *stranglehold* on us.

Although the United States holds itself up as a beacon of liberty and propriety, history and current research indicate that it is one of the more corrupt industrial democracies. In the 2003 Corruption Perceptions Index complied by the corruption-fighting organization Transparency International, the United Stated tied Ireland for 18th place with a score 7.5 on a scale in which a score of 10 means the country is "highly clean." Top-ranked Finland had a score of 9.7. Iceland, Denmark, New Zealand, Sweden, the Netherlands, Australia, Canada and the United Kingdom were among those with better scores than the United States.

Corruption started becoming as American as apple pie probably before apple pie earned that distinction. Steve Allen noted in *Ripoff: The Corruption That Plagues America* that while corruption existed in colonial America, the Revolutionary War revolutionized financial trickery with the wholesale flooding of the colonies with paper notes that popularized the phrase "not worth a Continental."

"A case can be argued that despite the ideals of Thomas Jefferson and the signatories of the Declaration of Independence, the war itself — as is the case with all wars — greatly increased corruption," Allen wrote. "This included untrammeled profiteering by some 'sunshine patriots' who saw a chance to draw scarce precious metal sovereigns into their own pockets. Some farmers gladly did business with the British military simply because they paid in gold whereas Washington's armies made purchases with paper money. . . .

"Alexander Hamilton, father of the U.S. Treasury, troubled about the Continental notes, decided to restore order by paying off one cent of hard money to the dollar. When word of his intentions got around, certain politicians and their friends in the know profited."

But the crooks were, nonetheless, few and far between in early America, Allen notes, because of high ethical standards articulated by the nation's founders and in part because of a lack of opportunities for fraud. The young nation's most plentiful asset was land, so it's not surprising that is where much of the chicanery occurred.

The development of Ohio — the source of most of the corruption featured in this book — was a good example. The Northwest Ordinance of 1787 that legalized America's first expansion to the west, as William F. Poole, president of the American Historical Association, noted in 1888 "was drafted as a part of the scheme devised by the Ohio Company of Associates, formed in Massachusetts, for buying and settling a large tract of land in Ohio on the Muskingum River; and that it was enacted by the unanimous vote of Congress in furtherance of that scheme."

Shortly after the Ohio Company established Marietta as Ohio's first city, an offshoot called the Scioto Land Company was formed, and it purchased part of the Ohio Company's land to sell to wealthy people in France who feared they were about to lose their heads on the guillotine during the French Revolution. The Scioto Company's sales representative, an Englishman with the ironic name Playfair, circulated a brochure in France about the scenic "new El Dorado" along the Ohio River that boasted "trees that spontaneously produce sugar; [and] plants that yield ready-made candles." Buyers were also promised a territory that had "no frosts, even in winter, no taxes or military service." When the "French 500" arrived in October 1790, they learned that the deeds they held were worthless and that southeastern Ohio was far from "new El Dorado."

Some nonetheless decided to stay in a settlement they called Gallipolis, or "French city." But Ohio was hardly like France, and Gallipolis proved to be as hostile as revolution-torn Paris. Few of the French settlers survived for long. Accounts of who benefited from this ripoff vary, but it's safe to say that some of Ohio's founding fathers certainly weren't hurt by it.

When a much larger wave of poorer immigrants started arriving in New York City 50 years later, they received a much warmer welcome as long as they were willing to play politics. In the 1850s, the Democratic Party began winning elections by accepting bribes, awarding patronage jobs to supporters and making naturalization increasingly easy for Democratic-leaning immigrants. William "Boss" Tweed's Tammany Hall "machine" soon became all-powerful and plundered the city treasury until *The New York Times* exposed huge cost overruns in the construction of the Lower Manhattan courthouse that bore his name. Tweed was convicted of theft and died in jail in 1878. But urban corruption did not die with him. In 1903, muckraking journalist Lincoln Steffens wrote a scathing series of articles about how corruption had spread to cities across the country. When the articles were published as a best-selling book, *The Shame of the Cities,* in 1904, it inspired attempts to enact political reforms, but the political machines kept cranking out corruption.

Ironically, the reform movement's push for the constitutional prohibition of alcohol created a massive market for bootlegged liquor and spurred the growth of organized crime, whose leaders made the old political bosses look like Boy Scouts. The mob generated a new breed of politicians that it controlled and made virtually invincible. In many cities and states, honest citizens abandoned the political arena altogether, and corruption became a self-perpetuating enterprise. By the late 1950s, an estimated 15 percent of local and state campaign funds came from the underworld.

The hope that the growth of middle class would eventually kill off corruption was dashed by the Watergate scandal in 1972 that led to President Nixon's resignation in 1974. Watergate inspired a plethora of investigations of political corruption. One of those caught in the feeding frenzy was Vice President Spiro Agnew, who was forced to resign in 1973 for taking bribes from construction companies when he was governor of Maryland.

That was an early sign that corruption had spread to the private sector and led to revelations of huge illegal political contributions by major corporations. The Enron scandal nearly 30 years later showed that the reform efforts of the 1970s had done little or nothing to stem the growth of corporate corruption any more than it did political corruption.

The continuing corruption of law enforcement was equally insidious. Victor E. Kappeler, Richard D. Sluter and Jeffrey P. Alpert pointed out in *Forces of Deviance: Understanding the Dark Side of Policing,* that the kind of police corruption that plagued Mansfield is nothing new. "To study the history of police is to study police deviance, corruption and misconduct," they wrote in their 1994 book.

On the other hand, the nature of police corruption has evolved from taking payoffs, selective law enforcement and collusion to active involvement in drug-dealing, organized crime and violent gang activity, of which the activities of the Sheriff Weikel's inner circle of deputies was a precursor. The 1997 report of the Chicago Commission on Police Integrity cited the history of police scandals in New York City as an example of how things had changed over two decades. "In the 1970s, New York's Knapp Commission on Police Corruption identified two general forms of corruption — police officers involved in relatively low level forms of corruption and misconduct, and those officers involved in large-scale corruption," the report said. "Twenty years later, New York's Mollen Commission revisited the issue and found the face of corruption had changed. Their primary problem was "crew corruption," wherein groups of officers protect and assist each others' criminal activities.

"The Mollen Commission identified the predominant patterns of corruption in New York City as police officers committing outright theft from street dealers, from radio runs, from warrantless searches, from legitimate raids, from car stops, from drug couriers and from off-duty robberies. They also discovered cops protecting and assisting narcotics traffickers as well as cops dealing and using illicit drugs themselves. A pattern of perjured police testimony and false crime reports was also identified. . . . New York is not the only city to experience a drug-related police corruption scandal. Virtually every major U.S. police department has confronted similar problems."

As was the case in Mansfield, police brutality seems to be a common byproduct of corruption.

"Police abuse remains one of the most serious and divisive human rights violations in the United States," a Human Rights Watch report concluded in 1998. "The excessive use of force by police officers, including unjustified shootings, severe beatings, fatal chokings and rough treatment persists because overwhelming barriers to accountability make it possible for officers who commit human rights violations to escape due punishment and often to repeat their offenses. Police or public officials greet each new report of brutality with denials or explain that the act was an aberration, while the administrative and criminal systems that should deter these abuses by holding officers accountable instead virtually guarantee them impunity."

Amnesty International came to the same conclusion in a report later that same year. "Systematic brutality by police has been uncovered by inquiries into some of the country's largest urban police departments," the Nobel Peace Prize-winning organization said. "In each case the authorities had ignored routine abuses. In each case police officers had covered up misconduct by fellow officers, hiding behind a 'code of silence.' . . . Many people have died, many have been seriously injured, many have been deeply traumatized. Each year local authorities pay out millions of dollars in compensation to victims, yet successful prosecutions of police officers are rare.

"Behind the walls of prisons and jails, largely hidden from outside examination, there is more violence. . . . Some prisoners are abused by other inmates, and guards fail to protect them. Others are assaulted by the guards themselves. Women and men are subjected to sexual, as well as physical, abuse."

Both reports emphasized that the overwhelming majority of America's law-enforcement officers are honest professionals trying to do a good job under difficult circumstances. "Human Rights Watch recognizes that police officers, like other people, will make mistakes when they are under pressure to make split-second decisions regarding the use of force," the Organization said. Even the best recruiting, training, and command oversight will not result in flawless behavior on the part of all officers. . . . Yet, precisely because police officers can make mistakes or allow personal bias or emotion to enter into policing — and because they are allowed, as a last resort, to use potentially lethal force to subdue individuals they apprehend — police must be subjected to intense scrutiny."

That is particularly true of sheriffs and their deputies, a subject I continued to investigate after leaving Mansfield. I eventually documented my findings in my 1995 book *Tin Star Tyrants,* which began with these dramatic examples: "In Mexico, a gunman later identified as a sheriff from Texas bursts into a hospital and uses an AK-47 to fatally shoot a prisoner handcuffed to his bed. In West Virginia, a sheriff is paid $100,000 to turn the job over to a known criminal who opens the county to his drug-dealing relatives. In Kentucky, a sheriff convicted of conspiring to kill two political opponents runs his office from prison. In Ohio, two politically powerful attorneys return to Columbus from Washington, D.C., where they gain assurances a much-feared sheriff targeted by a federal grand jury would not be indicted, then meet with a federal judge who "put the pressure on." In Mississippi, a sheriff sentenced to 20 years in prison for drug smuggling shrugs and tells the angry judge, 'That's showbiz.' "

"That's the sheriff biz, too, judging from how many of those who hold the powerful office use their tin stars as a license to lie, cheat, steal, beat, torture and kill."

As shocking as the situation was then, it has actually gotten worse. In 2002, former DeKalb County (Georgia) Sheriff Sidney Dorsey was convicted of plotting the murder of his successor, who was gunned down in his driveway after winning the 2000 election on a promise to rid the suburban Atlanta department of corruption. Dorsey was found guilty of murder and 11 corruption-related charges and sentenced to life in prison.

The 2002 election campaign in Kentucky spawned the murder of two more men. In March, Harlan County sheriff's candidate Paul Browning Jr. was found shot to death in his burned-out pickup. About a month before his murder, Browning was secretly videotaped accepting a large amount of cash from a man who had been charged twice with selling cocaine. As he collected the money, Browning told the man that if he won the election he would protect some drug dealers. At this writing, Browning's murder remains unsolved. Investigators reportedly were pursuing theories that Browning was killed by drug dealers he had been pressing for similar campaign donations or that other officials hired a hit man to prevent him from exposing their own corruption. Ironically, Browning was mentioned in the above-quoted first paragraph of *Tin Star Tyrants* as the sheriff who ran his department from prison while serving a sentence for conspiring to kill two political opponents.

One month after Browning's murder, Pulaski County Sheriff Sam Catron was killed by a sniper at a campaign rally. In 2003, former Sheriff's Deputy Jeff Morris, who was running against Catron at the time, pleaded guilty and was sentenced to life in prison for helping plot the sheriff's murder. As part of his plea bargain agreement, Morris agreed to testify against supporter Kenneth White, who allegedly was upset with Catron's crackdown on drugs. The actual triggerman pleaded guilty to murder earlier and received a life sentence.

But corruption doesn't stop with local law enforcement. It goes all the way up to the once-sacrosanct FBI. In 2002, former FBI Agent John Connolly Jr. was convicted of protecting Boston-area mobsters, including James "Whitey" Bulger, who was on the FBI's "Ten Most Wanted" list because of his suspected connection with a mere 21 murders.

One year later, H. Paul Rico, a former FBI colleague of Connolly's, was charged with involvement in the 1981 murder of Oklahoma businessman Roger Wheeler. Investigators said Wheeler was murdered because he questioned whether money was being skimmed from the gaming company World Jai Alai in Florida, which he had just bought. Rico was retired from the FBI by then and the company's security director. Prosecutors said Rico gave a Boston hit man Wheeler's schedule so he could be killed.

In 2001, Rico denied during testimony before a congressional committee that he and Connolly helped cause four innocent men to be convicted for a 1965 mob hit for which they spent 30 years in prison. "What do you want, tears?" Rico sneered when a representative complained of Rico's lack of remorse. Investigators said Rico's arrest was a big step toward closure in the investigation of Boston-based FBI agents' criminal involvement with informants, which one member of Congress said was the worst law-enforcement scandal in American history.

While law-enforcement officers are always in the forefront of corruption schemes, other public officials and business executives are also active participants. Corruption is often at its worst when the three unite. That happened on a small scale in Mansfield in the 1970s. It happened on a statewide scale during the administration of Ohio Governor George V. Voinovich in the 1990s. Behind the scenes was the governor's jail-building businessman brother Paul Voinovich. The front man, though, was Sheriff Earl O. Smith, who looked, talked and acted a lot like Mansfield's Sheriff Thomas E. Weikel.

Smith wasn't in the same league as Weikel when it came to corruption and brutality, although his eight-year reign of terror had its share of both. What made Smith so sinister was his political power. As a Republican and the top law-enforcement official in GOP-dominated Franklin County, home of Columbus, the Republican-controlled state capital, Smith had the kind of connections Weikel could only dream of. And that gave Smith a particular air of arrogance that would eventually be his downfall.

A short, swaggering man with oversized ears and an ego to match, Smith all but invited an investigation in 1989, when he told the Cleveland *Plain Dealer*, "You can call me a crook, but sooner or later you're going to have to prove it." Smith's belligerent attitude prompted the anonymous author of a booklet about him to write that Smith "personifies the law-enforcement entrepreneur who regards corruption as business and scandal as civil disobedience for public officials."

"Like all successful politicians," the booklet continued, "he developed a cartoonish alter ego: tough, glib, direct, unpredictable, macho, old shoot-from-the-hip, crisis-of-the-week Sheriff Earl, a combination of Huey Long, [former longtime Columbus] Mayor M.E. Sensenbrenner, Eva Peron and Wyatt Earp. He seized the county computer. Demanded his own armored personnel carrier. Seduced criminals with an atmosphere of easy sleaze, and John Q. Voter with a defiant disdain for desk-bound bureaucrats and rogue cops.

"But to federal prosecutors, political reporters and many law-enforcement colleagues, Earl Smith is a modern-day Sheriff of Nottingham, [a] corrupt and cynical manipulator of a squalid fiefdom, who politically shames his party and profession."

Two *Plain Dealer* reporters spent several weeks in Columbus trying to determine if Smith was indeed the crook many suspected. They found lots of smoke, but no fire.

But those who testified later that year before the third federal grand jury to investigate Smith since he had taken office in 1985 thought they had produced enough evidence to make him eat his words. In fact, a former chief deputy who had quit in disgust in 1987 said an FBI agent assured him there was enough evidence to warrant Smith three indictments, and a source who reviewed Smith's file said there was enough evidence there for *five* indictments.

But it was another former chief deputy and two Smith fund-raisers, not Smith himself, who ended up getting convicted in an honorary deputy badge-selling scam, first exposed by private investigator Jim Silvania, despite the following kinds of evidence against him:

• Copies of several suspicious checks, including one for $2,500 from an auto dealership made out to "cash" by Smith's later-convicted badge-selling crony. Smith admitted, without explanation, during a July 1992 hearing before the State Personnel Board of Review that he had cashed the check and deposited it in his personal account.

• Smith's use of a van provided at no charge by another auto dealer who, along with his brother, were made honorary deputies.

• Smith's alleged violation of the civil rights of an independent candidate for president of Teamsters Local 284 in Columbus. Smith conspired with incumbent officers to have the candidate arrested on trumped-up drunken-driving charges. The candidate lost the election amid rumors about his arrest.

• Allegations that Smith and two since-convicted cronies once discussed taking over an area massage parlor and funneling some of its profits into his political campaign chest.

• Allegations that Smith once discussed planting cocaine in the car of Dewey Stokes, the Columbus-based national president of the Fraternal Order of Police, because Stokes dared to fight Smith's attempt to replace the FOP with a patsy union to which a state hearing officer ruled he gave "unlawful support."

Speculation about how Smith escaped indictment began to circulate immediately. But the first time it surfaced in print was in an April 12, 1991, memo written by Joseph N. Gilyard, director of the Governor's Office of Criminal Justice Services. Gilyard's memo to Lieutenant Governor (now U.S. Senator) Mike DeWine was written to summarize numerous allegations that had been made about Smith's controversial Drug Enforcement Network, for which Gilyard had temporarily suspended funding.

Among the allegations Gilyard reported were drug use by agents; the improper use of juveniles; overtime fraud; the leasing, without the required bidding, of space from a national union whose president was convicted in the badge-selling scam; the leasing of five undercover cars, also without the required bidding, from an auxiliary deputy; money laundering; alcohol abuse funds; obstruction of justice; and tampering with evidence.

The head of the drug task force then was Ernie Cook, a convicted felon who also was indicted in 1978 on charges of receiving stolen property. The latter charges were dropped, however, by then-Prosecutor George C. Smith, who later became a federal district judge. Cook was one of 23 present or former Smith employees, campaign contributors or holders of auxiliary, special or honorary commissions from the sheriff identified as convicted criminals by *The Plain Dealer* in 1989. Shortly after Gilyard had suspended the Cook-led drug unit, Smith was heard saying he was "going to get Gilyard's black ass." Three months later, the spiteful sheriff did just that. Smith's successful vendetta, and what prompted it, is worth reviewing at length. For it shows how the power and influence of a renegade sheriff can reach to the very highest levels of government in a state capital and Washington.

As one of the highest-ranking blacks in state government, Gilyard was making $63,500 a year until DeWine fired him in 1991 amid a flurry of accusations and counteraccusations that rocked the state capital for several months. Gilyard's nightmare started as a dream come true in January 1991. Then the director of the Ohio Court of Claims, Gilyard was actively recruited by the newly elected administration of Republican Governor George V. Voinovich. He eventually was appointed director of the Governor's Office of Criminal Justice Services, which coordinated planning and funding for Ohio's law-enforcement and corrections agencies. "Joe clearly has the skills and experience needed for the Criminal Justice Services Office," said DeWine when he announced the appointment. "His management abilities are enhanced by his sensitivity to victims of crime."

But DeWine drastically changed his tune when Gilyard came under fire from two powerful forces. One was Smith. The other was the governor's brother Paul after Gilyard questioned the propriety of his prison-construction company's lobbying efforts. The roof caved in on July 22, when DeWine fired Gilyard for allegedly concealing an overturned misdemeanor conviction for the assault of a Department of Youth Services resident in 1975. DeWine's action came three days after Smith filed his heavily publicized theft charges against Gilyard for allegedly having an aide drive him to Cleveland to spend the night with a woman at state expense and one week after Gilyard wrote a memo about being pressured for contracts by the Voinovich Companies.

But the lieutenant governor insisted that neither issue affected his decision. There's no denying that Gilyard struck a juvenile inmate in 1975, which is why he said he never tried to deny it. He added, however, that he did so only after the youth kicked a tray from his hands in the tense aftermath of a foiled escape attempt.

"I'm human, just like everybody else," Gilyard said. "I made a mistake, even if the appeals court said it was justified. I just tried to live with it and learn from it. And then, after 15 years of solid performance in public service, that minor mistake was used as an excuse to fire me because I stepped on some toes while trying to do what was right and proper. It just doesn't make sense. But it happened."

Gilyard also insisted — and a confidential source in a position to know confirmed — that he told DeWine about the incident when he was interviewed for the Criminal Justice Services job. "I told DeWine about my past problem at Youth Services, just as others who interviewed me at that time said I told them," Gilyard said. "When I did, DeWine laughed and said, 'He probably had it coming.' He just resurrected the issue as a matter of convenience when I got too hot to handle."

Many of those who watched Gilyard's rapid fall from grace from the inside agreed. Former Ohio Inspector General David D. Sturtz, who conducted an exhaustive investigation of Gilyard's firing, took the middle ground. Although he found Gilyard's termination technically justified, he said Gilyard was also an unfortunate victim of circumstances. "Joe Gilyard got caught up in something that was bigger than Joe Gilyard," Sturtz said. "Too many things came together, and it all got dumped on him. And when it did, the people he thought would come to his aid disappeared."

Gilyard's problems began shortly after taking office when he agreed to meet with Bennett J. Cooper, who held the same job under Governor James A. Rhodes, and Phil Hamilton, head of Governor Voinovich's transition team. As Gilyard soon learned, Cooper and Hamilton were also lobbyists for the Voinovich Companies. Gilyard said Hamilton, who also was a paid consultant to Sheriff Smith, was "the glue that holds what happened to me together." As Gilyard related in a July 15, 1991, memo to DeWine, his February 1 "get-acquainted meeting" with Hamilton and Cooper — who held an honorary deputy commission from Smith — soon turned into a discussion about the Voinovich Companies' interest in "participating" in the state jail construction program.

"I listened and told them I did not know whether there was a conflict or problem, but that their participation raised a 'significant question' as to its propriety," Gilyard wrote. This was especially true, he said, in light of Governor Voinovich's pledge that his brother's company would receive no state contracts and a 1990 Ohio attorney general's opinion that the kind of grants being sought were state contracts.

In the following days, Gilyard claimed he received several visits and phone calls from Hamilton and Cooper, during which they kept bringing up jail contracts. "I kept telling them they should get an Ethics Commission ruling on the conflict-of-interest issue, but they wouldn't listen," Gilyard said. "I was afraid this would blow up in the governor's face someday without one."

On March 22, 1991, Gilyard unwittingly stepped into another minefield when he took the first of numerous calls about alleged improprieties in Sheriff Smith's Franklin County Drug Enforcement Network. As the allegations of financial irregularities and violations of the law mounted, Gilyard said he went to DeWine, who suggested a meeting with Smith, which Gilyard arranged.

In an April 12 memo to DeWine, Gilyard described his meeting with Smith as "very amiable." Smith apparently didn't see it that way. It was only a few days later that an employee of Gilyard's office heard Smith say he was "going to get Joe Gilyard's black ass."

When DeWine acted on his recommendation to suspend funding for DEN pending an audit on March 26, Gilyard said, Smith threatened to retaliate against him, DeWine and Voinovich. According to a memo written by Lieutenant Colonel Richard Curtis, assistant superintendent of Ohio State Highway Patrol, Gilyard discussed Smith's reaction with him and William Vasil, assistant director of the Ohio Department of Highway Safety, on April 8. Curtis' April 9 memo quoted Gilyard as saying he also had been warned Smith might bring criminal charges against him.

Gilyard was told to summarize the accusations against the task force in a memo to DeWine so the lieutenant governor could get Voinovich to approve a State Patrol investigation.

Gilyard prepared the memo for an April 12 meeting with DeWine, Vasil, Curtis and Charles Price, DeWine's chief counsel. As the participants discussed the memo, Gilyard claimed, he noticed the lieutenant governor reading ahead.

When he got to a paragraph stating that it was rumored that "the White House had stopped an investigation of Earl Smith's office because of political considerations during the Voinovich . . . gubernatorial race," Gilyard said, DeWine's face turned white. "Then he stood up, thanked everyone for coming, and collected the memos as they left," Gilyard said. "After closing the door, he told me to destroy all copies of the memo and to purge it from my computer." DeWine adamantly denied Gilyard's version of the meeting. But a witness — with considerable hesitation — admitted to me that "there was talk of destroying the memo."

Before leaving office on December 30, 1992, Smith cut off his own department's investigation of DEN to rush through a mild reprimand of task force leader Cook. Despite that, the probe greatly validated Gilyard's accusations. The reprimand concluded that Cook had sex with a paid informant; used a juvenile to buy drugs; drove a county car while intoxicated; failed to report an accident; planted evidence in a suspect's car; and "didn't properly administrate the task force."

Sheriff James A. Karnes, who upset Smith in the November 1992 election, suspended Cook for 30 days when he took office and demoted him to corporal after a new probe concluded, among other things, that Cook had driven an undercover car to another county to intervene in a domestic dispute involving one of his paid informants.

A confidential state investigative document also lent credence to Gilyard's money-laundering allegation. Of the $1,600 a month the task force spent to rent office space in a union's national headquarters building, the document speculated, "$800 came back to Earl Smith's pocket." The union head reportedly admitted much the same thing during testimony before the National Labor Relations Board.

Credible as his memo on Smith's task force might have been, Gilyard apparently put one foot in his political grave by writing it. He apparently put his second foot in the grave on July 15, 1991, when he sent DeWine a memo questioning the propriety of the lobbying efforts of Voinovich Companies. In rapid fashion, Gilyard was suspended and then fired by DeWine. Then, after *The Plain Dealer* reported that state background checks had referred to Gilyard's 1975 conviction and that a State Patrol document had confirmed the existence of his memo, DeWine admitted Gilyard had made "casual reference" to the 1975 accusation and that he may have seen his memo, which at first he said didn't exist.

DeWine still insisted he didn't have a copy, though. Then he said he found one — which was suspiciously one line off from Gilyard's on every page — in his desk at home. Finally, DeWine said he didn't ask Voinovich to approve the investigation the memo recommended because the State Patrol was reluctant to conduct one — a charge the Patrol denied. And through it all, DeWine kept calling Gilyard "a liar."

The administration also suggested Gilyard had written the memo on the Voinovich Companies when he knew he was going to be fired so it would look like that was the reason. But a subsequent State Patrol investigation indicated Gilyard had first raised the question several weeks earlier and that DeWine requested the memo.

The weapon with which Smith beat Gilyard into personal humiliation and political destruction was an anonymous letter that had been mailed to several state officials in the preceding months.

How that letter came about is anybody's guess. But here are the facts:

• On December 10, 1990, Gilyard warned Court of Claims employee Patricia Wingard-Carson that he was going to recommend that she be terminated if her performance hadn't improved by the end of her six-month probationary period in late January.

• On December 12, Reginald Wheeler, who worked beside Wingard-Carson, wrote what he initially told investigators later was one of "tons" of fictional letters he had typed to improve his limited writing skills. The letter, which he addressed to Johnnie Miles, president of the Ward 4 Street Club in Cleveland, confirmed that Gilyard would speak to the club at 7 p.m. on December 18, 1990.

• On January 15, 1991, a person later identified as Jeffrey Carson, Wingard-Carson's husband, sent an unsigned letter to Governor Voinovich. Hiding behind a veil of righteous anonymity in pursuit of revenge and money, Carson accused Gilyard of ordering Wheeler to write the attached "fake letter" to Johnny Miles "alleging" Gilyard would speak to his non-existent club. Carson, a deputy inspector of the Ohio Department of Rehabilitation and Correction, said the trip's real aim was for Gilyard to "meet his girlfriend, on state time and in a state vehicle in a hotel in which the state paid for, to have sex." Carson's letter also alleged that "Gilyard receives frequent joy at sexually harassing women and will be sued personally and in his official capacity."

• On April 19, Carson's wife filed a sexual-harassment complaint with the Ohio Civil Rights Commission that accused Gilyard of making sexual advances and telling sexually oriented jokes.

• On May 9, Sheriff Smith ordered his son, Lt. Earl O. Smith Jr., and Detective Robert West to investigate the allegations in Carson's letter. Smith had gotten a copy of the letter from Cornell McCleary, a leader of the maverick Columbus Coalition of Concerned Black Citizens. Smith said he asked McCleary to send him a copy of the letter after McCleary — whom Gilyard said was a friend of the Carsons' — kept complaining about Gilyard's alleged indiscretions. The minion McCleary, who once told me Smith was the only honest law-enforcement official in Franklin County and that I would never find anything about him that was corrupt — later arranged for the detectives to meet Carson.

The investigation was supervised by Personnel Director John Downs, a protégé of Voinovich Companies lobbyist and Smith consultant Phil Hamilton, even though it was beyond the realm of his duties.

On June 19, Earl O. Smith Jr. requested a copy of Gilyard's driving record and found that Gilyard had accidents in 1984 and 1989. After obtaining the full 1984 accident report, a license check was run on the car driven by Gilyard. The license number came back registered to a woman named Anna from Cleveland. Bingo! The dense detectives had Gilyard's "girlfriend" — or so they thought.

Armed with Anna's name, Smith Jr. and West interviewed Wheeler, who wrote the "fake letter" and accompanied Gilyard to Cleveland on the date in question. The Cleveland native told them the document was a practice letter. Wheeler also expressed uncertainty about seeing Gilyard with a woman.

After being reminded of an outstanding arrest warrant against him in Georgia, however, Wheeler recalled that he had seen Gilyard talking to a woman. But West and Smith weren't about to stop there, as the transcript of their interrogation shows:

Smith: You don't remember her name, right?

Wheeler: No, I don't.

Smith: If I told you a name, would it, it might remind you. . . . Does the name Anna . . . sound familiar?

Wheeler: I'm not sure. I don't remember ever hearing the girl's last name. Anna, yes, no. I can't really say for sure. . . .

Smith: And Mr. Gilyard met Anna, or met a girl there. Did he tell you anything about this girl?

Wheeler: Afterwards, the next day, on our drive back to Columbus.

Smith: Did he say much about her?

Wheeler: He told me he had met her, she was from Chicago, just moving to Cleveland area, lived in Elyria. I believe they had dinner, and that's the only thing I know he told me.

After telling him Gilyard supposedly once had an accident while driving Anna's car, West prodded Wheeler to go even further.

West: With everything you know, can you see where this information here was given to you to write for the purposes of Mr. Gilyard going to Cleveland and meeting this Anna?

Wheeler: If he knew that Anna prior to, yes.

West: Which all indications are that he did, since at least 1984, when he had an accident in her car.

Wheeler: Yes. . . .

West: Do you feel that he used you now for the purposes of . . . going on this rendezvous?

Wheeler: Yes . . . .

Smith: And he introduced you to this lady as Anna, right?

Wheeler: I believe that's what her name was, Anna.

Smith: Sounds right?

Wheeler: Yeah.

It took detectives almost a month longer to get around to contacting Anna herself. And they did so by a letter mailed July 17, 1991, the same day they closed their investigation.

Sheriff Smith filed theft-in-office charges against Gilyard two days later. But the sheriff's case began to crumble quickly. On July 22 — the same day Gilyard was fired — Anna called in response to the letter. Records show that Anna strenuously denied knowing Gilyard and insisted that she was not with him on December 18. The next day, an angry Anna called again after hearing news reports that she had slept with Gilyard. Anna insisted she was sick and pregnant in December 1990 and that she didn't own a car at the time of the 1984 accident. After her call, Sergeant Michael Flynn checked the case file and discovered that two letters in Gilyard's license-plate number had been transposed, which is how the car came up registered to Anna rather than to . . . *Lenore Gilyard.*

Yes, Joe Gilyard was driving a car registered to his wife, Lenore Gilyard, and not Anna when he had that accident in 1984.

Once the detectives figured out they had been on the trail of the wrong woman, they tried desperately to find the "right" woman. They never did. Which, along with the testimony of two people Gilyard had met on state business while in Cleveland on the date of the alleged sexual rendezvous, persuaded Franklin County Municipal Court Judge Richard H. Ferrell to dismiss the charges against Gilyard immediately after hearing the "evidence" against him.

But that didn't happen until June 30, 1992, almost a year after the charges had been filed and Gilyard had been fired and physically, financially and emotionally destroyed at the hands of a racist sheriff and greedy, ambitious and unprincipled blacks.

In the interim, Jeffrey Carson received a letter of reprimand on September 11, 1991, after a Department of Rehabilitation and Correction investigation concluded that he had misused his position by requesting a state background check on Gilyard and had been untruthful when first confronted about it.

Then Patricia Wingard-Carson sued the Court of Claims on December 4, 1991, once again accusing Gilyard of sexual harassment. Records show that the state agreed to settle the suit in December 1992 for $28,000 while stipulating that it "expressly disclaims liability as alleged in the complaint." That marked the second time Wingard-Carson, with the help of her husband, had successfully sued the state over her termination. Wingard-Carson soon got another state job.

Wingard-Carson later had the audacity to write a book, *Peculiar Pain: A Close Look at Black on Black Sexual Harassment and Its Impact*, about her alleged victimization, although she didn't have the courage to mention Gilyard by name. Jeffrey Johnson, a black state senator who wrote a complimentary foreword to the book, was later convicted of violating the federal Hobbs Act for extorting money from a Cleveland businessman.

Gilyard, once a rising star in the Ohio Republican Party, wasn't as fortunate as Wingard-Carson. He was relegated to selling used cars and similar jobs until he died suddenly in 1998. The cause of death was listed as a heart attack. But it would have been just as accurate to attribute his death to a *broken* heart.

An optimist by nature, Gilyard initially clung to the belief that Voinovich wasn't aware of what had gone on behind the scenes. So he went to one of his mentors, David B. Bailey, a Cleveland Republican ward committeeman, lawyer and political confidant to both Voinovich and longtime Cuyahoga Republican Party Chairman Robert Hughes. Bailey arranged a meeting with Hughes, who expressed concern about the potential scandal Voinovich might face if his aides kept making the decisions for him and promised to arrange a meeting. A short time later, Hughes was dead, the apparent victim of accidental carbon-monoxide poisoning.

"It is very hard for me to understand this whole situation from the point of view of Governor Voinovich," Bailey said. "Joe Gilyard talked to me more than once about whether the governor's brother should be involved in building jails, especially since it had been pledged that he wouldn't be. For what it's worth, both Joe Gilyard and I thought that kind of commitment meant more because he was George Voinovich, and that when he said there would be no jails built by his brother, he meant it. As far as we were concerned, we thought it was real, honest-to-God dynamite. . . . So Joe came to me on the last weekend of July (1991) and asked me to arrange a meeting with Bob Hughes. And at that meeting, Bob was taking lots of notes, and one of the things Joe told Hughes was that DeWine had told Joe to destroy all copies of that memo. The effort was for Hughes to talk to Voinovich. Whether he had ever gotten to talk to George Voinovich, I don't know. I know he said he was going to try, and Bob Hughes almost always did what he said he was going to do. Obviously, he was not successful in reversing things if he did. . . .

"From the Republican Party's point of view, the destruction of Joe Gilyard by those wonderful people in Columbus was an absolute disaster," Bailey said. "We lost one of the greatest possibilities of cutting into the black vote that there ever was. I happen to think that Joe Gilyard could be a tremendous asset to the state of Ohio. . . . Joe Gilyard was in politics for all the right reasons. He wanted to do something for America. We've lost somebody who could really make a hell of a difference in this country."

With Gilyard out of the picture, Paul Voinovich started getting the state contracts he wanted, and they ultimately destroyed his company and possibly contributed to his premature death. The whole fiasco seemed to lend credence to the adage to "be careful about what you wish for, because you just might get it."

In 1992, Jefferson County hired the newly named V Group to design a 140-bed jail in Steubenville. The company's responsibilities later were expanded to include assisting in the supervision of construction. When construction of the jail was completed in January 1998, it was almost 19 months behind schedule and its cost had risen from an estimated $15.8 million to more than $25 million.

In 1999, a federal jury ordered the V Group to pay $13.3 million because of problems with its work on the jail. The verdict came at the end of a nine-week trial over allegations of cost overruns, delays and shoddy workmanship.

In 1996, phone records surfaced in court records that seemed to establish a link between Paul Voinovich and a man indicted on charges of trying to bribe a public official in 1993 to secure a contract for Voinovich's company.

Voinovich claimed he didn't know the indicted man, Vincent Zumpano, but the records showed phone calls were made between Zumpano and Voinovich's suburban Cleveland home during the previous three years. When Zumpano pleaded guilty, he said he attempted to make the bribes on behalf of Voinovich.

In 1997, a state audit of the sanitary district found the V Group had received excessive profits from construction work in the district that supplies water to Youngstown and Niles, Ohio. State Auditor James Petro also questioned why Gilbane Building Co. — which won a multimillion-dollar contract with the district — subcontracted the work to Voinovich's company and gave the firm a huge profit.

The Plain Dealer also reported that Voinovich's firm was part of a federal investigation into a landfill where debris from the Steubenville jail project was dumped under state permit. The newspaper said the Ohio Environmental Protection Agency granted the permit at a time when it had frozen most such permits.

That same year, Paul Mifsud, the governor's once-powerful former chief of staff, who was vice president of the Voinovich Companies before moving to the statehouse was convicted of obstructing official business and violating state ethics law in a $100,000 remodeling project on his future wife's home.

The scandals involving his brother didn't keep George Voinovich from being elected to succeed John Glenn in the U.S. Senate in 1998.

But on election eve, word leaked that Secretary of State Bob Taft had filed complaints with the state Elections Commission alleging that Voinovich conspired to launder $60,000 in campaign funds to reimburse his brother and a statehouse lobbyist for money spent on his 1994 re-election campaign. Taft, a Republican who succeeded Voinovich as governor, said the allegations came from a federal grand jury investigation. According to grand jury testimony and FBI interview reports filed with the commission as exhibits in the case, statehouse lobbyist Michael Fabiano hired labor leader Anthony "Ray" Gallagher to do campaign work. Fabiano paid Gallagher by reducing the monthly payments he made under a contract to Paul Voinovich's company, and Paul Voinovich later asked to be reimbursed. During a meeting at which the governor was present, according to his former campaign treasurer, Paul Voinovich suggested the campaign reimburse him the money paid Gallagher by steering the money through a consulting firm. The former treasurer, Vincent Panichi, told the grand jury the governor agreed. Although this appeared to be a clear violation of election law, nothing came of the allegations, and George Voinovich's reputation as a Teflon politician was further enhanced.

But brother Paul was not as lucky. Facing a bankruptcy judge's order to liquidate his companies to pay the $13.3 million judgment to Jefferson County, Paul Voinovich died on July 8, 2002, at the Cleveland Clinic after suffering a stroke the previous night at his home. He was 59.

I can visualize the always upbeat Joe Gilyard greeting Paul Voinovich at the Pearly Gates with a warm handshake, then saying: "I tried to tell your people you were asking for trouble by pushing for state contracts, and no one would listen. But you start over with a clean slate up here, so let's talk about the future rather than the past."

Yet another whitewash

When former Ohio Inspector General Sturtz investigated Gilyard's firing, he came across disturbing evidence to substantiate rumors that two politically prominent Columbus attorneys traveled to Washington to head off an indictment of Smith. Sturtz turned his findings over to Richard J. Hankinson, inspector general of the U.S. Department of Justice, after he became convinced then-U.S. Attorney Michael Crites wouldn't pursue them any more than he had previous allegations against Smith.

Hankinson responded by dispatching Assistant Inspector General Jerome Bullock and Roger Williams, assistant special agent in charge, to Columbus. Bullock and Williams reportedly promised a full-scale investigation of the handling of the case against Smith after a lengthy secret meeting with several of Sturtz's sources.

Sturtz said that "full-scale" investigation turned out to be a walk-through appearance by an inexperienced FBI agent who "whistled through the graveyard" and disappeared.

"I don't think they did a very thorough job," Sturtz added. "I don't think they talked to the right people and I don't think their level of interest was very high. There was enough information there that the right people should have looked into it more than they did."

When Smith's former chief deputy and the two fund-raisers were indicted on charges of selling honorary deputy badges for a total of $4,500, U.S. Attorney Crites stressed that no other indictments would be issued. A confidential state investigative document possibly explained why. It reported that a source close to Smith had "advised for certain" that Smith and his attorneys — one of them the son of a former U.S. attorney general — had gone to Washington to argue that Smith was the victim of a witch hunt. After they returned to Columbus, the document said, the attorneys met with U.S. District Judge George C. Smith, who "put the pressure on."

"I don't know what Crites was told by Washington," Sturtz said in 1992. "All I know is that Crites has since been given sufficient information on Smith to at least command his interest, and I'm as curious as you are as to what happened to it. I haven't heard a peep."

Former Chief Deputy Charles Cotton said he first began to suspect that any federal investigation of Smith wouldn't go anywhere in January 1987, when David Cassens and Douglass Ogden, then the top-ranking FBI agents in the Columbus office, informed Smith in his presence that FOP President Dewey Stokes had given the FBI evidence that Smith was being paid off to protect a reputed gambler.

According to Cotton, Cassens told Smith that Stokes' tip was the result of "petty politics" and wouldn't be pursued. Cotton said he was so dismayed by the agents' action and the lack of aggressiveness by the U.S. attorney's office that he wrote confidential complaints to FBI Director William Sessions and U.S. Attorney Richard Thornburgh.

"I was later told by an FBI agent that my letter was faxed right back to the local office," Cotton said. "Seeing a case compromised at such a high level shattered my beliefs in law enforcement, to which I had given 30 years of my life."

Cotton, one of the few chief deputies under Smith to resign without being on the verge of criminal conviction, also minced no words about what he thought of Smith in testimony before the State Personnel Board of Review in July 1994. Cotton said Smith was "dishonest" and "a crook." Cotton, a former state trooper and Grandview Heights, Ohio, police chief with a sterling reputation who quit his job in disgust in 1987, also testified that he believed Smith's department had been involved in "a conspiracy to violate certain federal and state statutes."

Former Columbus Police Chief Dwight Joseph testified at the same hearing that Smith had obtained, through deception, a confidential police document containing allegations about Smith from his department's organized crime bureau. Joseph also said his department's relationship "started off on the wrong foot when [Smith] became sheriff and went downhill from there."

A State Employee Relations Board hearing officer found, in an unrelated case, that Smith "was not a very credible witness. His testimony was repeatedly contradicted by other witnesses and by the documentary evidence."

As the much-feared Smith headed toward his stunning electoral upset in 1992, his department had come under yet another investigation over its alleged use of the state law-enforcement computer system to check on political opponents and to provide pre-employment checks for a private employer.

Those whose licenses were checked that year joined a growing list of former employees and political foes — as well as an FBI agent and an assistant U.S. attorney — to be followed and otherwise intimidated by Smith's loyal employees.

One reason for that loyalty was because Smith had raised nepotism and cronyism to an art form. The best example of that was the head of his powerful internal affairs department, Earl O. Smith Jr. In Sheriff Smith's eight years in office, his namesake rose from the position of a civilian radio room employee once captured on videotape wrestling with a co-worker while on duty to the rank of lieutenant.

"What am I supposed to do, hold him back because he's my son?" Earl Sr. asked in 1986, after he gave Earl Jr. a salary increase almost as large as the $11,400 salary he had started at four years earlier. While Earl Smith Jr. was starting his meteoric rise in 1985, Earl Smith Sr. also hired his son-in-law, Mark Ely, as a jail administrator. At one point, he also had his nephew and his nephew's wife on the payroll, but his nephew wasn't a chip off the Smith block and left.

Smith's rapid promotion of his son and hiring of his son-in-law may not have been in technical violation of the law, but the hiring of his granddaughter almost certainly was. The Ohio Ethics Commission issued an advisory opinion in 1985 that said state law "prohibits a county sheriff from authorizing or otherwise using the authority or influence of his office to secure approval of a contract for the employment of his spouse or a family member . . . in the county sheriffs office." The commission's executive director told me a sheriff has the right to promote a family member already on the department's staff, and that a son-in-law and nephew are not direct members of the family. But Smith's hiring of his granddaughter was a clear violation of the law, she said. Smith, unfortunately, wasn't listening. His granddaughter stayed.

Not every Smith in the sheriffs department was related to the sheriff, of course. George C. Smith Jr., for example, who worked there for three years, was the son of U. S. District Court Judge George C. Smith and later became a state representative. Judge Smith reportedly angered the U.S. attorney's office in 1990 when he imposed a mere 30-day sentence on convicted racketeer Lester Compton, who was alleged in a Columbus Police Department document to have been paying the sheriff $1,000 a week to protect his gambling operations.

Despite his promise of more testing and better standards when he was running against an incumbent in 1984, Sheriff Smith hardly established the highest standards once elected.

Exams were haphazardly given, if at all, and the results were usually destroyed so they couldn't be challenged. As a result, cronyism and boot-licking became the rule rather than the exception.

And some of the people Smith personally hired raise serious questions about his judgment. Shortly after taking office in 1985, for example, Smith hired as a secretary a woman who had failed several tests, including a drug test in which she tested positive for cocaine.

She later told an informant that she often transported cocaine for a large contributor to Smith's 1984 campaign who was later convicted of cocaine trafficking. When Smith was asked why he would hire such a person and place her in a position in which she would have access to sensitive documents, he said she was actually an "informant."

Smith also hired, "per phone conversation" and under a thirty-day "emergency appointment," an unnaturalized Laotian immigrant who worked at the same auto sales lot that would later be implicated in the illegal sale of auxiliary deputy's badges. Smith later killed an investigation into allegations made in two anonymous letters that the Laotian was a former member of the violent communist Pathet Lao organization. Smith said he had made his own check and found the accusations to be unfounded. No evidence of such an inquiry could be found in the deputy's personnel file. Nor was there evidence in the file that any action was taken on a memo from another deputy that said two informants had identified the Laotian as a drug dealer. Without the full background check these allegations seemed to call for, the Laotian was kept on past his 30-day emergency appointment, and eventually was promoted to detective.

While the good deputies who were driven out of Smith's department were often harassed and emotionally or financially destroyed afterward, those who gained his special favor had less than stellar backgrounds. Charles Austin was one of them.

Austin, who rose to the rank of lieutenant, became embroiled in controversy in April 1988 when he fatally shot a mentally disturbed man four times. A wrongful death suit filed by the family of the shooting victim resulted in a $79,000 out-of-court settlement in 1991. Austin and Chief Deputy Al Clark, who was with Austin at the time of the shooting, were also named in a 1988 false-arrest suit in which the plaintiff was awarded $3,900 in compensatory damages and $250 in lost wages by the Franklin County Board of Arbitrators.

Austin commanded the sheriff's pride and joy — the high-profile Tactical Entry Team — some of whose members reportedly made up to $30,000 a year in overtime. Among TET's supposedly highly trained members was County Commissioner Jack Foulk who, I revealed in *Columbus Alive,* lacked the required state certification for police officers. That meant every time Foulk participated in a TET raid he was violating laws against impersonating a police officer and carrying firearms.

Foulk was also operating in defiance of a 1981 Ohio attorney general's opinion that the roles of a part-time deputy and county commissioner "are incompatible due to a conflict of interest."

Another deputy Smith favored, was Ross L. Staggs, Jr., whom he promoted to lieutenant shortly after Staggs allegedly assaulted two inmates. Staggs, a former member of the department's notorious "goon squad," had three letters of reprimand in his personnel file at the time of his promotion.

One of the reprimands accused him of using force on an inmate in 1982 "that was neither reasonable, necessary, nor justified under the circumstances" and of "bringing discredit and ridicule against the department."

Just before his promotion in 1992, Staggs reportedly punched a restrained inmate several times in the back of the head as he was surrounded by three deputies and two supervisors. "Can you feel that? Can you feel that?" one deputy said Staggs kept repeating as he slugged the inmate. "He was hitting hard, too," the deputy said. Staggs reportedly cut his ring finger in the process, but later said "it was worth it."

In the other incident, Staggs allegedly started "smarting off as he always does" to an arrestee at the county jail's front counter, just as he reportedly did to former heavyweight boxing champion James "Buster" Douglas after he was arrested on drunken-driving charges of which he was later acquitted. When the newly arrested inmate responded to Staggs' insults, a deputy said, "Staggs grabbed him by the throat and picked him up" off the ground. The deputy said the much smaller inmate managed to yank away from Staggs and was about to punch him when he was restrained by other deputies. Neither incident apparently was reported to the department's internal affairs bureau. One deputy who witnessed both of Staggs' alleged assaults said he tried to get another witness to file a complaint with him, but she refused.

The most tragic case of abuse involved Richard Williams, a father of three whose estate sued the Franklin County Sheriffs Department and the Columbus Division of Police in 1992. According to the suit, Williams died of head wounds in May 1991 after deputies and police officers held his face down on a wooden table for 20 minutes even after he had lost consciousness and control of his bowels and bladder. The well-dressed Williams had been arrested for littering, hardly a capital offense.

In a brief filed in U.S. District Court, Cleveland attorney Christian Patno claimed the 31-year-old, 150-pound Williams was held "an unreasonably long time" in a Columbus Police paddy wagon. After he was taken to the jail, Patno said, Williams was "savagely beaten with a flashlight, his head [was] slammed repeatedly into a wooden table, he was Maced, smothered and finally suffocated while handcuffed. The ultimate physical and mental abuse is evidenced on videotape . . . by one 300-pound-plus and one 200-pound deputy, who jammed Mr. Williams' face first into a large plastic-covered pillow on top on an intake counter," Patno contended. "The deputies brutally forced and leveraged Mr. Williams' already elevated handcuffed hands even higher over his head and pushed him even further into the pillow and down on the counter so that his feet were caused to be removed from the ground, and knowingly squeezed the life from his shackled, restrained and helpless body." During Williams' last seconds of consciousness, Patno's brief said the videotape revealed, he gasped, "You're choking me! You're killing me!" The deputies ignored his pleas.

In another brief, Patno claimed that "at no time did Williams do anything worse than tell a Columbus police officer that he was mistreating a woman transported to the jail in the same paddy wagon as Williams." Williams' attempt to defend the woman apparently irritated the officer, Patno contended, and he took his revenge — with the aid of two deputies — once the paddy wagon arrived at the jail.

After Williams lost consciousness, he was hog-tied and taken to a Columbus hospital in a paddy wagon rather than an ambulance despite the seriousness of his condition, Patno said.

When Williams died three days later, Patno added, Columbus and Franklin County officials began to cover up evidence of the negligence and mistreatment Williams had endured. What's worse, Patno said, officials had been warned of the possibility of the kind of tragedy that befell Williams by former Deputy Duane Lephart during a 1986 disciplinary hearing.

A transcript of that hearing quotes Lephart as saying he was being subjected to unfair discipline because he did not condone the physical abuse of inmates that occurred at the jail during the third shift. "Eventually someone, somewhere is gonna have their head slammed and somebody might die," Lephart warned.

It cost Columbus and Franklin County dearly for not heeding Lephart's warning. In 1994, the Williams case ended in the largest civil-rights settlement in Ohio history.

Dana Kitchen, one of the two deputies restraining Williams at the time of his death, was reprimanded for excessive use of force in two other incidents within six weeks of Williams' death. In the first incident, which occurred nine days after Williams' death, Kitchen was found to have "failed to use force in accordance with law . . . by grabbing [Christopher] Petty by the throat." In the second incident, it was concluded that Kitchen "did use unnecessary and excessive force in shoving inmate [Ryan] O'Keefe in the neck/shoulder area."

Kitchen was also reprimanded in February 1993 for operating a motor vehicle while intoxicated. Kitchen said he had consumed sixteen or more beers on November 5, 1992. He had an alcohol concentration of 0.179. The legal limit in Ohio was 0.10. An Ohio State Highway Patrol trooper said Kitchen went off the road at 3:21 a.m. on November 6 and just missed a patrol cruiser in the median strip. (Another trooper told investigators "they really didn't want to arrest Kitchen because he was a deputy but did so because of the circumstances," their report says.) Kitchen pleaded guilty to operating a motor vehicle while intoxicated. He was put on three years' probation and ordered to spend three days at a substance-abuse clinic.

Deputies claimed many abuses at the jail under Smith went unreported out of fear of the kind of retaliation other whistle-blowers had suffered. A deputy who filed a complaint in 1990 against a sergeant for kicking an inmate in the ribs with all the force his 280-plus pounds could deliver while the inmate was being restrained on the floor, for example, was transferred between shifts and departments so much — five times in one week — that she finally quit. The sergeant, whose victim had to be taken to the hospital, eventually received a mild reprimand for using "unnecessary force on an inmate."

The beginning of the end for several other deputies began on September 13, 1989, when they decided at a Fraternal Order of Police meeting to begin demonstrating to make their grievances public. Smith reportedly threatened to fire anyone who participated in the protest, and he kept his promise. The demonstrating deputies and members of their families soon were being followed and having their own cars vandalized.

One fired deputy even had his dog poisoned on a day the department knew he and his wife would be away. By the time the third anniversary of their demonstration came around, most of the dedicated but disgruntled deputies were gone — and feeling betrayed by a profession they once admired.

"I used to think cops were cops and robbers were robbers," said one former deputy who went on to pursue a college degree. "Now I'll tell you what I think of a lot of cops: I think they're scum. I'm not talking about all cops. I'm talking about 20 percent of them — and the higher up they are, the more crooked they are."

Hard feelings like that were about the only legacy Smith left behind. Informed sources said Smith made sure of that by ordering the shredding of hundreds of potentially incriminating documents the day after he lost his bid for a third term.

To add insult to injury, Dwight Radcliff, the longtime sheriff of neighboring Pickaway County and a former president of the National Sheriffs' Association, appointed Smith an auxiliary deputy. Smith's 1992 campaign brochure had quoted Radcliff, a Democrat, as saying that Smith, a Republican, was "the best sheriff I've ever seen."

But beauty is in the eyes of the beholder. And Sheriff Karnes said that what he found when he took over from Smith in late December 1992 was not a pretty sight. Karnes, a big bear of a man with a booming voice and quick wit, had been with the department of which he was then in charge for 29 years before retiring and deciding to run against Smith.

Asked what kind of department he inherited, what he had done about it and where he was at that point, Karnes said: "Well, I inherited an office that was in much strife and turmoil, which was evident the night of the election. And when I say grown men cried, grown men did. Their fear of the tyrant, their fear of harassment was now gone." But not forgotten. When Smith tried to unseat Karnes in the 1996 election, claiming that a "pack of lies" I wrote about his department for *Columbus Alive* was the only reason he lost in 1992, he lost badly. Voters apparently didn't miss the scandals and controversies that dominated Smith's years in office.

One of Karnes' first acts when he took office was to remove a number of dubious auxiliary deputies, including the illegally serving County Commissioner Jack Foulk. Sheriff Gary K. DeMastry, sheriff of neighboring Fairfield County, quickly appointed Foulk to the same position.

Foulk and DeMastry seemed to be made for each other. Within months, Foulk was convicted on hit-and-run and failure-to-yield charges. In 2001, a Fairfield County jury convicted DeMastry on 32 counts, including engaging in a conspiracy to engage in a pattern of corrupt activity, theft in office, tampering with evidence, obstructing justice, receiving unlawful supplemental compensation and filing a false financial disclosure statement with the Ohio Ethics Commission.

Audits showed that DeMastry, who was indicted on more than 300 charges, misspent more than $213,000, including more than $600 on dinner at a fancy Pittsburgh restaurant.

But DeMastry was hardly the top central Ohio crooked politician. In 1998, Jesse D. Oddi Jr. resigned as Franklin County clerk of courts after being arrested for the theft of $448,621 over a 13-year period. Oddi later pleaded guilty to 49 criminal charges and was sentenced to six years in prison. Yet politicians like DeMastry and Oddi were petty thieves compared with their counterparts in the private sector. A good central Ohio example is Daniel S. Wiant, who in 2001 was sentenced to 13½ years in federal prison for embezzling almost $8 million from the Ohio division of the American Cancer Society.

But Wiant was a piker compared with Toledo's Martin Frankel. The son of a respected judge, Frankel's $215 million embezzlement schemes rocked the nation's insurance and investment industries. On May 16, 2002, Frankel pleaded guilty to 24 federal corruption charges. Frankel faced 150 years in prison and $6.5 million in fines. A lawyer, an accountant and a Roman Catholic monsignor with connections to the Vatican were among several people Frankel got to help him with his schemes to also be convicted.

Which all goes to show that Mansfield *is* typical, at least of Ohio. And since Ohio is often portrayed as a microcosm of the nation as a whole, it's likely that the kind of corruption I encountered in Mansfield can occur almost anywhere, and often does. As Martin Shefter, a Cornell University expert on the subject, put it: "The amount of corruption discovered is a function of the resources put into its discovery."

Investing in such resources is, sadly, something the nation's news media seems increasingly less likely to do, as policing the police, keeping government officials honest and holding business leaders accountable has given way to covering trivialities and celebrities.

America's news outlets are also increasingly owned by a few conglomerates with a vested interest in the status quo, and America's watchdog is becoming a lap dog as a result.

The rapidly growing alternative press countered this trend during the 1980s and 1990s, but by the new millennium its owners seemed to be just as collusive, profit-oriented and eager to be part of the club as their mainstream counterparts.

Longtime *New York Times* columnist Tom Wicker warned of the consequences of this growing tendency in his 1978 book *On Press,* when he wrote: "My belief is that the gravest threat to freedom of the press is not necessarily from public animosity or mistrust, legislative action or court decision. . . . At least a great a threat, I believe, comes from the press itself — in its longing for a respectable place in the established political order, in its fear of the reaction that boldness and independence will always evoke. Self-censorship silences as effectively as government decrees, and we have seen it far more often."

The result has been just what James Madison, author of the First Amendment warned: "A popular government without popular information, or the means of acquiring it, is but a prologue to a farce or a tragedy, or perhaps both."

It increasingly seems that we have both. As mystery writer K.C. Constantine noted in the foreword to *Pittsburgh Characters*, an irreverent underground best seller in the Steel City a decade ago:

"Our history is sanitized, our news is sanitized. There are people who actually believe Sam Donaldson is an obnoxious person because he asks 'hard' questions. The only thing Sam Donaldson knows about 'hard' questions is that if he ever asks one, he's going to have to get a real job. The Sam Donaldsons of this world get paid to sanitize the news by talking about the dumb stuff. While the Sammys of TV-land prattle on about AIDS and race and abortion — all subjects the ruling class wants the Sammys to prattle about — the ruling class has found another hole in the laws they pay to get looped so they can steal another couple hundred million."

But the real culprits in the spread of corruption and its harmful by-products aren't the crooks or the news media. To find who is really responsible for this unfolding tragedy, all most Americans have to do is look in the mirror.

Far too many Americans directly or indirectly support the country's crooks, and many of those who don't choose to look the other way rather than speak out. A good example of how this plays out is Las Vegas, the capital of venality created by and — no matter how much we try to kid ourselves — still controlled by America's darker elements. Sally Denton and Roger Morris documented the thriving ugly underside of America's fastest-growing city in their 2001 book, *The Money and the Power: The Making of Las Vegas and Its Hold on America.* "The city has been the quintessential crossroads and end result of the now furtive, now open collusion of government, business and criminal commerce that has become — on so much unpalatable but undeniable evidence — a governing force in the American system. In that, of course, Las Vegas was never the exception it seemed. Ever brazen, the city was simply less covert than the country it mirrored too well. For all its apparent uniqueness, all the hype, the garish town in the southern Nevada desert has always been more representative of America than either wants to admit."

When I encountered corruption in Mansfield, many of its residents told me Mansfield had been called "Little Chicago." I've had the residents of countless other cities tell me the same thing about their town. But Chicago is an outdated metaphor. If America's corrupt, drug-and-vice-infested cities are a little anything, they are a "Little Las Vegas." And the biggest "Little Las Vegas" is Washington, D.C. While Washington may be the nation's official capital, Denton and Morris make a strong case that Las Vegas has become a possibly more powerful "shadow capital." It did so, they say, "because the rest of America made it so by embracing the ethic of greed and exploitation." By 2000, Denton and Morris write, "the national surrender of democracy to oligarchy in the United States — the submission to house rules, as they might put it on the Strip — had simply come into the open, where it had long been in Las Vegas."

As I noted previously, corruption costs Americans more than money that ends up in the pockets of crooks, crooked politicians and their cronies. It also unjustly costs some Americans their lives or their freedom. Ultimately, corruption could cost us the American dream. It is time to wake up before that dream becomes a nightmare for the comfortable many as well as the downtrodden few. That's what was starting to happen in Mansfield, Ohio, when I arrived there. It's what could happen anywhere or everywhere else if given a chance.

About the author

Martin D. Yant began his career at *The Pittsburgh Press* after graduating from Georgetown University. From 1972 to 1977, Yant served in a variety of editing positions at the *Chicago Daily News* and the *Chicago Sun-Times.* In 1978, Yant became editor of the Mansfield *News Journal.* An award-winning investigation he launched there eventually led to the conviction of the sheriff and seven deputies on corruption and brutality charges, the resignation of the county coroner and the electoral defeat of several public officials.

In 1981, Yant joined *The Columbus Dispatch*, for which he was commentary editor and a columnist. Yant resigned in 1991 to devote full time to independent journalism and private investigation. Since then, he has discussed investigative topics on numerous TV and radio talk shows; had investigations featured on *Unsolved Mysteries, 48 Hours, American Justice* and *The CBS Evening News*; aided in the release of several innocent inmates, including one who originally had been sentenced to death 26 years earlier; and successfully self-litigated a public-records case in the Ohio Supreme Court.

Yant also was a consultant for *Final Appeal,* an NBC-TV series on wrongful convictions, in 1992. That same year, an exposé on misconduct in the Franklin County Sheriff's Department that he wrote for *Columbus Alive* was credited with causing the defeat of the powerful incumbent sheriff in the November election. A series of articles he co-wrote on the controversial John Byrd death-penalty case for *Columbus Alive* in 2001 and 2002 won the Ohio Society of Professional Journalists' award for criminal-justice reporting.

As a licensed private investigator, Yant has conducted numerous pre- and post-trial investigations. The evidence Yant helped develop on a jailhouse beating death of a man arrested for littering resulted in the largest civil-rights settlement in Ohio history in 1994.

Yant has written four other books: *Presumed Guilty: When Innocent People Are Wrongly Convicted; Desert Mirage: The True Story of the Gulf War; Rotten to the Core: Crime, Sex and Corruption in Johnny Appleseed's Hometown; Tin Star Tyrants: America's Crooked Sheriffs.* His web page can be found at www.truthinjustice/yant.org.

9 780964 278028